THE TERRAN ALLEGIANCE

TERRAN MENACE
BOOK 3

J.R. ROBERTSON

Cover design and illustration by Jeff Brown Graphics

ISBN: 978-1-7359259-5-0 (paperback)

PROLOGUE

Junior Lieutenant Tarok Na'al swept his gaze over the devastated village of Ter S'kel. Fires burned through a number of structures around him, set alight by the fury of his soldiers' plasma carbines. Everywhere he looked, the dead and dying littered the ground, left where they'd fallen to serve as carrion for the local wildlife after Na'al and his men returned to their ship.

In another life, this place had been his home. Now it was his objective.

The small community was considered quaint by modern standards. Stick-built homes were nestled alongside the few shops and businesses lining the short main thoroughfare through town. The entire area was barely a few hundred meters in radius before civilization gave in to the inhospitable wilds of the Imperial colony world of Gallo-4. While the colony world was one of the oldest in the Imperium, it had always been considered a backwater, and the near-prehistoric nature of villages such as Ter S'kel served only to reinforce that narrative.

Which was precisely what the inhabitants of this village had wanted. It was a facade that had served them well for generations, allowing them to weave their dangerous plots beneath the notice of the Master and its agents—plots that Tarok Na'al was a part of.

They should have known that you could not hide from the Master forever. None of them would survive to pass this lesson on to the next generation. None, that was, except for the one responsible for their slaughter.

A sharp crack echoed between the shattered buildings of the central square, silencing the strangled plea for mercy from one of the Imperium's enemies that Na'al and his men had been sent here to root out and destroy. Through the millennia, many had sought to escape from beneath the yoke of the Master and its Imperium. They had all failed, and this small cluster of resistance to Imperial order was no different.

"Sir, that was the last one," Fleet Sergeant Delvak Rei reported, jogging up to Na'al's side.

Rei was the only other Th'aloki in Na'al's detachment. The rest of the men were all the shorter-statured Th'aloori combat troops that were so common among the reconnaissance and infiltration units of the Imperial military. While the two closely related species appeared quite divergent with respect to external morphology—the Th'aloki being much larger and more powerfully built—they shared the same organ systems, general bone structure, and a common language, having evolved side by side eons ago.

"Drone scans confirm only Imperial Navy personnel remain at this location," Rei said.

Na'al nodded. "Very good, Rei. Have the men conduct another foot search, just to be sure. These vermin have proven to be remarkably resourceful, given how long they evaded detection by the Master and its agents."

"Your command, sir!"

Rei turned to leave, but Na'al stopped him. "Sergeant! On

second thought, I will accompany you. I find it's good for the men to see their officers getting their hands dirty every now and then. Don't you agree?"

Surprise played across Rei's face. "If you insist, sir. But I should warn you: it's not a pretty sight in most of those buildings. The boys were... enthusiastic when it came to dispatching this trash." The sergeant spat on the ground to emphasize his words. "Traitors like these are the worst kind of scum."

Na'al struggled to fight back a wave of fury, but the twitch of his brow told him he hadn't succeeded in keeping his emotions off his face. Thankfully, Rei appeared to take his CO's reaction as agreement about the nature of the "traitors," and he simply nodded before starting toward the group of imperial marines that were milling about in the village square. A moment later, the burly sergeant was blistering the air with a profanity-laced fury that only a marine NCO could muster, and the rest of Na'al's troops flew into action in the vain hope of avoiding Rei's notice.

Na'al unlimbered his carbine from his shoulder and trotted after his sergeant, angling toward the north side of the square, where a side street led to a series of homes that hadn't yet caught fire. He pointed toward the six members of First Squad as they tried to sneak around the periphery of Rei's vision. "You men are with me," Na'al said, motioning for them to follow. "We're going to clear these buildings again—another sweep for survivors and intelligence. I don't need to remind you of what happens to those who displease the Master."

"Sir!" the members of First Squad shouted in unison, suddenly appearing much more attentive and enthusiastic after Na'al's mention of the Master's wrath.

As they approached the first of the buildings, Na'al slowed and turned to his marines. "Split up. Two to a building. Clear it and search for intel—anything at all that seems useful or suspicious. Mark the building clear on the tacmap when you're done and move on to the next." Na'al pulled up the surrounding buildings on the small semiflexible display attached to the armor over his left forearm and quickly assigned his team to their first buildings. "Here are your assignments. We'll meet up back at the square once we've cleared this block."

"What about you, sir?" one of the junior marines asked.

"I'm the odd man out and will go it alone," Na'al said. "The risk is minimal, as these buildings have already been cleared. Besides, it'll be good practice for me. It's been too long since I've had a chance to get some real-world breach-and-clear experience." He double-checked his carbine's status, then looked back up at his marines. "But don't let that stop you from bailing my butt out if I run into trouble, clear?" He left the members of First Squad to chuckle and crack jokes at his expense as the team broke up to clear their structures for a second time, but his self-deprecating smile fled the moment he turned his back on them.

Boots crunching lightly on the dusty road, Na'al braced himself for what he knew he would find inside the small house in front of him. The tacmap on his forearm listed three enemy KIA, along with a few other miscellaneous notes made by the team that had cleared this house a mere hour before. His heart began hammering faster as he approached the worn wooden steps. Faded gray paint peeled from years of exposure to the sun and the wind that blasted this forsaken planet year-round and without mercy. The groaning of the second step as his weight settled onto it triggered a memory: a young boy giggling quietly from behind one of the large flowerpots at the top of the steps, waiting to jump out and surprise his grandfather, who was just returning from a long journey.

Na'al stepped lightly over the shattered remains of that same ceramic pot on his way to the front entrance. His carbine came up to high-ready, and he smoothly stepped over the threshold and past the shattered door hanging drunkenly from one remaining hinge. His eyes quickly swept the interior of the first level, moving past the still form of a Th'aloori woman he didn't recognize, her lifeless body crumpled at the base of the stairs leading to the second level. He quickly and methodically cleared all the rooms on the main floor, then did the same upstairs, never allowing his eyes to stop moving. Another body lay amid a charred and bloody tangle of clothing in an upstairs closet, though Na'al didn't recognize this one, either.

That meant his search would end with the third—and final—body, which was in the basement.

Na'al didn't waste time searching the rest of the upstairs spaces and instead quickly descended to the main level, making a beeline for the basement door off the kitchen. The tacmap displayed a complete layout of the house, but Na'al's eyes didn't once consult his forearm display; he knew every board, fixture, and pane of glass in this house intimately. His eyes flicked to the mission clock in one corner of his helmet's visor. He needed to move faster.

Throwing the door aside, Na'al vaulted down the basement staircase, letting the power-assist actuators in his lightweight recon armor deal with the strain of the landing. A single light in the ceiling illuminated the mangled corpse along one bare wall, and Na'al's heart stopped.

He'd known what he would find here and thought he'd been adequately prepared to face it. But his carefully sculpted persona of an unflinching, fiercely loyal Imperial Navy officer crumbled to dust the instant his gaze took in the shattered remains of the elderly Th'aloki against the far wall. He stumbled forward a few steps, then sank to his knees in despair. After seeing the first two strangers upstairs, Na'al had dared hope the body he found here wouldn't be who he knew it must be.

Kroz Tibbedal wasn't really Na'al's biological grandfather, but the elderly Th'aloki had raised the boy once known as

Daloth Venz as his own after his parents were killed in an orbital shuttle "accident." Officially, the cause of the crash was never truly determined, but Kroz had long believed it was the work of one of the Master's agents; shuttles didn't just fall out of the sky for no reason. And from that day forward, Daloth's path in life was set.

Kroz had raised him, trained him to be a deep-cover operative for the resistance, and went to extraordinary lengths in an effort to change Daloth's identity; if the resistance's best operative was to remain undetected, the Imperial Navy must never be able to link Tarok Na'al to this backwater planet. But in the end, one could only hide from the Master and its agents for so long, and Kroz's time had run out.

His plan had nearly worked, too. Junior Lieutenant Tarok Na'al was one of the fastest-rising officers in the Imperial Navy. His unflinching loyalty to the Master and the Imperium, combined with a rigorous discipline and attention to detail, ensured he was fast-tracked for advancement, despite a genetic condition preventing him from taking advantage of modern neural implants—something that was seen as a severe handicap by his peers. A few decades more, and the plans Kroz and the other resistance leaders had worked for centuries to bring about might have been possible. But now, all was for naught.

In an attempt to obfuscate its true disposition and mitigate the inevitable security breaches, the resistance was nameless and operated in cells. To maintain operational security, only a few leaders from each cell knew how to contact the others... which now posed a problem. With Kroz and the rest of Ter S'kel wiped out, Na'al had no way of letting the other cells know he was still an asset in play. If only Kroz had made it...

Na'al's radio crackled with an incoming transmission, forcing him to jam his thoughts to the back of his mind and transform himself back into the heartless Imperial officer he was supposed to be.

"Sir, we've reached the end of the block and are heading back to the square," First Squad's leader reported. "Are you alright? I see you haven't finished clearing your structure yet."

Na'al glanced at his mission clock again, cursing internally when he saw how much time he'd wasted on his knees, giving in to his despair. He toggled the channel open. "I'm fine. More rust built up than I thought. I've just completed my sweep and will join you in the village square shortly."

First Squad clicked an acknowledgment, and their personnel trackers on the tacmap moved off toward the central square. Na'al quickly bent over and rifled through Kroz's pockets in the vain hope the kill teams had overlooked something that might assist the resistance operative in contacting the other cells, but the old man's pockets were empty, save for a small, well-polished stone. Na'al stowed the pebble in one of his thigh pockets and rose to leave, but before he could take a step, his visor lit up with a warning indicator: his combat suite had detected the sound of a weapon being readied nearby.

Acting on instinct, Na'al rolled to his left, away from the direction of the indicated threat, and brought his carbine up in a flash. But there was nothing before him aside from a dust-covered shelving unit and the wall behind it. The air was deathly still for several heartbeats, and then Na'al had an idea. He took his support hand off his weapon and slowly reached into one of the admin pouches on his chest rig, fumbling briefly with the small device he stashed there for times just like this. His thumb found the activation toggle, and his comms and visor display went dead.

"You can come out," he said to the wall. "I've activated a suppression field that will scramble Imperial technology for a short time. You will not be recorded by my combat suite, nor will it transmit your presence over the tacnet."

Several seconds passed with no activity, and Na'al began to wonder if he'd made a mistake. He lowered his weapon and tried one last time. "Please. It is imperative that I find out if Kroz left any sort of message or information for me."

A muted rustle tickled at Na'al's ears, and a moment later, a small seam appeared in the wall directly next to the shelving unit. A door slid silently to one side, and Na'al found himself staring down the business end of an ancient projectile weapon. The eyes of the young Th'aloori girl sighting down the barrel were wide with terror, and the weapon trembled in her hands.

"Who are you?" she squeaked. "How do you know my grandfather?"

Na'al reeled back slightly. To the best of his knowledge, Kroz didn't have any biological children, and the old man hadn't told him of any other wards. Then again, it had been many years since the two of them had spoken, so perhaps the old man had taken in yet another child orphaned by the Master or its agents.

Na'al safed his weapon and slowly lowered it until it hung limply from its sling, then held his hands out in a friendly manner. "Fear not, child," he said, quickly glancing down to see how much longer the suppression field would be active. He didn't have much. "I was once like yourself. I was orphaned and taken in by Kroz Tibbedal—a man I, too, called grandfather. He raised me, and now I serve the resistance as a covert operative within the Imperial Navy. I was unable to warn our grandfather about this attack, but I've come in search of information that will allow me to continue my mission for the resistance.

"Please," Na'al added, lowering himself to a squat and reaching a hand toward the girl, "did Kroz give you anything that could help me?"

The girl didn't lower her weapon, but after a moment, she

nodded almost imperceptibly. "Grandfather told me to hide when the Master's soldiers came. He put me in here and told me to wait until someone from the resistance came. He said to not trust anyone that didn't know the password. Do you know the password?"

Na'al froze. He'd been given a coded passphrase in the event he ever needed to contact Kroz, but he doubted it would be the same as the password the girl was looking for. He eyed the slug-thrower the girl still had trained on him, judging that his armor should be able to stand up to at least several shots from the ancient weapon, should it be necessary, but he'd prefer to not put that theory to the test.

"When the flowers of the field have returned to the earth, so we, too, shall meet again, my love."

The gun clattered to the hard basement floor, and the girl flew toward Na'al, sobs wracking her tiny frame. He wrapped her up in his arms, unsure of what to say. While she was clearly an adolescent and likely capable of taking care of herself, she'd just been through a terrible trauma. But Na'al had no way to care for her. He needed to rejoin his marines and dust off for orbit, and the girl would immediately be put to death merely for being present in Ter S'kel.

"Listen to me, girl." Na'al put just enough of an edge on his voice to cut through her hysteria. "We don't have much time. I need to rejoin my command before they become suspicious about my absence. I cannot take you with me, but I am certain other members of the resistance will come once they learn of what's happened here. But I need whatever Kroz gave you, and I need it right now."

The girl pushed away from him, and the relief that had washed away the fear in her eyes suddenly receded. "You're not here to rescue me?" she asked in a pitiful voice. "But grandfather said—"

"I am not the one of which he spoke," Na'al cut her off, checking the suppression field emitter again. Less than a minute remained before all his gear would come back online. "Hurry! Give me what I seek and return to your hiding place. My team will be alerted to your presence in less than a minute if you don't."

A hard look settled on the girl's face. "Fine!" she shouted, retrieving a framed photo from the secret room and throwing it at Na'al. "Take your stupid picture and be gone! If you aren't going to help me, I'll just do it myself! Go back to your stupid mission!"

Na'al reeled back, barely managing to catch the small, framed photo the girl had hurled at him like a missile. He quickly thrust it into a pouch on his armor and looked up, only to find the secret room was once again sealed and the girl was gone.

"My name is Daloth Venz," he said to the once-again seamless wall before him. He dared not give his current name to this girl, lest she fall into the wrong hands. The other cells would likely have a record of Daloth Venz and be able to determine that Na'al was still operating undercover for the resistance. It wasn't ideal, but it would have to do, unless the photo he'd received turned out to be more than just the keepsake it appeared to be at first glance. "Please tell the other members of the resistance what happened here. Good luck, girl."

With that, Tarok Na'al took one last sorrowful look at the lifeless body of his grandfather, then turned and made his way out of his childhood home for the last time.

1

AWAKENING

"HE'S COMING AROUND. INFORM THE ADMIRAL."

The voice was close and sounded surprised. It had an odd timbre, higher-pitched, with a trilling undertone. But something was... *off*, Ben realized. It was almost like the unfamiliar voice was speaking another language, but Ben's brain was translating it into English in real time.

Ben commanded his eyelids to open, but unlike all the other times he'd forced his way out of unconsciousness, his lids glided open with almost no effort at all.

"Benjamin Hutchins?"

A bright light shone into his eyes, and he blinked to escape the pain from his overloaded visual cortex.

"Benjamin Hutchins, can you hear me?"

"Shut that damn light off, will you?" Ben growled, attempting to roll away from the blinding irritant, but not a single muscle below his chin even twitched in response.

Panic welled up in Ben's mind at the realization that he was paralyzed from the neck down. But wait... that wasn't quite right. He could feel the rest of his body, from the tips of his toes all the way up to his rapidly thumping heart; he just couldn't force any part below his mouth to move even the slightest bit. And even more odd, it felt as though he were floating. Try as he might, Ben couldn't detect any sense that gravity was pulling him down onto the exam table he must be on, given the person standing over him. But how had he gotten like this?

There was a vague sense that he was in a medical facility, somewhere, but he had no memory of what idiotic stunt he'd pulled to get here. He wracked his brain, scrambling to come up with some idea as to the series of events that had landed him in his current predicament, but to his growing horror, he realized his memory was a blank slate. There were odd, ephemeral notions of who he was and the life he'd led up until now, but anytime he tried to grasp one of those thin threads of his past, they effortlessly slipped through his mental fingers.

The light snapped off, and a head covered with a surgical mask and cap appeared in Ben's line of sight.

"Welcome back, Terran. My master has been looking forward to meeting you," the man said. He reached up and removed the mask, revealing a huge smile stretched across his face.

A face with a wide mouth and large, glassy black eyes.

That did it; the sight of his enemy mere inches from his nose unlocked the mental barrier keeping him from accessing his memories, and an entire lifetime of experiences exploded outward, filling his entire sense of being. Time simultaneously sped up and slowed to a crawl as Ben's heretofore unused brain sprang to life, rapidly restoring his memory from the backup file his APEX had fired off in the seconds before his death. But there was something new there as well.

Intermingled with his memories and sense of self was… access to some sort of ability? It had a familiar feel to it, as though he'd tapped into a much cruder form of this thing in the past. It was similar to what he experienced when linking with his armor, when the squishy, biological bits of his brain finally got out of the way and let the hardware his dad had shoved into his head all those years ago really stretch its legs and go to work. Now, staring directly into the face of the enemy—an enemy that had him lying paralyzed on a table in some sort of laboratory or medical facility—Ben reached out in desperation for this new ability and the tantalizing power it promised him.

In an instant, his sphere of awareness expanded by orders of magnitude. He now knew that he was actually suspended in midair by some sort of anti-gravity field, which also served to restrain his ability to move. This new level of situational awareness brought with it a host of tactical options, which his brain assessed and prioritized seemingly on instinct. He searched for a way to release himself from whatever force was restraining his movement, and a moment later, he *felt* how to release himself. A quick mental command, and Ben felt gravity reassert its pull on him, and control of his limbs returned.

The alien had remained over top of him, looking expectantly into his face, but its expression quickly morphed from a fanatic's excitement into shocked surprise. A host of alarms began blaring from the equipment lining the walls of the small, isolated medical bay, and the alien scrambled back as Ben crashed to the floor.

As control of his body returned, so did his ability to flip his mental switch from "normal" to "extreme violence." He snarled, exploding to his feet and launching himself at the small, unarmed alien that was desperately trying to flee the hellbeast it had awoken. Ben slammed into the smaller alien, driving it to the floor. He straddled the mewling creature, ignoring its cries for calm and understanding, and crashed his fist into the side of its head. Ben grabbed the collar of its sterile, white uniform in an iron grasp and prepared to reprise his hand-to-hand fight with the Imperial trooper back at the High Council complex on Hai'alla, when he'd bashed said trooper's skull into paste against the unyielding stone of the courtyard. Ben surged power into his arms and upper body as he prepared to unload his fury on this poor bastard.

Then he stopped.

The pathetic creature had given up pleading for Ben to calm down and switched to cries for mercy. The meaning of its chittering words pierced the fog of bloodlust smothering Ben's conscious mind. And that was the problem: he could understand the alien's strange language, perfectly.

Slowly, Ben released his hold on the alien but kept his hands ready to strike again, should this be some sort of trick. The alien flopped back onto the floor, panting heavily.

"Why can I understand you?" Ben tried to say, but the words came out of his mouth as a broken mess of strangled vowels and bizarre tongue clicks, which didn't sound even remotely like human speech *or* the alien's native tongue.

The alien froze, its terrified demeanor melting away into a quizzical expression as it cocked its wide head to one side. Ben shook his head as if to clear the misfiring neurons in his brain and tried again.

"Why can I understand you?" he said, this time in his familiar North American–accented English.

The alien's mouth opened and closed a few times, but no sounds came out.

"Well? What the hell have you done to me?" Ben shouted. "And how did I end up here? The last thing I remember is being vaporized in a nuclear explosion, so you'll understand my confusion as to how I ended up *alive* and in an Imperial facility."

"Y-You…" the alien stammered out. "How did you… Never mind. We'll figure that out later. My name is Eelix Vor. I am one of the technicians responsible for returning you to life. Your father gave us your—"

"What did you say about my dad?" Ben demanded, focusing

his gaze like a laser, boring into the eyes of the alien—Eelix—with murderous intent as his hands regained their grip on his collar. If these bastards had hurt his dad in any way, Ben was going to ensure they all died a slow and agonizing—

"He gave us your engram!" Eelix squealed. "Please! Don't hurt me! Your father gave us your engram and genetic profile, and we worked together with your AI, Mabel, to reconstruct you! We are on your side and want to see the downfall of the Master, just as you do!"

The words crashed out of the medical technician so fast Ben had a hard time keeping up with him. He released his grip once again and rocked backward onto his feet, standing up and taking a few steps back while he tried to process the series of megaton-sized bombshells Eelix had just dropped on him.

Ben's head swam. Could the little alien be telling the truth? Or was he just stalling until help could arrive? The pieces began to settle into place as Ben thought about it. Unless the Imperium had some way to intercept the datastream from his APEX back to his dad—data being transmitted via entangled pairs of quantum particles, no less—he couldn't see how the Imperium would have acquired his engram. Ben's genetic profile wouldn't be that hard for the Imperium to dig up, if they really wanted to. But the engram? That was a different story entirely.

The panic that had initially flooded through Ben when he realized he was in the hands of the Imperium began to fade. Maybe, just maybe, this alien was telling the truth, and somehow his dad and Mabel had managed to escape from Hai'alla and hook up with some rebel faction. But that was an awfully big maybe.

"You'll forgive me if I don't take you at your word." Ben slowly edged his way over to a countertop with an assortment of technological devices neatly arrayed along its length. But he wasn't interested in any of the tech there.

Eelix sat up, rubbing the back of his head with one hand and cradling his jaw with the other. "That's perfectly understandable. I can't say I'd trust me in your position, either… What are you doing?"

Ben grabbed one corner of what appeared to be a textile cloth or blanket that the instruments were placed on. It was stiffer than it looked, but it would serve the purpose he had in mind for it. *Hospital linens are the same the galaxy over, it would appear.* He smiled at the thought as he grabbed the sheet with both hands and yanked the fabric out from under the expensive-looking instruments in one swift motion.

"What are you doing?" Eelix screeched in horror as every single piece of gear on the counter crashed to the floor, leaving Ben standing awkwardly with a sheet held off to one side like he was a butt-ass-naked matador.

"Huh," Ben said, junk flapping in the breeze and surrounded by a bunch of now-broken, expensive-looking instruments. "That's a lot harder than they make it look in the movies."

Eelix, now very much over his fear of being killed by the insane murder machine he'd brought back to life, rushed over and scrambled to pick up the alien gizmos and doodads Ben had knocked to the floor. Ben stepped back and wrapped the sheet around his waist, using it like a kilt to cover up his manly bits while the alien clucked indignantly as he examined each piece of tech in turn.

With each passing second, Ben felt more and more at ease. This alien wasn't acting like they were mortal enemies and he was only killing time until a full squad of Imperial troopers burst into the room to gun Ben down. He couldn't explain it, but like his ability to understand the alien's native tongue, he had an innate sense as to what Eelix's body language was saying—and nothing there told him the technician had been anything other than truthful the entire time.

"Oh hell," Ben said with a sigh, bending over and giving Eelix a hand. "I'm sorry, Eelix. Let me help you with that—ouch! What the hell?" Ben jerked his hand back after the diminutive alien slapped it away.

"You've done quite enough, Terran!" Eelix barked, then gestured to one corner of the room. "Go wait over there until the admiral gets here. Then you can make *his* life miserable and leave *me* alone. My job here is done," he said, then, under his breath, added, "And I did it a little too well, it seems. Never should have allowed Tellin to talk me into going along with those upgraded systems. 'Let's just stick with the approved design,' I said. But *noooo*, I had to let Tellin talk me into..."

Ben kept his gaze locked on the alien as he backed away. Eelix was now in the middle of a one-way conversation with himself, and Ben was beginning to wonder if maybe he'd hit the little technician a little too hard earlier. What had he meant by maybe doing his job "too well"? And "upgrades"? But his thoughts were interrupted when he bumped into something much bigger than himself—something firm and warm, but with just a little bit of give. Ben froze for a split second, then turned around slowly...

... and stared straight into the very angry face of a *very* large alien. One wearing an immaculate black uniform with gold piping and an Imperial admiral's crest on his collar.

"Ben Hutchins," the brute rumbled. "I am Tarok Na'al, former first admiral of the Imperial Navy. I'm also the leader of the rebellion. Welcome aboard my flagship, the battlecruiser *X'nec.*"

2

EAST MEETS WEST

DIMITRIY VOLKOV ABSOLUTELY HATED THE CITY HE'D CALLED HOME for the better part of the last twelve years. It stank of sweat and fermented vegetables. It was dirty, despite the constant vigilance of the army of forced laborers tasked with keeping the streets, sidewalks, and alleys clear of trash. But worst of all, it reminded him of the hellish concrete jungle he'd been born in back on Earth. Despite being filled with life, Lijia had no soul, and every day, Dimitriy could feel a little bit more of his own slip away into the concrete and asphalt abyss around him.

He reclined casually in one of the uncomfortable metal chairs placed outside of the small cafe for patrons to use as they enjoyed their overpriced, overly sweet tea and "coffee" drinks. With one hand wrapped around a steaming mug of said shit coffee, Dimitriy gazed idly at the tablet propped up in his other. This morning's edition of the Central Ministry's propaganda—commonly called "the news"—was the usual heaping pile of over-the-top garbage, carefully curated to always cast the Central Party in nothing but the shiniest of lights.

As a deep-cover operative for the Russian Galactic Intelligence Ministry, Dimitriy Volkov had led a thoroughly boring career. Once, he'd considered himself unbelievably lucky to attend the University of Southern California as a foreign exchange student and then be recruited directly out of college by the GIM. The age of human expansion was in full swing, and a life of wonder and excitement awaited those intrepid few who were willing to go out and conquer the stars. At least that was the bullshit his recruiters had shoveled at him as an incentive to sign on with Galactic Intelligence.

The truth was nowhere near as exciting. Instead of sneaking around star systems and infiltrating secret installations of geopolitical foes, Dimitriy had been relegated to a soul-crushingly boring role as a mid-level staffer for a string of completely useless bureaucrats within the beast that was the SRF's political structure. And for the last twelve years, he'd lived life pushing paper and filing the occasional status report with his handlers back on Earth at the GIM. At least until the fucking Alarians blasted it to hell for no particular reason whatsoever.

The Alarian War hadn't changed much. Instead of sending reports to Earth, Dimitriy had simply shifted to filing status reports with his new handler at the new GIM headquarters on Sukhovo, and his life had continued more or less uninterrupted by off-world events. But that wasn't to say life within the Sino-Russian Federation simply continued on with the status quo in the wake of humanity's first interstellar war with an alien race.

Before the war, the political powers-that-be within the SRF had gone to great lengths to project an air of unity within the enclave predominately comprised of people of Russian or Chinese heritage. The truth, however, was that the Sino-Russian Federation had always been an uneasy alliance, at best. Like the two other major Confed enclaves, the North American Commonwealth and the European Union, the SRF maintained two of the Confed's numbered fleets—the Third and Sixth. But while the NAC and EU operated two of the numbered fleets each, they were all closely aligned and more or less operated as one giant naval force: a stark contrast to those operated by the SRF.

Both Third and Sixth Fleet had been mauled during the Alarian War, but Third Fleet, in particular, had taken the worst of it. The Russian-aligned Third Fleet had been over Earth when the Alarian armada struck and suffered greater than ninety percent casualties. The Chinese contingent within the SRF political structure had acted swiftly afterward, taking advantage of the post-war societal chaos and sudden imbalance in military strength between themselves and the Russians. And just like that, the Russian-aligned faction within the Federation became second-class citizens.

While most SRF worlds had been left alone by the Alarians—something many believed to be a result of SRF-controlled space being located the farthest from Alarian space—the destabilization of the Confed government resulted in a reorganization of how the SRF's government was structured. The end result was a Central Ministry dominated by the Chinese People's Galactic Republic and only token representation within the Central Ministry for the Russian worlds. Perhaps worst of all, every Russian-aligned military or intelligence branch or agency suddenly found itself on the outside looking in, forced to fight over budgetary scraps and weakening them all, significantly.

Dimitriy's eyes flitted up to the sights and sounds of Lijia—the second-largest city on Lianmeng, the capital world of the Sino-Russian Federation. Everywhere he looked, people scurried along sidewalks with their heads down, oblivious to the stiflingly hot summer morning around them as they went about their days. Customers of the cafe were similarly mindlessly engrossed in their morning rituals, eyes locked onto screens scrolling the same bullshit "news" while sipping at their coffees and teas.

But the air of casual indifference that Dimitriy had worked

for years to perfect belied the rapid beat of his heart and the sweat that was steadily building on his palms. His eyes constantly darted through the crowd around him, searching for any sign that something was amiss, but the mass of humanity continued to wash through the city without even a casual glance in his direction... with one exception.

"Is this seat taken?"

Dimitriy glanced at the empty seat next to him, then up at the dumpy-looking man in a not-quite clean black suit and tie. He pretended to mull over the stranger's question before shaking his head. "Be my guest."

"Thank you," the stranger said with a grateful nod, dropping a worn leather briefcase on the ground. He wiped the beaded sweat from his brow with a handkerchief before settling his ample girth into the chair.

Dimitriy raised one eyebrow ever so slightly upon hearing the creaks of protest from the abused piece of furniture, but he said nothing more.

"Ahh, that's better," the stranger said, motioning through the front window of the cafe to the waitstaff inside. "I find that the older I get, the more my feet rebel whenever I need to walk any great distance. Of course," he said, patting his midsection for emphasis, "I suppose it could have something to do with all the coffee and scones. Have you tried the scones here?"

Dimitriy shook his head. "I try to avoid unnecessary sugar."

"Shame," the man said. "The scones here are the best in the entire city—no bullshit! I've tried them all, in my time, believe you me—ah! Mei, the usual, please," he told the waitress who had just appeared.

"Are you sure, Mr. Zheng?" the lanky teenage girl replied, slipping a small tablet from her apron. "We got fresh raspberries in this morning, and Ushi made raspberry chocolate chip muffins. The most recent batch is still warm."

"Say no more, my girl! One muffin, and my usual frozen caramel macchiato, please and thank you." The waitress bowed gracefully and retreated inside the cafe, and the man turned his grin back to Dimitriy. "So, then… Where were we?"

"Scones," Dimitriy said flatly.

"Right! Scones… This place has the best scones in the entire city," he said with a lopsided grin. "But the muffins are even better! Ha ha!"

Dimitriy offered the buffoon a polite grin that didn't reach his eyes, then glanced back at his tablet as the waitress returned with the guy's order.

"Funny," the man said, "for someone who was in such an all-fired hurry to get in contact with me, you sure don't say much." He'd switched effortlessly from Chinese to American-accented English.

Dimitriy looked up, unable to keep the surprise off his face.

"My god. You GIM guys really are bad at this whole secret-agent thing," the man said with a derisive chuckle. "It's no wonder I've been able to operate with impunity in this shithole for so long."

"*You're* my contact?" Dimitriy said skeptically, allowing his eyes to roam meaningfully over the man's grossly out-of-shape figure.

"Appearances can be deceiving, Agent Volkov. Or don't they teach you that at what passes for the GIM's secret-agent school these days?"

Dimitriy's eyes widened ever so slightly. He opened his mouth on reflex to deny his identity, but the man held up a hand.

"Don't bother. I have a jacket on you as thick as my thumb. You've been a good agent for the GIM, given how criminally they've mismanaged your placement within the power structure here, though you've perhaps slipped a little in recent years." The man shrugged. "Can't really say I blame you, given the fact the GIM parked a young, gung-ho agent like yourself in a dead-end assignment and left you to rot for nearly a decade."

"I don't think we should be discussing such things out in the open like this," Dimitriy said, glancing around in alarm.

"My dear Dimitriy, you don't really think I chose this cafe to meet at because I like their shit coffee, do you?"

Dimitriy narrowed his eyes. Nothing about this encounter had been what he'd expected. He'd kicked around the edges of some known Confed sources because the fingernail-sized data card he had sewn into the hem of his trousers contained information he needed to get off-world, and his usual methods for such things were no longer secure. The GIM knew the Confed had at least three different agents on Lianmeng, but so far, they'd been unable to identify any of them. It was Dimitriy's hope that one of the CID agents here might have a way to get his intel into the right hands, but everything about the man in front of him felt wrong. Either this guy really was a CID agent—and one in a whole different league than Dimitriy—or the wrong people had found out about the information he'd recently come to possess and this was all a trap to get it back. Without fully realizing it, Dimitriy had begun snaking his hand toward the pistol he carried in an appendix holster, just inside the waistband of his slacks.

"Relax, kid," the guy said with a chuckle. "I actually am the guy you want to talk to. No need to go for that gun in your crotch. You can talk freely here. This cafe sits in one of the few blind spots in the city's public safety monitoring network. Lianmeng internal security can't hear or see us right now."

"You're with CID?"

Zheng nodded. "Longer than you've been alive. You can call me Zheng, for now. So, what've you got for me?"

"I need to get some intel off-world." Dimitriy allowed

himself to relax slightly, though he kept his gun hand on his lap, just in case. "I have reason to believe that my usual means for such things have been compromised."

"Oh?" Zheng cocked an eyebrow in question. "And why would I help out a known GIM agent?"

"Because the intel I'm in possession of concerns both my organization and also the CID. I just don't have any way to make sure it ends up in the right hands within the Confed."

"And whose hands would those be?"

"CID Director Gideon or Admiral Robert Garland."

Zheng's cocked eyebrow shot straight up to his hairline, along with its partner on the opposite side of his face, and he let out a low whistle. "Now *that* is mighty interesting. But I'm afraid your information is out of date. Both of those men are out on their asses after the removal of President McGibbons—"

"I'm well aware of the political shakeups within the Confed, Zheng," Dimitriy interrupted. "And I'm telling you, I need to get this intel to Gideon and/or Garland and not the puppets that have been put in charge of our respective governments— puppets that are being controlled by a previously unknown alien race hell-bent on humanity's destruction."

3

ANSWERS

BEN SAT IN A CHAIR DESIGNED FOR TH'ALOKI PHYSIOLOGY—WHICH was to say it made him feel like a small child sitting in his father's office chair—and idly drummed his fingers on the polished, onyx-black conference table in front of him.

After his somewhat awkward introduction to Tarok Na'al, the leader of a group in open rebellion against the Imperium and honest-to-God former first admiral of the Imperial Navy, he'd been escorted here and then left to sit and stare at the barren walls around him. To make matters somewhat more awkward, nobody had bothered to find him a set of clothes. That was just over two and a half hours ago, according to his neural implant, which he apparently still had, despite having been atomized in a nuclear blast and then... grown? Assembled? Well, however the hell the Imperial mad scientists had put him back together, they'd evidently installed a new implant during the process. And given what he'd been able to do after coming to back in Eelix's lab, Ben couldn't help but wonder what else they'd crammed into his brand-spanking-new body.

So here he sat, with what amounted to little more than an oversized loin cloth covering up his manly bits, but at least these guys kept their ships at a comfortable temperature—about three degrees warmer than Terran normal, according to his implant. How it knew what the temperature in the room was without a data link to the environmental sensors, Ben didn't know; it was just one more question to file away until he started getting some answers from somebody.

He held his hands up and inspected them for the umpteenth time since he'd been left here. They felt and looked like his hands... mostly. The shape and skin tone were correct, if a little paler than he remembered, but the slew of small scars dotting his knuckles from his time working on a farm were gone, as were the calluses he'd built up after years of manual labor and martial training.

One of the first things Ben had done after being dumped in the conference room was ping his implant for the current date; he needed to know just how long he'd been dead and gone. He'd expected to find it had been months, if not years. After all, somewhere along the line, his dad had hooked up with Admiral Na'al and the rebels, and then they would have needed to somehow come to terms and arrange bringing him back. Much to his disappointment, however, his implant returned an error when he queried it for the current date and time. His only guess as to why was that the rebellion docs that'd installed the implant either hadn't bothered to sync it to a Terran standard timekeeping system or hadn't had access to one in the first place.

Ben's brain hopped from question to question almost faster than his conscious mind could fully form the thoughts. How long had he been gone? What happened to *Indomitable* and the Alarian fleet over Hai'alla? His dad had been aboard the big battlecruiser, and if what Eelix had said about his dad giving his data to the rebels was true, that must mean he was still alive, right? So had *Indomitable* been able to escape that firestorm in orbit? Or had Ramsey and the Alarians pulled off a miracle and defeated the Imperial fleet that had shown up? And what about his team? Not only had Kravczyk and Mabel been with Klaythron, and some of the Pathfinders, but Tess and Valdez had also crashed the party toward the end. Tess...

God, he wanted to see her. It'd been months since they'd seen each other even *before* he blew himself up. How long had it been now? Had she survived the fight with the Imperium? How was she coping with his death? That last thought brought on a physical ache that welled up from somewhere deep in his chest as he considered the grief she must've felt, and more than anything else, he wanted to be near her again.

But those were the only questions Ben allowed himself to dwell on. His mind wanted desperately to spend some time thinking about what it meant that he'd died and been brought back to life. Was he the same person as before or just an empty copy of the real Ben Hutchins? But he forced that line of questioning to the back of the line. Something told him those were things better left addressed when he had some support nearby. Ben had always been confident in his sense of self, but sitting here, looking at the pristine skin on his hands, he was starting to have doubts about who he was *now*.

A high-pitched, almost static-like sound emanated from the hatch, interrupting his ruminations, and a moment later, it whisked aside silently. Time froze briefly as a memory flashed through Ben's mind at the speed of light. Another noiseless hatch slid aside, only to reveal the face of his enemy mere inches from the faceplate of his APEX suit. His hand lashed out reflexively, aiming for the soft tissue of the alien's throat...

"Ben!"

Time lurched back into motion and the memory evaporated. Ben leapt to his feet, but it was too late. His dad slammed into him and wrapped him up in a bear hug so tight his ribs creaked under the strain. Ben returned the hug but jerked his arms away a moment later when his dad wheezed in sudden agony.

"Sorry!" Ben said with a sheepish grin. "I guess somewhere along the line of dying and coming back to life, I forgot how strong I am." It was a lame attempt at breaking the ice, but his dad smiled through the tears streaking down his face all the same. "Admiral." Ben nodded to the hulking Th'aloki who was standing silently just inside the hatchway. There were others still out in the passageway behind Na'al, but before Ben could get a good look at them, his dad hugged him again.

"I thought I'd really lost you this time, Ben," he said, shifting his grip to Ben's shoulders and squeezing affectionately as he looked him up and down. His smile faltered when he saw Ben's hastily improvised kilt, and only then did he seem to register that his son was basically naked.

"Admiral," his dad said, turning to Na'al with a not-quite-friendly set to his eyes, "what's the meaning of this?" He gestured toward the scrap of tablecloth Ben had wrapped around his waist. "Why haven't you supplied him with any clothing? Surely, you must have something more suited for a human than a towel."

"My apologies," the big alien rumbled, stepping around the far end of the conference table and pulling out a chair for himself. "We initiated the reanimation process as our two teams agreed, but your son's integration didn't exactly go according to plan. He viciously attacked my chief medical officer, who was overseeing the procedure, and we immediately placed him in here as a precaution. I thought it best to wait until you arrived before we attempted to interact with him again. I feared the ramifications to our tentative alliance, should Ben have injured or killed one of my people or been injured himself due to a misunderstanding."

Ben's ears perked up at the mention of an alliance. So his dad had actually somehow managed to find and make friends with a rebel Imperial faction, and they were working together now? That juicy bit of intel had him chomping at the bit to get this show on the road and get the answers coming.

He watched as several more aliens filed into the room after Na'al, with Eelix being the last one in. All three of the newcomers cast wary glances toward Ben, choosing seats as far from the unstable Terran as possible. Ben smiled and cast a jaunty wave to Eelix, who returned the greeting with an annoyed glare.

His dad took a step back and cocked an eyebrow at Ben. "You did what?"

Ben held up his hands innocently. "I'd just been vaporized, then woke up—somehow *alive*—with an Imperial mad scientist standing over me. What was I supposed to do?" He waved a hand in Eelix's general direction, feeling his cheeks flush with a sudden rush of anger. "It's his own damn fault for not making sure the guy—whose last memories involved murdering the absolute shit out of evil aliens that happen to look *exactly* like him, by the way—was properly restrained."

Eelix squawked indignantly, but Ben ignored it. He'd gone from equal parts overjoyed and cautiously curious to seriously hot under the collar, but he couldn't quite put his finger on why. He didn't really blame the rebel doctor for what'd happened. During the time Ben had been cooling his heels here in the conference room, one of the things he'd spent some time reflecting on was just how fast and effectively he'd been able to flip that mental switch over to his warrior's mindset.

Given the information he'd had at the time, overwhelming violence had pretty much been the only real option if he'd wanted to escape. How was he supposed to know that the lab-coated Th'aloori standing over his newly awoken self was friendly? *You'd think they'd have taken some precautions to keep me sedated or otherwise restrained...* Ben's thought's flashed back to that bizarre suspensor field he'd been trapped in when he first came to, but a commotion from the opposite side of the room broke him out of his reverie.

"I did have him restrained!" Eelix shouted, standing up so fast that his chair tipped over with a crash. "He was contained within an anti-gravity suspensor field, and we'd installed a neural shunt to disable all motor functions below the neck. But he somehow broke through the lab's isolated near-field datanet and released himself before I'd finished the procedure!"

Ben's dad cocked his head at Eelix, and a moment later, his eyebrows knit together in confusion as he turned to look at the irate Th'aloori scientist. "How?" he said, casting a sidelong glance at Ben, then back to Eelix. "The Mk. VI implant Ben has shouldn't be able to crack your wireless security, unless he's integrated with Mabel. Ben's a special case when it comes to his mastery of our implant technology, but what little I know about your own systems tells me even *he* can't break your security on his own."

Eelix froze like a prey animal. "I... I don't know."

Something about the alien's body language signaled to Ben that he was lying his scaly little ass off, which triggered the memory of something Eelix had muttered to himself back in the lab.

"What did you mean earlier when you were talking about 'upgraded systems'?" Ben asked, narrowing his eyes in suspicion. "Back in the lab, I mean."

Eelix's eyes went comically wide, and his mouth silently opened and closed a few times. Finally, a strangled ticking sound emanated from the little alien's throat. Eelix's gaze flashed to the Th'aloori sitting next to him, then to Admiral Na'al, who'd been silently taking in the exchange like a predator studying its prey before an attack.

"Wh-What do you mean?" Eelix squeaked out. "I-I didn't say anything like that."

"Tellin," Ben said, addressing the Th'aloori next to Eelix. He was making an educated guess, but the guilty look the two aliens had just shared—coupled with the name Eelix muttered back in the lab during his little pity party on the floor—had Ben relatively sure his guess was on the mark. "Since Eelix doesn't seem interested in answering my question, how about you? After all, Eelix said the whole thing was your idea in the first place."

"He what?" Tellin exclaimed, turning to glare at Eelix. Eelix began to splutter, but an irritated growl from Na'al silenced the room.

"Enough!" the admiral barked. "This chaotic back-and-forth only serves to confuse the reason we're here. We will proceed with this meeting in an orderly fashion. Any irregularities that may or may not have occurred during Hutchins's integration procedure can wait until later, along with any potential causes thereof." Na'al shot a withering glare at the two bickering scientists before turning his gaze to Ben and his dad.

"Please, gentlemen," the admiral said, gesturing to a pair of seats, "sit down. I've already instructed my crew to bring some suitable garments for Ben. For now, I'd prefer to simply give Ben a broad overview of the events that have transpired since my fleet's arrival over Hai'alla and instead spend most of this time dedicated to determining our next moves in our shared struggle against the Master and its thralls. I suggest any Terran-related topics not strictly applicable to that fight wait until the two of you return to your ship."

Na'al was all business. Ben's overall impression of the alien commander thus far was that he was a rigidly disciplined, fiercely intelligent, no-nonsense type of leader. But there was something else in there—a burning hatred for the Master that peeked out when the admiral mentioned the entity that ruled the Imperium with an iron fist. He seemed the perfect ally for humanity's fight against the Imperium, but a wave of disgust washed over Ben as he considered Admiral Na'al. After all, this was someone who was openly committing treason against the Imperium. How long had Na'al been planning his little rebellion? He also seemed to only care about his personal fight against the Master, and Ben got the feeling he, and Terrans in general, were nothing more than a means to an end for him. Could they really trust someone like that?

"I have no objections to that," his dad said, sliding a chair out from under the table and taking a seat. "Ben?" He raised an eyebrow in question.

"Yeah, sorry," Ben said quickly, retaking his own seat. He made an effort to push his suddenly strong emotions aside, and they evaporated almost as quickly as they'd come upon him. "I've got a lot going on up here right now." He rapped a knuckle against the side of his head. "Whatever you guys did to put me back together has left me feeling a little, I don't know… off."

"To be expected," Eelix said with a sniff, having retaken his seat. "Considering that jumbled disaster of an engram file we were given, it's a miracle you're even able to walk and speak at the same time. My team and I spent many a sleepless night laboring to reconstruct you, Terran, and we still have a number of tests to run before you'll be cleared to leave my custody."

"Don't get me wrong," Ben said, holding up a placating hand, mostly to stop himself from acting on the urge to strangle the imperious little shit, "I'm grateful for your efforts. It's just that this is the first time I've ever been blown up and brought back to life, and it's proving to be a little more challenging than I might have expected. I don't really know what the playbook is for something like this."

"Maybe that's the best place to start," his dad said, looking first to Ben, then to Admiral Na'al. "With your permission, Admiral, I'd like to give Ben a quick summary of the events that took place during and after the Hai'alla operation, leading us up to where we are now."

Na'al inclined his head in assent. "As you wish."

His dad shifted in his chair so he was more directly facing Ben, then leaned back and let out an explosive breath. "Okay, where do I start here? Ben, what's the last thing you can remember?"

Ben had given that question a lot of thought over the past couple of hours, but he still wasn't sure what to tell everyone. The very last thing he could remember wasn't his fight with the agent in the server room or anything from his link with Saryf, the once-biological consciousness upon which the agent was built. The *actual* last fragment of a memory he had kicking around in his newly grown head was the warmth of his mother's touch—a touch that couldn't possibly have been real.

So he went with a lie of omission.

"The attack on the datacenter on Hai'alla," he began. "But before I continue, there's something I really need to know... How long have I been gone?"

His dad smiled. "Not as long as you might think, thanks to the admiral here. It's been just shy of four months since you and the Pathfinders assaulted the datacenter on Hai'alla."

Ben rocked back in his chair. Four months was all it'd been? He would have bet good money on that figure being closer to a year or more. Just how fast had his dad been able to find Na'al and work out their partnership?

"Wow..." Ben said, shaking his head in near disbelief. "That's significantly less time than I'd assumed." He looked from his dad to the rebel admiral and back. "I really want to hear exactly how this happy little alliance came to be, but I suppose that can wait for now. The question of how long I'd been gone has been eating at me something fierce for the last few hours, and just having an answer is a relief." Ben inhaled deeply and sighed away the tension that'd been building while he'd been waiting for someone to come tell him what was going on.

"Right then," he said, leaning forward and getting back to what he could remember. "The agent had us pinned down. Its troops were pounding the marines at the back of the facility, and after a bloody fight, my team and I had fought our way to the central control room. But the agent had already isolated itself from the planet's datanet, which effectively took Mabel out of the fight before she even had a chance to get into it."

Ben paused for a moment as a wave of fresh memories washed over him. Images blurred through his mind so fast that it was like looking at a deck of cards being shuffled: the agent's Reaper avatar, video feeds of the marines getting hammered by Imperial shock troops, a hulking construct controlled by the agent. Ben blinked a few times and shook his head, attempting to clear the cascade. He looked down at the table and became aware that he'd been unconsciously bouncing one of his legs.

"Ben?" his dad said softly, placing a gentle hand on his shoulder. "Are you okay?"

Ben cleared his throat and looked up, meeting his dad's gaze. "Yeah. Sorry..." He shook his head again, and his mind finally focused and came fully back under his control. "Just had a bunch of memories flash through my head for a minute there."

"It's alright, son," his dad said, dropping his hand away from Ben's shoulder. "I'm sure it's not easy. We've all had some time to process and move on from that battle, but for you, it must be like it just happened."

"Pretty much." Ben smiled grimly. "Um, anyway," he said, continuing with what he remembered, "the marines were getting hammered at the loading dock and the agent was threatening to unleash chaos on Hai'alla if I didn't surrender myself. The only way I could see saving the situation was to buy time for my team and the marines to break contact and evacuate. I figured I could keep the agent distracted long enough for everyone to make it out before the nuke we brought as a last resort detonated.

"You see, the agent assumed Mabel would be on board my APEX since I'm the only one we have that can link with her. He figured it could get both of us at the same time if I surrendered myself. But what the agent didn't know was that Chief Kravczyk's APEX had been modified to carry her matrix as well. The chief can't link with Mabel, but he could at least give her a ride out of there. So before I surrendered myself to the agent, I transferred her matrix to his armor via an inductive connection that I passed off as an extended handshake while I said goodbye. I also transferred a quickly composed text file with instructions on what I needed them to do. With the agent monitoring the control room, I couldn't tell them verbally.

"Then, while I went to go play tag with the agent's construct in the server room, Klaythron armed the bomb while the chief let Mabel do her thing in the control room. I figured if the agent was tied up with me, then she could quickly ransack any useful data from the onsite databases and hopefully figure out how to shut down the electronic jamming that was blanketing the area. Then they were to high-tail it out of there and get clear before the place went boom.

"As plans go, it wasn't exactly a masterclass in tactics," Ben admitted with a shrug. "I was just trying to get everybody out of there and, most importantly, keep Mabel safe. Being able to take the agent with me was just a bonus."

He leaned back in his chair and looked around the room, debating whether or not he should share what he learned about the agent and the biological consciousness that was shackled inside it. How would Na'al and the others react to him knowing one of the deep, dark secrets of the Master's agents? Did they know what the agents really were? Or would his bringing it up only serve to muddy the waters? While his dad apparently trusted Na'al and his crew enough to collaborate with them to bring him back to life, Ben was finding it difficult to trust these aliens at all. As far as his memories were concerned, the beings across the table from him were mortal enemies; it was going to take some time for him to entrust them with more intimate knowledge than what he'd already given them.

"Hmm," Na'al rumbled thoughtfully. "Neither we nor anyone from your assault force has any records of what happened in that server room after the Mabel construct withdrew from the facility's datanet and your team evacuated. Can you tell us how you managed to hold the agent's focus for the length of time you did? My people were able to identify the construct the agent used as a safe harbor from the rest of your team's sensor data—a very powerful piece of hardware, indeed. The Master's agents frequently use them whenever they require a physical shell capable of enduring combat or extreme environments. Your APEX armor, while a well-designed piece of technology in its own right, certainly wouldn't have stood a chance in a straight-up fight against a Reaper-class armored drone controlled by an agent."

Ben shifted in his chair and tried to keep his discomfort with the admiral's line of questioning from showing on his face, but the raised eyebrow from his dad indicated that he hadn't been all that successful.

Turning to his dad, Ben said, "Exactly how much did you share with our new friends here about my abilities while I'm wearing my armor?"

"Everything," his dad said without hesitation. "I figured they would already have a pretty good picture as to your abilities, thanks to the agent's long-time presence in our datanets, as well as the various times you interacted with their forces since the beginning of the war. And then, when we decided to move forward with the project to bring you back, I gave them every-thing we had regarding you. I wanted to make sure they had every scrap of information possible in order to minimize the chance that something might go wrong."

Ben nodded. He'd kind of figured as much, given that Na'al and his people clearly had access to Terran implant technology, Ben's complete genome and neural engram, as well as some sort of access to Mabel. Still, he didn't love the fact that these aliens now knew every last one of his little tricks and secrets. It made him feel naked, in a way. Vulnerable.

"To answer your question, Admiral," Ben said, resigned to the fact that he couldn't just skirt by with the barest of details about his fight with the agent, "I used the integrated combat blades in my APEX to pierce the armored casing of the construct the agent was controlling. Once I'd managed that, I was able to forge a link with the construct's systems and essentially do to the agent what it had done to me back on Elizabeth." He stopped for a moment, realizing Na'al and his people might not be familiar with the incident in question. "Are you familiar with the opera-tion I took part in on Elizabeth to neutralize one of the agent's slipspace transceiver facilities?"

The big alien smiled wryly. "Yes. I'm well aware that the agent ambushed your team at the site, as well as your apparent penchant for setting off nuclear devices on capital worlds."

Ben winced, but he did have to admit that he *had* kind of established an MO when it came to hunting down the agent. "Water under the bridge, as the Terran saying goes," he quipped, casually waving off the fact that everywhere he'd gone recently had ended up a radioactive wasteland.

"Okay," he said, getting serious again. "So, on Elizabeth, the agent ambushed Mabel and I when we attempted to link with a system it was residing in. We weren't prepared for it, and the agent managed to isolate Mabel in my armor while pulling my consciousness into some kind of virtual prison."

Na'al and the two Th'aloori scientists next to him nodded in understanding. *Well, isn't that interesting,* he thought. *So they're at least aware that the technology exists to digitize a biological consciousness. And if that's the case, then they probably know what the agents really are...*

"Well," Ben said with a nonchalant shrug. "I did the same thing on Hai'alla—bushwacked the son of a bitch and gave him a taste of his own medicine. I severed the agent's connections to all the input that defined its reality and locked it in a box, which held it in a kind of stasis long enough for the nuke to go off, and *poof.*" Ben simulated an explosion with his hands. "No more me. But most importantly, no more agent."

The smile that had been slowly stretching across the big Th'aloki admiral's mouth as Ben finished explaining how he defeated the agent sent a shiver down his spine. There was something feral residing just out of sight behind those razor-sharp, conical teeth.

"Finally..." the admiral said in a whisper so quiet Ben wasn't really sure he'd actually heard it. Eelix and Tellin exchanged excited looks with each other, then gazed back at Ben with something not unlike a zealot's fervor. The whole thing was creepy, and Ben couldn't shake the feeling that he'd somehow just become some sort of mystical object in their eyes.

"Uhh," he said guardedly. "I feel like I'm missing something here." Ben glanced at his dad to see if he could get a read on what he was thinking, but his dad just seemed confused by the whole thing, his eyes rapidly shifting back and forth between Ben and the aliens.

"Ben," Na'al said quietly. "Do you have any idea how long my people have been searching for an individual that can cross the plane of existence between what we perceive as reality and the digital realm? The realm where only those like the Master and its agent can exist?"

Ben just stared at the admiral. He had a bad feeling about where this whole thing was going.

"Millenia," Na'al said. "We've been waiting for thousands of years, hoping that, someday, we would encounter an individual like yourself: someone who can delve into the depths of the Master's realm... and kill it once and for all."

4

SENATE SHELLACKING

ADMIRAL ROBERT GARLAND QUICKLY DUCKED TO THE SIDE AS A bevy of photographers and reporters rushed in his direction. Questions were shouted and camera flashes strobed as the capital's security forces struggled to push back the rabid mob. Thankfully, none of the vultures appeared to have noticed Garland. Instead, the crowd was focused on the procession of senators and their aides that had just walked through the ornate doors leading out of the main senate chamber, led by that smug, conniving bitch Cynthia Mercer.

Garland was sporting a newly grown beard and neatly tailored civilian suit, having been forcibly retired after the ouster of former president Martha McGibbons. Her VP, Jasper Cunningham, had taken the reins and immediately gone to work cleaning house. The majority of the senior civilian and military leadership that had served under the McGibbons administration was summarily thrown out on their asses without so much as a "thank you for your service," and then the real fun had begun.

Mercer and her allies had needed to focus the chaotic beast that was the Confederated Terran Systems in the wake of the unprecedented events that had led up to this point, and they'd immediately gone to work raking the previous administration over the coals in front of very public hearings. Everything from the Alarian War right down to the high price of basic groceries was blamed on McGibbons and her people, and as with all political show trials, Mercer and her allies were sprinkling in just enough cherry-picked real facts to make the more ridiculous accusations seem credible. Today was merely a continuation of the same bullshit the senate had been crowing about for the last two months, without having actually accomplished anything other than improving their chances for reelection.

The whole thing disgusted Garland. What nobody was talking about was the fact that they were engaged in an actual, real-life shooting war with a previously unknown alien race, and it was happening *right now*. But the Imperium situation was all classified. The details surrounding the devastating losses the Confed suffered during the Battle of Icarus, the revelation that the Imperium had orchestrated the Alarian War, the fact that the Alarians were now allied with the Confed—all of it had been buried under a shroud of secrecy so thick Garland thought it was actually a minor miracle the new administration hadn't simply ensured he suffered an "accident" shortly after having his command ripped out from under him.

Then again, his opponents had been ready, pushing the narrative that the horrific losses attributable to the Imperium were actually suffered at the hands of the Alarians. Naturally, that explanation, of course, resonated well with a general public still suffering from nightmares about Alarian bombs falling in the middle of their cities. If he or any of his allies tried to expose the real truth here—that the Confed was at war with an unknown, highly advanced alien civilization hell-bent on their destruction—they would sound desperate, at best, or completely nuts, at worst.

Then he'd gotten the summons from the senate, and he'd

understood: they were going to make him a scapegoat. They were going to parade him in front of the cameras, assassinate his character, and trample his reputation with blatant lies, then look on with smug satisfaction while he sat there mutely, because no matter what he said, nobody would believe him. Or not enough, at least. Well, if that was the game they wanted to play, then so be it; he had his own allies he could call upon, and Garland had a few surprises of his own up his sleeve.

"Bob!"

Garland turned to face the familiar voice shouting over the din. Mark Gideon waved to him from half behind the corner of a hallway that led to the senate's gymnasium, locker rooms, and a host of lesser offices. Gideon inclined his head down the hallway and slipped around the corner, out of sight. Garland reversed course and followed.

"What's up, Mark?" Garland said with a wry grin. "Mercer and co. call you up for your ritual flogging today, too?"

Gideon grunted. "Yeah. I'm slated right after you. But that's not what I need to talk to you about. Come on." He stepped quickly down the hall and dove into an unoccupied office a few doors down. "Shut the door." He pulled a palm-sized device from his pocket and swept it in an arc around the room.

Garland did as instructed, glancing both ways down the hall to see if anyone was taking a special interest in them before closing and locking the door. "What's this all about, Mark? If the press see us sneaking around the capital for a talk like this, I can only imagine the creative stuff they'll come up with."

"We're clear." Gideon pocketed the device and turned to Garland. "We've got one hell of a big problem, Bob. And I'm not talking about the dog and pony show going on out there." He gestured in the direction of the senate chamber. "I got word this morning that one of my deep-cover agents on Lianmeng needs an emergency extraction, but I don't have any way to get him out."

Garland didn't bat an eye when Gideon referred to the agent as "his." Both men still considered themselves on the job, despite recent events. Still, neither of them had any authority with either CID or the navy anymore, so Garland couldn't see how this was in any way a problem involving him.

"Mark, I don't have any pull at CENTCOM right now, so I don't see what I can do here. Is CID working this?" Garland inquired.

"No," Gideon said, shaking his head. "My guy went outside the normal channels for this, using a back-door quantum link that goes directly to a small team that reported to my office for times when something is so sensitive that the reporting agent doesn't want to risk it going through the normal chain of custody. The handler that fielded this particular contact is someone loyal to us, and she quietly killed the report at the CID and passed it along to me directly."

Garland's eyes widened slightly. It was one thing to have someone on the inside feeding you information—he had his own back-channel contacts within CENTCOM doing just that, even now—but to have someone kill an emergency report like this? Whatever information Gideon's agent had called in must be radioactive.

"How bad is it?" Garland said.

"I don't know exactly, as my source didn't send much in the way of hard intel yet, but the status codes given indicate it's got something to do with the Imperium and its agents, the imminent threat of military action, and compromised command structure."

Garland swore softly. "What do you need from me, Mark?"

"I need to get my guy out, and I have nobody I can send. Is there any chance you can get word to our friends on Hai'alla and see what they can do?"

Garland pursed his lips and absently massaged his chin, thinking hard. He'd been completely locked out of CENTCOM's network, including both his official and personal comms accounts. He had a few trusted friends left that might be able to get word out to *Indomitable* via a comm drone, but that would surely flag in the system, as it would need to be a logged flight. He and Gideon were both nominally free men at the moment, but their travel had been restricted to the surface of Columbia until such a time as Mercer and her goons were done wringing them for all the political capital they were worth or they were charged with some trumped-up crime.

Finally, Garland shook his head and looked at the floor, feeling defeated. "I'm sorry, Mark. I don't have anything imme-diately available to me, but give me a day to think on this. There has to be some way to get this done." He checked his watch, then reached a hand for the door. "I'm out of time. I'll touch base with you tomorrow morning, one way or another. In the mean-time, keep working it from your end, too."

Gideon visibly deflated. "Damn." He sighed heavily. "I really hoped you might have a back-channel in place with Hutchins. I figured direct comms with *Indomitable* was a long shot, but with Hutchins out there, too, I guess I just thought you'd have a way to reach them."

Garland opened the door and quickly checked the hallway, then turned back. "Sorry, Mark. We'll talk tomorrow. Gotta go."

The admiral straightened his suit jacket and stepped out into the hallway, leaving Gideon behind. The feeding frenzy in the hall had mostly broken up now. Small detachments of reporters remained, huddled in groups around a few senators that were either eager to get their point of view out to the citizenry or had been cornered and were trying desperately to escape. Garland expertly weaved his way through the traffic, making sure he didn't draw any attention to himself as he navigated the media minefield. He took a right-hand turn just before the doors leading to the main senate chamber and followed the curved wall around to the east wing of the building, where he was scheduled to appear before a closed-door session of the senate's security subcommittee.

As he approached the secure conference room where the hearing was taking place, a pair of guards from the Senate Security Forces stopped him and checked his ID against the roster of approved personnel. While he waited for them to clear him through to the waiting area just ahead, a familiar face appeared. Commander Matthew Evans, whom Garland had once assigned to babysit Henry during his self-destructive phase a couple of years back, was just emerging from the overly large doorway to the hearing room. The man looked completely drained, but he still held his head high as he strode out from the lion's den. When he saw Garland standing in the hallway, however, his friendly face cracked a warm smile.

"Admiral," Evans said, reflexively beginning a salute but smoothly transitioning to a handshake upon realizing Garland was in civilian attire.

"Good to see you, Matt," Garland boomed, crushing the affable officer's hand in a heartfelt handshake. "I hope that pit of vipers didn't go too hard on you."

"It wasn't so bad, sir. Senator Jarrett went to bat pretty hard for us. He was in rare form today."

Garland grunted. "Sounds about right. He and Mercer have been at each other's throats for decades. I'm sure he's loving the opportunity to shit all over this witch hunt of hers."

"Admiral, you're up."

Garland looked up at the subcommittee's secretary, who was gesturing for him to join them in the hearing room. He nodded at her. "Coming," he said. Then he turned to Evans again. "Are you here in the capital for a bit longer, Matt, or are you heading back out to Archimedes?"

"I'm here for the next twelve hours. Then I'm headed back to Kerner. It seems the new powers-that-be are content with sticking me at Archimedes and letting me continue trying to wrangle all the scientists there." Then Evans chuckled, as though a thought had just occurred to him. "Although, I must say, it's not nearly as tall an order now that I don't have to babysit Henry all day. But…"

Garland watched the man's face as his mirth quickly faded, replaced by a mix of sorrow and disgust. This conversation had only served to remind them both that Hank was stranded in Alarian space—persona non-grata to the new administration, along with everyone aboard the three ships Garland had sent there to parley with the Alarians. While they'd been successful in getting the Alarians on board with an alliance, they were now stuck there, effectively exiled by the new administration because the news they would bring back would very likely undo all the political maneuvering Mercer and Cunningham had done over the last couple of months.

But something Evans had said tickled the back of Garland's brain. Then, a moment later, his eyes flew wide open when the adrenaline rush hit him. He clamped onto Evans's shoulder so tight the man winced.

"Matt," Garland boomed. "It was great to see you. Let's catch up over lunch, after I finish thrashing this pack of jackals. I'm buying."

5

UPGRADES

"YOU DID WHAT TO MY SON?" HENRY EXPLODED.

Ben stood up and put a hand on his dad's shoulder in an effort to calm him down. Despite the bombshell Eelix had just admitted to, Ben couldn't help but smile inwardly at the role reversal; historically, *he* was the one that usually needed to be calmed down in a situation like this.

"Chill out, Dad. This isn't the first time I've had untested tech jammed into my skull." Ben gave his dad a meaningful look. His dad winced and went silent, and Ben said, "Let's hear him out on just what, exactly, they did and why."

His dad's face was flushed, but after a moment, his shoulders sagged and he sat back down. "Very well," he said with a noticeable edge to his voice, and Ben realized he must still be harboring guilt about the fact that he'd used his only son as a science experiment once upon a time.

Ben retook his seat and gave his dad a reassuring pat on the back. "Look, Dad, if Eelix says what I think he's about to say, this could end up being a huge boon and will probably explain how I was able to break through the measures they'd put in place to restrain me when I came to." Then he looked up at the Th'aloori medical officer. "Right, Eelix?"

Eelix nodded meekly, stealing a glance at Admiral Na'al, who'd reacted with a similar level of outrage as Henry when his chief medical officer admitted to using an unapproved implant design in Ben that incorporated a number of Imperial materials and technologies. "That's right... Should I continue?" He looked first to Ben and his dad, then at Na'al.

Receiving nothing but unfriendly stares, Eelix cleared his throat awkwardly, then continued. "As I was saying, Tellin and I were not impressed with the specifications of the Terran Mk. VI implant your father requested we use, so we examined some alternatives to utilizing the Mk. VI as designed. We ran a number of simulations to determine if we could modify one of our own implants for your physiology or if we should instead attempt to integrate some of our more advanced materials and technology into the Mk. VI. However, neither Tellin nor I were familiar enough with Terran physiology or technology to feel confident in our results, so we consulted with the Mabel AI construct aboard your vessel, *Indomitable*. When we explained to her what we wanted to do, she was not only very helpful, but also quite enthusiastic—"

"Of fucking course she was," Henry said with a sigh, resting his elbows on the table and massaging his temples.

Ben couldn't help but chuckle. Mabel had always been prone to doing things without asking, but she'd really started to become quite the rebel once she and Ben started spending so much time together during their training evolutions after the Battle of Icarus. In fact, Ben recalled his dad saying something about needing to get him and the chief away from her for just that reason.

"I'll deal with Mabel after I return to *Indomitable*," his dad said resignedly. "Please, Eelix, continue."

"Uh, yes," Eelix said uncomfortably, having just realized he'd unwittingly outed another of his accomplices. "As I was saying, the Mabel AI was very helpful. She was primarily responsible for the redesign of the standard-issue Mk. VI implant, upgrading it with a number of modern Imperial materials, as well as designing the interface that allowed us to use our most advanced generation of quantum processing cores. The end result is an implant that is one hundred percent safe for Terran physiology and will integrate seamlessly with existing Terran technologies such as your APEX suit. The materials used for neuronal signal conduction are twenty-six times more efficient than the carbon composite nanotubes you were previously using, and we expect the processing core to be at least a hundredfold faster than your current Terran-designed processors, though we won't know the exact improvement until the implant fully integrates and we can test it under real-world conditions.

"There are a few other modifications that were made to the design: improved near- and far-field wireless capability, improved power generation and storage for the implant, as well as a significant expansion of the onboard memory capacity. However, Mabel and I both agree these improvements were necessary to prevent some of the issues Ben experienced in the past, such as the current bleed-through event that left his biological nervous system severely damaged, as well as to prepare him as best we can for any future encounters with an agent or even the Master itself." Eelix finished, slumping back in his chair and looking like a naughty kid that had just confessed to a grave sin he'd been keeping secret for a long time.

For his part, Ben wasn't actually all that impressed. In his mind, it made perfect sense to maximize his potential. They were building him up from scratch, so why not take the opportunity to correct some flaws and give him every advantage they could? Based on how skittish the little aliens had been after being caught red-handed, Ben was expecting them to admit to cramming him full of a bunch of alien weaponry or other gizmos. His mind had been conjuring visions of Wolverine-like blades sliding out of his hands or advanced cybernetics throughout his body. Heck, he wouldn't have been surprised to find out he wasn't actually flesh and blood anymore, but some sort of biomechanical construct instead.

So to hear that all this fuss was over some upgraded material and processing cores being incorporated into a run-of-the-mill neural implant? It was a bit of a letdown.

"So, wait," Ben said. "Everybody's freaking out because Eelix, Tellin, and Mabel went outside their chain of command to make sure I was given the best implant I could possibly receive? You'll have to forgive me, but I'm really struggling to see why what they did wasn't the course of action in the first place. You guys had the perfect opportunity to build me up into the most potent weapon you could, but you settled on remaking me just the way I was?" Ben asked, a bit of incredulity working its way into his tone.

"That's not the point, Ben," his dad said, using that irritating lecturing voice he'd so frequently used when Ben was a kid. "Modeling is all well and good, but we only had one shot at this and didn't want to risk using hastily designed, untested technology. There are so many things that could have—and still could— go wrong here that it was deemed too risky."

Ben snorted derisively. "This from the guy who jammed a prototype implant into his only child without any kind of oversight whatsoever."

"That was different!" his dad shouted, slamming a fist onto the table.

"Was it?" Ben fired back. "Because as far as I can see, Eelix and Mabel did the *exact* same thing you did five years ago! Look, I don't blame you for what you did, Dad. Desperate times and all that. But to pretend that we aren't in the same exact situation now looks a lot like someone sticking their head in the sand and pretending the reality around them doesn't exist."

Ben waited a moment to see if anyone wanted to object, but they all just stared at him passively, save for his dad, who looked like he couldn't figure out which emotion needed to be the dominant one: guilt or anger. Since nobody else wanted to chime in, Ben took the opportunity to unload some of the baggage he'd been hauling around for the better part of a year.

"Dammit! Yes, we got bushwhacked by the Alarians five years ago thanks to the agent pulling the strings. Yes, we barely had our feet back under us after the war before the Imperium sent in the cleanup crew to finish the job, leaving us with barely more warships than could fit in a string bag. But I'm so sick of all the pussyfooting around! We're staring down the extinction of our entire species—and the Alarians, too. The Imperium isn't just going to leave us alone because we gave them a bloody nose. They're going to come back, again and again and again, until all of us are wiped out or enslaved. I've seen that movie, and it isn't pretty. Now isn't the time for caution. Now is the time to swing our enormous iron balls around and go for broke.

"No more half-assed measures. No more politicians promising action, then turning around and going back to sitting on their thumbs because they're worried what the voters will think. We need to mobilize for war. *Really* mobilize—like we mean it. That means throwing everything we have into building ships, recruiting every ornery son of a bitch out there and giving him a rifle, making a concerted effort to lock down our cybersecurity so the Imperium can't pull the same shit twice, and if we need to bust some heads to get it done, then so be it. But I'm done patiently sitting back and waiting to be told what to do. I've seen what awaits us if we fail, and there's no way in hell I'm going to let that happen, if I can help it."

Ben realized he'd been directing his little diatribe directly at his dad, and he took a moment to look around the room and see how the admiral and his people were reacting. Na'al had a predator's gleam in his eye, but Ben couldn't tell if that was a good thing or a bad thing. Eelix and his compatriots seemed genuinely shocked at the ferocity with which Ben had voiced his thoughts. "We can't wait," Ben said, looking meaningfully at Na'al. "If we're going to be any use to your rebellion, Admiral, we're going to need some help getting our own house in order first. I will not be a weapon for you to sic on the Master until after we get my people moving in the right direction."

Na'al's expression darkened somewhat at that, but a moment later, he nodded. "Very well. My fleet will assist you in this, but only for a limited time. My betrayal will have kicked off events in Imperial space that *will* require the presence of my fleet and myself before long."

"It's not going to be that easy, Ben," his dad said. Something in his tone had that little voice in Ben's head screaming bloody murder that shit was about to hit the fan. "After Hai'alla, there was a coup within the Confed. McGibbons was removed from office, along with Bob Garland and a number of other higher-ups that supported action to prepare for war with the Imperium.

"The new administration is pinning everything from the high cost of groceries to the Alarian War on McGibbons and her administration, and they're quietly trying to sweep everything related to the Imperium under the rug. Not only do we lack the support we would need in the senate to do what you propose, but you and I are effectively exiles. If we were to fly back to Terran space, *Indomitable*, the *Wraith*, even the *Robert Morris*, which is just the fleet tender that brought me out here with spare parts for *Indomitable*, would all be immediately quarantined and shuffled off to some backwater holding facility where nobody could make any trouble for the new administration and their...

messaging," he finished, coating that last word in so much contempt Ben thought he might have been able to physically touch it.

"So... what?" Ben asked, his head spinning with the news that he'd apparently gone from humanity's savior to one of its most wanted. "We're stuck out here with no support whatsoever? The Confed is just going to plug their ears and scream 'lalala, can't hear you' at the top of their lungs until the next Imperial fleet shows up to burn them to ash?"

His dad sighed heavily and glanced down at the table in defeat. "Pretty much," he said flatly. "I'm sure Bob is doing everything he can to salvage the situation, but we haven't even had any communication from him for over a month. And if that's not happy enough news for you, Elyria tells me her people are threatening to pull their support and circle the wagons." He met Ben's eyes. "Ben... everyone on Elizabeth thinks you're dead, including those who are on our side. We need to shake things up, give people hope again. Our hope is that you can do that. Just the fact that you're alive—the man who went head to head with the Imperium, not once but twice, and came out on top—that kind of thing can take on a force all its own.

"Right now, our alliance is fractured and the Confed is in turmoil. We need someone who can rally the troops just by being seen. The things you and your team have accomplished are incredible, and while the general public are unaware of what you've done, the power brokers that make things happen within the Confed know exactly who you are and what you've done. Those big iron balls you so eloquently spoke about a minute ago? You're the one who has them. And I think if you wheel them right down the center aisle of the senate chamber in front of God and everyone, people will listen to what you have to say."

Ben sat in stunned silence for a moment, trying to process

how everything could have possibly gone to hell so fast. Then, as his dad's words really began to settle in, the bottom fell out of his gut when he realized what his dad was talking about. "*Fuuu-uuuck,*" he whined. "I'm going to have to go be diplomatic again, aren't I?"

His dad smiled for the first time since their reunion hug at the start of the meeting. "Don't be such a baby, Ben. Considering how quickly you got the Alarians to agree to an alliance, I'd say your diplomatic track record is pretty good."

Ben buried his face in his hands. "You should have just let me stay dead."

6

ESCAPE FROM LIJIA

"Just leave it, Vasily," Dimitriy said to his partner, who was scrambling to detach a series of data drives from a workstation. "We don't have time. Zheng's message said we're burned. We have to go now! Just wipe the drives and initiate the fail-safe."

The GIM agent pulled two nondescript backpacks from a pair of hooks on the wall next to the apartment's door and tossed one to Vasily. The younger man—a recently graduated agent on his first assignment, whom Dimitriy had been helping find his stride —caught the pack and slipped his arms through the straps, then tapped one last series of commands into the secure laptop computer that housed all their local mission files. The screen went blank a moment later, followed by wisps of acrid black smoke that curled from the seams of the case.

"It's done," Vasily said. "Let's go."

Dimitriy swept his gaze around the barren apartment one last time, making sure they hadn't forgotten anything. This place was a designated safe house for GIM agents, and the only place in Lijia that Dimitriy had spent more time in than his office at the Central Ministry's annex complex just adjacent to the city center. Satisfied they'd completed every step of the evacuation protocol, he checked the camera feed from outside the door one more time to make sure their escape route was still clear. It was, so he unlatched the dead bolt and opened the door.

Dimitriy stepped half into the hallway and glanced in either direction, but his eyes told him the same thing the camera feed had—it was deserted. He stepped out fully and turned right, headed for the fire escape leading to the alley behind the apartment building. Vasily was right on his heels.

The two men walked quickly down the hall, past boarded-up doors, water-stained wallpaper, and gang graffiti. A deep bass beat thundered out from an open doorway about halfway down the hall, and Dimitriy merely nodded at the tattooed muscleman guarding the door of one of the local drug dens. The brute raised his chin in greeting, and then the two agents were past him. They reached the end of the hall and slipped into the stairwell. Signs in multiple languages warned that an alarm would sound if the door was opened, but the alarms had long since been disabled, if they'd ever even worked at all.

When they reached the ground floor, Vasily cracked the door open and glanced around the alley. His eyes took in nothing more than the usual clutter of trash cans and a few drug addicts reclined against the dirty masonry with glazed expressions on their faces. He opened the door and walked into the alley, heading for the busy street nearby—and the ground car that was supposed to be waiting for them just around the corner.

When they turned the corner at the intersection, Dimitriy was relieved to see the car Zheng had promised. The driver was parked in a loading zone, casually reading a tablet and smoking an e-cigarette. Vasily opened the back door facing the sidewalk, and Dimitriy unslung his pack and tossed it inside before climbing in himself. Vasily sat down beside him and closed the door, and the driver put down his tablet and shifted the car into drive.

"Everything go okay?" the driver said over the faint hum of the electric motors as they accelerated out into traffic.

"Yes," Dimitriy replied.

"Good. We've got a ride waiting for you at the commercial spaceport south of town, by the industrial zone. I'll drop you off at one of the cheap hotels across the street, and you can make your way over there on your own. One of our guys will be manning the main gate when you arrive, and he'll get you squared away from there. Got all that?" the driver said.

Dimitriy looked over his shoulder, paranoid about the possibility that they were being pursued. "Understood. Is Zheng meeting us there?"

"That I don't know," the driver replied as they turned away from the heart of the city and headed toward the outskirts of town. "I'm just the—shit!"

Dimitriy was thrown forward against the back of the driver's seat as their car struck something with tremendous force. Fireworks exploded behind his eyes with the impact, and the world around him suddenly went silent. His vision began to clear a moment later, but at first, he couldn't make out much of anything through a dense white smoke that filled the passenger compartment. A pair of hands roughly dragged him out of the back seat, and he managed to snag one of his pack's straps as he was pulled out of the car. He landed hard on the ground and threw his elbows back to catch himself.

Vasily's face appeared in front of him. The man was yelling, but all Dimitriy heard was a high-pitched ringing. Vasily shook him by the shoulders and pointed at something. Dimitriy followed his partner's outstretched finger and saw the blood splattered across the inside of what was left of the car's windshield. Something in his head clicked, and the world started to come back into focus. His gaze fell on the driver, slumped over the wheel and missing the left half of his face.

"Come on, Dimitriy! They've found us!" Vasily pulled a short-barreled PDW from his pack and unfolded the stock.

Dimitriy struggled to his knees, fumbling with the zipper on his own pack, but his movements were uncoordinated and sluggish, and he had a pounding headache.

"Run!" Vasily shouted. Then he opened up with the PDW, using the crumpled remains of their car for cover. The muzzle blast from the unsuppressed weapon hammered at Dimitriy's ears, but he did his best to block it out and focus. He glanced around, finally seeing his surroundings with some sort of clarity.

Their car had been struck by a garbage truck, but the hit hadn't been as clean as it should have been, thanks to the driver's quick reflexes. Instead of plowing directly into the side of the truck, the driver had managed to veer to the side just enough that they'd only clipped the truck's rear end. The impact at speed had killed the driver and sent their car spinning off the road. They'd come to rest wedged up against an alley next to a convenience store, the remains of their car acting like a barricade.

Dimitriy stood on shaky legs and stumbled into the alley. The sound of gunfire thundered through the confined space around him, but he managed to finally slip his arms through the straps on his pack. The alley ended at a chain-link fence, but the rotting carpet draped over the top of the fence and the dumpster pushed up against it told him this was a well-traveled alley among the street gangs that claimed this part of town as their turf.

Dimitriy stole a glance over his shoulder as he fled. Vasily was still hunkered down behind the car, trading fire with whoever was attacking them. The young agent nimbly ejected a spent magazine and fished a full one out from his pack. He slammed it home and slapped the bolt release, chambering a fresh round as he rose to fire again.

Then his head exploded. ·

Dimitriy looked on in horror as what remained of the young agent collapsed to the ground, blood pouring from the horrific wound.

The violent death of his partner jolted his concussed brain, allowing Dimitriy to operate on instinct. His instructors had beaten survival skills into him mercilessly when he'd trained to become an agent, and though he hadn't needed to call upon those skills in over a decade, they came naturally to him now. He turned back down the alley and ran toward the chain-link fence with renewed energy. When he reached the dumpster, he vaulted onto it and launched himself at the fence. His hands gripped the carpeting laid over the barbed wire strung atop the fence, and his feet scrabbled for purchase among the links.

Shouting erupted from behind him, followed immediately by gunfire. Bullets snapped through the air all around him, a few sparking as they struck the hardened alloy links of the fence. Dimitriy crested the top and dropped to the ground on the far side, the dumpster's bulk serving to absorb most of the rounds fired at him. He stayed low as he sprinted for the end of the alley, his heart pounding in his chest as a roaring filled his ears; the adrenaline dump was finally catching up to his concussed brain.

Just as he reached the alley's exit, something stung the outside of his thigh. He staggered as he exploded out onto the sidewalk, the burning sensation in his leg already ramping up in intensity. He knew he'd been hit, but he couldn't stop to check the damage. Dimitriy angled to the side and out of the line of fire from the alley, then continued running, ignoring the shouts of anger and surprise from the pedestrians he shoved aside in his mad dash to escape. He spotted a public trolley just crossing the intersection at the end of the block, and he put on a burst of speed, veering out onto the street as he closed with the intersection and angling for an intercept with the trolley. He leapt onto the rear platform just as the trolley cleared the intersection, headed away from his pursuers, and he looked back at the alley. Several men dressed in black tactical clothing burst out into the daylight, armed to the teeth.

Then he was out of their line of sight, a building interposed between him and the men who were trying to kill him as the automated trolley continued on its route.

————

"DIMITRIY? WE THOUGHT THEY GOT YOU," Zheng said, looking relieved as Dimitriy was escorted into a private hangar at the commercial spaceport. A run-down microfreighter stretched from one end to the other, its marker lights on and its engines already beginning to spool up. "When I heard what happened, I was sure the ministry's goons had nabbed you." Zheng raised his voice so he could be heard over the growing din. "How did you escape?"

"Vasily sacrificed himself to buy me time to get away," Dimitriy said wearily. "It was close, but I was just able to evade their tac team after the ambush. I'm sure we don't have much time before they track me here, however. I was forced to use some public transportation to get here."

Zheng nodded and looked up at the freighter's cockpit, twirling a finger in a circle above his head. He put an arm around Dimitriy's shoulder and guided him toward a boarding ramp. "No time to waste, then. Let's get the hell out of here."

Once aboard the ship and strapped into a utilitarian seat just aft of the freighter's cockpit, Dimitriy finally allowed himself to rest. Zheng was leaning through the cockpit door, talking to the flight crew, but Dimitriy couldn't make out any of what they were saying. His exhausted body and abused brain screamed for him to relinquish all control and let him sleep, but something told him that was a bad idea.

"Zheng," Dimitriy said. When the CID operative turned around, his questioning look rapidly changed to one of concern when he took in Dimitriy's face. "I think I need medical attention." Dimitriy slurred the last few words as darkness crowded his vision.

"Dimitriy!" Zheng shouted, kneeling in front of him and examining the Russian in detail. "You're hit," he stated when his eyes landed on the bulge over Dimitriy's thigh from the bandage he'd hastily applied to his wound. Zheng peered closely at Dimitriy's pupils, apparently seeing something he didn't like. "Don't go to sleep! Do you hear me, Dimitriy? Don't. Sleep."

Dimitriy felt his shoulders sag, and the rest of his body went limp. Then, mercifully, sleep claimed him at last.

7

SECRET AGENT STUFF

COMMANDER MATTHEW EVANS KNOCKED BACK THE LAST FEW SIPS of his coffee, then pushed his chair away from the table and stood up, leaving his tray for the staff of the officers mess to clean up. Being back on Archimedes Base certainly had its advantages, especially considering the fact that he'd been left in his current role as the officer in charge of liaising between the civilian scientific staff and the Confed military... at least for now.

The senate hearings had been the miserable clusterfuck he'd expected from what amounted to a political show trial, but he'd managed to at least escape with his job intact. He didn't exactly love his prospects for further advancement. Hell, if he was being honest with himself, he fully expected to be left here to rot until he couldn't take it anymore and retired. But a few more years of babysitting civilian scientists, followed by a nice, quiet retirement would end up as nothing more than a pleasant dream if he was caught doing what he was on his way to go do right now.

Evans exited the mess hall and hooked a left, heading in the direction of the transit tube that would take him to the civilian residential complex, where all of the base's nonmilitary personnel were quartered. Despite the fact that he'd walked this same route hundreds if not thousands of times over the past year, his heart was hammering in his chest. Garland had asked him to do a very simple favor. But he couldn't help feeling like the admiral had asked him to switch his MOS to that of an intelligence operative.

Evans showed his ID to the pair of marine guards manning the security station at the entrance to the civvie dorms, and they waved him through without a second glance. He emerged into the building's atrium—a significant upgrade in aesthetics compared to the dorms that housed the base's military personnel. After all, one had to keep the civilians happy so they'd continue to grind out cutting-edge technology for the war effort.

Evans headed straight past the small botanical garden in the center of the atrium and stopped at a bank of elevators along the back wall. A soft chime emanated before his finger could press the call button, and the doors to his left whisked open. A scene flashed through his mind: armed marines storming out and tackling him to the ground before slapping cuffs on his wrists and leading him away to the brig. But the only people to step out of the lift car were a pair of middle-aged men chatting quietly with each other.

The two men didn't even acknowledge Evans's presence as they strode toward the security station, and Evans quickly slipped into the elevator car before the doors slid shut. He pressed the number for the top floor, and a faint hum filled his ears as the car was lifted toward his destination. Two minutes later, he was standing outside a plain-looking door with *H. Hutchins* printed on the nameplate.

Evans glanced down the hall in either direction to make sure the coast was clear, then keyed the door open with a generic security override code. If anyone checked the logs later, all they would know was that someone associated with either command or base security had accessed this room. While he would almost certainly be a suspect, at least his personal ID wouldn't flag in the system and furnish the authorities with a giant, flashing neon arrow pointing directly at his face.

The locking bolt retracted with a soft click, and Evans hurried inside.

The lights came on automatically as soon as the room sensed motion, and Evans looked around the mostly tidy quarters. The bed was made—not quite up to navy standards, but close enough—and everything was neat and orderly, save for a few small items still resting on the desk in the corner. The new administration was still in the process of cleaning house within the various levels of military leadership, and they'd either been too busy to have someone come by to bag and tag all of Henry's stuff, or they simply hadn't cared. The man was effectively exiled more than a hundred light-years away, and they already had access to all of his research files because he'd been working for the military up until his departure.

Evans strode over to the desk and pulled open the bottom right-hand drawer. A plain black metal box, about twenty centimeters square and no more than five or six in height, stared back at him. The standard tablet docking port on the top of the metallic box sat empty, however. *Of course,* Evans thought. *Henry never goes anywhere without that beat-up datapad of his.*

Evans quickly pulled open the other desk drawers and rifled through their contents. When he pulled open the center drawer, he hit paydirt. What looked like hand-drawn schematics for some piece of tech Evans didn't recognize lay front and center, but it was the datapad—so new it still had the plastic protector sheet stuck to the screen—that caught his attention. He pulled the small device out and ripped the plastic off. Thankfully, the battery was still charged, and the datapad came to life as soon as he swiped at the screen. Evans snorted in amusement when the datapad displayed the initial setup screen asking for the user's language preference. He quickly worked his way through the setup menus until the device displayed the generic home screen that graced all government-issued computers and datapads.

Evans wasted no time, opening up a new text file and quickly hammering out as concise a message as he could manage while still including all the details he thought they'd need. When he'd finished, he marked the file *Extremely Urgent* and saved it. Then he stuck the datapad on the docking port of the quantum link module in the bottom drawer, which had been cleverly designed to allow him to read the screen and input commands, despite the fact that the link module was affixed to the bottom of the drawer.

A prompt appeared, informing him that the device didn't have the necessary software to utilize the QE link and asking if he'd like to install it. He tapped *yes*, and a few seconds later, another prompt appeared, letting him know the install was complete and the system was ready for use. He closed the prompt and tapped the new icon that had appeared on the home screen. The UI was extremely simple, opening a window that asked him to select the file he wished to transmit. Evans selected the text file he'd just typed out and tapped *OK*. A new window popped up with a progress bar, and a soft blue line began crawling across the screen.

Evans leaned back in the chair and exhaled an explosive breath. He'd done what he could, and when the link module finished transmitting in a few seconds, it would be up to Henry, the SEARs, and the rest of their people to figure out where to go from here. He didn't envy them one bit—they were going to have their work cut out for them in the coming days and weeks.

He just hoped and prayed they weren't too late to act on the information he'd just sent them. Because if they were, a whole lot of people were probably going to die.

8

HANDS

"GODDAMMIT!" BEN SHOUTED IN FRUSTRATION AFTER READING THE red text of the alert his HUD was flashing in front of his eyes. He ripped off his helmet and tossed it onto an adjacent workbench. "What the hell is the problem this time?"

His dad didn't immediately answer. Instead, the furrow in his brow deepened as he continued to swipe his fingers across a datapad. Ben waited, impatiently tapping one armored foot on the floor.

"Please stop that," his dad said without looking up.

Ben growled. "Fuck it," he said, unlocking his gauntlets and ripping them off. He tossed them on the table next to his useless helmet, then set about extricating himself from the rest of his brand-spanking-new APEX armor. "We've been at it for six hours with jack shit to show for our efforts. Something somewhere is screwed up, and we're not going to have a fix figured out until we can sit down and really dig through the data to figure out where the issue lies."

Finally, his dad stopped tapping away on his tablet and looked up. "You're probably right, Ben. I just don't understand it, though. Everything checks out. All the self-diagnostics show green. Your implant appears to be linking up with the suit's hardware just fine. I can't for the life of me see anything that would be preventing the APEX from responding to any and all of your commands."

A pair of *Indomitable*'s engineering techs cracked the seals on the armor around Ben's torso and pried off the backplate, allowing him to finally peel himself out of the rest of the armor that encased his upper body. "Mabel, what are you seeing?" Ben asked, glancing at a nearby holotable, where her familiar dot matrix cube avatar was pulsing her usual soft blue color.

"Everything appears to be normal, at least insofar as I can tell, Ben," she replied. "But I'm forwarding the data over to *X'nec* to see if any of Admiral Na'al's people might have an insight as to what the problem may be."

"Do you really think they'll know what to look for?" his dad said. "They don't have much experience with the APEX armor systems."

"True," Mabel said, "but they have extensive experience when it comes to integrating neural implants with advanced technology among their own people, and their engineers were furnished with complete schematics on both Ben's APEX and his implant during the project to bring him back. A fresh set of eyes can't hurt, Henry."

His dad sighed and then tossed his datapad onto the workbench next to Ben's discarded helmet and gauntlets. "No, I suppose not," he admitted. "Do me a favor please, Mabel, and have copies of all the data we've collected sent to the workstation in my quarters. I'm going to take Ben down to the mess deck for some lunch."

"Sure thing, Henry," Mabel said. Then her avatar evaporated into thin air as she left the lab.

Ben nodded his thanks to the two techs as they pulled the last of his APEX free and returned it to the nearby assembly rack.

Then he jogged over to a set of lockers nearby and grabbed a clean set of ship's utilities and a pair of boots. After stripping off the APEX skinsuit, he quickly donned the utilities, then sat down on a bench and pulled on the boots.

Ben finished cinching the laces but paused. He stared at his hands, deep in thought. He flexed his fingers slowly. The dimensions and physical sensations were all correct, but they didn't *feel* like his hands. He sat up slowly and rubbed a thumb over the knuckles of his left hand, where there should have been a series of small scars from several years spent tearing himself up on the farm. But the skin covering the joints was pristine. The frustration that had been building over the last few hours evaporated, replaced by a deep unease that flirted with the border of dread.

He'd been kept aboard *X'nec* for almost a week after they'd brought him back. Eelix and his team had run a truly impressive battery of tests during that time, and when the poking, prodding, sampling, blood-drawing, and scanning were finally finished, the little Th'aloori medical officer had pronounced Ben better than new and fit to rejoin humanity. But while Ben's DNA was identical to his old self and his memories seemed to all be there, intact, something was off.

He'd been brought aboard *Indomitable* in the dead of night and hustled off to a secure section of the ship. An army of the navy's medical people had immediately launched a full-scale assessment of his health—both physical and mental. And after several days of enduring *their* poking, prodding, sampling, blood-drawing, and scanning, they'd pronounced him fitter than any human alive and cleared him for duty.

So then why didn't he feel like he belonged here?

"Ben? Are you okay?"

Ben inhaled sharply, suddenly aware that he hadn't been breathing for an unknown length of time. As his lungs filled once again, his thoughts cleared, somewhat. "Yeah," he said, though his ears told him he'd failed miserably at his attempt to conceal his unease. He turned to look at his dad, who'd been patiently waiting by the hatch leading out of the lab, hoping he hadn't picked up on Ben's distress.

His dad frowned with concern and strode over, taking a seat beside him.

Busted.

"Questioning who you really are now?" his dad asked gently.

Ben's heart rate ticked up a notch. Was he really that transparent? He'd always thought he was better at hiding his true feelings from his dad, but his old man had seen through him with ease.

"How'd you know?"

A shadow passed over his dad's face for just a split second before it was replaced with a sad little smile. "Because I've seen that same look on my face every day since Admiral Na'al told me they had a way to bring you back." Then he looked away. "I almost didn't do it," he finished, his voice so quiet it was almost a whisper.

Ben put his arm around his dad's shoulders. "I'm not sure I'm glad you did," he said quietly. Now it was his turn to look at the floor.

The two men sat in silence for a long minute. Every part of Ben screamed at him not to say the things he desperately needed to, because voicing them out loud would mean admitting his fears. His pride as a Hutchins man demanded he bottle this shit up and get on with what had to be done, but the chaos raging in his head was becoming so much of a distraction that he knew he'd have to unpack his thoughts with someone… and soon.

As much as he loved his dad, this was something he didn't feel comfortable talking to him about. So he'd been putting it off, waiting for Tess and the SEARs to get back from the surface. As strange as it seemed, Ben thought they'd understand infinitely better than his dad could, despite the fact that they'd apparently been kept almost entirely in the dark about the effort to raise Ben from the dead. Hell, they were due back aboard the *Dame* in less than a day, and they still had no idea he'd be here to meet them when they stepped off the ramp.

The SEARs had been planetside the entire time he'd been back, along with what remained of the Pathfinders, participating in a training evolution with the Alarians. In the wake of everything that happened on Hai'alla a few months ago, the Alarians were scrambling to shift their military doctrine to something geared toward fighting Imperium shock troops instead of the Confed. But the lack of familiar faces other than his dad's and Mabel's had only served to make Ben feel even more like an outsider since his return to *Indomitable*.

"I don't know who I am, Dad," Ben said, his voice breaking as tears began to well in his eyes.

"Ben—"

"No," Ben said, shaking his head. "I really need to just unload this stuff without interruption. Sorry," he added, finally looking up to meet his dad's eyes. He took a deep breath, and the words started pouring out. "I look the same, my DNA is identical, all my memories are here"—he tapped the side of his head—"but I don't *feel* the same.

"I look in the mirror and I see my face. I hear my voice when I talk, and I feel my body move and respond how it should… but I'm *not* the same, Dad." He held his hands up in front of his face, then flipped them around so his dad could see his knuckles. "These aren't my hands!" he said, shaking them for emphasis. "Look!" He stabbed a finger toward the knuckles of his left hand. "There are supposed to be scars here! Two years after the bombs fell, I ripped the skin completely off of these three knuckles. I was in the middle of the west vineyard, on my back and underneath the flail mower, trying to clear a piece of wire that'd been sucked up and got jammed in the drum. When the fucker finally came loose, this hand slipped and smashed into the blades. And let me tell you what, even though I had everything shut down, those fuckers are more than capable of tearing your ass up.

"Where are they?" Ben asked rhetorically. "I'll tell you where. They're scattered all over that planet below us, along with the rest of me." Tears were flowing freely from his eyes now, but he didn't bother to wipe them away. "So if *I* am scattered all over that fucking planet as a collection of radioactive particles, then who the hell's hands are these?"

His dad sat in stunned silence for a moment, tears running down his own face. Then he wrapped Ben up in his arms and whispered in his ear, "My son's." His dad released his embrace and took Ben's hands in his own. "These hands belong to my son, Benjamin. And don't you ever forget that."

9

CONTACT

HENRY APPROACHED A FIERCE-LOOKING MARINE WHO WAS STANDING beside the hatch to one of *Indomitable*'s secure briefing rooms. The military types called it a SCIF—the acronym for sensitive, compartmentalized information facility—but Henry just called it a pain in the ass.

"Corporal," he said, nodding politely. "I believe I'm expected."

About an hour ago, *Indomitable*'s comms officer had contacted Henry and informed him that Captain Ramsey requested his presence at a high-level briefing to discuss the current state of affairs within the Confed. While Henry wasn't exactly a political animal, he was responsible for the development of some of the navy's most important technologies. He was also best friends with the man who was spearheading their fight against the machinations of the Cunningham administration and its allies in the senate—Admiral Robert Garland. Not to mention the wild card that Ben now represented, though exactly what his son would be able to do for them was still in question.

Ben was exceptional when it came to killing aliens and breaking their stuff; he was decidedly less exceptional at diplomacy. Henry had given him a big speech about being needed to help sway the politicians back on track and unite humanity, but in reality, that was probably a long shot, at best. Lately, the situation had been feeling more and more desperate, and Henry wasn't delusional enough to believe that Ben would be seen as some sort of white knight, there to rally the troops and lead them to victory. In fact, he thought, it was more likely that Ben would be cast as the villain, given how much support Cunningham and his cronies had managed to build among the general citizenry. But what he knew for sure was that just sitting out here, doing laps over Hai'alla, wasn't going to help them in the slightest. They had to try something.

The sentry took Henry's ID and checked it against a list of authorized persons. After a few glances between Henry and his datapad, he handed back the ID and tapped out a few commands.

"I'll need you to place any personal belongings in here," the marine said, indicating an open lockbox on a rack next to the hatch. Henry knew the drill for entering a SCIF, so he'd taken only his personal datapad and ID with him. After tossing his stuff in the box, he held his arms out to his sides so the marine could sweep a security wand over his person to make sure he didn't have anything hidden away somewhere.

Satisfied that Henry wasn't secretly a terrorist, the marine nodded at him. "You're good to go, Mr. Hutchins. They're waiting for you inside."

"Thank you, Corporal," Henry said with a polite smile. Then he ducked through the hatch after the marine keyed it open. Inside the SCIF, Henry was greeted by four familiar faces, two strangers, and one softly glowing blue dot matrix cube, which was suspended in the air over a conference table that made a valiant effort to look like it was made from real cherrywood. But he was most interested to see Captain Collins from the *Wraith* sitting there. She'd taken her ship back to Terran space to do some poking around and see if they could get a better read on the political situation back home.

A comm drone had come in carrying a message from CID Director Gideon a couple weeks after the assault on the data-processing facility, and the message it brought had been short and maddeningly vague. All they knew for sure was that President McGibbons had been impeached and the new administration was purging everyone associated with her. Worse, both the new administration and a powerful coalition of senators were doing their damnedest to sweep the Imperium mess under the rug and blame everything on the Alarians and a small rogue faction within the Confed military—namely, Garland and anyone associated with Henry and Project Blackthorn. The SEARs had been burned, along with Collins and her entire crew. Ramsey and *Indomitable*, along with Major Davis and his Pathfinders, had been officially declared AWOL.

In the message, Gideon intimated that he and Bob were both likely to be removed from their posts within the week and that the small contingent of Terran forces over Hai'alla should stay well away from Terran space for a while. That message, coupled with Garland's last-minute play to keep their little three-ship force as an ace up his sleeve for the coming political shakeup, had left the Confed forces over Hai'alla in limbo for the last several months. Henry knew Collins had finally taken the *Wraith* on a fact-finding mission a few weeks ago, but he hadn't heard a word about where she was taking her ship or when they were due back.

"Henry," Captain Ramsey said, rising out of his chair and reaching across the table to shake Henry's hand. "Thanks for coming. How's Ben getting along?"

"A bit of a mixed bag, I'm afraid," Henry said, returning the captain's firm handshake. "Everything checks out with him, but we're running into some bugs when it comes to getting him back into his armor. All our diagnostics show he, the armor, and his link with the hardware are good to go, but for whatever reason, he isn't able to do so much as lift a finger in it. I'm confident we'll get it all nailed down, but it's been a frustrating couple of days for both of us."

"Well, let me or Commander Russell know if there's anything else we can do," Ramsey said, retaking his seat. "Whatever you need."

Henry nodded his thanks. "I suspect the problem isn't related to the armor or his new implant, but a mental block on Ben's part. I'm hoping the return of some familiar faces today will help him get over whatever is going on in his head and let him focus, but in the meantime, I've sent copies of all the data we've collected over to *X'nec* to see if Na'al's engineers can spot anything we're missing."

"I can only imagine what Ben must be going through," Ramsey said sympathetically. "Let's hope you're right and the return of the SEARs and the Pathfinders help him clear whatever demons are lingering from his ordeal. I believe they're due aboard within the hour?" He glanced questioningly at his XO.

"Should be coming aboard any minute, sir," Russell confirmed.

Ramsey turned back to Henry. "And again, Henry, if there is anything we can do to help, you need only to ask."

"I appreciate that, Captain. Thank you." Henry then turned his attention to the others in the room. "Commander Russell, Captain Collins, Major Davis," he said, greeting the other people he was already acquainted with either with handshakes or polite nods, depending on their places around the table. "Major, I'm surprised to see you up here already. I'd assumed you'd be coming up with the rest of your marines."

"I was going to," Davis admitted, "but Captain Ramsey

asked if I could make this meeting, and if I'm being honest, I'm really not all that useful when it comes to getting marines to line up and board a dropship. That's what the Marine Corps has sergeants for."

Henry smiled good-naturedly. "Well, it's good to see you again, regardless." His gaze shifted to the two unfamiliar people at the far end of the table: a dour-looking brown-haired woman with captain's bars and a youngish-looking lieutenant commander with bright blue eyes and biceps nearly bursting out of his uniform. "And I'm afraid I haven't had the pleasure…"

"I'm terribly sorry, Henry," Ramsey apologized. "I completely forgot that you haven't had the opportunity to meet my counterpart aboard the *Robert Morris*, Captain Felicia Stanz and her XO, Lieutenant Commander Ashland."

"Nice to meet you." Henry pulled a chair out from under the table and took a seat next to Captain Collins. He had, in fact, had the opportunity to meet Captain Stanz and her XO when he'd flown out here aboard the fleet supply ship, but neither of them had ever bothered to make their way down to guest berthing to meet *him*. He'd spent most of his time going over all the work they needed to do to repair *Indomitable*'s QE link with Shelly, so it wasn't like he'd made the effort to be social, either. And given the unflattering things he'd overheard from the *Morris*'s crew, he didn't really *want* to get to know Captain Stanz.

"Eh-hem."

Henry smiled. "And hello, Mabel," he said to the pulsing cube overhead, noting her color had shifted ever so slightly toward purple-blue. "It's good to see you, too. How's everything in your cozy little corner of *Indomitable*'s network?"

"Very good. Thank you, Henry," she replied, a touch of amusement in her voice.

"I don't think I'll ever get used to that," Captain Stanz said.

The scowl on her lips told everyone in the compartment just how she really felt about dealing with an AI.

Henry's immediate instinct was to get defensive at Stanz's statement. Mabel was the culmination of his life's work, after all, and he wasn't about to just sit there and let some unhappy shrew of a woman take shots at her. But before he could retaliate, Mabel put the *Morris*'s captain in her place, with authority.

"If you'd like, Captain Stanz, I could ask Captain Ramsey for a few days of leave. I'm sure it wouldn't be too much trouble to have my matrix transported aboard your ship, and we could spend some time getting to know each other a little better. I might even be able to assist your chief engineer in correcting the harmonic resonance issue your ship has been experiencing for the past week.

"I suspect the problem lies with a containment field misalignment. Those old type-II tokamak designs are getting pretty long in the tooth at this point, and it wouldn't surprise me to find some of the superconducting magnets have degraded to the point that it's causing an issue. I can crunch the data and put together a plan to help your engineering section compensate for the unequal field strength, if they're having a hard time nailing down the adjustments on their own."

Her tone had been light and friendly, but Henry's long experience with the AI helped him detect just the barest hint of sassy bitch buried in there—as if calling Stanz's ship old and her engineering crew incompetent wasn't a dead giveaway. By the time Mabel was finished, Henry had a few different emotions warring inside him. On the one hand, he was deeply embarrassed that his creation would speak to a naval officer in such a manner. On the other, the red flush of Stanz's face as she barely controlled her fury was *deeply* satisfying. And when he surreptitiously glanced around the table to see how everyone else was taking the exchange and he saw hints of smiles and/or general mirth lighting up their eyes—including on the face of Stanz's own XO —Henry decided that Stanz probably had it coming. He allowed smug satisfaction to win out, and he made a mental note to congratulate Mabel on her expert use of passive-aggressiveness

"Unfortunately, Mabel," Captain Ramsey said, trying to steer the meeting back on track, "I'm afraid we'll all be too busy to indulge in any sleepovers. Which brings me to the first item I'd like to discuss now that we're all here. Captain Collins, would you be so kind as to share what you found out on your mission?"

The last trace of the smile she'd been suppressing after Mabel dropped the hammer on Stanz had vanished, replaced by a grim expression. She looked around the table, and the atmosphere of the room shifted to all business when everyone saw the look on her face.

"I'll get right to it," Collins said. "The situation is far worse than anything we anticipated. We were aware the new administration is trying to pin everything from the Battle of Icarus to the nuke on Elizabeth on us and the Alarians, but they've also gone so far as to recall nearly all active naval forces and place all those ships and crews on standby for an indefinite period of time, meaning we have almost no fleet presence outside of Columbia and Kerner.

"Ostensibly, they're conducting an official review of all military personnel—trying to root out traitors and sympathizers and the like—but I think something else is going on. You don't just pull all of your ships back to your two remaining naval bases and leave virtually every other system undefended. Seriously, you should see the fleet assembly stations in Columbia. They've got so many ships jammed into the docks or at anchorages nearby that it looks more like a mothball fleet than anything else. Reactors are all spun down, and crews have been gutted via forced leave or reassignment or mandatory training evolutions dirtside. I've never seen anything like it. The fleet has gone from a full wartime footing to acting like there's not a single threat anywhere in the galaxy. It's truly bizarre."

Henry was astonished, and judging by the looks of utter shock on the faces of everyone else, so were they. When *Indomitable* had been sent out here to see what could be done about forging an alliance with the Alarians, the political situation back home had been a little uncertain, but he couldn't imagine how things had veered so far off course in such a short period of time. Henry had been around the galaxy for more than half a century; he'd seen the various political factions' power ebb and flow time and time again. But so dramatic a shift had never occurred so fast. This kind of thing usually took several years of building rhetoric and huge media pushes to even get the ball rolling in the direction of change, not just a few short months. Not in the Confed, at least.

"All fleet assets?" Ramsey asked. "Even the permanent guard forces around Earth and Valkyrie?"

"Pretty much," Collins replied. "Earth has a token force remaining—based on what comms we were able to intercept, at least. The *Wraith* is an incredibly stealthy ship, but we weren't able to make it more than about a half an AU from Elizabeth, so the intel we collected is a little thin. However, we also made a stop at Newman's Rock, as it's still nominally located in an unaligned system, and the long-haul freighter crews were much more forthcoming with information, like the fact that Valkyrie has been stripped of everything except the cutters and gunships that the Planetary Defense Force operates."

"What the hell is going on?" Major Davis muttered to himself, shaking his head in bewilderment.

"Well, that probably explains why we haven't received any further communication from Admiral Garland or Director Gideon," Ramsey speculated. "If CID and CENTCOM have the fleet locked down that tight, it's unlikely they'd be able to take advantage of their remaining support network and get word to us using official assets. But I'm still surprised we haven't heard a single word through official channels as to our status. One would think they'd at least want to get *Indomitable* back in their hands, if nothing else."

"But doing so would cast doubt on their narrative," Henry chimed in.

"What do you mean?" Stanz asked, furrowing her brow.

Henry shrugged. "If the new administration's story is that a small group of renegades stole a few ships and partnered up with the Alarians, then how would they explain reaching out to those same renegades and ordering them to come back in? At the very least, the crew of the ships they sent to fetch us would have questions as to why we weren't being blown out of space on sight. And if they sent a comms drone, there's an entire chain of people involved with sending that drone that would know where it was headed. Questions would be asked," Henry said matter-of-factly. "And if Bob and his allies in the senate and within CENTCOM are fighting the fight I'm sure they are, those questions would only bolster their side of the story.

"So they're going to leave us out here to rot. Think about it. We're more than a hundred light-years from Terran space. You couldn't ask for a better place to store your inconvenient dirty laundry. We don't have enough ships of our own to even think about using force as a solution, and even if we did, all it would do is galvanize the citizenry against us. And if we try to politely knock on the door and return home, we'll all be arrested and thrown in a deep, dark pit somewhere unpleasant until we can be disposed of quietly.

"Cunningham is playing hardball," Henry continued. "And what's worse is we didn't see it coming, and now we've lost almost any chance to effectively push back. In politics, the first liar is almost always the one that gets believed by the public, and we most certainly were not first. But the real kick in the nuts here is I don't see how we can realistically expect to be able to get Ben or our new Imperial friends in front of the senate to open some eyes and try to expose—"

He broke off mid-sentence when the locking bolts to the hatch thunked open and a muted-but-incessant beeping spilled into the briefing room. The marine guard poked his head into the compartment, looking apologetic.

"My apologies, sir," he said to Captain Ramsey, looking a bit flustered, "but Mr. Hutchins's datapad is making a heck of a racket, and it won't stop."

Every eyeball in the room was suddenly staring straight at Henry. "Uh," he said, looking sheepish at having forgotten to set the device to silent mode before locking it up. "I guess I'll just step out and see what's going on. Be right back."

He pushed his chair back from the table and headed for the hatch.

"I'm sorry to interrupt, Mr. Hutchins, but I thought it might be important," the marine said as Henry ducked through the hatch.

Henry searched his memory but couldn't think of any reason why his datapad would be sounding continuously like it was. The tone emanating from the lockbox was the one he'd set to alert him to an emergency, but the fact that there were no alarms blaring throughout the rest of the ship nixed that option; his datapad was connected to the ship's wireless network and nothing else. If it was signaling an emergency alert, the only place it could be coming from would be the ship. Well, that or...

Realization dawned on him, and he threw the storage box open as soon as the marine finished unlocking it. He quickly pulled out the datapad and swiped at the screen. A notification popped up, informing him that a text file had just been uploaded via the quantum comms link back in his quarters at Archimedes. He opened the file and scanned the message, his eyes going wide.

Without a word to the marine, Henry bolted back into the SCIF, datapad in hand.

"We've got a problem," he said. "A *big* fucking problem."

10

NO TIME FOR REUNIONS

Ben leaned his head back against the cool steel of the bulkhead adjacent to one of the airlocks allowing access to the big battlecruiser's flight deck and closed his eyes. A mighty boom reverberated through the deck plating, followed a moment later by strobing yellow lights accompanied by a warning klaxon. Ben opened his eyes and focused on the gauges mounted next to the airlock's hatch. The one showing the atmospheric pressure of the flight deck was creeping up toward the green with agonizing slowness.

He didn't know exactly how he felt. He was excited, certainly. There was also a healthy dose of joy at the prospect of seeing the people he cared about for the first time since the attack on the agent, as well as an eagerness to feel that sense of brotherhood that went with being a member of an elite team of badasses.

But overshadowing all the positive emotions was a thick pall of anxiety. How would his friends react? How would *Tess* react when he strolled casually across the flight deck with a smile on his face like nothing had happened? Would they be just as happy to see him as he was to see them? Or would they fear him?

Would they fear the ghost that was about to walk back into their lives? Or worse, what if they couldn't see him as the real Ben Hutchins? What if all they saw when they looked at him was a hollow shell, a cruel mockery of the friend they'd lost?

The strobing yellow light snapped off, and a voice came over the intercom, announcing that the flight deck was repressurized and personnel were cleared for entry. This time of day—or, more accurately, night, according to ship's time—there wasn't much activity on and around the flight deck, save for the various crews that were required to secure and service the spacecraft that had just arrived. Most of the engineering shops and maintenance teams that made this area of the ship a hive of activity during the day were off duty now, so Ben was the only one that stepped into the small auxiliary airlock in front of him, which he'd chosen for just that reason.

His heart hammered in his chest as he toggled the control to equalize the pressure in the airlock with that of the flight deck. He peeked through the small viewing port and out into the flight deck area but couldn't see much, thanks to the limited field of view offered by the small circle of glass. He stepped back and waited. The airlock cycled quickly, but it still felt like the pumps took forever to equalize the pressure. Finally, the indicator above the hatch turned green, and the locking bolts retracted.

Ben opened the hatch and stepped out onto the flight deck. The airlock he'd used was nestled in the corner of a maintenance bay, so he stepped quickly to the mouth of the bay and looked around. The flight deck of the Colossus-class battlecruisers was absolutely massive and reminded Ben of the time his crippled shuttle had been brought aboard the carrier *Halifax*, back when he'd been fleeing to Earth after the outbreak of the Alarian War. Everywhere he looked, aerospace craft were crammed into every nook and cranny. Saber strikefighters, Griffon assault dropships, and a few small personnel shuttles were all stuffed into their various bays and tied down securely. But lined up along the centerline of the flight deck, still hissing and smoking from their transatmospheric flight and subsequent transition from the vacuum of space into the pressurized atmosphere of the flight deck, sat two huge Marine Corps MS-88 Condors.

A veritable army of crew chiefs, maintainers, and other personnel were swarming around the transports, rapidly going through the post-flight protocols that needed to happen before the ramps could be lowered and the people inside were let out. Ben did his best to stay out of the way, following the painted line on the deck designating the path for people to transit the flight deck so they wouldn't be run over by equipment, trip over fuel lines and the like, or be roasted to a crisp behind an MPD.

He knew which direction the marines, Valdez, Kravczyk, and Tess were going to head as soon as they exited their ships, because he'd done this drill a half dozen times a few months back when he'd been one of them. So Ben posted up in a spot they would all have to file past on their way to the transfer airlock that would take them off the flight deck and toward the assembly area, where they would dump their gear and check their weapons. His plan was to stand there with a shit-eating grin on his face and act like nothing had happened, but as he'd learned time and time again, no plan survived contact with the enemy.

Ben's gut was doing a truly remarkable job of finding new and interesting ways to twist itself into knots, and a wave of anxiety-induced nausea washed over him. He crossed his arms in an attempt to hide how badly his hands were shaking.

The flight deck crews backed away from the tail ramps of the Condors, and the big slabs of alloy began to descend with the whine of hydraulics. In just a few short seconds, Ben would find out which, if any, of his fears were valid. He steeled himself for any gut punches that were about to come his way and watched as a bunch of exhausted-looking marines in full kit tromped down the ramps and turned in his direction.

Interestingly enough, he didn't see any Alarians mixed in with the Terran Pathfinders. Due to the horrific losses they'd suffered at the hands of the Imperium on Hai'alla, and the fact that the Confed had cut them off entirely, the Pathfinders had been forced to fill out their ranks with Alarian marines if they were to remain an effective fighting force. Fortunately, Klaythron and Major Davis had overseen the integration of the Alarian marines with the Pathfinders starting just a month after the operation to take out the agent, after it became clear the Pathfinders weren't likely to receive any kind of replacements from the Confed. Not wanting to be caught at barely half strength, Davis lobbied for a combined force to at least give the alliance a full company of special operations troops without having to rely exclusively on Alarian forces.

To the surprise of everyone but those who'd fought shoulder to shoulder with Klaythron and his commandos on Hai'alla, there'd been almost no friction between the two races outside the expected and inevitable cultural issues. In a story as old as time, those in the profession of arms had quickly rubbed the rough edges off each other before buckling down and getting to work. It helped that both the Pathfinders and the Alarians chosen to join them were a cut above the average infantryman, having been forged into true professionals in the fires of their respective training programs. The weary marines trudging toward Ben were returning from their final training exercise with the Alarians, and the word on the street was that they'd soon receive the nod of approval to move forward as an integrated unit.

Ben inched away from their line of travel, allowing plenty of buffer space between where he was standing and where the marines were about to file past. He scanned the Pathfinders as they approached, but they were all wearing their helmets, full chest rigs with weapons slung, and big rucksacks strapped to their backs, and it was hard to make out many facial details as they quickly filed out toward the airlock. Then, suddenly, his heart leapt into his throat.

There, striding down the ramp with a fluid grace that Ben would never be able to match, was Tess. Her APEX was beat up and dirty, and the color of her left pauldron and one of the armored fairings below it didn't quite match the rest of her armor, indicating it had been replaced at some point. But what really caught Ben's attention was the *way* in which she moved— her body language. Something wasn't right. Ben remembered her gait having more life to it. She still had that fluid grace he remembered so vividly; it just seemed less energetic now.

She reached the bottom of the ramp and turned, waiting for Valdez and Kravczyk, who emerged side by side, their heads bobbing toward each other as if in conversation, which they were, judging by the chief's enthusiastic arm waving. The two reached the bottom of the ramp, and all three of them began their trek to the airlock.

The first group of marines was already past him and cramming themselves into the big service airlock used to move large quantities of people and supplies at once. Nobody appeared to have recognized Ben, though he noted a few familiar faces, but no one he was particularly well acquainted with. The first group looked to be mostly made up of marines from Third Platoon, which Ben hadn't had much interaction with in the past. He took a moment to scan the marines again and spotted Dominguez, who was currently trying to get Ybarra to agree to join him in the showers when they finally got to their berthing area, but she was having none of it.

Ben looked away, suddenly averse to the idea of drawing attention to himself. Standing here on the sidelines in a set of nondescript utilities, he was just another faceless swabbie, as far as the marines were concerned, and they didn't even give him a first glance, let alone a second. Ben had worked so hard to prove himself to the Pathfinders, first in training on Elizabeth, then in combat as they took on the Imperium and hunted down the agent. And just like that, he was an outsider all over again, unworthy of the marines' attention. It stung his pride, but what was worse, it filled him with even more doubt about who he really was now. Ben quickly glanced up to see where the SEARs were, contemplating making a hasty exit before he could intrude on their lives.

Three onyx-black faceplates were staring directly at him, their owners rooted in place halfway between Ben and the Condor they'd just walked off of.

Time slowed to an agonizing crawl as Ben stared back, a deep, soul-sucking dread washing over him. He wanted to run, but the terror gripping his heart wouldn't let him. All his fears, all the doubts he harbored about himself—it felt like they were all laid bare the instant his gaze connected with theirs.

Then Tess was running, a blur of motion approaching so fast even Ben's shiny new Ferrari of a nervous system had a hard time tracking her. He stood there, unable to do anything but worry about what she would say.

She stopped three paces away, guarded and leaning away from him slightly as if she expected him to attack at any moment.

"Ben?"

Her voice came through her suit's external speakers, barely more than a choked whisper. Ben fought to swallow, but the ball of iron in his throat made it impossible.

"Hey, Gorgeous," he said, lips briefly curling up into a sad little smile. "Miss me?"

Ben remembered the sound of her helmet hitting the deck, but any and all other details of what happened before and after that were forever lost to him. The next thing he knew, Tess was on top of him—all hundred and fifty armored kilos of her—and her lips were warm on his. They each tried to pull the other in closer as they kissed for the first time in forever. Tears streamed down Tess's face as she pulled away at last, and Ben blinked away tears of his own as he looked up into her beautiful green eyes.

"You have got to be fucking kidding me," Kravczyk boomed from over Tess's shoulder, where he and Valdez were standing with their helmets off. "I really thought I'd actually managed to get rid of you for good!" The big SEAR turned to Valdez. "Boss, I'm formally requesting a transfer." He stabbed a finger at Ben. "This dude is way more trouble than he's worth, and I want nothing to do with him... again."

Tess stood up and Kravczyk reached down to help Ben to his feet. Ben took the proffered hand and was immediately yanked off the deck and into a crushing bear hug. A pitiful, high-pitched wheeze was all Ben could manage as Kravczyk made him feel like a small child in his massive arms.

"You son of a bitch!" the big SEAR bellowed. "You tricky son of a bitch! You actually did it! You came back!" Then the chief froze as a sudden revelation hit him. "Oh... shit," he said, looking resigned. "This means I'm actually going to have to pony up for those beers I promised, now doesn't it?"

Ben merely wheezed again in response.

The crushing force on his ribcage eased a bit, and Ben gulped in a lungful of air. He shook his head. "Chief, I don't really care about the round you owe me," he said before his eyes locked onto something strapped to Kravczyk's back. At the sight, he curled his lips up into his best grinch smile, then looked back at the big SEAR. "But I *am* going to make you give me my favorite boomstick back."

Kravczyk dropped Ben and backed away with his hands out,

pleading. "No," he said desperately. "Anything but that. You name it, it's yours. Just don't take Ethel away from me."

Ben blinked a few times, the smile disappearing from his face. "Ethel?" he said flatly. "You named my custom-built XM-93, tailored specifically to my unique abilities and physiology... Ethel?"

Before Kravczyk could respond, a commotion from around the big service airlock caught their attention, and they all turned to see what was going on. Ben's eyebrows rose a few notches when he saw his dad hurrying toward them, accompanied by Captain Collins and another pair of fleet officers Ben didn't recognize.

"Hello, Ben," Captain Collins said, walking up with a warm smile. "It's great to see you again." To Ben's surprise, she leaned over and gave him a brief hug. "I'd love to stay and catch up, but we're in a bit of a hurry, I'm afraid." She indicated herself and the two officers Ben didn't know. "See you soon."

And before Ben could get even a single word in, she was gone, heading straight toward one of the Condors the marines had just arrived on, with the two strangers hot on her heels.

Ben turned to look at his dad. "What was that all about?" he said, looking to the SEARs to gauge whether or not they knew what was going on.

"We've got a problem, Ben," his dad replied, deadly serious. He swept his gaze around the SEARs before it landed back on Ben. "I'm afraid we're out of time for reunions. It's time to get back to work."

11

REVELATIONS

A HARD THUMP JOLTED BEN OUT OF HIS REVERIE, AND HE FINALLY looked up from the well-worn deck plates of the Griffon's cargo bay. Valdez stared back at him from across the aisle, over all the crates of gear secured on pallets in the center of the bay.

"Docking clamps," he said. "Stay strapped while they bring us in."

Ben nodded and leaned his head back. The cool surface of the alloy spar helped him feel more grounded to where he really was. He and the SEARs had been kept in the dark as to the exact nature of the emergency that required them to quickly pack their gear and prepare to transfer to the *Wraith*. All his dad had said was that they were needed for a mission and time was short. The next several hours had been a whirlwind of packing their gear and getting ready to deploy. When Ben tried prying details out of his dad, he got nowhere. Even Mabel wouldn't give him any juicy bits as to what was up, other than to say she didn't think it would involve any direct combat, which was good, considering the fact that Ben couldn't actually use his multimillion-dollar powered armor suit to do something as simple as a push-up, let alone go into combat with it.

Then his dad had disappeared along with Mabel and a bunch of gear, leaving Ben to stew in the dark a little longer. The chief and Tess had taken the first flight over to the *Wraith* a few hours ago, with Ben and Valdez left to make sure the rest of their gear was accounted for and made it over to the little spy ship. It was everything Ben had come to hate about life attached to a military unit: hurry up and wait, coupled with a complete and utter lack of information as to why you were hurrying up just to wait. But eventually, the order finally came down for him and Valdez to shuttle over.

So for the last half hour, as the small dropship ferried them to the *Wraith*, Ben had been lost in his own little world. Fortunately, he found it easy to not dwell on all the questions he had about their mission. Unfortunately, that was because his thoughts had been endlessly looping through a chain that started with his body being built from scratch and having his mind transplanted into it. It ended with the possible root causes for his inability to use the thing that, over the last year, he'd come to think of as part of himself: his APEX. Questions that threatened an existential crisis—like whether or not he still had a soul and was "real" —aside, Ben was sure the answer to his current problem was in there somewhere.

By all measurable metrics, he was better than he'd ever been. The team that worked to bring him back had solved the dueling nervous system issue with better materials and proper coding for the dendrite production. Not to mention being able to grow dendritic pathways in a controlled environment under constant, expert supervision, as opposed to letting a damaged implant run amok through an unaware teenager in the aftermath of alien Armageddon. His implant was more powerful than anything else in Terran space and had been custom tailored to his unique physiology and skill set. Hell, they'd even gone so far as to perform some gene editing to correct some of his genetic predispositions toward several different cancers and other maladies that still plagued humanity. Ben was presently the single healthiest human being to ever exist, and every possible diagnostic that could be run on him, his implant, and his armor's hardware, software, and firmware showed that everything was working perfectly.

So then why the hell couldn't he even make his armor so much as twitch a finger?

Experience had taught him that the answer was probably something obvious, but in a place nobody had thought to look yet. Unfortunately for Ben, he, his dad, Mabel, and a host of specialists, both human and alien, had been wracking their brains trying to find the place where that obvious fault lay, yet their combined efforts had yielded nothing more than a shrug of confusion. It was maddening.

Another jolt ran up Ben's spine as the docking clamps finished retracting, completing the process of pulling the dropship into the *Wraith*'s small flight deck, and Valdez nodded to him, unbuckling his restraints and standing up.

"Alright, Ben," he said. "Showtime."

Ben cast off his own restraints and stood up just as the loadmaster hit the control to drop the ramp. The whine of hydraulics and rapidly expanding sliver of light that spilled in over the lowering ramp sent a wave of nostalgia coursing through Ben. He hadn't been aboard the *Wraith* since he, Mabel, and the SEARs pulled off one of history's greatest surprise attacks during the Battle of Icarus—a feat that served to snatch victory from the jaws of defeat and routed the Imperium's first incursion into Terran space.

Ben and Valdez made their way aft, then walked down the ramp after it kissed the deck. Ben looked around, taking in the familiar sights of the small intelligence ship's flight deck. One corner of his mouth curled upward into a lopsided grin as a series of memories from the last time he was aboard paraded through his mind's eye. Then he caught sight of the welcoming party waiting for them, and his grin turned into a full smile.

"Dominguez!" Ben exploded. "You son of a bitch! I didn't know you were going to be tagging along with us on this one."

The Pathfinder looked like he'd seen a ghost, and Ben realized the marines must not have received news of his resurrection yet. The short-statured marine approached cautiously and with his mouth agape, weaving through the frenzied traffic of the deck crew as they went about the task of bringing a ship aboard. He stopped two paces away, looking like he wasn't sure if Ben was friend or foe—a reaction Ben had seen a half dozen times since his reintroduction to Terran society. It was understandable, given the situation, and he was more or less used to it by now.

Dominguez shook his head in disbelief. "No way... No fuckin' way," he said in awe. "You're dead."

"The tales of my demise have been greatly exaggerated," Ben said with a reassuring smile.

"So it would seem," Dominguez said hesitantly. He stretched out a hand, but Ben ducked inside the marine's guard and lifted him off the floor in a bear hug.

"Fuckin' A, man," Dominguez wheezed after Ben set him back down. "How the hell did you get *stronger* by dying?"

"Trade secret, buddy," Ben said with a laugh. "I could tell you, but then—"

"Yeah, yeah," Dominguez interjected, rapidly coming back onto a level keel and warming up into the smart-ass Ben knew and loved. "I know. Secret science project shit. You could tell me, but then you'd have to kill me."

"Nah," Ben scoffed, then added, "I'd have Chief Kravczyk kill you."

"Sergeant," Valdez said with a nod of greeting. "Congratulations on your promotion."

Dominguez, suddenly remembering where he was and why, straightened up and saluted. "Yes, sir, Commander. Thank you. I'm here to make sure your gear gets stowed and you two are to report directly to the command-level briefing room on—"

"Deck three, across from CIC," Valdez finished, returning the salute. "We know where it is. Thank you." Valdez motioned for the three of them to step aside as a team of people from the *Wraith* marched up the ramp and began the process of unloading all the gear stuffed inside the Griffon's cargo bay. "Do me a favor, Sergeant, and make sure our gear gets to the SOCOM detachment armory unmolested." He eyed the unloading crew, and Ben caught the excited gleam in the eyes of the two men about to lift the transit case containing Valdez's APEX. "The last couple of times we were here, these spooks couldn't keep their grubby mitts off our equipment."

"Don't you worry, Commander," Dominguez said with a smile. "I'll make sure all your gear arrives safe and sound, then tuck it in and sing it a lullaby, personally."

Valdez looked at Ben and inclined his head toward the airlock leading into the heart of the ship. Ben threw a jaunty wave at Dominguez. "Later, buddy."

"See you, Ben," the marine said over his shoulder as he headed up the ramp to oversee the unloading.

Ben followed Valdez across the flight deck and into the ship. Then the two of them weaved their way through the cramped interior spaces of the little spy ship. They were just a few frames away from their destination when the pitch of the ship's engines changed. Ben and Valdez looked at each other in question.

"Are we jumping to warp?" Ben asked.

"Sure feels like it," Valdez said, but before he could say anything else, the *Wraith* shuddered briefly, followed by the reactor noise spooling back down to its previous mild thrum.

"Well, that's new," Ben said, going from curious to alarmed.

Ships didn't just jump to warp from deep within a star system, unless it was an emergency. Space was unfathomably big and mostly barren, but the odds of the ship striking something too big for the forward distortion wave to shoulder aside increased significantly as you went farther down the well toward the primary star. He couldn't think of any reason why Collins would have transitioned to warp, unless something was terribly wrong.

Ben and Valdez both knew this, and they resumed their trip to the briefing with renewed urgency. When they arrived at CIC a few moments later, they ducked through the hatch opposite the *Wraith*'s nerve center on high alert.

Five people were already seated around the conference table when they arrived, all looking perfectly calm and collected. If their transition to warp was caused by some kind of emergency, nobody had told the people in this room about it.

"Captain," Valdez said, looking around the room in confusion. "Did we just transition to warp?"

A look of understanding dawned on Captain Collins's face. "Relax, Commander," she said with a reassuring smile. "*X'nec* passed along a real-time map of any and all hazards within the system before we transitioned. It allowed us to plot a course out and depart the system nearly a day before we otherwise would have been able to. Our current mission is extremely time-sensitive."

Valdez visibly relaxed at the explanation. "That's good to hear, ma'am. For a minute there, we thought maybe the jump to warp was necessitated by an emergency."

Ben felt the tension leave his shoulders, then paused when the true meaning of what Collins had said really sank in. It seemed like such a simple thing; they were merely taking advantage of the advanced sensor capability of the modern Imperial warship, but if Na'al was willing to share the secrets of their technology with the alliance, this could revolutionize space travel. Intra-system warp hops would cut in-system transit times down from days to mere hours. It was a small thing, but for the first time since he'd been told about the rebellion joining forces with the alliance, Ben was beginning to think about how that event could change the big picture of Terran and Alarian society, beyond the scope of their fight against the Imperium.

Putting the false alarm behind them, Valdez and Ben quickly took the two open seats closest to the hatch. Ben smiled at Tess and the chief, then nodded at his dad and Captain Collins before catching the look of shock on Lieutenant Harris's face. Harris was the CO of Dominguez's Pathfinder platoon, and he had the same look on his face as everyone else when they met a dead person. Ben nodded politely at him and settled back in his chair, ready to get this show on the road and find out just what was so damn important that he and the SEARs had to be hustled over here less than twelve hours after being reunited.

"Alright," Captain Collins said with a genuine smile on her face. "Now that we're all here, I can finally give you all some answers regarding the urgency of the last few hours."

Her expression turned serious and she tapped a few commands into the terminal built into the table in front of her. The MFD on the far wall came to life, the official crest of the CID displayed across the entire screen. A few more taps and the crest disappeared, replaced with a high-resolution video feed from *X'nec*.

Admiral Na'al's onyx-black eyes surveyed the room, and he bowed slightly. "Greetings," the big alien rumbled. "I thank you for including me in this briefing."

"Admiral Na'al," Collins said, addressing him directly. Her voice was as official-sounding as Ben had ever heard it. "Welcome. How does the feed look on your end?"

"Nominal," Na'al stated curtly.

Collins nodded in reply, then turned back to everyone

around the table. "Admiral Na'al is joining us via a quantum link module we've supplied to him. The rebels are not participating in this operation, but we may find the admiral can provide some context for a few things."

Ben's brow furrowed. If the rebels weren't going to be involved, that meant whatever this mission was, it was strictly a Terran matter. But then why did Collins think Na'al might be able to supply context to what they'd be doing?

The captain looked at his dad. "Henry, why don't you start."

Ben cocked an eyebrow when Collins deferred to his dad. He expected, based on the fact that he and the SEARs had been told to pack all their combat kit, that this was going to be a military operation of some sort. The presence of at least a small detachment of Pathfinders aboard the *Wraith* only reinforced that notion. But if his dad was giving the briefing, then this wasn't a run-of-the-mill special ops mission for the Alarians or the Confed.

His dad tapped a few commands into that beat-up datapad he'd had as long as Ben could remember, and one of the wall displays came to life, showing a simple text file.

"Less than twenty-four hours ago, I received this communication from Commander Evans, who is the navy's liaison with the civilian researchers at Archimedes Base," he began. "Matt is also a good friend to both myself and Admiral Garland, having served as my handler for several years after the Alarian War. He sent me this via my personal quantum comms terminal, located in my quarters back at Archimedes and not registered or monitored in any way by the Confed. Being the guy who invented the system has its perks," his dad quipped with a small grin.

"You'll all receive copies of this text file with your mission packets," he added, "but the important part is this: a CID deep-cover operative called in a request for an emergency extraction. We were fortunate that the request came in via someone at CID who is loyal to Director Gideon, and they passed the request on directly to him before erasing all traces of it from the official record."

"The reason for that," Collins said, seamlessly taking over the briefing, "is the operative in question has information relating to the current political shakeup within the Confed, including the wholesale house-cleaning at the top levels of CID and CENT-COM, and it's a worst-case scenario."

Ben's blood ran cold. He didn't know how he knew, but he was certain he knew what information the operative had come across.

Collins continued. "The operative claims to have information that proves someone or something from the Imperium is directly influencing both the SRF leadership and the Cunningham administration, and we're the only assets Director Gideon and Admiral Garland have access to right now. So it's our job to go extract the operative and the information in his possession and get it into the right hands back on Elizabeth."

Something was itching in the back of Ben's mind, like a lost memory that was trying to reestablish a connection with his consciousness. He focused on it, and something clicked, unlocking a previously unknown store of data.

"The Master is pulling the strings," he blurted out.

Every eye in the room locked onto him, including Collins's, but it was the predatory glare suddenly coming from Na'al that unnerved Ben the most.

"That's our guess," Collins said, surprised. "How did you know?"

"And not just within the Confed," he continued as though she hadn't even spoken, suddenly unable to contain the flood of new information that had just popped into his memories out of nowhere. "The Imperium has been working something within the power structure of the SRF for a while now. A backup plan, maybe." Ben shut his eyes tight and cocked his head, simultane-ously trying to stop the torrent of information but also suss out the details. It was like someone had pulled a single brick out from the base of a dam, and now there was no hope of bottling the torrent of information back up. Just the act of trying to mentally slow the flow led to a brain-splitting migraine.

"Not an agent, though," he continued in a strained voice, the details starting to filter through the static. He groaned. "Ugh. Something else... Still AI, but more like a series of programs intended to mind the shop while the agent is away." The thing he was looking for was so close, but the true meaning kept slip-ping out from under his mental grasp, like he was trying to stab a grape with a fork. Finally, he managed to wrangle the errant information and shouted in triumph. "STOPs! Specific task-oriented programs. That's what they're called, right?" he said, looking at Na'al for confirmation.

The rebel leader was utterly dumbstruck, but he dipped his chin in confirmation.

"This operation has been in the works for so long," Ben continued, "that it's more or less self-sustaining at this point—just like what happened immediately leading up to the Alarian War. The agent already did all the hard work, getting things lined up and put into motion, and now it's only a matter of time before things kick off. Ugh." He clutched his head, trying to keep his skull from exploding. "But I don't know what the trigger is."

The flood of information ceased as quickly as it had started, and with it went the pain. Ben gasped as the agony receded, his chest heaving like he'd just run a marathon. He opened his eyes and saw nothing but shock and concern staring back at him. No one spoke.

"What the hell did you people do to me?" Ben demanded of Na'al. "How do I know that?"

All eyes shifted to the rebel commander.

"We did nothing that could explain this," Na'al said, and for some reason, Ben believed him. The expression on his face and the tone of his voice told Ben the alien was being sincere. "But I find it most interesting that you are somehow aware of all that information, Ben. In fact, you just related some details that even *I* was unaware of."

The eyes were all back on Ben now, and he looked around helplessly. "How do I know that?" he repeated, searching their faces for any kind of answer. The splitting headache was gone, but in its wake was a building light-headedness. Ben looked back at Na'al. "And how do I know that you're not lying, Admiral? I can tell—your sincerity is written all over your face and in the tone of your voice. When did I magically gain the ability to expertly read alien body language and interpret vocal inflections? And—" Ben broke off, realization hitting him.

Na'al's feed was coming in directly from *X'nec*, and everyone's implants were handling the translation duties. That was the beauty of the standard-issue neural implants—as long as the correct translation matrix was loaded in, the implants would process and translate it in real time, then send the corrected impulses to the auditory cortex. The end result was someone hearing their native language, even if the actual speech was in an alien tongue. What the person heard wouldn't match up with the mouth movements of the speaker, but it would still be a virtually flawless translation in the correct tone of voice. But what Ben was hearing from Na'al matched the alien's mouth movements *exactly*, meaning he wasn't hearing a translation, but his brain was directly attaching the correct meaning to the alien's speech without any input from his implant.

Which meant he now had an innate understanding of the Imperial common language.

A whole series of interlocking pieces suddenly clicked into place in Ben's mind. Somehow, he had a fundamental understanding of all things related to the species that comprised the Imperium—their speech patterns, their mannerisms, their body language, and a host of other cultural and social cues. He didn't need his implant to do the work for him; he just *knew*. It was like he'd grown up as one of them, and his brain had made all the correct connections to completely integrate with them. But the same was also true when it came to the Terran equivalents. Ben was completely at home in either environment, and he was sure that if they dropped him off in the middle of an Imperial city, he could navigate the situation without batting an eye. *That* was definitely not a thing he'd had before he went and blew himself up on Hai'alla, but if Na'al and his people hadn't done it to him, then where had this all come from?

"Ben?"

Ben shook his head in an effort to clear the cobwebs, but it was getting harder and harder to focus. He realized that his dad was standing with his hands on the table, trying to get his attention. A bone-deep weariness descended on him, and Ben rested his elbows on the table and cradled his face in his hands.

"I think my brain is broken," Ben groaned, his hands muffling the words. "Chief," he said, looking up at the big SEAR. "The next time I decide that blowing myself up and letting a couple of alien mad scientists put me back together is a good idea, please beat some sense into me."

The last few words sounded slurred to Ben's ears, and he tried to sit up, but the room spun violently around him when he did. Darkness seeped in around the edges of his vision, and Ben knew what was coming next. He opened his mouth to warn everyone what was about to happen, but he was too late.

Something dark loomed in front of him, followed by a sharp crack from somewhere close by. Then everything went black.

12

MARCHING ORDERS

"I can't keep our fleets bottled up forever. Too many people are already asking some... uncomfortable questions. Plus, if we continue to keep our forces from patrolling the non-core systems, we run the risk of undoing all the hard work we just put in to bring them back into the fold after the Alarian War."

"That is not my concern," the Master rumbled dismissively. "If you are too incompetent to maintain your position of power, *President* Cunningham, then perhaps I need to find someone more suitable."

Cunningham shuddered inwardly. He knew exactly what replacement would mean—he'd been forced to order the "replacement" of several people from key positions already. For the thousandth time since he'd so readily crawled into bed with the devil, he wished he could go back in time and warn his past, naive self.

"That won't be necessary," he said quickly. "I'll manage. I just wanted you to be aware of any potential obstacles we may face in the future."

"I'm sure," the holographic shadow in the center of the room stated, its crimson eyes narrowing ever so slightly before reset-ting. "But the trivial failings of your administration are not why I'm here."

A chill ran up Cunningham's spine. He'd feared that the unexpected appearance of the Master's avatar signaled that the entity had a new mission for him, and the Master never appeared in person for trivial matters.

"One of your deep-cover operatives within the Sino-Russian Federation has uncovered information that, were it to fall in the wrong hands, could jeopardize our little arrangement. He contacted CID headquarters and requested an emergency extrac-tion, but someone within CID killed all mention of it immedi-ately, so it never entered the proper chain of command. Admiral Garland and his allies received word of this through their network of people still loyal to them. I have reason to believe they intend to pass instructions for his rescue to Henry Hutchins and your exiled forces over Hai'alla.

"With your fleet assets so badly out of position, it is unlikely they will be able to intercept the agent in time to secure the infor-mation he possesses and eliminate the threat. That is not your concern—I have other resources available to perform that task. What *is* your concern, however, is the means by which Garland was able to obtain this information and communicate it to Hutchins. Track down the leak within CID and eliminate it. Then ensure that whatever avenue of communication Garland has with Hutchins and your forces is permanently closed.

"I have not been impressed by your ability to control your own government, President Cunningham. This is an opportunity for you to prove to me that you have worth. Do not fail."

The Master's avatar evaporated before his eyes, and Cunningham let out a shaky breath. He spun his chair away from his desk and reached for a decanter filled with bourbon sitting on the small table behind his desk. As he removed the stopper, his hands were shaking so badly that the cut-crystal plug chattered musically against the neck of the decanter. He poured a generous amount of the high-end alcohol into a rocks glass, then knocked half of it back in a single gulp.

The president of the Confed turned his chair back around and set the glass on his desk. One hand worried at his scalp as his mind raced, trying to come up with some way out of the hell he'd so willingly plopped himself into. If only he'd known... Never had he imagined things would spiral so completely out of his control. He'd been so sure he and his compatriots had been in the right when they conducted their political blitzkrieg against Martha McGibbons and her allies. She was the one fucking everything up—her and that buffoon Garland.

But how wrong he'd been.

And now he was stuck. There was no way to backtrack. It wasn't like he could publicly admit what had really happened—the real reason he wanted power. Cunningham wasn't a fool. Anyone could see that the Confed didn't stand a chance at taking on the Imperium, even if Garland's cockamamie plan to ally with the Alarians worked out. It would have been David versus Goliath, except this time Goliath was bringing starships and plasma weapons against David's rock and sling. So Cunningham had done the only sane thing and struck a bargain with the Master, all in the name of ensuring humanity's survival. It was a shit deal, but it damn sure beat being wiped from existence.

At least that was what he'd told himself, back before he'd seen the true nature of the being that ruled the Imperium and realized, too late, that he'd been suckered into swallowing a poisoned pill. Cunningham could see the writing on the wall; the Master wouldn't allow him to live one second past the point at which he was no longer useful. And worse, he suspected the same could be said for the rest of the Confed as well. Even now, the most powerful military force in human history was withering away, and Jasper Cunningham was the one who'd ordered it. Too late, he'd realized the moves he'd made weren't allowing the Confed to slink off with its tail between its legs, content to live in obscurity in its small part of the galaxy. Instead, his orders had ensured they were meekly walking like lambs to the slaughter. He knew what had to be done if they were to have any chance at all of extricating themselves from the disaster he'd gotten them into.

But Jasper Cunningham was a coward.

His actions had allowed the Master to run roughshod over any and all of the Confed's digital infrastructure, undoing in a matter of days what Garland and his people had accomplished over the last year, and at great cost. If Cunningham tried to back out of the deal now, the Master's retribution would be swift and merciless. It claimed not to have sent another of its agents to keep an eye on things, and the president of the Confederated Terran Systems had believed it. After all, why would the Master need to send an agent when Cunningham and his people were willingly giving it complete access to all their most secure systems, a nonnegotiable condition of his contract with the devil?

So here he was, stuck between a long, drawn-out certain death and a painful, more rapid certain death. Cunningham couldn't just pull a one-eighty and try to undo everything. Not only would the Master ensure his immediate—and likely violent —murder, but the public would crucify him when they learned his administration had made up their story from whole cloth. Garland's unchecked warmongering, which resulted in horrific losses, compounded with his criminal mismanagement of their naval forces, was a major talking point. Henry Hutchins and his rogue AI project setting off nukes on Elizabeth and McGibbons's complete and utter incompetence were just a few of the others.

Well, Cunningham mused darkly, that last one actually was kind of true. For the most part, though, it was all bullshit. A story, expertly crafted to fit the facts and enrage the public enough that the people would be screaming for heads to roll. And Jasper Cunningham was the heroic vice president who, at great personal risk, brought everything to light and ensured a plan was in place to right the ship.

Cunningham's musing on the topic of Garland and Hutchins gave him pause, and he absently reached for his neglected glass of bourbon. It was true that he'd stupidly ensured the Confed no longer had the ability to take action against the Master without devastating consequences… but what if there was another option? He sipped the alcohol and thought back to what the Master had said about Garland having a secret channel of communication open to Hutchins and the small contingent of Confed forces stranded in the Alarian home system. Was it possible to assist them in some way? If Cunningham could point them in the right direction, it might be possible that they could do his dirty work for him. The president was certain Hutchins would do whatever it took to exact some small measure of revenge on the Imperium after the Master's forces had overseen the deaths of both his wife and son. And *Indomitable* was a force to be reckoned with, not to mention whatever fleet the Alarians had left after their defense of the system against *another* Imperial armada.

How they'd managed to defeat another of the Master's strike forces *and* take out the agent, Cunningham didn't know, and the Master had shut him down immediately when he'd asked. Garland had only played dumb when he'd been questioned about it, giving up only the same information that Cunningham's agents had found in the initial reports received by CENTCOM—reports Garland had tried to erase when he found out about McGibbons's imminent removal. Why the admiral tried to cover up those reports was a mystery, but Wheaton's people at the CID had managed to recover the original files. Unfortunately, all that was in them was a brief status report from *Indomitable*'s CO, saying all three Terran ships had survived, but nearly half the marine Pathfinders had been killed in action on the planet, along with Ben Hutchins and his AI. The Alarian Home Fleet was battered but still an effective force, and the Imperial force had been defeated in detail.

It all beggared belief, but if he had to guess, Cunningham would say Ben Hutchins and the AI must have pulled another miracle out of their ass to give the defenders a decisive edge, reprising their role from the Battle of Icarus. The Master had been downright gleeful when Cunningham told him about the demise of Ben and the AI on Hai'alla—something that, in retrospect, was probably the thing that planted the first seed of doubt in the president's mind about his deal with the entity that controlled the Imperium. If the Imperium really was the unstoppable force Cunningham had thought it was, then why did it seem like a single kid and an AI had been such a threat to it?

Well, Ben and the AI might have been lost, but the man responsible for creating the unique abilities they'd possessed was still alive. Maybe, just maybe, Cunningham could get them the intel they'd need to finish what they'd started. If he played his cards right, that embodiment of pure evil, the Master, would never know he'd been working against it.

A knock on the door to his office shattered his train of thought, and he dropped his glass in surprise, cursing as the spilled booze soaked his slacks.

"Mr. President?"

"Oh, Jane," Cunningham said with relief when his chief of staff poked her head around the door. "Come in. Sorry, I was lost in thought and your knock jolted me, is all." He quickly swiped at his pants in a useless attempt to clear some of the spilled liquid, then picked the rocks glass off the floor, set it off to one side of his desk, and returned his attention to her. "What can I do for you?"

Jane VerBeek looked around the office before turning around and closing the door. "I'm sorry to disturb you, sir," she said, approaching his desk with a leather folio cradled in one arm, "but I just came in to tell you that Senator Mercer called and asked if it would be alright to reschedule your meeting with her for tomorrow afternoon. Apparently, today's hearings are going to take longer than anticipated, and she doesn't think she'll be able to make your meeting for this afternoon."

The mention of Cynthia Mercer brought Cunningham's mind right back to the Master's orders and the impossible position he was trapped in. Then he looked at his new chief of staff... and remembered what happened to those who crossed the Master.

"Is everything okay, Mr. President?" Jane said hesitantly. He'd let his dark thoughts show, and the sudden change in mood hadn't gone unnoticed.

"No," he admitted. "I had another visit from *it*."

Her expression rapidly shifted from concern to terror. As his chief of staff, Jane was fully informed about the deal he'd struck with the Master. She was also very much aware of what happened to the people who didn't do everything in their power to ensure the Master's orders were carried out to the letter or, worse, actively tried to undermine them.

"What did it want?" she said, her voice trembling. The last time the Master made an unexpected appearance, it was because someone from Cunningham's office had gotten cold feet and tried to leak their secret to the press. Felicia Keller's eyes and tongue had arrived in an ornate wooden gift box an hour later. Cunningham still didn't know whom the Master had kill his former chief of staff, and he was too terrified to try and find out.

But the message was clear: cross the Master, and you die horribly —it didn't matter who you were.

"It told me we have a leak, and it wants it plugged," Cunningham said seriously. "I need you to get me a meeting with Russ Ogden, Jane. Tonight."

13

ROADBLOCK

"I REALLY NEED TO STOP WAKING UP LIKE THIS," BEN GROANED AS he took in his surroundings.

He was lying in the same medical bed in the *Wraith*'s sickbay he'd been in when he woke up after having his brains scrambled by the Imperium corvette's controlling AI back during his escape from Earth. *God, that feels like ancient history*, Ben thought. In reality, it'd only been about a year, but he'd managed to pack a decade or more's worth of experience into that time. Ben quickly pinged his implant and was surprised to see he'd only been unconscious for a few hours—way better than going dark for days or weeks like he usually did.

Remembering a pleasant detail from the last time he'd awoken in this bed, Ben sat up and looked at the far bulkhead. Last time, an angel had been sleeping softly in the chair in the corner. This time, however, a rather unattractive gorilla was sleeping in that chair. *Well, that explains why I can't move my feet.*

"Hey, dickhead," Ben said, the volume of his voice a solid notch or two above a socially acceptable "inside voice." "Get your gigantic fucking clod-stompers off my legs!"

His aim was true, and the pillow he'd thrown at Kravczyk

poofed into the sleeping man's face with a bit more of a thwack than he expected. The big SEAR's arms flailed about as a muffled shout rang through the compartment, but most importantly, his size-twelve boots jerked off of Ben's legs, allowing him to free himself from the uncomfortable medical bed and stand up. He stretched his arms and rolled out his shoulders.

"What the hell, Ben?" Kravczyk said indignantly, rubbing the back of his head with one massive hand. "Are you trying to kill me?"

Apparently, that thwacking sound Ben heard when the pillow hit the chief was his head cracking against the bulkhead. Just how hard had he thrown that pillow?

"Sorry, Chief," Ben apologized. "I guess I'm still trying to get used to this shiny new body." He looked down at his hands as he spoke, flexing his fingers a few times and really paying attention to the strength they seemed to have. Whatever Eelix and his team had done to make sure his muscle tone was in tip-top shape for his rebirth had really been effective. He'd been up and about for a couple of weeks now, but thus far, he hadn't really had a chance to test his strength and stamina by working out hard. It was one of the things he was itching to do, but *Indomitable*'s medical people had insisted on him easing into it over a period of weeks so they could monitor how his new body responded to the stress. Ben shrugged mentally and let his hands drop. It was just another advantage to having a wealth of advanced technology available to them, he supposed.

"Damn, man," Kravczyk complained as he stood up. "That shit hurt."

The privacy curtain walling off his little corner of the sickbay whisked aside, and good ol' Doc Adams glared in at the two men, looking imperiously down his nose through the spectacles he always wore. Ben noted that the *Wraith*'s chief medical officer looked noticeably more aged than the last time he'd seen him.

Deep lines creased the corners of his eyes, and his once uniformly brown hair was now streaked with gray.

"I should have known better than to leave the two of you unattended," he said. "Every time the two of you come into my sickbay, the rest of my patients can't get any rest. At least it seems you suffered no permanent brain damage from your episode, Mr. Hutchins."

Ben and the chief quickly exchanged amused glances, then put on their best attempt at looking sheepish. Ben's mind quickly flashed back to something Dr. Maynard—*Indomitable*'s chief medical officer—had said about her CID counterpart the first time Ben met her. *Such an insufferable ass.*

"So am I cleared to return to duty?" Ben asked hopefully. Whatever had happened to him during that briefing, he'd rather not try to figure it out here in sickbay. He was sure his dad and Mabel would have been working nonstop to figure out what had gone wrong, and with their live link back to *X'nec*, they could also consult with Na'al's people on the issue. The important thing was that he was back on his feet, and every part of him seemed to be working just fine.

Adams let out a frustrated sigh. "Yes. You're healthy as a horse—at least insofar as my equipment can determine. I don't know what those Imperium doctors did to grow you that new body, Mr. Hutchins, but there's nothing wrong with it that I can see." He pulled a datapad from one of the oversized pockets in his lab coat and tapped at the screen for a few seconds. "Your father wants you to check in with him as soon as you leave here. He said he'd be in the SOCOM detachment's quarters."

"Thanks, Doc." Ben gave Adams a friendly smack on the shoulder as he walked over to take the pile of clothes Kravczyk was holding out for him. Adams grumbled something under his breath and turned on his heel.

As the man walked away, Ben tossed the clothes on the foot

of the bed, then stripped off the itchy hospital gown he'd woken up in. He reached for the fresh pair of boxer briefs on the top of the stack of fresh clothes, then paused when he saw the chief looking him over with an… appraising eye.

"No," Ben deadpanned.

Kravczyk looked up and met his gaze. "What's that?" he said innocently.

"No," Ben repeated. "You can't touch them." He pointed to his midsection and flexed his newly acquired and absolutely spectacular abs. "These are for Tess. Not you."

Kravczyk looked crestfallen. "But," he protested, "they're so… amazing." The big SEAR reached out one tentative hand.

Ben couldn't do it anymore. He laughed and slapped away the chief's hand. "Fuck you, dude! Let me get dressed in peace." He pointed toward the exit, still chuckling. "I'll meet you there."

"Aww, man," Kravczyk whined and turned away resignedly, unable to let the charade go until well after the joke had been played out, which was par for the course. The big man ducked through the hatch and was gone a moment later, leaving Ben to dress in peace.

Or so he thought.

"Any chance you can get your buddies on *X'nec* to give me a set like that?" Kravczyk asked, sticking his head back in through the hatch. "I mean *damn*! I've worked my ass off for like fifteen years to look like this." He flexed one bulging bicep for demonstration. "But those things are on another level, man. Hey, Doc!" he queried an annoyed-looking Adams, who sat behind a nearby desk. "What's his body-fat percentage right now? Like, three percent or something?"

"Good*bye*, Chief Kravczyk." Adams emphasized the "bye" part of the word enough that even someone as dense as Kravczyk couldn't miss the implied threat.

"Well, you're no fun," Ben heard Kravczyk mumble as he headed off down the passageway for good.

"How in the name of all that is good and holy do you put up with that man?" Adams asked, cradling his forehead in one hand and massaging his temples.

Ben finished pulling on his utility top and sat down in the chair to start getting his boots on. "Honestly, Doc," Ben said seriously, "I couldn't." When Adams frowned in confusion, Ben flashed him a sardonic smirk. "Why do you think I blew myself up?"

———

"WHAT THE FUCK IS THIS SHIT?" Kravczyk exclaimed, seeing the contents of the transit case containing Ben's new armor.

"My armor," Ben admitted after a long moment.

"No." Kravczyk held up one finger like a schoolteacher correcting a particularly dense student. "Your armor is big and black and has lots of power cells and fancy processors and circuits integrated into it, just like mine." He pointed down at the open crate at his feet. "*This* is regular old marine-issue hard-shell—AKA, shit."

Ben shifted uncomfortably and nodded. "It is. I'm having some… issues."

"About that," his dad said, ducking through the armored hatch leading into the SOCOM armory, eyes glued to the beat-up datapad in his hand, as always. "I've got some good news and some bad. Which do you want first?"

"Good to see you, too," Ben said, a wave of consternation washing over him when his dad wandered in like his son hadn't just experienced a brain-melting event during a classified briefing.

His dad looked up, and his expression softened. "Sorry, Ben. I really am glad you're up and about so quickly."

"But..." Ben interjected, knowing it was coming.

"*But...* while the event you experienced during the briefing was scary at the time, I consulted with Na'al's people, and they said they believe you experienced a sudden memory flash as the result of a related stimulus—something we knew might happen. And after reviewing all your vitals and brain scans, neither Dr. Adams nor the specialists on *X'nec* can find anything wrong with you. However, they warned that while this is the first time they've reintegrated a human, our physiology is similar enough to a number of other species they've performed the operation on in the past, and they said it's highly unlikely that another event will occur. Their experience is that a traumatic memory flash like this usually only occurs with memories that were created immediately preceding death. Eelix said it's a one-and-done kind of thing as the brain attempts to reconcile what should be short-term memory actually falling on the long-term side of things because it was processed out of short-term during the reintegration process." His dad looked at him expectantly.

"And I forced the agent into a link right before the bomb went off," Ben said, the lightbulb suddenly flaring to life in his head. "Meaning I probably pulled in a bunch of data from its onboard memory without realizing it, and that information was, what, filed under a different folder in my gray matter than my brain expected it to be in?" His dad nodded, and Ben finished running through the logic train he'd been following. "And that's how I miraculously have knowledge about some sort of operation within the SRF," he finished. "Because my subconscious ransacked the agent's files while I was busy trying to hold it at bay until the nuke could go off."

"That's the most likely explanation," his dad confirmed.

Ben sighed. Why he'd thought dying and being brought back

to life would be a relatively simple thing, he couldn't fathom. On the surface, it didn't seem that complicated. Well, once you got past the inherent technological hurdles. All they had to do was clone a new body for him from his DNA, then load his neural engram into the new body. It looked great on paper, but there always had to be some stupid complicating factor, like his brain assimilating piles of data from a malevolent AI in the moments before his death.

"Figures," Ben mumbled to nobody in particular. Then, to his dad, he said, "So is that the good news or the bad?"

His dad squirmed, and the little bit of hope Ben had that things could only get better from here vanished.

"Neither, actually."

A loud screeching made both Ben and his dad flinch, and Ben turned to look at Kravczyk, who was in the process of pulling a stool out from under a workbench.

"Sorry," the big SEAR said as he settled his bulk down on the stool. "It just seemed like this was about to turn into the kind of conversation that's going to get really long and technical, and I didn't see any reason to continue standing for it."

Ben smiled. He'd missed having the chief around, if for no other reason than the man always helped keep the mood light. Ben stepped around the armor crate on the floor and leaned back against the workbench, next to his friend. He looked back at his dad and nodded.

"Alright, Dad. Hit me with it. What did you figure out?"

"Well, I heard back from Eelix," he began. "Remember how Mabel said she forwarded copies of all the data we collected while trying to troubleshoot your APEX integration problems?" Ben nodded. "Well, he spotted something we didn't—though to be fair, it's not something we thought to look at, either."

"And that is?" Ben said with a raised eyebrow, the tiniest bit of hope beginning to creep back into his chest. If Eelix had nailed down what the problem was, then they could move on with finding a solution.

His dad looked back at his datapad and tapped out a few commands. One of the wall displays next to him came to life, and he pointed at two side-by-side images showing a bunch of wavy lines. "This," he said, pointing to the image on the left, "is what your brainwaves used to look like, with your old body." Then he pointed at the image next to it, which had a whole lot more going on. "And this is what it looks like now.

"My first thought, when Eelix brought it up, was that the waveforms are just more complicated as a result of the upgraded implant you received, but Eelix and his team don't think so. He said it looks to him like there are actually two distinct neural patterns here." His dad tapped one of the lines on the display, and Ben saw what he was talking about. Instead of a chaotic jumble of waveforms, as it had looked like a moment ago, he could now see two distinct patterns overlaying each other.

"When Eelix and his team went through the data from your attempts to operate your APEX, they found what looks like conflicting inputs—almost like two different people were trying to move the armor simultaneously." His dad tapped another command on his datapad and cleared the display. He turned back to Ben. "And that's why you haven't been able to do anything with your armor, Ben.

"The suit is receiving conflicting instructions from your implant, and it's going into vapor lock, for lack of a better term. The command impulses are being interrupted before the armor can respond, so the suit's processors are canceling the action and resetting. We didn't see it when we ran our diagnostics because those are all automated signal checks between the various components, which are working just fine."

Ben pursed his lips, trying to figure out both why this was

happening and what the solution was, if there even was one. "Okay," he said, "so that's the bad news. What's the good?"

"Actually," his dad said, "that *was* the good news. We now know what the problem is. The bad news is that neither Eelix nor I can think of any solution to correct the issue, and Mabel is just as stumped." He flashed Ben an apologetic look. "I'm sorry, Ben, but unless we can figure out a way to stabilize your neural wave-forms, this means you can't use your APEX."

Ben's heart sank as the realization of what this all meant hit him. "Fuck," he said. "If I can't run with my armor, then I can't link with Mabel, either…"

His dad shook his head solemnly. He knew what that meant, too.

Ben looked at the chief for a moment, seeing a raised eyebrow from the big SEAR, then back at his dad before he said the worst part. "So then what the hell good am I now?"

14

FENG

"RELAX," SAID AN ANNOYED ZHENG. "THERE'S A WHOLE LOT OF light-years between here and Columbia, Dimitriy. It's going to take some time for my people to put together an extraction. So stop worrying about the fact that we've been here a grand total of three days without anyone making contact. We may need to hunker down here for a few weeks, depending on what assets were available at the time I requested an extraction."

Dimitriy stopped lapping the small apartment where he and Zheng were hiding out until someone from CID came to get them and sat heavily onto the musty-smelling sofa along the back wall. "I'm sorry," he apologized to the more senior agent, who was settled in an overstuffed "leather" armchair opposite the sofa, sipping on a mug of freshly brewed coffee despite the fact that it was nearly midnight. "It's just that I've never been in a gunfight before. The GIM training program put us in simulators and ran us through plenty of live-fire scenarios, but a decade of living life as a paper-pushing bureaucrat didn't exactly reinforce my martial training."

"It's okay." Zheng waved off Dimitriy's apology. "You did

pretty damn good, kid. You got bushwhacked, but you kept your head on straight and made it out alive. Don't kick yourself over it. Learn from it. Then, maybe next time around, you see it coming—or at least manage to avoid getting shot." The older agent indicated the bulge under Dimitriy's left pant leg, where a heavy gauze bandage was wrapped tightly around the gunshot wound he'd suffered during his escape.

"One would hope."

Dimitriy absently rubbed a hand gently over the wound, the images from the ambush popping once again to the forefront of his mind. The microfreighter they'd hitched a ride on had a fairly extensive medical bay on board—something the crew had explained was a necessity, as they occasionally made multi-week hauls to remote systems. They'd been able to treat Dimitriy's concussion, as well as his leg wound. The leg actually wasn't that bad. The bullet had punched a hole through the meat of his left thigh, but there hadn't been any damage to the bone or any arteries. The concussion had actually been the most serious injury he'd sustained, and it took nearly a week for the brain fog he'd been experiencing to fully clear and his memories of the event to return in any coherent fashion.

"How long do you think it will be before the ISB catches up to us here?" Dimitriy asked.

Zheng pursed his lips and bobbed his head back and forth slightly as he thought about it. "Probably another couple of days, at least," he finally said. "*Cloverston*'s departure from Lijia had been scheduled for a while, so it's unlikely the ISB will look too closely at them until the other, more obvious suspects don't pan out—of which there were at least five or six. *Cloverston*'s skipper has run some jobs for me in the past, but it's always been low-level stuff and hasn't flagged with the ISB, as far as I'm aware, so I don't think they would've had the ship under observation."

The big man set his empty mug on a side table and rose to his feet. "Still, the fact that they tried to smoke you guys in broad daylight and in the middle of a busy intersection tells me they're in an all-fired hurry to get that data of yours under wraps as soon as possible." He walked to the apartment's single window and peered out at the street four stories below through a gap in the drapes. "Which isn't good news for us. They'll have a lot of manpower running down leads and trying to pinpoint where we went. *Cloverston* is pretty quick, despite her age, but it still took eight days for us to get here and the ISB has access to ships that can get a team out here in a little over half that time. Even if they flagged *Cloverston* immediately, it would take a few days, at least, for the ISB to get their team together and find a ride for them. Then they'll need to figure out what part of the city we're in before they can get down to the business of trying to sniff us out.

"Newman's Rock may officially be a neutral world, but the folks around here aren't exactly big fans of the SRF. That business between the Black Dragons and the SEARs a few years back didn't endear the Federation to the locals, and since the Alarians didn't bother to send a force to an unaligned backwater like Newman's Rock during the war, that Quantum Tiger clusterfuck is pretty much the worst thing anyone around here remembers."

Dimitriy nodded in understanding. "So the ISB is going to have to tread lightly. The Federation still acquires a lot of hard-to-get raw materials from the auction house here, meaning the ISB will be on a tight leash while they're here. If they come storming in here and start gunfights in the street, the planetary government might just decide to shut off the supply of refined metals and rare minerals the Federation uses to build our starships."

Zheng winked and fired a finger gun at Dimitriy. "Now you

see why my extraction plan required us hiding out here until a team arrives to pick us up. The locals might get all kinds of ornery whenever the NAC or some of the other enclaves come calling, trying to snag themselves another resource-rich system, but they also remember what the SEARs did for them six years ago. If it comes down to an us-versus-a-bunch-of-spooks-from-the-ISB kind of situation, the locals will almost certainly throw in with us. And considering the fact that everyone who lives around here is a miner or in a related profession, you don't want to be facing off against a bunch of pissed-off rockers."

Dimitriy let out an explosive breath and sank back into the couch. "So we wait," he said.

Zheng nodded and walked back to his chair. "We wait," he said, sitting down. "Don't worry, kid. We'll be off this rock before you know it."

———

Senior Agent Feng Wu of the Central Ministry's Internal Security Bureau stared at the planet below with disgust. He'd set foot on Newman's Rock only once in his entire life, and he still bore the shame of that failure. As he looked down on the unremarkable world from the bridge of the bulk freighter currently serving as a covert transport ship for his team, the memories of Operation Quantum Tiger came flooding back. At the time, he'd been a lieutenant in the Federation Marine Corps—specifically, a member of the elite Black Dragons commando unit. They'd been given the jobs the regular Federation military units couldn't execute for deniability reasons and the intelligence services didn't have the manpower for.

Feng glanced down at his left foot and absently flexed the pseudomuscles of his prosthesis. The sensation of his toes curling within the highly polished boot was there, but muted. The loss of his foot and subsequent life with the best artificial replacement the Federation could afford had never really bothered him before. But now, seeing that cursed planet for the first time since his utter defeat at the hands of that brutish SEAR, Kravczyk, the lack of definition in the sensation coming from his prosthesis grated on him.

"Sir, flight operations report the shuttle will be ready to take us to the surface within the hour," the freighter's ops officer said.

Feng broke his gaze from the main bridge display and turned his attention to the young officer. "Thank you, Ensign. Please inform the rest of my team that I'm on my way down and we will be departing shortly." The ops officer acknowledged his order, and Feng turned to leave the bridge.

Somewhere down on that planet, his quarry had gone to ground. Feng knew that Volkov had help from the Confed, but so far the Central Ministry's intelligence services hadn't been able to ID the man who went by the alias "Zheng." The man was suspected to be a CID operative, but the ISB hadn't been able to confirm that. The driver of the car Feng's team had ambushed in Lijia didn't have any identifiable marks on him, and his DNA profile wasn't in any database. That alone was a good indicator the CID had been prowling around in his backyard, but Feng couldn't prove it. However, the fact that Volkov was a GIM agent meant Feng couldn't rule out any of his own enclave's in-house intelligence services. All he knew for certain was that Volkov and Zheng were down on the surface, and he needed to find and detain them before they could slip away again.

Feng ducked through the bridge hatch and headed toward the habitation module where the rest of his team was gearing up. The clock was ticking. It'd been nearly two weeks since he'd failed to stop Volkov from fleeing Lianmeng, and time was running short to find and capture the GIM agent. And if he couldn't capture Volkov, Feng would need to kill him and make sure that whatever data the man had was destroyed. It was going to be a challenge, but the senior ISB agent was determined to make sure this mission didn't end as poorly as the last one that'd sent him to this rock.

15

THE FIRST DREAM

"SARYF!"

Ben's heart froze as the piercing scream reached his ears. He raised his head just enough for his eyes to clear the barricade he was taking cover behind, and what he saw horrified him.

A sea of fire.

Black smoke billowed toward the heavens, driven there by the roiling flames. The skeletal remains of a dozen charred transports burned with the intensity of a star. And in the middle of it, he saw his wife.

"Leika!" Ben howled, his voice hoarse and cracking, just like the heat-blasted soil beneath his feet.

She turned her face toward him, and he saw that she was clutching their daughter to her chest.

"Leika! Run!"

Ben vaulted over the barricade, flinching in pain as the searing heat of the flames hit him full in the face. He leaned into the hellish wind that fought to drive him back, and he forced his way forward. He had to reach them. He was their protector. He couldn't fail.

Leika looked directly into his soul.

"Avenge us, husband."

Then the flames pressed in. Her flawless lavender-colored skin smoldered briefly before turning black with char and crumbling to dust. The bodies of his wife and child fell apart, revealing a pair of crimson eyes.

"No!" Ben screamed, his heart rending at the loss of his family.

"Yes, Saryf." A deep voice spoke directly into his mind. The eyes flared brighter, an ephemeral body of shadow and will forming around them. Then it charged directly at him.

Ben raised his hands in an attempt to ward off the specter, but it passed effortlessly through his armored hands and straight into him. A blinding pain flared inside his skull, and Ben dropped to his knees, clawing at his head. He needed to get it out, for if he didn't, it would consume him.

He howled as excruciating pain lanced through him, and he collapsed fully to the ground, writhing in agony. Ben struggled for what felt like an eternity, unwilling to give in to the influence's demands. But in the end, he was simply too weak.

He yielded.

The pain faded, along with the inferno before him, and Ben pushed himself up onto his hands and knees, panting heavily. He opened his eyes to the view of shattered glass littering the ground beneath him, and he saw his reflection in every single piece of it.

Two crimson eyes stared back at him, and he smiled.

16

CAPTURED

"HEY, MAN, YOU OKAY?" KRAVCZYK SAID, NUDGING BEN WITH AN elbow.

Ben turned to face the big SEAR, who was strapped into a web seat next to him. "Yeah," Ben said unconvincingly. "I've been having some weird dreams lately. I was just... pondering whether they have any meaning or not."

"Pondering, huh?" Kravczyk said. "Looks more like whatever you've been dreaming about has you spooked."

"It's fine, Chief—" Ben broke off as the little civilian cargo shuttle they were strapped into jerked violently to the side as they hit the roughest part of atmospheric entry. "I'm good," he said after renewing his grip on the oh-shit handles next to his seat. "It was just a dream. How are you doing?"

Now it was Kravczyk's turn to lie. "I'm good."

"Uh-huh," Ben said with a sardonic smirk. "You and me both. Totally fine."

Kravczyk's expression darkened a little. Then he turned his head and pretended to examine the transit cases that were lashed to the deck. Ben left the big man to deal with his demons in peace and turned his attention to the world they were dropping on.

Their ride continued to shudder and bounce around as it screamed through the atmosphere over Newman's Rock. The shuttle was similar in design to the corporate cargo transport that carried Ben safely away from Isadore back at the outset of the Alarian War. They were headed for the civilian spaceport on the outskirts of Landing, the creatively named capital city of the sparsely populated world, built on the site where Sylas Newman had first set foot on the then-unclaimed planet.

Newman, a self-made billionaire and outspoken critic of the Confed, had loudly proclaimed that, as the first person to set foot on the planet, he was the rightful owner of the world, and he and his modest group of colonists immediately set about erecting a settlement. The SRF had thrown an absolute shit fit when word of Newman's settlement reached them, and they immediately lobbied the Confed to recognize the world and the system it was in as Federation space. The demand wasn't without merit, as a Federation autonomous probe had actually cataloged the habitable world before Sylas Newman settled on it, but the SRF hadn't made a claim on the world before Newman arrived.

As if that wasn't drama enough, the NAC threw their hat in the ring and petitioned the Confed to grant them ownership of the system, as Newman was a citizen of the NAC, along with every single one of the people that went with him. For his part, Sylas Newman staunchly maintained that he and his people were beholden to no part of the Confed, as they'd all renounced their NAC citizenship the day they settled on an unclaimed planet in an unclaimed system. The whole mess was tied up in the courts for more than a decade before the SRF decided to take matters into their own hands and tried to tilt the scales in their favor… by conducting a false flag operation that resulted in the deaths of hundreds of the world's population.

Only the timely intervention of SEAR Team One kept the Federation plot from achieving its aim. Both Valdez and Kravczyk had been part of that team, but Valdez had been injured badly after things went south in a hurry, leaving only a very green Kravczyk to deal with a rabid bunch of pissed-off Chinese commandos. The fight hadn't been pretty, and Ben could tell the chief was having a hard time dealing with his return to the scene of that battle.

"Touching down in a couple minutes, Dagger," the shuttle's co-pilot announced over the intercom. Ben couldn't help but smile when he heard their call sign. "Dagger" had been Team One's call sign during their mission to rescue Ben from Earth, and they'd recycled it for their insane boarding operation during the Battle of Icarus. The last time Ben heard that call sign, he and the SEARs pulled a miracle out of their asses. Their current mission was supposed to be relatively low key and free of explosions, but despite the promised cakewalk, he couldn't help but feel better knowing a little piece of his past success was coming with him on this op.

Kravczyk had noticed Ben grinning like an idiot and was staring at him with a raised eyebrow.

"What?" Ben said. "It's a badass call sign. And you can't deny the fact that we were demonstrably badass the last time we used it."

Kravczyk sighed. "Just promise me you won't go all Sith lord on us again, okay?"

"No promises."

Ben sat at a small cafe table, sipping on a cup of honest-to-God fresh-ground coffee. He reclined casually in a polymer chair, a mini personal data tablet in one hand as he mindlessly scrolled through the various news headlines. The weather was cool and crisp, reminding him of an October day back home on the farm. Except instead of working like a man possessed, thrashing to get the fruit off before the botrytis trying to take over the Pinot Noir really got out of hand, he was sitting here, alone, in front of a small cafe in the residential area of Landing.

The casual passersby saw a good-looking guy in his early twenties with his head in his mini PDT, scrolling through social media, which was exactly what he was going for, and judging by the disgusted looks and muttered talk about "oblivious kids" coming from the pair of old guys playing chess three tables down the sidewalk, he was nailing it. A trained eye, however, would've noticed how he'd positioned himself such that nobody could sneak up behind him, and the panes of glass lining the shopfronts along the strip next to the little park allowed him to keep track of nearly everyone within fifty meters of his position. And for the people he couldn't track from his position, he had Tess and Kravczyk.

"I've got eyes on someone that might be our target," Tess called out over their secure comms. "Asian male, approximately one hundred and seventy centimeters, wearing a dark green jacket with the hood up and sunglasses. He just turned south into the park from the corner of the main boulevard and is heading straight for you, Ben."

Ben didn't reply or otherwise indicate he'd heard anything at all. The small sling pack at his feet contained a comms unit that relayed the line-of-sight laser communications directly to his implant. He heard everything that came in over the team channel, and he could even fire off text replies via the implant, but he avoided doing so out of fear that he would inadvertently ruin his carefully maintained facade.

"I've got him," Kravczyk reported. "Looks good. At first blush he seems casual, but I can see the tension in his shoulders from here. He's majorly stressed about something. He's also twitching his head side to side, like he's checking his flanks but trying not to be obvious about it."

Ben's eyes flicked up to the plate-glass window next to him. It took him a moment, but he soon locked onto the individual in question. Tess was right; he was angling across the park, directly toward Ben's position.

"I thought Collins said the guy we're here to pick up is an experienced deep-cover agent," Tess said, sounding like she was no longer sure of their target. "This guy doesn't appear to have the finesse I was expecting."

The old guys a few tables down wrapped up their game, and the larger of the two stood ponderously and shook his opponent's hand.

"Great game, George," the guy said, turning to walk past Ben's table. "I'll get you next time!"

"Not likely, Chet," his opponent said with a huge grin. "That's four in a row. I'm on a hot streak!"

Ben glanced back up to check the position of the target Tess had called out. The guy was halfway across the park and still headed straight for him. Ben dropped his eyes to his tablet again and took a sip of coffee.

"Excuse me, son," the old guy said, having stopped next to Ben's table, "but I have to ask…"

Ben looked up to meet the man's gaze, sweeping his eyes over the window for another glimpse of their target—another thirty seconds and he would reach Ben's table.

"What's that?" Ben said, plastering a friendly smile on his

lips as his heart rate started to climb. He was only supposed to sit here and wait until their target arrived, then catch his attention and lead him to their getaway car, which Valdez had parked a block and a half away.

"Have you tried the scones here?"

There was something in the old guy's expression. Ben's spidey sense went on high alert the instant before he realized the man's easygoing smile didn't reach his eyes, and he tensed involuntarily.

"No," Ben answered. "I'm afraid I haven't. I've read that too much processed sugar isn't good for you."

The old guy let out a hearty laugh, and Ben was surprised to find that it sounded genuine. "God, you young'uns are all the same," the guy said, pulling out a chair next to Ben and sitting down. He peered into Ben's coffee cup and nodded in approval. "Good call on taking it black. They grind the beans fresh before making the coffee, and it would be a shame to cover up the flavor of the roast."

"Ben, get rid of that old geezer," Kravczyk said urgently. "The target is less than ten meters from you."

"Don't worry about him, son," the guy said, still smiling that friendly neighborhood smile. "I'm the one you're here for."

Ben tried to check his reaction, but his eyebrows shot up without his express permission.

"Ben, what's going on?" Kravczyk said over the team channel. "Get rid of that dude!"

Ben didn't respond. On the off chance this was all some sort of ploy, he didn't want to out the rest of his team. The old guy's smile faded to a faint grin, and he narrowed his eyes slightly. He raised a finger and wagged it, like he'd just realized something and was about to give Ben a rundown on his findings.

"You're not with CID, are you, son? No," he said quickly

when Ben opened his mouth to respond. "Let me guess... Not CID, but you're also not trying to kill me right now, which rules out most of the Federation intelligence services. You've got a good idea as to what you should be doing for a covert meeting, but your execution is all wrong."

The guy rubbed his chin as he thought through the logic chain in his head. "But if you're not CID, then you would have at least been tasked with my extraction *by* CID, which probably means military. Not naval intelligence, as they tend to stick more to the analysis side of things. The regular marines don't really do this kind of thing, so that leaves the Pathfinders or SEARs. Your arms aren't long enough to drag your knuckles on the ground, so I'm going to go with you being a SEAR."

The guy leaned back in his chair with a satisfied grin, just as the man in the green jacket walked right past their table and entered the shop next door. "So how'd I do?"

Ben leaned back himself and returned the grin. "None of the above."

The guy's smile faltered and his face screwed up in a combination of surprise and confusion.

"I'm a civilian." Ben took the last sip of his coffee and set the empty mug on the table. He swiped his tablet over the near-field wireless terminal built into the center of the table and transferred a healthy tip to the cafe staff. "Let's go."

With that, Ben grabbed his sling pack and stood up, then walked down the sidewalk in the direction of a waiting Valdez. The fat old guy pushed himself out of his chair with surprising dexterity and hustled after Ben.

"I'm not alone," the guy said after he'd fallen into step next to Ben. "I have a GIM agent with me. He's the one we really need to get off-world and then put him in touch with either Admiral Garland or..." He trailed off, then tensed.

Ben had seen it, too. Green jacket guy had emerged from the shop next to the cafe shortly after the two of them had passed, and he was coming up fast from behind. Ben and the old guy were only a few steps from the corner of the park. There wasn't much traffic transiting the side street they were approaching, but there was enough that they couldn't just run across without risking one or both of them being hit, so Ben hooked a right at the corner, which would break their pursuer's line of sight for a few moments.

"Run!" the old guy whispered harshly as soon as they were around the corner.

Both Ben and the old guy made a break for it. Ben tried to fire off a quick call for help over the team channel when he realized he hadn't heard anything over comms since green jacket guy had passed their table and headed into the shop.

The screeching of tires on the road next to them drew Ben's attention, and time seemed to slow down as the full scope of what was happening hit him all at once. A nondescript panel van was angling onto the sidewalk, skidding to a stop a few meters ahead, and the sliding side door was wide open. Two men with Asian features and dressed in tactical gear were squatting on either side of the door, their eyes locked onto Ben and the old guy.

Ben hit the brakes, intent on taking his chances with green jacket guy to the rear. He grabbed the old guy's arm and forcefully spun him around, nearly yanking him off his feet in the process.

Green jacket guy was ready for them, though. Ben saw something streak through the air toward both him and the old guy. His brain told him what it was just as the barbs from the Taser dug into his flesh. Searing pain lanced outward from his chest, and stars exploded behind his eyes as his entire body went rigid.

A loud crack rang out from next to him, and out of the corner of his eye, he saw the old guy fold up like a rag doll.

The current pouring into his body from the Taser abruptly ceased, and two pairs of strong hands snaked around him from behind and jerked him roughly in the direction of the van.

"Fuck! This guy weighs a ton!" one of his assailants said in the Chinese common dialect, the translation coming in seamlessly thanks to Ben's implant.

His vision cleared after a split second, and control of his body was returning far faster than he'd expected. This wasn't his first rodeo being Tased, thanks to an inadvisable competition he'd once participated in with the Pathfinders while they were en route from Elizabeth to Hai'alla. Ben remembered the stun effect lasting for several minutes, and the guys busy trying to abduct him were acting like they expected the same thing.

Green jacket guy tucked the spent Taser into a pocket and rushed forward to help shove Ben into the van, and that was when Ben's noodly legs came fully back online.

He reared back and lashed out with a vicious straight kick, using the two goons holding his arms for support. His foot connected with Green Jacket's midsection, taking the guy off his feet. He landed in a heap, gasping for air. His sunglasses and hood had been knocked off his head, and Ben got a good look at an Asian man in his late thirties, eyes bulging in shock and pain as he clutched his stomach.

"Dammit! Get him in the van!" shouted someone from behind Ben.

Ben strained against the hands dragging him backward, an animalistic terror coursing through his veins. He roared, putting everything he had into tearing himself free.

One arm shot forward, a very surprised kidnapper still attached to it. Ben twisted his body, gaining momentum in an attempt to rip free of the bigger of his two assailants, who was just barely maintaining his control over Ben's left arm. Ben spun all the way around, whipping the hapless thug on his right arm in an arc toward the guy on his left, intending to use him as a meat bludgeon.

The collision between the two thugs resulted in a sickening crunch as bones broke and soft tissue tore free. Then the weight holding him back was suddenly gone as the two goons crumpled to the ground.

Ben had just enough time to see the bloody compound fracture of Lefty's forearm poking through his sleeve before his vision flared white hot and another sickening crack reverberated briefly around the inside of his skull. Then the world around him went black.

―――――

"Boss, we've got a problem!" Kravczyk shouted into the team comms as he broke from his overwatch position at the opposite end of the park from Ben.

All comms with Ben had gone dead shortly before the kid and the old guy he'd been talking to got up and headed in the direction of Valdez and the car. Kravczyk found it a little hard to believe that a dumpy old guy like the one Ben was with was the guy they were here to pick up, but the kid had seemed calm and collected when he made to get up, so he must be their target.

That wasn't the problem, though. The thing that had Kravczyk vaulting over the railing of the fire escape he'd posted up on and dropping the five meters to the alley below was the fact that green jacket guy had immediately reappeared behind Ben and their target, and he was closing in on them with a decided air of violence.

Kravczyk hit the ground hard, rolling with the impact before springing to his feet and sprinting off in Ben's direction.

"Chief, what's going on?" Valdez called over the team channel.

"The kid's hooked up with our guy, but they've got trouble inbound, boss," Kravczyk said as he exploded out into the park and began weaving his way through the pedestrian traffic. Out of the corner of his eye, he caught sight of McCollum as she emerged from the apartment building that she'd been on the roof of. The two of them angled toward the street corner at the far end of the park, where Ben and their target now appeared to be aware they had a tail and were just turning the corner to break line of sight.

"On my way," Valdez said curtly. The boss was a couple of blocks away in a car that was facing the wrong direction. That meant Kravczyk and McCollum were on their own for a few minutes before the boss arrived to back them up.

Ben and the old guy finished their turn around the corner and both took off running, but green jacket guy was running now, too. Kravczyk saw their tail pull a dark object from under his jacket just as a white service van coming down the road toward them pulled a one-eighty and raced up onto the sidewalk. The van screeched to a stop, cutting Ben and the old guy off from any avenue of escape, but the kid was quick.

Ben spun their target around and headed back the way he'd come, radiating pure violence and clearly determined to go right through Green Jacket, if that was what it took. Time slowed to a crawl, and Kravczyk watched helplessly as several black-clad thugs piled out of the van and chased after the kid. Then both Ben and the old guy stiffened, and Kravczyk realized the objects Green Jacket had pulled out were Tasers. The whole sequence from Ben turning the corner until now had taken only a few seconds, and Kravczyk wasn't even halfway across the park yet.

He wasn't going to make it in time.

"They're going to nab them!" he yelled over the comms.

The chief immediately went into combat mode, pulling a Mk. 27 out from its hiding place beneath his bulky sweatshirt. He unfolded the stock as he put on a burst of speed. He needed to get clear of the people occupying the park between him and the assailants before he could risk taking a shot.

Unfortunately, when a gorilla-sized man charged out of a dark alley and into a peaceful park and then pulled out a submachine gun, normal people tended to freak the fuck out.

Kravczyk cursed internally when the pedestrians nearest to him began screaming and running for cover. The good news was that he suddenly had a clear field of fire. The bad news was that the thugs already had the old guy halfway into the van and two more bad guys had just latched onto Ben. Kravczyk couldn't take a shot without potentially striking either Ben or the old guy, so he lowered the Mk. 27 and ran for all he was worth. McCollum was slightly ahead of him, but she was on the opposite side of the street and didn't have a shot, either. The two of them sprinted in a desperate bid to reach their teammate in time.

Then Ben was suddenly back in the fight, having shaken off the effects of the Taser faster than anyone Kravczyk had ever seen. In a truly impressive display of power, the kid reared back and booted green jacket guy so hard he briefly went airborne before crashing to the pavement. Ben followed up his strike by lifting the guy holding his right arm off the ground like he weighed no more than a small child, and then he swung the poor bastard around like a club. The kid smashed the two men together with such force that they both crumpled to the ground in a heap, one with his head canted at an unnatural angle to his body.

Kravczyk was nearly there, just another thirty meters. "Ben!" He shouted the warning as Green Jacket regained his feet and launched himself at Ben's back. Another sickening crack split the air as Green Jacket brought a sap down on the base of Ben's skull, and the kid folded like a puppet whose strings had been cut.

More bad guys appeared from the van and dragged their wounded teammates into the vehicle, the last one helping Green Jacket shove Ben's dead weight inside.

"Ben!" McCollum screamed from across the street as she broke from the sidewalk and ran out into traffic in a last-ditch attempt to reach the kid in time.

Green Jacket climbed into the van and turned around to shut the door, and Kravczyk came to a screeching halt. His blood froze as recognition hit him. Then it began to boil.

"Feng!" Kravczyk bellowed, overcome by a sudden onslaught of rage. His Mk. 27 came up in a flash, but he still couldn't risk the shot—Ben was on the floor of the cargo van right behind the former commando.

Feng finally looked up, realizing the two men he'd just captured had support close at hand. The two old enemies locked gazes for what seemed like an eternity, and Feng's lips twisted up into the mirror image of Kravczyk's rage-filled snarl.

Then Feng slammed the door shut, and the van roared away. Tess arrived on the scene a few seconds later, halting her desperate sprint right where the van had just been parked. She yelled something unintelligible at the retreating service van, then rounded on Kravczyk, who was still rooted in the middle of the sidewalk, Mk. 27 tucked into his shoulder pocket at high-ready.

"Why'd you stop?" McCollum demanded as she ran up to him. "You could've made it! Now they have Ben!"

Kravczyk shot her a withering glare but didn't respond before looking back down the street. He was singularly focused on the rapidly retreating vehicle. When the van made a quick turn onto another side street and he lost visual on it, Kravczyk finally lowered his weapon.

"Goddammit!" he raged, the vehemence in his voice so powerful that McCollum actually took an involuntary step back. "Feng!" he screamed down the street. "I'm going to find you and rip your fucking spine out, you murderous fuck!"

The red haze clouding his vision began to relent a few moments later, and Kravczyk made a conscious effort to take some deep breaths and get control of himself. That was when he realized Valdez was shouting into the comms.

"Chief! What the hell is going on?"

Kravczyk shook his head to clear the blood rage and quickly took in his surroundings. People were cowering behind anything solid enough to provide cover, and many of them had their comms units to their ears—calling the cops, no doubt. The precariousness of their situation hit him all at once; they needed to get the hell out of here before the local LEOs showed up and things got messy.

"Boss!" Kravczyk said into the comms. "Ben and the target were just nabbed by another team, and that asshole Feng was with them—the same guy from last time we were here."

There was a long pause before Valdez came back over the channel. "Understood, Chief. I'll be there in ninety seconds. Be ready to—"

Kravczyk didn't hear the rest of Valdez's sentence because a silver four-door sedan came flying up on them and screeched to a halt less than two paces away.

"Get in, quick!" the driver shouted out an open window. "I'm GIM. The ISB just took my CID partner and your teammate. We need to get the hell out of here before the police show up!"

Kravczyk exchanged a questioning look with McCollum, and they both shrugged. He thought it unlikely that this guy was playing for the other team, considering the fact that he had no visible weapons and was trying to pick up two people armed with some serious firepower. Most likely, this guy really was with the CID agent they were here for and had been hanging out nearby just like Kravczyk and McCollum had been. Damn lot of good it did for the kid.

"Why the hell not," he said, opening the rear door and piling in with McCollum right on his heels. Then he toggled the team channel open just as the first few notes of an approaching siren reached his ears. "Change of plans, boss. We've got our own ride. Steer clear of our position and let's regroup somewhere safe."

Valdez didn't question the change-up, simply replying, "Copy."

Their new best friend from the GIM stomped on the accelerator before Tess had even closed the door, and they roared off in the direction Feng's team had escaped in.

"Do you have any assets that can track that van?" the GIM guy asked.

"Not here, but if you can get us to our shuttle at Liberty Spaceport, we might have someone that can find where they've gone."

"It'll have to do," he said. "I'm Dimitriy, by the way. Dimitriy Volkov. The man those ISB thugs took, along with your teammate, was my contact with CID. While it's not good that the ISB have them, I am actually the one with the information they want."

Kravczyk felt a glimmer of hope. If Feng wanted what this guy had, then he would probably keep Ben and the CID agent alive in an attempt to find out where Dimitriy was. That at least gave them a little bit of time to nail down where they'd gone and attempt a rescue, but Ben was almost certainly in for a rough time. The chief glanced at McCollum, who was busy scanning for signs of pursuit. She paused for a moment when she saw him looking at her, and Kravczyk saw her fear for Ben reflected in her eyes.

"We'll find him, Tess," he said firmly. "Mabel is the best bloodhound in the business, and Ben is one stubborn son of a bitch. Those ISB assholes won't know what hit them."

17

INTERROGATION

"WELL, WHAT DID YOU FIND OUT?" FENG SAID AS HE APPROACHED his tech specialist, Field Agent Cheng Li.

Li looked up from the ruggedized laptop computer he'd been staring at for the last hour and shook his head. "Nothing."

"Not good enough," Feng said, a touch of acid in his voice. "He was working with the SEARs. There has to be a record of him somewhere."

Li didn't back down. "I've run his DNA profile through both CAFID and our own personnel databases. Whoever he is, he isn't in any way associated with the Confed military."

"Could he be a CID operative?"

Li shook his head. "The ISB maintains its own database of CID personnel. 'Zheng' is in there, though there is little more in his file than his alias, and some brief physical descriptors. But the point is, we at least have a record of him, and he's a deep-cover operative. Whoever the guy we grabbed along with Zheng is, he's neither military nor CID—I'd bet my pension on it."

Feng growled with frustration. "What about facial recognition?"

"Same," Li said, leaning back in his chair. "No matches in

either the ISB's databases or the Confed's. I've got the system cross-checking his scan against civilian records now, but..." He trailed off and shrugged.

"But there are billions of civilian records spread across a dozen different databases," Feng said, massaging his temples. "Even if a match exists, it could take hours or days for the system to find it." He turned to look at the door that led out of the small office they were using as a command center while in Landing, thinking about the enigma that was currently cuffed to a metal office chair in the room across the hall.

"I refuse to believe he isn't military," Feng said firmly. "His attempt at being covert was amateurish at best, but the speed with which he moved and the way he fought tells me he's received extensive martial training. A civilian isn't capable of reacting that quickly to a violent encounter. And then there's the fact that he managed to shake off fifty thousand volts from a Taser in just a few seconds."

"I concur," Li agreed. "But if he's not in any of our databases, that means he's either so new that his file hasn't been loaded into our databases yet or he's a part of some ultra-secret NAVSOC operation that we don't know about."

"Either way," Feng mused, "he's dangerous."

The office door opened, and Feng scowled when he recognized the face of his team's medic. "Senior Agent Wu, I need to examine your ribs."

"Not now, Chen," Feng said, waving off the medic.

"Now, sir," Chen insisted. "You won't be any use to the ISB if you die from a punctured lung or sepsis from a lacerated organ."

Feng growled in annoyance but took a step toward the door. "Li, when Kong is done with Zheng, tell him to get some answers from our mysterious friend. Do whatever it takes. We won't be taking him with us once we find Volkov and the data he stole."

Li nodded in acknowledgment, and Feng gingerly walked toward the door, one hand supporting the ribs on his left side. The senior agent had never come across an enemy that Li couldn't ID inside of ten minutes once he had his computer searching their databases for a match. The unknown agent *had* to be military—Feng was sure of it—and he was clearly Confed. Probably from the NAC. There was just no way they wouldn't have been able to get a hit on his DNA profile in that case. Even if he was from a colony world, the NAC kept impeccable DNA records of all their citizens, taken just after birth.

As Feng exited the small office and trailed after his team medic, the sounds of Kong's work interrogating Zheng reached his ears. He made a mental note to have someone work on the soundproofing of their hastily rigged-up interrogation room. The deserted warehouse they were using as a base of operations was in one of the industrial districts that ringed the city of Landing, and traffic out here was sparse. Still, it was better to be diligent when it came to making sure no errant cries from the tortured made their way to the attention of a sharp-eared passerby.

A few meters farther down the hall, Feng paused briefly outside the door to the room where their mystery prisoner was secured. Curiosity about the man's identity burned within him. He was unaccustomed to not having all the information in a timely fashion. Unease began to gnaw at the edges of his consciousness; the last time he hadn't been able to get answers when he wanted them, it resulted in a lost foot and a humiliating defeat.

Feng pushed his misgivings aside and continued down the hall. He would get his answers soon enough. His people were very, very good at getting information out of unwilling subjects. For a moment, Feng almost felt bad for what their mystery guest was about to experience. Then he remembered his broken ribs and the fact that one of his men was dead and another crippled, thanks to that Confed piece of shit.

I just hope Chen finishes patching me up before Kong gets the information. I want to see the look on that kid's face when he finally breaks.

———

"WAKE UP, BITCH!"

Ben's eyes popped open, and he immediately recoiled from the ammonia salts being wafted in front of his face. His sight cleared just in time for him to see the fist about to slam into the bridge of his nose. A loud crack rang out, and fireworks exploded behind his eyes. Tears immediately sprang from Ben's eyes as the fiery pain of a newly broken nose tore into his skull. He sucked in a breath through clenched teeth, doing his best to will the pain away from the forefront of his consciousness.

"Oh good, you're up."

Ben blinked rapidly to clear the tears welling in his eyes. A hard-looking Asian man in his late twenties or early thirties was standing a few paces in front of Ben, a sadistic grin stretched across his lips.

"Where the fuck am I?" Ben coughed out, feeling hot blood pouring down his face from both his nostrils. He leaned his head forward slightly to keep the blood from pooling and draining down his throat. "And who the fuck are you?"

"Hmm," the man said, sounding disappointed. "I expected better from one of the CID's operators."

"I'm not fucking CID, you asshole," Ben said derisively. "I'm just a civilian."

"I think not."

The guy's foot snapped out and struck Ben in the solar plexus. The little bit of air he'd managed to suck in after having his nose broken exploded out of his lungs, leaving him gawping like a fish out of water. The goon had moved like lightning, not that Ben would've been able to do anything about it, restrained as he was.

"Shall we try again?"

Ben struggled to take in a breath, his diaphragm spasming from the hammer blow it'd just received.

A fist slammed into the side of his head, followed an instant later by another on the opposite side. His vision went red and darkness crowded in around the edges. He let his chin drop to his chest as he fought to shake off a sudden wave of nausea. He felt consciousness beginning to slip away.

"Oh, no you don't, meat!" his tormentor shouted.

A fresh wave of agony lanced out from Ben's broken nose as he involuntarily scrunched up his face at the ammonia salts that had suddenly reappeared below his nostrils. He coughed and spat a glob of blood onto the floor, the world spinning around him in a disorienting haze.

Ben's head was jerked backward, and he struggled to focus on the eyes boring into his from just a few inches away.

"Who do you work for? Huh?" his captor shouted. Spittle flew from his mouth and sprayed across Ben's face. "Where is Dimitriy Volkov? Tell me!"

To stop the abuse, Ben wanted to tell him. But he didn't know what the hell this asshole was talking about. "Who the fuck is Dimitriy Volkov?" Ben slurred out through split lips. "Is he your boyfriend?"

Fury raced across his torturer's face, and the guy raised a boot off the floor and stomped it down onto Ben's left hand, which was firmly cinched to the arm of the chair with a flex cuff around his wrist. Bones broke, and Ben screamed as his torturer ground his heel into Ben's mangled hand.

White light flashed behind his eyes as the blinding agony fully hit him. He thrashed at his restraints, an animalistic need to escape burying all rational thought. His whole body strained, but his efforts were incoherent. His abused body refused to operate in a coordinated fashion. And all the while, his tormentor laughed at his struggles.

"Pathetic! Give me what I want, Confed trash! You're too weak to stand up to what I'm going to do to you! Tell me where Volkov is hiding, and I'll end your useless existence quickly."

Darkness again crowded Ben's vision, moving in faster this time. The pain began to fade as consciousness slipped away, but the part of his mind that was still barely holding on to reality was screaming at him to fight, to find a way out of this hell. As his head fell once again to his chest, a voice mocked him from the darkness.

"Go ahead and rest, meat. I'll be back soon."

18

THE SECOND DREAM

BEN ROCKETED BACKWARD, COVERING THE ENTIRE LENGTH OF THE server room before slamming into one of the last server towers in line. Agony flared in his chest where the agent's foot had collided with his breastplate, buckling the thick graphene polyalloy plating and splintering his ribs. His HUD exploded with injury notifications and fault codes, but he couldn't make them out.

Despite the blinding pain, Ben considered his impact with the server tower a blessing. The relatively fragile object sapped away most of his momentum before he crashed into the unyielding wall behind it. He collapsed to the floor in a heap, the pain causing an explosion of fireworks somewhere between his eyes and his brain. A metallic, coppery taste filled his mouth, and he spat a glob of blood and saliva into his helmet.

Get up, Ben… Get up!

Ignoring the flurry of warnings his HUD was throwing at him, Ben planted one hand on the floor and pushed himself into a kneeling position. Tears streamed from his eyes as he fought back a wave of agony-induced nausea. His faceplate had spiderweb cracks running through it, but the implant in his head transmitted the HUD directly to his brain, so the data on it remained crystal clear, even though the rest of the world around him was beginning to blur and lose color. Somewhere a long way off, he could just barely make out shouting through the buzzing in his ears.

"Had enough already?" the agent mocked him. "We've only just started!"

The agent stormed toward him. The massive Reaper-class armored drone, currently controlled by his enemy, seemed an utterly insurmountable obstacle. The sheer size and strength of the construct was unlike anything Ben had ever fought before. As if to reinforce that notion, the agent ripped a server tower from the floor and flung it across the room.

Ben had made a catastrophic error. The agent was just too strong. He'd hoped that the chief and Mabel would be able to escape along with the rest of his little team, but in order for that to happen, Ben needed to distract the agent for ten minutes. Instead, he'd barely managed to hold it off for ten seconds. He hadn't heard anything from the rest of his team since he'd dropped down into the server room to confront the agent, and dread filled his chest as he realized none of them were going to make it out of here. He was simply too weak. Ben had never lacked determination, but sometimes willpower simply wasn't enough to overcome the kind of true strength the agent possessed.

The agent drew closer. The sheer malice it radiated made it seem to have grown in height. Ben steeled himself for one last effort. It was a desperate gamble, but it was all he had left. He gasped in agony as he struggled to stand. The agent stomped ever closer. There was only one way Ben would be able to hold out long enough, and it sure as hell wasn't going to be here in the real. If he could get close enough, try to forge a link with the agent via his APEX, he might just have a chance to snatch victory from the jaws of defeat. But how to get access to its systems?

Ben's eyes locked onto the fairings that housed his integrated combat blades. Thirty centimeters of conductive alloy in each arm. He glanced back up to the behemoth now standing stationary a few paces away. Would thirty centimeters get deep enough?

"Well?" the agent said. "Is that it? I thought you were a fighter, Ben. But you're just like all the others I've broken over the millennia. Weak! Pathetic! Bow before your better, human, and I'll make your end quick."

Ben crouched painfully, eliciting a menacing chuckle from the agent. Then he launched himself at the devil before him, channeling every last ounce of augmented strength into his shaky legs. He triggered a burst from the grav harness, accelerating directly toward the jaws of death. His arms flashed out in front of him, and he sent one last command to his APEX. Twin thirty-centimeter blades forged from one of the hardest alloys known to man shot out of their housings in his forearms and drove directly into the agent's chest.

They shattered into thousands of razor-like fragments the instant they contacted the Reaper's heavy armor, exploding outward in every direction.

Ben screamed in agony as the bones in his arms splintered. He crashed to the floor in a tangle of limbs at the agent's feet, blinding agony tearing through his destroyed body. He rolled back and forth on the ground, clutching his ruined arms to his chest. Through the tears streaming from his eyes, Ben saw the Reaper squat down next to him.

A bony face leaned over his own and stopped mere inches from Ben's cracked faceplate, its crimson eyes flaring.

"Weak. Pathetic. Useless. What good are you to anyone, Benjamin John Hutchins?" the agent said rhetorically. "Do you understand now? Do you truly see my strength? The power that I command? *You* will never be able to do the things that *I* can do because you lack the resolve."

The agent paused, cocking its head in thought. "Or maybe you will… provided I show you the way."

The agent reached one massive hand down and placed it on Ben's chest. Something began tugging at the back of Ben's mind, and his consciousness recoiled in terror.

The agent was trying to force a link with him.

Ben tried to fight back. He urged his body to lash out, but he was too broken. His arms and legs refused to respond to his brain's commands. With growing horror, Ben realized the agent would get through, and there was nothing he could do to stop it. The unrelenting mental pressure assaulting his consciousness steadily increased. Ben thrashed inside his own mind, desperately attempting to stave off the inevitable.

"Stop struggling, Terran. Embrace the power that I offer, and no one will be able to stand against us."

The world around him began to fade away, and he knew he'd lost. Yet still, he fought, but his resistance to the agent's will rapidly lost its coherence. In the last instant before the agent crushed Ben's consciousness, he knew the fight was over, and he gave in.

The agent ripped a hole through the thin veil separating its digital consciousness from Ben's physical brain and roared into his mind, *You're mine now, Terran!*

19

BREAKOUT

TWO OF THE ISB TAC TEAM QUICKLY RESTRAINED ZHENG TO A METAL office chair with a series of stout flex cuffs. The old CID operative peered around his new cell through the one eye that he was still able to see out of, the other having been so thoroughly abused that he feared more than just the swelling was keeping him from seeing anything with it. The two ISB agents finished their task and exited the room without a word, the door slamming with a boom, followed by a metallic click of the hastily installed padlock on the outside.

The kid Zheng met in front of the cafe was secured to a similar chair on the opposite side of the small room, though his chair was also bolted to the floor for some reason. Zheng took a moment to get a good look at his cellmate. The kid was well built but not overly muscular. Instead of spending time in the gym overdeveloping the glamour muscles, like some operators Zheng had known, the kid across from him had focused on functional strength and speed, judging by his athletic physique, his low body-fat percentage, and the lean-but-powerful-looking cords of muscle that were visible in his forearms. He'd claimed to be a civilian, but nothing about the young man said anything to Zheng except "special operations."

Unfortunately, it looked like that sadist had worked the kid over pretty good, though not quite as severely as he'd worked over Zheng. At least not yet. The young man's nose was broken and he already had two black eyes beginning to show. His left hand sported several broken fingers, and the broken tooth lying on the floor at his feet told the experienced CID agent that, at least so far, the ISB hadn't used anything but their fists to soften the kid up.

Zheng glanced down at the fingers of his right hand. The bleeding had mostly stopped, or at least slowed to a trickle. The sight of the raw, bloody meat where his fingernails used to be brought the throbbing pain to the forefront of his mind. He shifted uncomfortably in his chair, trying to relieve some of the pressure on the ribs of his left side. The stabbing pain every time he inhaled told him he had at least one broken rib, courtesy of his torturer's right hook.

Despite it all, though, Zheng had been able to hold out, and he hadn't given up anything during his first "interrogation" session. He knew there would be more to come, and he was less certain of how much more he could take before he started to crack, especially as the ISB goons would only escalate their techniques as he held out longer. Hopefully, though, it wouldn't matter. The SEARs should have been able to hook up with Volkov by now, and with any luck, they would have both the GIM agent and the data he carried safe. That just left the question of whether or not the SEARs would be able to locate their teammate and Zheng before the ISB made that a moot point.

A pang of regret swept through Zheng as the realization hit him: the young man was suffering because of his overconfidence. He'd known the ISB would be on their heels, but his time on Lianmeng had made him complacent. He hadn't seen any evidence that the ISB was capable of being so efficient when it came to tracking him down, and he'd allowed his guard to drop in the eleventh hour. When he'd spotted the kid by the cafe and his two team members in their overwatch positions, Zheng had done what he'd always done and wanted to put the rookies in their place. He'd let his situational awareness slip, instead focusing solely on teaching the young man a lesson about things not always being as they seemed.

A bitter laugh escaped through Zheng's swollen lips. The irony was just too much.

The jingling of keys from the hallway brought Zheng's attention back to the moment. He shook his head at the ISB's attempt to get their prisoner's good and scared before they entered—nobody needed to fumble with keys for that long. The whole thing was meant to build the tension and fear of those chained up in the cell. Still, Zheng had to admit, it was an effective technique. He really didn't relish the idea of another round with the sadistic bastard that worked him over the first time.

Finally, the door opened, and two men walked in. Zheng immediately recognized his torturer from before, but it took a moment for his memory to call up the identity of the second man.

"Wu Feng," Zheng said, using the traditional Chinese order of family name first. The words struggled to form themselves properly, thanks to his abused larynx and swollen face. "I'm surprised you aren't cowering aboard your ship in orbit, haunted by your dismal failure the last time you dared to set your boots down on this planet." Zheng made a show of looking pointedly at Feng's left foot. "I hope setting your *foot* on Newman's Rock again meets with similar success this time."

Feng sneered briefly but quickly got control of himself. Zheng smiled at the lapse. It was the tiniest of wins, but small victories were all he had left at this point. He knew full well that, barring the SEARS pulling off a miracle, he would never leave this place alive. The real question, though, was whether he would be able to keep the information Feng wanted from escaping his lips.

Feng turned away from Zheng and approached the kid, examining his battered face and mangled hand. "What's your opinion, Kong?" he said to the one who had tortured Zheng earlier.

"He's not nearly as strong as I expected. I could see it in his eyes—he was unprepared for even a mild interrogation like this."

"I find that unlikely," Feng stated. "When—" He broke off as the door opened suddenly.

"Sir, we've got a lead on the SEARs. Their shuttle has been located at Liberty Spaceport, and Quon reports only the flight crew are present."

A feral grin spread across Feng's face. "Tell Quon to have his team move in and secure the craft. I'll join you in a moment." Then, turning to Kong, he said, "Make sure Zheng gets a good show when this one wakes up. We still need Volkov."

Feng quickly exited the cell, and the door slammed shut again. Kong approached Zheng and smiled.

"Did you hear that, my friend? Your ticket to escape is about to be revoked. Unfortunately, we still need to know the location of Volkov and his data. Don't worry, though. I'm not going to hurt you anymore. I'm going to hurt him," the sadist purred, pointing at the kid. "And you get to watch, knowing every second of agony he experiences will be your fault."

Zheng tried to spit in the man's face, but his parched mouth and swollen lips only managed a hoarse cough, followed by a small trickle of drool running down his chin. Kong roared with laughter, a power-drunk tyrant basking in the misery of his victims.

Then Zheng's gaze shifted back to the young man across from him, and his blood ran cold. The kid was awake and staring directly at their captor. He noticed Zheng's attention, and his eyes snapped onto him.

Those eyes. They weren't the same ones Zheng knew from before. There was something in them, something… inhuman. It filled Zheng with a terror unlike anything the ISB could threaten him with, and his brain screamed at him to get away from it.

Kong stopped laughing, having finally noticed Zheng's sudden shift in demeanor. He whirled around, going into a fighting stance, but the kid was already in motion.

The young man's muscles bulged, and for just a split second, it looked like the flex cuffs securing him to the chair were going to hold, despite the audible creaking and groaning from the metal chair and thick plastic of the cuffs. Then, his arms tore free in a rapid-fire series of loud snaps. Kong lunged forward in an attempt to catch the kid before he freed himself entirely, but the young man effortlessly batted the ISB operative's hands aside, then picked him bodily off the ground and hurled him into the wall behind him.

The kid went into a forward shoulder roll, using the leverage of the maneuver to break the cuffs securing his ankles to the legs of the chair. Kong crashed to the floor, a spiderweb of cracks spreading out from the human-sized dent in the wallboard above him. But despite the horrendous impact, the ISB agent quickly scrambled to regain his feet. He launched himself toward the kid, who lightly hopped up and turned to face him, hands coming up into a guard position.

Kong was faster than the kid expected, though, and the agent slammed into him, driving the kid off balance. They tumbled backward, landing in Zheng's lap.

He cried out as the two thrashing men crashed into his abused body. The sudden weight on his chest sent spikes of agony radiating out from every one of his cracked or broken ribs. Zheng struggled to focus through the pain, seeing one of Kong's hands snaking around the back of the kid's neck as the two men grappled. Zheng lurched forward and clamped his teeth down on the meaty part at the base of the ISB agent's thumb. Kong howled, jerking his hand away only to leave a chunk of meat behind in Zheng's mouth.

The ISB agent recoiling gave the kid an opening, however, and he didn't hesitate, lashing out with his free hand and striking Kong in the throat. The blow didn't have much power behind it, thanks to the awkward angle and limited range of motion he had while sandwiched between his attacker and Zheng, but it was enough. Kong reeled backward, choking and coughing as both his hands came up reflexively to clutch his wounded throat.

The kid sprang forward, moving like lightning. His hands grappled onto the sides of Kong's head, thumbs searching for the agent's eyes. Kong grabbed the kid's hands and desperately tried to pry his thumbs away. The kid drove his captor backward, using his bigger, more powerful frame to bully the smaller ISB agent. The two men smashed into the dent Kong had left in the wall mere moments ago, and in an incredible show of strength, the kid lifted Kong off the ground, pinning him to the wall by his skull as he continued to drive his thumbs into the agent's eyes.

Kong lashed out, attempting to strike the kid in the groin with a knee, but the young man anticipated the move and shifted his hips, taking the blow on his thigh. Blood flowed freely from deep lacerations on his wrists where the flex cuffs had cut into him before they'd finally snapped. Despite the injuries, his forearms bulged and rippled, looking more like he had cords of steel cable beneath his pale skin than muscles.

Zheng's stomach dropped as he was forced to watch the

horrifying scene, now utterly certain of the fight's outcome. The kid was an unstoppable force, completely unfazed by Kong's kicks and knees at his groin and midsection. His thumbs continued to drive forward, overpowering Kong's own grip millimeter by millimeter. The agent's grunts and growls as he fought with the kid suddenly shifted to an animalistic shriek, and his desperate attempts to strike the kid with his knees and feet turned into an uncoordinated flailing.

Blood and clear liquid erupted from the man's face, and the room was filled with the most horrible scream Zheng had ever heard come from a human being. Kong's body jerked and spasmed as he fought to escape his inescapable end. Then, with a pair of wet cracks, the kid's thumbs abruptly plunged all the way into the ISB agent's skull, sinking up to his palms as he broke through the bones of the orbital socket. Kong's scream abruptly cut off, and his arms dropped to his sides. The kid released his hold on the agent, and Kong's corpse crumpled to the ground, limbs twitching as his ruined brain fired off its last few errant commands.

Zheng stared on in horror. The kid hadn't made a sound during the entire fight—not a single grunt or shout as he mercilessly dispatched a trained ISB tac team operative. Even now, the only sound coming from the young man was his slightly heavier, more rapid breathing, brought on by the exertion of the fight. Kong had been a sadistic fuck and absolutely deserved to die, but the manner in which the kid had killed him displayed a level of brutality Zheng had never witnessed before. Even now, the kid was standing there silently, examining his hands, turning them around as he flexed the fingers. It looked as though he was studying them—like they were foreign objects he'd never used before. The mangled fingers of his left hand, in particular, received extra scrutiny.

"Quickly," Zheng hissed, forcing aside the overwhelming

urge to cower in fear and instead focusing on what needed to be done if they were going to escape. "Help me out of these restraints! I'm sure the rest of Kong's team are used to screams coming from his interrogation rooms, but they'll soon get suspicious at the silence."

The kid turned his head and studied Zheng. "Who are you?" he said.

"My name is Zheng. I'm a CID operative—*the* CID operative you and your team came here to extract." *The kid must've had his bell rung pretty good*, Zheng thought. Those soulless eyes stared back at him, showing no sign of recognition.

"Who is Dimitriy Volkov?" the kid asked. He nudged Kong's body with his toe. "This one demanded I tell him where Volkov and his data are, but my team was only told to extract you."

"He's a GIM agent," Zheng said. "He's the one who obtained the data we need to get to Admiral Garland or Director Gideon. He didn't have a way to get off Lianmeng, so he asked for my help. But we don't have time for this right now. Get me out of these cuffs!"

The kid nodded slowly, as if he had to think carefully about the action before making a decision. Finally, he turned and walked to Zheng's side, studying the flex cuffs securing him to the chair, as well as their placement. He reached down and grasped the closest cuff with both hands, applying pressure briefly, as if to test its strength.

A pounding began on the door, and both Zheng and the kid snapped their heads toward the room's entrance.

"Kong, are you done in there? I don't hear any more screaming. Did you kill them by accident?"

The kid opened his mouth, and Zheng was shocked when he spoke not only in a voice that very closely matched Kong's tone but also almost flawlessly matched the agent's native accent and inflections.

"Just taking a break," he said. "This little Confed bitch is weaker than any of us expected. I don't want to damage him too severely before he gives me everything."

A muffled laugh came through the closed door. "Well, hurry it up, will you? I bet Chen a week's pay that you'll break both of them in under three hours. That only leaves you with forty minutes!"

The kid stood up and walked over to the door, positioning himself such that he'd be hidden from the hallway by the door, if it were to open. "Fine. Give me a hand a minute, and we'll see if we can't make sure you hold on to your money."

There was a pause, followed by the clink of the padlock being removed. The door swung open, and another ISB operative stepped into the room with a carefree smile on his face.

"Do you really need—" He broke off when he caught sight of Kong's lifeless body on the floor, and his hand shot to the holstered sidearm on his hip.

The kid kicked the backside of the door so hard that one of the hinges tore loose. The door smashed into the agent's right side, the handle striking him in the elbow and sending him crashing to the floor with a scream. Before he could get his bearings, the kid was on top of him. The young man effortlessly put the agent into a rear naked choke, and the ISB operative's cries quickly died out as his airway was completely closed off. The agent struggled briefly, but his efforts quickly became less coordinated as his brain was starved of oxygen. A few seconds later, he lost consciousness.

As soon as his opponent went limp, the kid quickly shifted his grip and violently twisted the ISB agent's neck. A sickening crack rang out, and the kid dropped the body to the floor. He unsnapped his victim's holster and withdrew the sidearm the man had been going for mere moments ago. He checked the weapon, ensuring a round was in the chamber, and stood up.

"Pathetic creatures." The kid's words dripped with disdain as he sneered down at the body at his feet.

"What are you?" Zheng whispered, every millimeter of his skin crawling at the *thing* standing before him. He didn't know how, but while the body looked like the kid he'd met in the park, Zheng was positive it *wasn't* him.

The kid looked up, and as those cold, soulless eyes met his gaze, the CID agent knew he was about to die.

"I am merely an agent of my Master," the kid said flatly. "Just as you are, Agent Zheng." The warmth that had colored the young man's words when they'd spoken in the park was gone. All that was left in its place was a cold, flat, emotionless voice. It made Zheng think of a machine.

Shouting rang out from down the hall, but the kid didn't shift his gaze. His eyes continued boring right into Zheng's soul.

The gun came up, and the barest hint of a smile flickered briefly on the thing's lips. "Thank you for your service."

Zheng heard a thunderous boom and felt his head jerk backward. Then the world around him went suddenly—and eternally—black.

20

RAMPAGE

FENG WALKED QUICKLY DOWN THE HALL TO THE OFFICE HE'D SET UP as his team's planetside command center. The news that Quon and his team had located the SEARs' shuttle was excellent. Feng feared the Confed navy's favored children hadn't kept their transport dirtside and had instead sent their shuttle back up to whatever ship was supporting them. If that was the case, then setting a trap to nail them as they tried to get off the planet would have been difficult, at best, as a dropship could de-orbit and meet them nearly anywhere. If they had a shuttle parked at the Liberty, however, then Feng didn't need to have his men out searching for Volkov and the SEARs; he could simply wait for them to return to their ship and ambush them there.

Opening the door to the command center, Feng saw Li and Chen huddled around the array of displays the ISB team used to monitor the various information channels they had open at any given point in time. They'd also tapped into Landing's local utility datanet and now had access to all the civilian monitoring sensors like traffic cams, civilian air and space flight plans, and even immigration data. That Li's search algorithm hadn't flagged the SEARs themselves when they landed wasn't much of a surprise—they were probably using forged credentials, if they'd even bothered to go through customs at all—but it almost certainly helped Quon locate the ship they'd arrived on.

"How long before they move?" Feng said without preamble.

"Quon signaled they'll be ready to move on the target in thirty minutes. He doesn't believe taking the ship will be a difficult task. The flight crew are evidently more concerned with performing maintenance and trying to blend into the civilian traffic around them than they are with maintaining tight security."

Li leaned back in his chair and stretched his arms, yawning as he did so. Feng checked the time, realizing his tech specialist hadn't had a break in over twelve hours. "Take a break, Li," he said. "Go take a piss and grab some food. I'll keep an eye on things and call you back when Quon and his team are ready to move in."

Li nodded gratefully and stood, then checked to make sure his sidearm was still secured in the holster. He turned and headed for the door, rolling out his neck as he went. "I'll be back in ten," he said over his shoulder.

"Do you want me to give him something to help him stay alert?" Chen asked after the door closed and he and Feng were alone. "Li's been awake for nearly thirty hours without rest at this point."

Feng thought about it. The rest of the team had rotated sleeping shifts after they'd secured the compound, but Li had worked tirelessly to get them patched into the planetary datanet and make sure their command center systems were running smoothly long after their hideout had been physically secured. Next to Feng, Li had had the least amount of sleep of anyone on the team since they'd landed and began scouring the planet for Zheng and Volkov.

"Not yet," Feng said thoughtfully. "I don't like how jittery he gets when he's on stims. But keep an eye on him, and if he asks for something, go ahead and issue him whatever he needs. Li isn't prone to taking pills when he doesn't absolutely need them to do his job."

Feng slid into Li's chair and scanned the displays, paying extra attention to the one that had a split-screen array of all the surveillance cameras monitoring the immediate area surrounding the building they'd commandeered for their ground operations. Everything was nice and quiet, just the way Feng liked it.

A faint thump filtered in through the door, and the floor under his feet trembled almost imperceptibly.

"Sounds like our mystery guest is giving Kong more of a challenge than he anticipated," Chen said with a wry chuckle. "He usually doesn't start with the hard stuff until much later, unless his subject is pissing him off something fierce."

Feng scowled. He was well aware of Kong's proclivities, but that was a particularly noticeable thump, especially when he considered the extra work they'd put into the interrogation cells to mute the noise. When another, more pronounced crash reached his ears, Feng went on high alert. He swiped a hand across one of the displays to bring up the feed from Kong's room, and his eyes flew wide. Kong was in a bloody, crumpled heap against one wall, and Li was sprawled out by the door, head twisted at an impossible angle. The kid was bent over the tech specialist, in the process of pulling Li's sidearm from its holster.

Chen had seen the bodies, too, and he was already halfway to the door by the time Feng was on his feet. Feng winced and reflexively held a hand to his battered ribs as he twisted and bolted for the door. A gunshot rang out, and his hand went to the pistol on his hip. Another shot boomed down the hallway a split second later, and blood misted through the air. Chen's body flopped onto the worn floor, his head just peeking past the open doorway. The bloody hole between his eyes told Feng all he needed to know about what waited for him in the hall, and he changed course, pressing himself up against the wall adjacent to the door.

His heart hammered in his chest as he strained his ears, listening for anything that would give him a better idea as to the kid's location. Feng cradled his pistol to his chest, muzzle aimed at the door. His ears picked up a faint whisper from around the corner—stealthy footsteps, maybe? He strained his senses, trying to pick up some hint of a shadow approaching or the sound of the kid's breathing. That soft whisper tickled his ears again, closer this time, but it abruptly cut off. Feng tensed up, his decade-plus of combat experience screaming at him that a fight was imminent.

And he was right.

A foot exploded through the flimsy wallboard behind him and slammed into the small of his back. Feng cried out in surprise as the unexpected blow sent waves of searing pain lancing out from his broken ribs. The kick landed with such force that he was thrown away from the wall. Feng crashed to the floor, dazed by the unexpected assault. He struggled to roll onto his side, but his movements were hindered by the pain and a sudden ringing in his ears.

What seemed like an eternity later, his limbs came fully back under his control, and he managed to push himself onto his left side. By some small miracle, he'd managed to hold on to his gun, and he brought the muzzle to bear on the doorway just as the kid rounded the corner. Time seemed to slow down as the first waves of an adrenaline rush hit him. Feng squeezed the trigger as his front sight settled on the kid's chest, but even as the trigger broke under the pressure from his finger, he knew he hadn't been quick enough.

The kid moved unnaturally fast, altering his motion so that he simply spun past the open doorway instead of charging into the room. Feng's pistol barked, but the round passed harmlessly into the wall on the opposite side of the hall. Then the kid was gone, out of Feng's line of sight.

Feng sprang to his feet, keeping his muzzle trained down the hallway as he sliced the pie, strafing to his left to open up an ever-widening field of view down the hall. But the kid didn't reappear.

Shouting erupted from the direction the kid had come from, followed by a quick barrage of gunfire. Feng flinched back as balls of flame from the kid's stolen pistol strobed outside the door, just a few paces away. The shots were followed immediately by screaming and the thump of a body crashing to the ground. A quick follow-up shot from the kid and the scream cut off.

Feng ground his teeth in rage at the death the kid was dealing out to his team, but whichever of his men had just died at least helped Feng get a bead on the kid's location. He aimed at the wall to the right of the door, about where he thought the kid must be, based on the muzzle flashes. Feng fanned the trigger, sending a half dozen rounds tearing through the thin office walls and out into the hallway beyond.

His fire was immediately returned, and he had to dive to the side to avoid the hail of bullets and fibrous wallboard splinters that came with them. He rolled up into a crouch in the corner of the room and ejected the spent magazine from his pistol, quickly slamming home a new one from the mag pouch on his belt and sending a new round into battery.

Feng's heart hammered at his rib cage, and he strained his ears in an effort to pick up some indication as to where his enemy was and what he was doing, but all he heard was a high-pitched ringing that modulated in time with the thump of his heartbeat. Slowly, the ringing faded and Feng was able to make out the faint echoes of gunfire from the direction of the building's entrance.

Feng paused. The kid couldn't have made it that far so quickly, could he? The absence of screaming agony or the sound of a body hitting the floor out in the hallway would seem to indicate Feng had missed his mark, but it had only been a few seconds. There was no way the kid could have run down the hallway, down two flights of stairs, and then out the front of the building in that time.

Feng cautiously approached the doorway, slicing the pie as he moved and expecting his foe to make his move at any moment, but his movements revealed only empty hallway outside the door. Then, just as he was almost out of room to maneuver without exposing himself, he saw the blood spatter on the opposite wall, roughly in line with where Feng thought the kid had been when he'd opened fire.

So I did hit him, after all.

Feng froze, pressing his face up against the wall in an attempt to get a few more degrees of visibility; he still couldn't see enough of the space along the near wall. There wasn't any sign of a body on the floor, so it was still possible his quarry was waiting in ambush, hugging the wall and just out of sight. A fresh round of gunfire from the lower level helped make up Feng's mind on where the kid had disappeared to, and he made his move.

Feng repositioned himself to open up some room to maneuver, then exploded out into the hallway. Stepping over Chen's body, he quickly swept his muzzle around the corner, still expecting the kid to be just out of sight and waiting to strike.

It was clear. The kid really had fled.

Feng ran down the hall toward the stairs at the south end, but a warning scratched at the back of his consciousness, insisting something wasn't right. There were three more offices between the ISB's command center and the entrance to the stairwell that would take him down to ground level. All the doors were closed—a small measure Feng and his team had taken to minimize the risk of an errant scream reaching the industrial area around them via the thin exterior walls and windows, as well as to prevent any light from their operation from being seen at night. But it wasn't the closed office doors that had the alarm bells sounding in his head.

There's no blood trail.

Feng realized the problem too late, and the door to the office nearest to the command center flew open just as the ISB team leader stepped in front of it.

A hand shot out from his blind spot like lightning. Feng cried out in pain as a crushing force was applied to his dominant hand, and his index finger, poised over the trigger guard and ready for action, snapped with a sharp crack. The senior agent tried to shift the gun over to his off hand, but the kid's strength was otherworldly. Feng's arms were yanked upward as the gun was wrenched from his hands like he was a toddler whose parents had caught him with something he wasn't supposed to be playing with.

He turned into his attacker and lashed out with a knee, but the kid took the blow without flinching. Then Feng felt as though he were on skates as he was driven across the hallway. The kid clamped onto Feng's throat with his right hand and effortlessly lifted him off the ground as his other finally tore the gun free and tossed it away.

Feng clawed at the hand constricting his windpipe as he was slammed into the wall and something hard drove into his back, followed by the sound of breaking glass. He felt his grip weaken as his arms suddenly seemed to weigh fifty kilos each. Stars erupted in his vision as the back of his skull collided with the sheetrock and, unfortunately, what felt like a structural stud right behind it.

When his vision cleared a moment later, Feng found himself staring into a pair of cold, emotionless eyes, and his skin crawled as the kid's gaze bore into his soul and laid bare all his innermost secrets. His attacker cocked his head slightly, as if accessing a long-dormant memory. Then he spoke.

"You," he said. The kid's voice was nothing like Feng remembered—lower in pitch with a growling quality that made him seem borderline feral. But there was also an unyielding quality to it, as if every word spoken were an absolute truth in and of itself. "You're the pathetic meat puppet that couldn't execute a few simple orders the last time you were here. Do you have any idea how much your failure has inconvenienced me over the last six years? Decades of planning, all for naught because you couldn't hold this unprotected rock from a few SEARs?" The kid snorted derisively. "Useless."

Darkness crowded Feng's vision as the pressure the kid was exerting on his airway continued to build, and he struggled to pry just one or two fingers away from his throat. His lungs began to burn from the CO_2 buildup, and his diaphragm spasmed. Rational thought began slipping away, and Feng's hands fell to his sides; he no longer had the strength to continue fighting the freak of nature opposing him. His right hand smacked hard against cool metal and broken glass, and his oxygen-deprived brain helpfully informed him he'd been smashed against an inset fire extinguisher cabinet.

"Ben!"

The shout came from the direction of the south stairwell, and the kid's head snapped toward the approaching voice.

"Ben!" someone shouted again, more urgent this time, and the stairwell door burst open. The crushing force on Feng's throat slackened as his attacker's concentration was broken, and his chest heaved, sucking in a ragged breath of life-giving air. His vision cleared and the strength returned to his hands almost instantly. His left hand darted down to the small knife he kept concealed inside his waistband while the right fumbled around for the fire extinguisher behind him.

The tiny knife slipped free of its Kydex sheath and flashed upward. Feng buried the two-and-a-half-inch utility blade up to the handle in the kid's forearm. He didn't gasp or cry out, but in an instant, all pressure from the kid's hand ceased, and he reeled back a step in surprise, twisting away from the unexpected attack.

Feng capitalized on his sudden freedom and the kid's brief disorientation. The fire extinguisher came free of its mount, and Feng swung for the fences, putting every ounce of strength he still had into a vicious blow. The ten-kilo cylinder whistled through the air and smashed into the back of the kid's head. He folded like wet cardboard without so much as a grunt.

Feng rushed across the hall, into the open office the kid had just attacked him from, and hurled the fire extinguisher at the dirty window that looked out over the building's back parking lot. The window shattered in an explosion of tempered glass fragments, and Feng dove for the opening, catching the windowsill and using it to arrest his momentum and spin himself around as his body arced through the air outside.

Air exploded out of his lungs as he smashed face-first into the side of the building, and he nearly lost his hold on the sill. The massive adrenaline dump he was riding helped him ignore the agony and gave him near-superhuman strength as his fight-or-flight response pegged hard over to flight. Feng glanced down, seeing another window just a meter below his dangling feet.

Most of the second-story windows in the abandoned building were broken from years of teenagers throwing rocks at them, and this one was no exception; it was actually the reason Feng and his team had set up on the third floor. It seemed the limit of the local youth's arm strength was just below the level of the third-floor windows, and all but one were intact.

"Feng!" a voice boomed into the office.

With a sneer of impotent rage, Feng released his hold on the windowsill and dropped away from his nemesis. This wasn't over, not by a long shot.

21

RESCUE OP

"Mabel's got him, boss! Let's roll!" Kravczyk shouted to a fully armored Valdez, who was standing next to a nondescript delivery truck they'd "borrowed" from a commercial uniform supplier's parking lot a short while ago.

Things had moved fast after Ben and Zheng were abducted, but not fast enough for Kravczyk's liking. Dimitriy had turned out to be the real reason they were here—or at least the data he'd smuggled out of Federation space, which was now safely stashed aboard the team's cargo shuttle—but they couldn't exactly pack up and leave without rescuing Ben first. Fortunately, Dimitriy traveled light and didn't need to return to the CID safe house he and Zheng had been camping out at, so Kravczyk, Tess, and the GIM agent had simply met Valdez back at the spaceport to figure out their next move.

Mabel had been monitoring the situation from her specialized docking station that was rigged up aboard the shuttle, and she'd immediately gotten to work tracking down where that murderous fuck Feng and his team had taken Ben and the CID guy. Unfortunately, it turned out that the ISB was actually competent and had covered their tracks pretty well, especially when it came to Landing's public utility datanet, which hosted all the traffic and public security surveillance cameras. But the tenacious AI had been steadily working her way ever closer to Ben's location, and she'd finally struck paydirt.

Valdez turned and called out into the truck, "We're rolling!"

Kravczyk ran down the cargo ramp of their shuttle and hoofed it over to the waiting truck. Valdez was already in the back with Tess, and Kravczyk lightly hopped inside and swung the double doors closed as their new best friend, Dimitriy, hit the accelerator. The truck was already loaded with all their gear, and the SEARs were armored up in their APEXs and itching for a fight. Ben had only been nabbed a few hours ago, but that could already be too long, depending on what the ISB wanted from him.

Kravczyk didn't want to think about the darker possibilities that waited for them, so he instead focused his mental energy toward their new target.

"It's an abandoned commercial building in the industrial district, Volkov. Mabel will send you the directions," he said, reaching up to grab one of the built-in metal shelves in the back of the truck to steady himself as the wiry little Russian agent flogged the old delivery truck for all it was worth.

"She already did," Dimitriy said, pointing to the center display in the dash, showing their route overlaid on a map of the city. "I must say, you SEARs have all the best tools."

"Oooh," Tess said in warning, "I wouldn't ever let her hear you refer to her as a tool. Mabel has a nasty streak when it comes to us squishy humans not giving her the respect she deserves. And she's already all kinds of pissed off right now, so you'll probably want to get started on the apology right away."

Dimitriy wasn't fazed by the warning, clearly not understanding the level of excruciating pain Mabel was capable of inflicting upon an unsuspecting victim. "Yeah, well, if she's right and we're able to save Zheng and your teammate, I'll make sure I get her a nice thank-you card and some flowers."

"You'll do more than that, Agent Volkov," Mabel's voice cut in over their team channel. "*When* we return safely to the shuttle with my Benjamin and your missing CID friend, I expect a full-matrix massage to go along with your card and three dozen red roses. And don't skimp, either. I can tell the difference between proper florist roses and that trash you can pick up at any super-market. Then and only then will I consider not walking up there and slapping you into next week with the ridiculous meat hooks Chief Kravczyk calls hands."

Kravczyk couldn't help the grin that spread across his face. He could see the sudden lack of color in Volkov's wide-eyed face in his reflection off the rearview mirror. Why a delivery truck with no back windows had a rearview mirror, he didn't know, but it sure as hell made for a good source of amusement right about now.

But then he really thought back on what Mabel had said. Quickly toggling over to a private, onboard channel, Kravczyk whispered, "You can't really take control of my suit, can you?"

The pause before Mabel replied was just a little bit too long for his liking. "Not as far as you know," she said sweetly.

Mabel was riding shotgun in Kravczyk's suit, much like she had during their escape from the data processing facility on Hai'alla while Ben was busy playing patty-cake with the agent's Reaper combat drone. She'd insisted on being present with the team when they moved on the ISB, making a compelling argu-ment about the possibility that the team would need her to crack any number of unknown secure systems to facilitate their rescue of Ben. Kravczyk suspected they wouldn't come across anything their standard, onboard intrusion programs couldn't deal with and that Mabel's real reason for wanting to be with them was the same as everyone else's: she was worried about Ben and couldn't stand sitting on the sidelines while others did the work. And he couldn't blame her for that.

Valdez approached the pass-through to the cab and leaned his head in, addressing Agent Volkov. "How about you just worry about getting us to the location Mabel provided and leave the smart-assed commentary for later, Agent Volkov. Deal?"

The GIM agent nodded. "Got it."

Damn, Kravczyk thought, *the bossman is some serious kind of pissed.*

It was true; Valdez had taken Ben and Agent Zheng's abduction especially hard. Whether it was because he was still feeling the sting from the shitshow that the operation to capture the agent's slipspace transceiver complex on Elizabeth had turned out to be or because he cared about Ben a whole lot more than he let on, Kravczyk wasn't sure. Probably a combination of both. Either way, though, Valdez had changed in recent months. He'd always been a—mostly—straight-laced, by-the-book kind of officer when it came to operational details, but he'd never been quite so... bitchy.

It was just one more reminder of how much strain they were all under. Finding out the Imperium was not only a thing but hell-bent on humanity's destruction had been a shock to the system, especially in the wake of the Alarian War and all that entailed. But to then get hit with back-to-back-to-back nut punches with the nuke on Elizabeth, losing Ben, and then all the political bullshit going on with the Confed, it was just too much. They desperately needed something to go right, for a change, and thus far, that wasn't happening. If they somehow managed to lose Ben a second time, Kravczyk wasn't so sure it would even be worth trying to keep on fighting. Not that he would ever admit that to anyone.

"Commander," Mabel said, all business now, "I'm working on getting us eyes and ears on the location, but it looks like the

ISB has already taken steps to limit the ability of an outside entity to gain control of the local network at the facility. I'm afraid the best I can do for the time being is play around with the various public feeds they're tapping into for their own intelligence and try to keep them unaware of our approach."

"Do you have any idea how many bad guys we're dealing with, Mabel?" Kravczyk said.

"Not with any certainty," she replied. "But based on what information Agent Volkov gave me, as well as the data I received from Captain Collins before we deployed, I would guess we're dealing with a full ISB tactical team—probably around a dozen agents, plus a technical specialist, a team medic, and the team leader."

"What about orbital support?" Valdez queried. "I can't imagine they flew all the way out here on a shuttle like ours. They must have a ship in orbit somewhere."

"Unknown, but the *Wraith* didn't flag any known Federation military or intelligence vessels when we entered the system, and we haven't received any new threat bulletins from them," she said. "If I had to guess, I'd say they probably staged from one of the tramp freighters that frequent the planet. It would provide a sufficiently large vessel to operate from without raising suspicion. Any one of the medium-sized cargo vessels in the traffic pattern around the planet could be easily fitted with a specialized modular cargo container or two that would provide ample space to conceal the necessary manpower and materiel for a mission like this."

"Well, that's just great," Valdez groaned. "Make a note that we need to warn the *Wraith* as soon as we can, without jeopardizing our position, that there may be a damn Federation Q-ship somewhere up there."

"I can, um, *borrow* some broadcast bandwidth from one of the spaceport's tight-beam comms systems, if you'd like, Commander. The *Wraith* will be entering a comms window inside of an hour, and I'm fairly confident I can get a message off to them without anyone realizing it," Mabel said.

Valdez paused for a moment before replying, cocking his head slightly as he always did whenever he was considering a decision with potentially weighty consequences. "Cue it up, but don't transmit unless I authorize it. I want to try and get a better idea of what, exactly, we're dealing with before committing."

"As you wish."

"Sir," Tess chimed in. "If Mabel can send me all the orbital traffic data, I might be able to narrow down the list of suspects. I was born and raised on merchant ships—my family operated a quarter-million-ton long-hauler before I joined the navy. I know what the normal rhythm of freighter operations are, and I'll bet you that whatever ship the ISB has up there will stick out like a sore thumb to someone who knows what to look for."

"Mabel?" Valdez said.

"Forwarding the data now, Commander."

"Alright, McCollum, you've got thirty mikes to find me that ship. After that, we've got some doors to go knock on."

———

"Time's up. We're hot in three minutes," the boss said to Tess.

With the exception of a muttered, "Hey, Uncle Mike's here," a few minutes ago, she'd been completely silent for the entire ride around the city to the industrial district. Kravczyk had raised an eyebrow in her direction at the comment, but she'd been completely engrossed in her work and hadn't offered any further clarification.

"I think I've almost got it, sir," she protested. "I've narrowed the list of suspects to eight ships. Just give me—"

"No, Petty Officer. Shut it down. You can take another look on our return trip."

"Yes, sir."

Their trip had been uneventful. Kravczyk had checked and rechecked his kit during the ride—something that was very much out of character for him. Normally, he checked his gear before boarding the transport, then did his best to relax while inbound to the target, sure in the knowledge that he'd already done all he could to ensure he was ready for a fight. But this time was different. Kravczyk wasn't sure if it was because Ben's life was on the line or because he was going up against Feng again— and all the old baggage that dredged up—but either way, he just couldn't settle down.

And he wasn't the only one, either. While Mabel couldn't link with him like she could with Ben, Kravczyk could have sworn that he was picking up a nervous vibe from her, which seemed crazy, considering she hadn't spoken more than two sentences since they'd hit the freeway that ringed the city. On some level, though, he thought, maybe it wasn't entirely crazy. At the moment, she was still on board the armor his implant was synced up with, so who was to say it wasn't possible for there to be some kind of, like, bleed-through or whatever? Then again, while Mabel seemed especially lifelike, she was just an advanced AI, after all. Did she actually have real feelings? And why the hell was this a line of thought he was going down right now when there were going to be bad guys to kill in a couple of minutes?

"Chief?"

Kravczyk picked his gaze up off the floor of the truck, where he'd been intently studying the worn diamond plate while his brain ran around in circles. "Yeah, boss?"

"You okay?" Valdez asked. "I've never seen you this on edge before an op."

Kravczyk nodded. "I'm good. Just feels a little different this time, is all."

"I hear you," Valdez agreed. "Let's just go get our guy back."

"Fuckin' A," Kravczyk said, offering Valdez his fist. The boss bumped it with authority, and as if that were her cue, Mabel checked in with their final enemy disposition report.

"No change in detected enemy positions," she said over the team channel. "I've got access to all public and private surveillance devices that are connected to the datanet, and I'm covering our approach. I can't guarantee the ISB didn't set up their own detection grid, however."

"Do you still believe our best shot will be a direct smash-and-grab?" Valdez said.

"I do," Mabel said firmly. "I was able to track four ISB agents leaving the complex over an hour ago, and they have yet to return. If Ben and Agent Zheng are being actively interrogated, which I feel is a safe assumption, that only leaves a handful of tac team members that could be on guard at any given point in time. We know Ben killed one of them and wounded two others during his abduction, so I think it's likely you may only face armed resistance from five or six operatives at most."

"I agree," Dimitriy said over his shoulder. "The ISB is cautious, but their tac teams work alone and generally try to keep a low profile—something that will be even more important for them here on Newman's Rock, given the incident six years ago. At worst, you'll be facing a half dozen or so agents armed with sidearms and maybe submachine guns. They'll all be inside the building, in an effort to avoid the local traffic from noticing their presence. Hit them hard and fast, and they won't be able to organize a coherent defense until it's too late."

"Do you still think the third floor is the most likely place we'll find Ben, Agent Volkov?" Kravczyk asked.

"The building only has three floors and no basement levels,

so yes. They'll keep their interrogation rooms as far away from street level as possible so as to minimize the chance of noise reaching the wrong ears."

"Meaning torture," Kravczyk growled.

The GIM agent shifted uncomfortably in his seat. "Torture, yes," he confirmed. "The ISB tac teams usually have one or two agents who specialize in intelligence extraction. Their methods are usually... quite brutal. Please understand," he said quickly, "I'm not trying to anger you. I merely want you prepared for what you might find."

Their ride turned a corner and accelerated gently down a mostly deserted road. It was late evening in Landing, and the only traffic still out and about in the industrial district were the few people who'd put in a couple extra hours or were just leaving the couple of local bars that catered specifically to blue-collar workers after they got off their shifts. Their target appeared through the windshield, and like someone had thrown a switch, the worry and tension they'd all been feeling evaporated, leaving nothing but hardened professionals behind. They were on the job now.

"Showtime," Dimitriy said.

22

SHOCK AND AWE

THE BUILDING THEY WANTED WAS AN ABANDONED TEXTILE FACTORY. The corporate offices—where they suspected Ben and Zheng were being held—were in the three-story building on the north side of the complex. Two large warehouses sat a hundred meters to the south, with the main production facility that fed them directly to their east. Both the warehouses and the production facility were single-story, open-floor-plan buildings that, while massive, didn't really have any convenient places to stash prisoners or set up a base of operations.

The office building was a different story. Three floors of offices and conference rooms of assorted sizes, and only a few entrances. It was easier to secure, better equipped to set up a base of operations, and unfortunately easier to slap together makeshift interrogation cells, should the need arise. It was constructed of preformed aircrete slabs, with the outer rooms having windows.

Aircrete was a lightweight material that weighed one-third as much as concrete but had the same effective compression strength. It wouldn't stand up to the same level of abuse, but it was practically a miracle material when it came to quickly and cheaply constructing industrial buildings. It was also really good at blocking screams and the cracking of bones from being heard on the other side of it.

While their target complex was abandoned, the commercial park it was located in was not. So a laundry service delivery van driving by wasn't exactly the kind of thing that would immediately raise the alarm. Dimitriy casually drove by the complex's southern entrance, and Valdez signaled Kravczyk to stand by. Kravczyk posted up just inside the truck's rear doors, waiting for the right moment to throw them open and hit the ground running.

Dimitriy didn't have armor, so he was going to do a drive-by, and the SEARs were going to pile out the back and sprint the short distance to the office building. Their armor should be able to cope with any small arms the ISB had waiting for them, but Kravczyk just hoped the tac team hadn't anticipated the need to pack anything heavier. While the SEARs cleared the building and worked to extract Ben and Zheng, Dimitriy was going to stage the van a short distance away and await their call for exfil. He'd repeat the drive-by, and the SEARs, using the awesome speed afforded by their armor, would pile back in on the move, and they'd be off. Their shuttle was warmed up and ready for them whenever they got back to the spaceport, and they didn't intend to stick around any longer than they had to.

"Now!"

At the shouted command from the wiry little GIM agent, Kravczyk threw open the back doors and exploded out of the van. He was still moving nearly thirty kilometers per hour when his feet hit the ground, but his APEX stabilized his balance and allowed him to almost seamlessly transition to a sprint. He heard Tess and the boss hit the ground moments later, and the three of them tore across the parking lot toward the office building's main entrance.

"Threats identified," Mabel called out, and a series of target markers appeared floating in Kravczyk's vision. Even with his armor's systems augmenting his sight, he wouldn't have been able to spot the two ISB thugs sitting behind the receptionist's desk until he was much closer. But with Mabel working overtime to monitor and analyze everything his suit's sensors picked up, she'd spotted them almost immediately.

The ISB agents were just beginning to react to the three armored SEARs running hell for leather in their direction when Kravczyk's Mk. 27 snapped up to his shoulder and opened fire. The guy on the left was stitched from belly button to forehead by the first burst. Kravczyk immediately shifted his fire to the second, but the son of a bitch was damn fast. The second tac team guy threw himself behind cover, and the rounds tore harmlessly into the wall behind the reception desk.

Tess had always been the fastest member of the team when in armor, even after Ben really dialed in his freaky-ass, souped-up nervous system, and she put that speed on full display, leaving her two teammates in the dust. Kravczyk's fire had done a number on the laminated glass panes of the entrance's double doors, and Tess simply lowered a shoulder and charged through the one on the right. The second ISB agent popped up over the desk, sub gun at the ready, only to find the seriously pissed-off girlfriend of one of his captives less than a meter away.

Kravczyk winced as Tess went airborne, slamming into the poor bastard with her hundred and fifty armored kilos at damn near forty kilometers per hour. The results were... messy.

Valdez and Kravczyk charged through the front doors a moment later, wordlessly splitting up in their preplanned maneuver to cover more ground. Valdez headed for the north side of the lobby—and the stairwell on that side of the building —and Kravczyk took the south. Tess quickly extricated herself from the remains of the second tac team operative and joined

Valdez. The north side of the building had more rooms to cover, which left Kravczyk all by himself on the south. It was a risky gamble, but now that the ISB knew the SEARs were here, they didn't have time to stick together and methodically work their way through the building. Kravczyk was counting on his APEX to make up for the lack of a battle buddy, and Mabel would keep an eye on his blind spots for him.

The big SEAR quickly swept the handful of small offices between the lobby and the south stairwell. As he ducked into the last one before the stairs, shouting and gunfire rang out from behind him, but the synchronized barks from his teammates' PDWs quickly ended the threat. He finished his sweep of the room—nothing but a dusty desk and a few cardboard boxes of the usual office junk—and headed toward the stairwell.

"Chief," Mabel cut in suddenly, "I just detected what sounded like multiple pistol shots from upstairs."

Kravczyk threw open the metal fire door that led out into the stairwell. "Do you know which floor?"

"Based on the sound attenuation, I'm going to guess third."

Kravczyk vaulted up all eight of the steps in a single leap, pausing just long enough on the landing to reverse course and leap up the next set of steps. A quick glance out into the hallway of the second floor revealed no immediate threats, so he ducked his head back into the stairwell and jumped up to the next landing.

The staccato of rapid pistol fire, followed almost immediately by a second shooter opening up, reached his ears just as his feet hit the landing midway between the second and third floors.

"Ben!" Kravczyk shouted, then jumped the last half flight of stairs and tore the door open. "Ben!"

He exploded out into the hallway, catching sight of two men struggling about twenty meters down the hallway. It took him a moment to realize the brute that had one of the ISB thugs pinned to the wall by his throat was actually Ben, then another moment to see that Feng was the purple-faced rag doll Ben was in the process of strangling to death with one hand.

Ben's head snapped in Kravczyk's direction, and the chief froze. There was something in the kid's dead eyes that seemed to pierce straight into his soul, and he hesitated for just a split second. A chill flashed up Kravczyk's spine, and for a moment, he suddenly wasn't sure the man he was looking at was actually Ben.

Then Feng's hand flashed up, a silver blade glinting in the dim light of the hallway. The ISB agent buried the knife up to the handle in Ben's forearm, and the kid immediately lost control of his hand. Kravczyk brought his gun up, but Feng and Ben were too close, and he couldn't risk the shot. He started forward, watching helplessly as Ben staggered back while Feng yanked a fire extinguisher from a storage cabinet inset in the wall behind him.

The sharp crack as steel met skull filled the hallway. Ben's eyes rolled back in his head, and he folded up into a heap. Feng dove into the open office across from him, and Kravczyk poured on the speed, covering the short distance in seconds. He turned the corner into the office, catching sight of Feng's hands gripping the windowsill from outside the building.

"Feng!" he roared, lunging for the window.

Feng's fingers slipped away, and by the time Kravczyk reached the window and looked outside, the slippery ISB agent was gone.

"Goddammit!" Kravczyk raged, spinning on his heels and rushing back to where Ben lay crumpled on the hallway floor. Blood pooled beneath him, streaming out from the knife still buried in his right forearm, as well as from the back of his head, but at least he was still breathing. His face was battered and bruised, and his hands were covered with blood. A few fingers on his left hand were swollen and not lined up exactly right. He'd clearly been worked over pretty good, and it spoke to his skill and determination that he'd been able to not only get loose but hand Feng his ass. Well, at least until Kravczyk had burst onto the scene and distracted him.

"Hang in there, kid," he said softly. "Your girlfriend's gonna kick my ass something fierce if I let you die again."

"Chief," Valdez said over the team channel, "we're approaching the third floor now. What's your status?"

"I've got Ben, sir," Kravczyk replied, raising his Mk. 27 and taking a defensive posture over his wounded teammate. "I haven't cleared the floor, but we're in the middle of the street-side hallway and nobody's shooting at us right now. There are at least two bodies up here."

"Copy," Valdez said, and Kravczyk heard the north stairwell door creak open. "We're coming to you. Stay there."

Less than a minute later, the floor was cleared and Tess was kneeling next to Kravczyk and worrying over Ben's unconscious form while Valdez poked around in the office next to the one Ben was in front of. The boss stepped out into the hallway and signaled for Kravczyk to join him. Kravczyk jogged over and gave his team lead a questioning look.

Valdez opened a private channel. "Take a look in the room down the hall on the right. The one with the door ripped halfway off its hinges. Ask Mabel for her read on what you find in there."

"Boss?" Kravczyk said. His team leader was shaken up by whatever he'd seen in that room. Tess hadn't said anything about it, but now that he thought about it, Kravczyk remembered she'd cleared the office across from it and Valdez had declared it clear before she could enter.

"Just do it, Chief."

Kravczyk trotted down the hall and poked his head into the

small room. The body of one of the tac team was just inside the door, his head twisted almost 180 degrees from where it should have been. Zheng's body was secured to a chair with flex cuffs. The man had taken a serious beating—face beat up, fingernails removed—but it was the single bullet hole between his eyes that told the chief what had killed him. The powder burns on the man's face indicated that the gun had been mere inches away when it'd been fired.

Then he saw the empty chair on the other side of the room and the body against the wall. Kravczyk stepped over and examined the chair, finding no fewer than six pairs of heavy-duty flex cuffs that had been snapped. There were some minor blood spatters on the chair, but nothing really of note. He moved to the body and took a knee next to it, finding another of the tac team operatives that had died horribly. The blood and brain matter that seeped from his destroyed eye sockets spoke to a seriously brutal fight. It was a terrible way to die...

Kravczyk looked back at the body on the floor by the door. Most people didn't realize just how much force it took to break a human's neck, especially if the guy in question was a trained operative and actively fighting back. The same went for how much force it took to punch through the back of the orbital sockets and get to the squishy bits behind them. Ben was in great shape, thanks to his shiny new and improved body, but Kravczyk was having a hard time reconciling the feats of strength he was looking at with the fact that the kid had been knocked unconscious and dragged here by the ISB.

He looked at the broken flex cuffs and shook his head. He knew how hard those were to break; it could be done if you knew how to take advantage of biomechanics and the proper application of force, but to do so with six sets of cuffs fast enough that the people keeping an eye on you wouldn't be able to react before you got all the way loose?

"Mabel, what's your read on this?" he said to his unusually silent passenger. "Because I'm having a hard time figuring out just how Ben managed to break all those cuffs, then kill both of these guys with his bare hands. Not to mention that it looks like he did it all *after* having been worked over at least once during questioning."

"I can't explain it, Chief," she replied. "The amount of force required to break those cuffs should have been far in excess of what Ben is capable of. Even you, with your immense strength, likely would not have been able to break free. And even if you did have the strength for it, the amount of pain you would need to endure from the cuffs cutting into your wrists and ankles would be a strong deterrent."

Kravczyk was silent for a long moment. His mind flashed back to when Ben had looked at him after he'd exited the stairway, and he remembered how his skin had crawled at the expression on the kid's face—or lack thereof, to be more specific. He didn't know what these ISB assholes had done to Ben, but he was sure he didn't know whose eyes had been staring at him then.

Kravczyk let out an explosive sigh. They needed to get off this godforsaken shithole and back to the *Wraith*. This planet had a bad habit of changing people for the worse, in his experience, and based on what he'd seen back in the hallway, it looked like Ben might be its latest victim.

Kravczyk stood and headed for the door. That Feng had escaped again galled him, but judging by what he'd seen here, that piece of shit might well be the least of their problems. He hoped he was wrong and Ben would be able to recover without any lasting trauma, but the sickening feeling that was building in the pit of his stomach told him there was no way he'd be that lucky.

23

CHANGE OF PLANS

"I'VE NARROWED THE LIST OF SUSPECTS DOWN TO THREE SHIPS, SIR," Tess said. "That's the best I can do."

Kravczyk looked up from his kneeling position on the floor of the truck, next to Ben. He was doing his best to stabilize the kid during their return trip to the spaceport; despite Dimitriy's best efforts to drive smoothly, the old delivery truck's stiff springs were making the journey rougher than any of them would've liked.

"That's still a heck of a lot better than the several dozen possibilities in Mabel's initial list," Valdez replied. "Good work." Turning to face Kravczyk, the boss nodded at Ben. "How's he holding up?"

"Mabel says he's stable, boss, but that's all she knows for sure. Without him in armor, she can only see his vitals over the near-field data connection with his implant. He hasn't even twitched since we loaded him up, though."

"Mabel's already called the situation in to Collins and the *Wraith*," Valdez said. "They're moving into a lower orbit to expedite our exfil. We'll be back to the shuttle in about five minutes, and the flight crew will have the bird ready for dust-off as soon as we're aboard."

Ben was lying on the floor of the truck, a C-collar immobilizing his head and neck. They'd been able to get the bleeding under control, but he'd still lost a lot of blood. Deep lacerations to both wrists and ankles—most likely from the cuffs that'd bound him to the chair—several broken or dislocated fingers on his left hand, burns on his chest from the Taser shot he'd taken during his abduction... But it was the wounds Feng had inflicted that worried Kravczyk the most.

The back of Ben's head was a bloody mess, courtesy of the fire extinguisher. The kid definitely had a concussion—it didn't take a doctor to figure that out—but Kravczyk suspected he probably had a fractured skull to go along with it. Being unable to wake the kid was a bad sign. Plus, Feng's knife was still lodged in Ben's forearm, having been driven through the muscles between the radius and ulna. There were several nerves and arteries buried in there, and no one wanted to risk severing one by withdrawing the knife. So they'd wrapped the wound as best they could, and Kravczyk had been tasked with making sure nothing happened to the arm that would cause more damage than had already been done.

Once he'd had a chance to properly check the kid over, Kravczyk had been absolutely shocked to see all the damage Ben had soaked up. It was a testament to the kid's sheer determination and willpower that he'd not only still been on his feet when the SEARs arrived but was actively stacking bodies during his escape. But then again, Ben had never been short on grit and determination when the situation required it.

There'd been a brief discussion among the SEARs on whether they should just call in the locals to help them secure the complex and get Ben to one of Landing's hospitals with a proper trauma center, but with Feng and at least four of his team still on the loose, they couldn't risk it. As much as it pained them all, they still had a mission to accomplish, and the longer they remained on the surface, the more chances Feng and his thugs had to take out Dimitriy and the data he'd acquired. With Mabel ensuring them that Ben was at least stable for the moment, they'd made the call to load up the kid and Zheng's body and hightail it out of there, leaving the ISB to try and clean up the mess the SEARs and Ben had left for them.

The spaceport finally came into view as the old delivery truck ate up the kilometers of roadway at what felt like a snail's pace, and Kravczyk squinted at a large plume of black smoke that was curling into the sky. The boom of an explosion reached their ears a few seconds later, and the bottom dropped out of Kravczyk's gut as the SEARs exchanged worried looks.

"Mabel, what the hell was that?" Kravczyk said urgently.

"I don't know for sure, but I just lost my datalink with the shuttle."

"Mabel, get me eyes on our shuttle," Valdez commanded. "Dimitriy, don't take the exit. If the ISB just took out our ride, I don't want us anywhere near that spaceport."

The GIM agent nodded curtly, his knuckles going white as he squeezed the steering wheel harder.

"I was using the shuttle as a routing point for my connection to the local datanet," Mabel reported. "Give me a minute to see if I can figure out a way back in. I'm now limited to the onboard processing power of the chief's APEX, and it might not be enough for a high-bandwidth connection."

"We need to assume we just lost our ride," Valdez growled in frustration. "I'm open to suggestions."

Silence lingered for several moments, but then Tess spoke up. "I have an idea—give me a second." Her eyes glazed over as she accessed something via her implant. Finally, her eyes refocused, and she looked at Valdez. "I think I know where we can find another ride off the planet, but we need to hoof it over to the commercial spaceport, where the big cargo-haulers land to load the processed ores."

Valdez exchanged a knowing glance with Kravczyk, then looked back at Tess. "We know the place. What's this idea of yours?"

"Give me a minute to make a quick call, sir," she said. "Mabel, can you look up the comms node address for the bulk freighter ISF *Gambler's Fortune* and connect me, please? Their transatmospheric cargo hauler was parked at the commercial spaceport when I last checked."

"Do it, Mabel," Valdez said.

"Stand by, Tess... Done," Mabel reported.

There was a moment of silence as they waited for the call to be answered, and Valdez and Kravczyk once again looked at each other, neither with any clue as to what McCollum was up to.

Then a gruff voice came over their suit comms. "Yeah? Who the hell is this, and what do you want? I've got another twenty tons of heavy shit to load and secure, and I'm already an hour behind schedule. So make it fuckin' snappy."

"Hey, Uncle Mike," Tess said.

The line went dead silent for almost ten seconds. Then that gruff voice whispered back as if he were talking to a ghost. "Tessie? Is that you?"

"It's good to hear your voice, too, Uncle Mike. I know what you're probably going through right now, and I'm sorry to have to cut to the chase, but I need a favor..."

———

DIMITRIY PULLED their borrowed delivery truck onto the loading pad where the *Fortune*'s transatmospheric cargo mule had just finished loading the last of her cargo aboard. The big truck's brakes squeaked as it rolled to a stop at the base of the mule's massive forward-facing cargo ramp, and Tess threw the back doors open and jumped out. Valdez followed a few steps behind, leaving the chief in the back of the truck to keep an eye on Ben.

A grizzly bear of a man was waiting for them a few meters away, arms crossed with a hard set to his jaw. The guy had to have been in his early sixties, but the fire in his eyes made him seem quite a bit younger. He didn't even flinch as two APEX-armored SEARs strolled up to him, and the Pathfinder tattoo on his right forearm hinted as to why. Tess's uncle Mike looked to have once been a seriously bad hombre, in Kravczyk's experienced opinion.

Tess stopped in front of the man and reached up to remove her helmet. The moment her matted auburn hair was revealed by the powerful lights illuminating the pad, the old guy's stern expression melted. Tears welled in his eyes, and he reached out a shaky hand and lightly cupped her cheek.

"Tessie?" he said, voice cracking. "My god, it's really you, isn't it?"

Tess responded by wrapping the old guy up in a careful bear hug, her helmet clattering to the ground at her feet. Then Kravczyk's eyebrows shot up when Uncle Mike's huge forearms returned the hug and the grizzled freighter captain lifted her armored bulk off the ground without so much as a grunt of effort.

"Goddamn it's good to see you," he boomed, placing her back down on the ground and taking a step back. "When I heard what happened to your family, I just assumed you'd been with them."

Tess's gaze dropped to the ground at the mention of the pirates that'd captured her ship and murdered her entire family before taking the then-teenaged Tess as a sex slave. "I was," she said softly.

The old guy's expression hardened again. "I hope you made the fuckers pay, Tessie," he growled.

She nodded softly. "It was James Tipton and his gang."

Mike leaned back at the statement, and his expression softened. "I heard he was found gutted like a fish in his own bed." He turned and spat on the ground. "Good fucking riddance."

"The chaos that ensued after his death ripped the Tipton gang apart when several of his lieutenants went to war over who was going to take over. They've spent the last five years trying to pick up the pieces... You saved a lot of lives, Tessie—they were so busy killing each other that they couldn't be bothered to raid the major shipping lanes anymore. What's left of them has been relegated to harassing mining outposts and the like in the fringe systems, but last I heard, they weren't having much success."

Tess sniffed and wiped a tear from the corner of one eye. She cleared her throat and picked up her helmet, then gestured at the back of the truck. "This is the rest of my team," she said, changing the subject. "Like I said earlier, I can't give you any details, but we need a ride off this rock ASAP."

"Commander Ramiro Valdez, Captain," Valdez said, extending a hand in greeting.

The freighter captain's meaty paw swallowed Valdez's armored hand and pumped it several times in greeting. "Captain Mike Micholson, Commander."

"Captain, we've got a wounded man and some critical intel we need to get back to Columbia, and there's at least part of an ISB tac team still hunting for us. I hate to put a civilian in danger, but Tess insisted you could help us."

The old freighter captain snorted in disgust. "Get out of here with that 'civilian' bullshit, Commander," he said, waving away Valdez's concern with one hand. "I'd storm the gates of hell with a smile on my face if that's what my Tessie needed. Now, get your people loaded up, and we're out of here. My ship is already maneuvering to a transfer orbit, and we can be clear of the well within a few hours after we're aboard."

Valdez nodded curtly and turned back toward the truck. Kravczyk stepped around toward the front of the truck, and together, he and Valdez carefully picked Ben up on the makeshift stretcher they'd cobbled together by ripping one of the delivery truck's metal shelves out of its mounts. They gingerly carried the unconscious kid out of the truck, and Dimitriy stepped up to stabilize Ben's arm as they moved him. Tess jumped into the truck as Kravczyk and Valdez carried Ben straight up the waiting cargo ramp and into the well-lit cargo bay of the mule. If the old guy was surprised at Tess emerging from the truck with Zheng's bloody corpse over her shoulder, he didn't say anything.

Instead, the former Pathfinder hopped into the truck and drove it a short distance away, clearing the pad for takeoff. A stout middle-aged woman in dirty coveralls met them at the top of the ramp and directed Valdez and Kravczyk toward an airlock along the rear bulkhead. Another crewman in the same uniform waited for them just inside the crew compartment of the mule, and he quickly led them down a short passageway to a pair of bunkrooms.

The heavy-lift cargo mules weren't warp-capable and were primarily used to ferry equipment and cargo to and from the large freighters that remained in orbit, but they were also outfitted for medium-range intra-system work. As such, they were equipped with the barest of necessities for a cargo run that could take a week or two, moving material between a planet and its satellites or hauling raw ore from the larger mining rigs to a processing station.

"You can secure him here," the crewman said, indicating a

single bunk that doubled as a sick bed. "I'm trained as a medic and will get him hooked up to the monitors we have on board and work to keep him stable until we dock with the *Fortune*."

Dimitriy moved aside in the cramped space and the two SEARs set the makeshift stretcher on the bunk. The *Fortune's* medic immediately went to work getting Ben secured to the bunk and immobilizing his head and injured arm. Valdez nodded toward the hatch, and the three men made their way back to the cargo bay, where Captain Mike was headed their way with Tess hot on his heels.

"Follow me," he said, brushing by them without slowing down. "We've already received our clearance for departure, and the engines are warming up. It's time to blow this popsicle stand."

"McCollum?" Valdez said, an unspoken question riding on his tone.

"He's secured against the bulkhead over there, sir." She indicated the starboard side of the cargo bay, behind a stack of huge transit cases that were marked *Freedom Group Mining, Ltd*. "Mike said the cargo bay will remain pressurized, and I thought it was probably best to secure Zheng's body somewhere that would be easy for the crew to clean after we dock."

Valdez nodded. "Understood. Let's go."

The three SEARs hurried after the freighter captain, and Kravczyk could feel the deck plates begin to tremble as the mule's engines began to power up. They had their ride off the planet. Now they just needed to meet up with the *Wraith* and get out of the system before the ISB could swoop in a ruin their day again.

24

AN UNEXPECTED ALLY

GARLAND LOOKED UP FROM THE NO-GOOD, USELESS TURD OF A goddamned lawnmower-shaped heart-attack-inducer he'd been working on when his wife called his name through the house and out into the backyard. She'd used *that* tone and inflection combination on the word "visitor," and the disgraced admiral went straight to DEFCON 1.

"I'm out back, Gale," he bellowed in his best command voice. "Send whoever the hell it is around the side of the house."

He heard something that sounded like an acknowledgment from his wife, then planted one hand on the nonfunctional shitbox before him and used it to help himself stand up. Garland's knees both creaked in protest as they were called back into duty, and he let out an explosive, effort-induced grunt-groan hybrid as he levered himself up to a standing position. Finally back on his feet after his expletive-laden though sadly fruitless attempt to repair the brand-new lawnmower that Gale made him buy once she found out he was going to be home for the foreseeable future, Garland wiped the sweat from his brow with a shirtsleeve. Turning to the strategically placed cooler next to him, he opened the lid and pulled a fresh beer from its icy depths.

The top of the frosty bottle had only just hit the grass at his feet when quite possibly the last person he ever wanted to see again strolled casually around the side of the house and into the backyard.

"You've got some big fucking brass ones, showing up here," Garland growled dangerously. "What, no security team this time, Russ? Or did you make that sniveling little CID shit wait in the car?"

Admiral Russel Ogden was the new chief of CENTCOM and Garland's replacement. He'd been there with his partner in crime, acting CID Director Charles Wheaton, when they'd had the marines escort Garland out of his office after McGibbons's ouster. And the worst part of the whole thing was that Garland had once considered Russ Ogden to be a close friend and a damned level-headed commander. But that had all gone out the window as soon as the man threw in with Cunningham, Mercer, and their band of usurpers.

Ogden held his hands out wide in a gesture indicating he'd come in peace. "I suppose I deserved that, and I know you're pissed, Bob. Frankly, I can't say I really blame you."

"You deserve the end of a fucking rope," Garland muttered, just loud enough that Russ was sure to have heard it, but not so loud that it could be considered a real threat.

Ogden's neutral expression hardened, and he took a calming breath before speaking again. "I'm not here to pour salt on open wounds, Bob," he said, then looked pointedly at the ice-cold beer in Garland's hand, then at the still-open cooler and half dozen bottles still nestled in ice. "I don't suppose you have an extra beer to share, do you?"

Garland looked down at the cooler, then slapped the lid closed. "Sorry, Russ. I'm all out."

Ogden stood there awkwardly for a moment, then swept his gaze around the neatly manicured backyard of the Garlands' suburban home. "Is it safe to talk back here?"

Garland narrowed his eyes. "Why?"

Ogden shot him a grave look. "I think you know why, old friend."

"Yes," Garland stated flatly. "But cut that 'old friend' shit out. You lost the right to call me a friend when you stabbed not only me but the entirety of the human race in the back."

"I know."

Garland rocked back on his heels slightly at the matter-of-fact admission. The man seemed to deflate right before his eyes, suddenly looking more weary than Bob had ever seen him. *Goddammit*, he sighed internally. Opening the cooler, Garland pulled a bottle from the ice and tossed it to Ogden.

"Looks like I've been restocked, Russ." He inclined his head toward a pair of Adirondack chairs sitting next to a firepit a few meters away. "Come on, then," he said, turning and walking over to the chairs. "Take a load off and tell me all about whatever it is that has your panties wadded up."

Ogden sat down while Garland cranked open a shade umbrella to take the edge off the summer heat. Elizabeth wasn't a particularly hot planet, but the summer months around Elizabeth City were almost always humid, thanks to the large amount of surface water in the region, whether that be the host of inland lakes, either of the two large rivers that straddled the city, or the ocean they flowed into just forty kilometers to the southeast. Once the umbrella was up and angled to give the two senior navy men a reprieve from the midday sun, Garland settled heavily into his chair, took a long pull from his beer, and finally looked up to meet Ogden's gaze.

"Okay, Russ. Hit me with it. How bad are we fucked?"

———

THE SHORT ANSWER was that they were completely, utterly, inescapably fucked.

Garland sat in silence for nearly a minute, his mouth hanging open in complete shock at the utter stupidity on display. Not only had Cunningham cut a deal with the devil directly, but the conditions he signed off on essentially did all the Imperium's hard work for them: pulling the entirety of the Confed navy back to just a few bases, cutting new enlistment and training programs, slashing budgets and killing new construction. Jesus fucking Christ, the new administration was leading humanity straight into the slaughterhouse, and they intended to do it not kicking and screaming, but whimpering like meek little lambs that didn't know any better. You couldn't ask for a more perfect setup for annihilation.

Garland looked down at the long-empty beer bottle in his hand, then stood without a word and walked over to the cooler. Grabbing the handle on one side of it, he dragged it over to the firepit, threw open the top, and pulled out three fresh bottles. He handed one to Russ, then opened the other two for himself. He chugged one down, tossed the empty bottle over his shoulder, then took a measured sip of the second before finally opening his mouth to speak.

"I'm going to be brutally honest here... I don't know what the hell you expect me to do with this shit sandwich, Russ. You guys have spent months on a full media blitz to discredit myself, McGibbons, Mark Gideon—everyone and everything even remotely connected to the Imperium, the Master, or the agent that's been pulling our strings for decades... everything. I have no pull left within CENTCOM, thanks to your efforts, and the general public are largely against the fantastical notion that we've been getting played by another alien race all along.

"Don't get me wrong. I'm happy to hear you and Cunningham have finally opened your damned eyes and acknowledged the giant fucking train that's about to smash us into a bloody paste, but fuck, couldn't you have done it before you *completely* screwed us over?"

"I know." Russ buried his face in his hands for a moment before worrying at his scalp. "I know, Bob. I know we screwed ourselves, and I know the fact that I truly believed negotiation was the best option was the wrong tack to take. I understand all of that, now. The president really did think he was doing this for the good of the Confed, too. I can't speak to Cynthia's motivations, and I know Charles was only in it because he wanted to be the big fish in a little pond at CID, but the president is asking for your help here."

"And again," Garland said, "I don't know what the hell you expect me to do. It's not like you guys can just hold a press conference and say, 'Whoops, we fucked up, and everyone who was screaming about Armageddon from a vicious alien race was actually right. So we're undoing all the stuff we just did and putting them back in charge. Sorry, everyone!'"

"Don't be so fucking glib, Bob. I'm serious here."

"So am I," Garland exploded. "You overthrew the rightfully elected president of the Confed based on mistruths and outright fabrications, stripped the people who were actively working to fight the Imperium of their commands, and then exiled the few people who actually understand this enemy and might be able to make a difference. The cupboard is bare now, Russ—we don't have anything to work with anymore!"

Russ sat back in his chair and took a pull of his beer. Holding it by the neck, he rubbed his thumb around the bottle's crown in thought for a moment. "I know you have a line of communications open with Henry Hutchins and *Indomitable*, Bob. There has to be *something* they could do to help us out here."

Garland leaned back. He hadn't wanted to admit that he *thought* he had a way to get messages to Hank, because a small part of his mind warned him this whole conversation might be a ruse to get him to expose the tiny fraction of control he still had over the situation. The truth was, he had no idea if Evans had been able to get through to Henry or not.

"I don't know what the hell you're talking about, Russ. I haven't spoken to Hank since before he left Archimedes and headed out to Hai'alla, and that's the God's honest truth."

"Don't bullshit me with semantics, Bob," Russ bit out. "The Master dropped in on the president unannounced a few days ago and told him all about the emergency recall notice that the CID received from one of their agents on Lianmeng. It knows the handler that fielded the request quietly killed it and then passed it along to Mark, and it also knows Mark immediately came to you with the information. And there's only one reason Mark would bring that to you. So stop pretending you don't know what I'm talking about."

Garland sighed, drained his bottle, then looked longingly at the cooler before passing on the idea of another beer. It looked like he was going to have to come clean and pray that Russ was on the level with him. If this was all a trap, well, it wasn't like he was able to do much to help Hank out right now, anyway. But if Russ was being honest, and the administration was trying to find a way out of this mess, then Garland might just have the support he needed to try and right the ship.

"I may have a way to get a limited amount of information to Hank, but it's not here, nor do I have direct access to it," he finally admitted. "I had someone pass the intel from Mark along in the hopes that the forces we have out in Alarian space could retrieve the agent in question. We believe the intel he has in his possession could potentially give us the firepower we need to fight back against Mercer and her witch hunt in the senate.

"But what I really want to know," Garland said, shifting to the offensive, "is how exactly the Master knows everything it does. You said it dropped in on Cunningham? Does that mean it's here?"

Russ shook his head. "No, it only drops in every once in a while, using the last remaining slipspace transceiver its agent constructed. Essentially, it's making a long-distance vid call whenever it wants to talk."

Garland's ears perked up, the gears in his strategist's mind beginning to churn out the first parts of a possible plan. "And is that how it's getting information relayed back to it?"

Russ nodded. "It's got some kind of information-gathering AI programs that it left behind to keep tabs on everything we do. My understanding is that's how it's staying informed."

"So it sent more agents?" Garland said, alarmed. It had taken nearly everything they had just to kill the first one.

"No," Russ said quickly. "It told Cunningham that it didn't see the need for an agent to be present and that its monitor AIs were more than sufficient. Personally, I think that's bullshit and it either doesn't have any agents available to send to Terran space or it's gun-shy about possibly losing another one, given that we've already demonstrated the ability to kill them."

Garland cupped his chin, thinking hard. If the Master wasn't sticking around in Terran space and was only getting its intel via a single transceiver, then it might be possible to cut off its influence and blind it in a single stroke. With no naval assets and no agent around to fight back, the transceiver should be a relatively soft target, as long as they could locate it.

"Do you know where this transceiver is?" he asked.

Russ nodded hesitantly. "We do, but I can see what you're thinking, and it's not going to be a simple matter of just blasting it from orbit, Bob."

"Why not?"

"Because the minute we try to mobilize any of our fleet assets to strike the transceiver, the Master will find out about it and act to ensure that doesn't happen. It may not be present here on Elizabeth, but anyone who even steps one toe out of line has ended up dead, and we don't know how. We assume the damn thing is paying someone to do its dirty work—mercs, gangs, pirates... It doesn't really matter. The point is that I've seen the body parts the Master had sent to Cunningham's office. Which is why we need someone outside all the chains of command, but even then, the transceiver is located in a populated area and under heavy guard."

Garland's brow furrowed. "Where is it, and who's doing the guarding? It can't be that hard of a target."

"It's on Isadore," Russ said. "Buried beneath ExoDyn headquarters on the outskirts of the city."

Garland's mouth dropped open. How the hell could Hank not have known? For the briefest instant, he questioned if maybe Hank had been in league with the agent this whole time, but that was absolutely absurd. The agent had proven its ability to pull off some pretty incredible tricks, right under their noses. And actually, the more he thought about it, the more it made sense to him. ExoDyn headquarters was where Hank and his people performed all kinds of cutting-edge research. The facility had its own onsite fusion plant for power generation, and anomalous EM readings from a slipspace transceiver would probably be overlooked as a byproduct of one of the weird projects ExoDyn had in development.

Then he realized how close to a major city the facility was, and images of the nuclear fallout from the transceiver the agent blew up just a hundred kilometers from where the two men were sitting flashed through his mind. That transceiver had been located in the dead zone left after the Alarians nuked the original Elizabeth City back during the war. What if someone set off another explosion of that magnitude but did it directly adjacent to a city that still had a million people living in it, like Arcadia?

"Fuck me," Garland said under his breath. "Okay, Russ, so we can't just blast the site from orbit and call it a day, but you didn't answer my question about who is responsible for security at the facility. So why can't we send in the SEARs and Pathfinders Ramsey still has available to take the site and neutralize it that way?"

"The few people we have left on Isadore report the facility is guarded by no less than a company's worth of soldiers. They aren't ours, and they don't go out and mingle with the general population, so we've had a hard time ID'ing them. We suspect they're from one of the more disreputable PMCs or possibly one of the larger organized crime syndicates. Unfortunately, we've had to pull nearly all of our military assets out of the system, so getting good intelligence has been difficult, and we're left relying on field reports that come in over a quantum link."

Garland shook his head in amazement. Russ had just openly admitted that the Confed had almost no way of knowing what was happening on one of its most industrialized worlds. "Well, that's just fucking great, Russ," he said derisively. "But fortunately for you, we happen to have more than just a handful of Pathfinders and a few SEARs to throw into the mix."

Ogden's brow furrowed, and a sly smile spread across Garland's face. "There's something you don't know, Russ." He let the statement hang in the air for a moment, savoring the confusion on Ogden's face. "You see, I knew you'd be coming to kick my ass to the curb long before you actually showed up with the marines in tow, so I pulled a fast one on you guys.

"I assume Wheaton had his people dig through my deleted files after I was removed?" Russ nodded once without commenting, so Garland continued. "Well, then they found Ramsey's report on what happened during the operation to take out the agent and its transceiver on Hai'alla, which is exactly what I wanted them to find. However, I made sure there was one big item that was omitted from that report. Are you ready for this?" He sat back, feeling an immense sense of petty satisfaction at the fact that Ogden was now hanging on his every word.

"Ramsey and the Alarians didn't miraculously defeat another Imperium battlegroup. The goddamned first admiral of the entire Imperial Navy switched teams and kicked off his own little rebellion, and the first shots were fired over Hai'alla. He worked *with* Ramsey and the Alarians to take out the loyalist members of his battlegroup and then agreed to ally with us. Russ, Ramsey and *Indomitable* didn't just get us one ally in our fight against the Imperium when they went to Hai'alla. They got us two. And one of those is the big dog himself."

Garland produced a cigar from a tube he'd had sitting in his pocket and clipped the end off before sticking it in his mouth, smiling triumphantly. "You wanted a force that can tackle the transceiver complex beneath ExoDyn HQ?" He pulled out a torch and puffed the cigar to life. "I've got one for you. You just need to tell me where and when to have them make their move and figure out a way for me to get a message to Archimedes Base on the sly. My people will take it from there."

25

HOT EXTRACTION

"Ma'am, one of the targets the SEARs flagged as a possible Federation Q-ship has broken from the traffic pattern ahead of schedule."

Captain Samantha Collins looked up from her command multi-function display and raised an eyebrow at her operations officer, Lieutenant Seymour. She'd ordered her ship into a lower orbit when the SEARs called in an update to inform her that they'd successfully recovered Ben and Zheng—though the CID agent had been killed before they got to him. At present, the SEARs were high-tailing it back to Liberty Spaceport for a dust-off to orbit. Given that Collins and the *Wraith* had been loitering well outside any of the established shipping lanes to ensure they avoided detection, it was going to take the better part of an hour to get into position for a quick intercept of the SEARs' shuttle.

"Did they inform Newman's Rock orbital control, or does it look like they're trying to make a run for it? It's possible they just got word of the SEARs hitting their team on the ground, and they're trying to make a run for it before the planetary government becomes aware of their presence."

"Neither, ma'am," came the reply, and Collins frowned.

"They appear to be transferring to a different orbit that will bring them to within a thousand kilometers of us soon after we pick up the SEARs, but they're taking their time about it."

"Put the tracks on the big screen, please," Collins said, and her frown deepened after her ops officer sent the predicted orbital tracks to the main bridge display.

The *Wraith* was stealthy enough that they very likely had remained undetected by the ground-based tracking stations that monitored shipping traffic in and around Newman's Rock, despite the burn required to insert her ship into its new orbit. Indeed, the lack of any hails from either the civilian orbital control authority or the Newman's Rock Territorial Defense Forces after the *Wraith* fired her engines would seem to indicate just that. But Collins wasn't inclined to believe it was a coincidence that one of the few ships Mabel flagged as a possible Federation intelligence vessel was suddenly on the move and working to position itself above and behind her ship at the same time the SEARs should be making their way back to the shuttle for extraction.

So what to do? Collins could order her ship out of orbit and make the shuttle rendezvous with them somewhere else—it did have limited facilities for an extended flight, after all. But that would put them at risk of being picked up or picked *off* by their adversary. She could also try to lose them by taking advantage of her ship's remarkable agility to shift orbits when they went over the horizon, then rely on the *Wraith*'s excellent stealth capability to keep them from being spotted again until it was too late.

"Still no word from orbital control regarding her shifting position?" Collins asked.

"Not yet, ma'am, but the spacelanes are so crowded right now it might take a bit for them to get around to posting a notice, if it's not an immediate hazard to anyone."

Collins nodded absently. She wished she could get an update

from Mabel and the SEARs—to see if they could offer any insight—but they were just heading over the horizon and about to lose line-of-sight comms with the shuttle. There was still the chance the whole thing was simply an innocent maneuver. For that matter, it was still possible the ship in question wasn't even the ISB's vessel at all. She stared at the plot a few moments longer, watching the marker that designated the ISF *Crescent Dawn* inching its way closer and closer to an orbit that would put them spitting distance away before too long.

How in the world is she able to maintain such a low orbital profile at her tonnage? Collins mused. It could be that *Crescent Dawn* currently had no cargo aboard, which would make it easier for her crew to hold the ship in a lower orbit without needing to burn her engines continuously. Then again, if she was an ISB vessel, then it was likely that she'd been significantly modified to make her less massive while simultaneously giving her substantially more thrust. Either way, she still massively outgrossed the *Wraith*, which meant *Crescent Dawn* would have the high ground, unless Collins wanted to put her ship farther out from her team, and there was no way she was about to put a potential enemy ship between herself and her people on the surface.

"Keep an eye on her, for now, Ops. Let me know if orbital control puts out a bulletin on it."

"Aye aye, ma'am."

"And Ops," Collins added, "ask CIC to run an analysis on the *Crescent Dawn*. I want to know how she's able to maneuver in so close to the planet at her size."

The *Wraith* went over the horizon, and Collins cursed the hard laws of physics that meant she would periodically lose direct contact with both her people on the ground and their suspected opponent. But such was the reality of operating in space, and until someone could convince the rebels to part with the secrets of their reactionless propulsion technology, humanity would just have to deal with the vagaries of Newtonian physics.

Twenty-three minutes later, as her ship was coming back over the horizon and was once again within comms range, all hell broke loose.

"Captain! There's been an explosion at Liberty Spaceport. We've lost contact with our team on the ground!" Seymour called out.

Almost simultaneously, her command display lit up with a flurry of notifications from CIC, and her comms officer informed her the planetary datanet was starting to fill up with reports of weapons fire at the civilian spaceport. Her eyes flashed back to the main bridge display, which still showed the position data on both her ship and the *Crescent Dawn*.

"Comms!" Collins barked. "Find a way to contact our people down there. Even if the Feds took out the shuttle, the SEARs could still be alive. Their APEX armor has integrated comms suites, not to mention the fact that Mabel was riding shotgun with Chief Kravczyk. Ops," she said, turning to her ops officer, "bring us to Condition-1. Tactical, keep a bead on the *Crescent Dawn*. I don't want them slipping a missile in on us while we're busy trying to sort through the chaos on the ground and working to reestablish contact with our people down there."

Her bridge officers went to work, and Collins took a moment to scan through the notifications on her console. She cursed internally as she quickly took in the data. The hit on their shuttle must have been coordinated; the attack occurred less than a minute after the *Wraith* went over the horizon and lost comms with the shuttle. The silver lining was that it seemed unlikely that the SEARs were back at the spaceport before the attack happened, given their last known position and the time the shuttle had been attacked. She hoped and prayed they'd be able to make contact soon, because there wasn't much the *Wraith* could do until then.

Collins swept her gaze past the plot showing the orbital track for the ISF *Crescent Dawn*. The freighter was still lumbering its way toward its new orbit, not showing any sign that something was amiss. Maybe she was mistaken and they were focusing on the wrong target, or maybe the *Dawn* really was the ISB's support ship but they hadn't actually spotted the *Wraith* yet. It could be the *Dawn* was doing the same thing Collins had ordered her ship to do: move to a lower orbit and prepare to pull their people off the surface. The orbits in question did provide the best balance of least-time-intercept with a shuttle burning for orbit and ease of escape afterward.

"Contact from Mabel, Captain," came the report from Comms, and Collins allowed herself to breathe an internal sigh of relief. At least they hadn't lost the whole team. "She reports the ISB hit the shuttle before they were back to Liberty, and they've rerouted to the big commercial spaceport that's operated by the planetary government to handle the sale and transport of all the planet's mining production. Evidently, Petty Officer McCollum has a contact with one of the cargo haulers operating there, and they believe they can find transport to orbit. They'll update us once they meet up with their new ride."

Finally, a stroke of good luck. This day had been nothing but one disaster stacked on another, ever since Ben and Agent Zheng had been abducted by the ISB, so Collins was grateful for the good news. "Understood, Comms. Any word on the status of the shuttle's crew? We had three people on that bird."

Her comms officer's face fell, and he shook his head. "Sorry, ma'am."

"CIC sent an update stating they believe all three of the shuttle's flight crew were aboard at the time of the attack," Seymour added. "The odds of there being survivors are, well…" He trailed off.

"Copy that, Ops," Collins said, her voice stony. Lieutenant Evers, the shuttle's pilot, had been part of her crew since before this whole mess with the Imperium. She'd lost people before, but this time felt different. Her team had just been bushwhacked right under her nose, and that was going to be a tough pill to swallow. First, though, she needed to get the rest of her people safely off the surface—something that was now very much *not* a sure thing.

As the *Wraith* prepared to go over the horizon again, Collins eyed the ever-closing *Crescent Dawn*, a frustrating cocktail of suspicion and doubt mingling in her gut. The big freighter still hadn't made any hostile move, but a nagging feeling tugged at the back of her mind. Something about this whole situation didn't feel right. It made sense that the ISB would want to take out the SEARs' only means of transport, because that would give them another shot at intercepting them and retrieving the data Agent Volkov had in his possession.

Whatever that intel is, the ISB really don't want us getting our hands on it, Collins mused.

With no new threats presenting themselves in surrounding space, Collins and her ship didn't have anything to do, except stay vigilant and wait to hear from the SEARs. She watched the plot as her ship slipped over the horizon again, hoping their next trip around the planet wouldn't reveal some other fresh hell she'd have to contend with.

———

IT TOOK NEARLY an hour and two more complete orbits, but that new fresh hell Collins was worried about finally struck. The

Wraith was once again just heading over the horizon and out of line of sight to Landing City when the ISB ship made its move.

"Vampire, vampire!" her tactical officer shouted. "Multiple launches detected from ISF *Crescent Dawn*. Missiles are tracking toward the heavy-lift cargo transport the SEARs are aboard!"

"Time to target?"

"Approximately twenty-one minutes, ma'am."

"Can we take them out?" she asked, already knowing the answer as she saw the missiles' positions update on the plot.

"Negative. There's still too much atmosphere between us and them—our point-defense lasers don't have the power needed to burn through it and still put enough energy on target to disable all the missiles before they strike."

Collins quickly ran through each of the weapon systems available to her for missile defense, but the damned ISB had timed their attack to perfectly coincide with the *Wraith* being out of position again. The point-defense railguns didn't have the range or the angle, her own missiles would take too long to make the intercept, regardless of whether they were fired ahead of the *Wraith*'s orbit or in retrograde, and her ship's lasers didn't have the power to burn through the upper layers of the planet's atmosphere *and* all the missiles' casings in time. They might get a few of them, but there were currently a dozen missiles closing with her team.

"Tactical, target those missiles with the laser batteries and take out as many as you can. Even degrading their performance a little might buy us the time we need. Ops, tell CIC to start throwing every electronic countermeasure we have at them until we lose contact. Comms, let our team know they have incoming and broadcast a general warning to all local shipping across the planetary and system-wide emergency channels," Collins barked. Then, turning to her command console and bringing up the screens pertaining to orbital navigation, she called out, "Helm, stand by for orders."

Hands flying over her console, Collins quickly ran through several course and speed options. The safety margins for what she planned to attempt were so far beyond razor-thin that they were practically microscopic. She was relying heavily on the *Wraith*'s navigation computers and risking her ship on the accuracy of their sensor data.

"Helm! New course and speed are coming to you now—no time for questions," Collins said, tapping the command to commit the new course and velocity information to the helm.

Her helmsman visibly stiffened when he saw what she was ordering him to do, but he didn't hesitate. "Course laid in, ma'am. Executing first maneuvering burn in twelve seconds."

"Ops, tell CIC to clean us up—anything protruding from the hull that can be retracted needs to be stowed before we breach the atmosphere! And Tactical, if this works, you'll need to be ready for a quick acquisition and engagement of the targets. Don't worry about sparing the taxpayer dollars. If we lose that team, we lose the war."

"Aye aye, ma'am." Her tactical officer took a moment to flex his fingers and crack his knuckles. "No pressure," he muttered under his breath.

The *Wraith* began vibrating harshly from the military emergency thrust her engines were suddenly pouring out as her nose angled alarmingly down toward the planet. "Restraints on!" Collins said, and the few people on the bridge that weren't already strapped in quickly donned their harnesses. "Ops, sound collision."

A strident klaxon blared throughout the *Wraith* as the little spy ship brushed up against the first hints of the planet's atmosphere. Collins said a quick prayer. Her eyes darted to the hull temperature readout, which was beginning to climb rapidly as her ship continued to drive itself into ever denser air.

The *Wraith* tore through space, rapidly chewing through the last thousand kilometers of exosphere before plunging into the planet's thermosphere. The speed at which the altimeter was dropping began to slow as the helmsman shallowed out their dive. When their altitude broke through the planet's Karman line, the ship was shaking and buffeting so bad Collins feared she'd killed them all. A ventral hull temperature north of two thousand degrees Kelvin all but confirmed it. Her command displays were awash with angry red warning indicators, but she ignored them; they were committed now, and whatever happened couldn't be helped.

"We're max q!" The helmsman had to practically scream to be heard over the horrific noise assaulting their senses.

The idea that a spaceship—*space*ship—like the *Wraith* would ever need to endure a max q event was utterly insane, but here they were. Collins had just ordered her five-thousand-ton ship to perform an orbital maneuver that actually dipped down into the upper atmosphere of Newman's Rock, forcing her command to contend with atmospheric friction for the first and—God willing —only time in her service to the Confed. While the density of the air at eighty-five kilometers wasn't exactly as thick as molasses in winter, the unholy velocity at which the *Wraith* was currently tearing through it was enough to leave a fiery streak across the planet's sky.

Then their altitude began to climb, passing back above a hundred kilometers as their blistering pace of more than ten kilometers per second through the ionosphere caused the little ship to skip off the planet's atmosphere. As the violent shaking died down, Collins was again able to clearly make out their positional data on the main display. It was going to be close, but she thought they would have just enough of a window to take out the missiles that should still be streaking toward the cargo lifter her SEARs were aboard. Unfortunately, they were going to be limited to using the *Wraith*'s laser batteries, as their interceptor missiles would need to bleed off too much of their inherited velocity before they'd be able to engage either the enemy's missiles or the *Crescent Dawn* herself.

"Thirty seconds to line of sight. Standing by to acquire targets," her tactical officer reported, his voice still a little shaky after they just narrowly escaped disintegrating in a planet's atmosphere.

"Your show, Tactical," Collins said in a reassuring tone. "And Lieutenant Davis?"

"Ma'am?"

"Good hunting."

26

TWO CAN PLAY AT THAT GAME

"WHAT THE FUCK DO YOU MEAN WE HAVE MISSILES HEADING OUR way?" Captain Micholson shouted over the open comms channel. "Can't you CID spooks do anything about them with that fancy-ass ship my tax dollars paid for?"

Kravczyk exchanged a worried look with Valdez, but the two SEARs kept quiet. If they had incoming, Micholson and his copilot were about to have their hands full, and bombarding them with questions wasn't a good way to help.

The two SEARs were strapped into a pair of well-worn jump seats at the back of the lifter's small cockpit. Squeezing into the restraints while still armored up had taken some creative thinking, but they'd managed it. The cargo lifter had a passenger compartment one deck below, but Valdez had wanted to be in the cockpit, should the need arise for him to coordinate with Collins and the *Wraith* or answer any questions the old freighter captain might have. And with McCollum playing nursemaid to the still-unconscious Ben, Kravczyk had taken the last open seat on the flight deck.

"Judy, get the *Fortune* on the horn and get them moving! Tell them to bring the targeting array online and send us a feed so we're not flying blind when the *Wraith* goes over the horizon—no point trying to keep a low profile anymore," Micholson said to his co-pilot, and one of Kravczyk's eyebrows ticked up a few notches. It would seem that McCollum's "uncle" Mike was more than just a space truck driver if his ship was carrying something that could utilize a tactical search array.

The woman didn't even bat an eye at the sudden danger they were in, instead calmly tapping out a series of commands on her display.

"I hope you boys are strapped in tight," the big freighter captain said over his shoulder, "because this ride's about to get a lot more exciting."

"Who's doing the shooting?" Valdez said, finally breaking his silence.

"Some twats in an old Orion-class bulk freighter," Micholson stated evenly. "Your people seem to think it's the support ship for your ISB friends down on the surface. Seeing how they just launched a dozen ASMs in our direction, I'm inclined to agree. A dozen seems a bit like overkill, though, considering their target is just an innocent little cargo lifter like us."

There was something in Micholson's voice that made Kravczyk's ears perk up. The freighter captain had definitely been around the block a few times, and Kravczyk was sure he'd had his fair share of run-ins with the less-than-friendly types that frequently preyed on commercial shipping, especially in the more remote systems, but the man was *too* calm, given their situation.

"How long do we have?" Valdez asked.

"The *Wraith* says about twenty minutes, which is well before we'll be able to join up with the *Fortune*, turn around and make an emergency descent back to the surface, or wait for your ship to come back over the horizon and provide defensive fire... Those Fed bastards timed their shot pretty well."

"So what are you saying?" Kravczyk said, unable to keep his mouth shut any longer. "We're down to rude gestures and harsh language?"

Micholson shrugged. "Unless you want to lean out the airlock and try to shoot them down with that buzz gun strapped to your chest, sure. I suppose it can't hurt anything—oh, hey! That's some damned fine gunnery there! Those CID spooks sure do know their shit," he said, switching tack halfway through a sentence. "The *Wraith* managed to pop a few of the incoming before they went over the horizon. Gotta say, I'm impressed. Too bad we still have nine missiles to contend with, though."

"Mike," Judy said, finally looking up from her console and turning to Micholson, "Laura Beth says she'll do what she can, but they're not in the best position to offer support. If we alter course and burn hard, we should be able to buy ourselves a little time, and the *Fortune* will be in a much better position to cover us."

She paused, like she had something else to add but didn't want to voice it out loud.

"But..." Micholson said, irritated at her hesitation. "Spit it out, woman. We don't have all day."

"Mike, I don't think the mains will take the abuse. They're already almost a hundred hours overdue for a depot-level overhaul."

"We don't have a choice." Micholson reached up to snug his restraint harness down a little more. "Update the nav computer with the new course and burn profile. She'll hold together," he said confidently, then toggled over to the ship-wide comms channel. "Hang on to your butts, people. We've got some hot shit coming down the pipe, and the ride's about to get a lot more lively. Secure all hatches, keep your vac kit handy, and depressurize all nonessential compartments. Hard burn imminent!"

"Course and burn profile updated," Judy said.

"Send it!"

The old freighter captain stabbed his finger down on the big MFD panel in front of him, and Kravczyk felt like he'd been simultaneously kicked in the ass by a pissed-off mule and sat on by an elephant. His armor squeezed around his lower extremities in response to the sudden, crushing g-load, doing what it could to keep oxygenated blood flowing to his brain. The flight couches Micholson and his co-pilot occupied were designed to alleviate the effects of high-g maneuvers, but the fold-out jump seats the two SEARs were currently plastered into weren't designed for it in the least.

At first, the efforts of his APEX, combined with his own anti-g straining maneuver, managed to stave off the worst of the effects of the hard acceleration, but as the seconds dragged on, Kravczyk noticed the color begin to drain from the world around him. After a minute, darkness started creeping in on his now black-and-white world, pushing in from the edges and inexorably compressing his field of view to just a narrow circle. Then his visual reality winked out entirely, leaving him only a vague sense of the hellacious noise and shaking of the ship as he clung stubbornly to the last vestige of consciousness.

"Goddammit! Come on, you ancient piece of rusted shit! Give me just a little more!"

Kravczyk inhaled sharply as his blood resumed its regular circuit around his body. The muted world around him sharpened after just a few seconds, and he shook his head to clear the cobwebs. The splitting headache that assaulted him an instant later made him immediately regret doing so.

"That's it, Mike," Judy said softly. "We just lost the mains. We're down to maneuvering jets only."

Micholson seemed to deflate in his seat, shoulders slumping in defeat. "It wasn't enough, Judy," he said, eyeing the plot on one of the cockpit displays. "They're gonna smoke us."

"How long?" Valdez croaked out, having just regained consciousness himself.

"Oh hey! You boys enjoy your little nap?" Micholson chuckled ruefully. "At current rate of closure? About six minutes, give or take. But that assumes the missiles aren't programmed to execute a final evade and sprint maneuver, so it could be less. And before you ask, no, my ship won't be able to cover us in time. The interceptor missiles the *Fortune* carries are meant for defending the ship herself, not another vessel as far away as we are, and her point-defense cannons don't have the range."

"What about Newman's Rock planetary defense?"

The big man snorted derisively. "That bunch of yokels? They couldn't find their asses with both hands, let alone shoot down nine modern anti-ship missiles with no warning. Hell, they don't even have any of their gunboats in the black right now. They only roll them out when the big annual auction happens, and even then, they're only used for crowd control. There's a reason the fucking Dragons were able to take the planet with just a company of grunts with rifles.

"No," Micholson said, practically sighing the word out as he loosened his restraints and leaned back, kicking his feet up on the console. "Best we can do now is sit here and relax for the last few minutes we have—"

A shrill alarm from the console cut him off, and the freighter captain's feet leapt off the console like he'd been electrocuted. He scanned the new data flashing on his displays, then shot a finger toward his co-pilot. "Tell Laura Beth to forget about us for the time being and concentrate on pursuing the *Crescent Dawn*! Weapons free—whatever she deems necessary. I want that fucker dusted!" Micholson leaned over his displays and stared intently at the tactical plot. "You guys think you're so big and bad with your sneaky little missile pods?" he growled. "Well, two can play at that game."

Judy leaned over her consoles and started hammering out commands while she called the *Gambler's Fortune*, and Micholson twisted around in his seat, grinning maniacally at the two SEARs. "When this is all over," he said, "I need you to introduce me to that captain of yours. That woman is absolutely out of her damn mind... I think I'm in love."

———

"HELM, GET US SLOWED DOWN," Collins said, her voice strained from the massive adrenaline dump she was riding. "Tactical, I want some good news."

The *Wraith* had come over the horizon to discover the SEARs' lifter had executed its own hard burn in an attempt to evade the incoming missiles. The little craft had altered its course significantly and picked up a ton of extra velocity, but now it appeared to be on a ballistic trajectory, unpowered. Their desperate maneuver hadn't been in vain, however, buying them precious seconds that made it possible for the *Wraith* to come around the planet and take one last crack at the missiles. But Collins could see that her ship was carrying so much speed after their slingshot around the planet that they only had a tiny window of opportunity to down all the incoming missiles and clear the skies for the SEARs.

Davis didn't respond right away. The man's hands were a blur of motion across the various MFDs arrayed around him at the tactical station. Collins's ears picked up the high-pitched whine of her ship's laser batteries dumping terawatts of power into space before cutting off and going through a quick-charge cycle, only to fire again a few seconds later. As their distance to the missiles began to increase, thanks to their orbital escape trajectory, the pulses became longer as the beams scattered more and more, putting less energy on target with each passing second.

The red inverted V's denoting the enemy missiles winked out one after another, leaving a line of red X's that marched closer and closer to the heavy lifter with Ben and the SEARs aboard. Collins and the entire bridge crew held their breath as the last two missiles closed to within ten kilometers of the lifter. The nearest one winked out, followed by the last a moment later.

Cheering erupted from every bridge station as the tactical plot displayed clear space around their besieged ground team, at last. Collins exhaled a shaky breath and stood from her command chair. Walking over to the tactical station, she reached down and squeezed Davis's shoulder firmly. He looked up at her, face pale and beaded with sweat, and grinned.

"All missiles destroyed, ma'am. The skies are—"

A warbling alarm from his console cut him off, and both he and Collins scanned the displays.

"What the…" Davis muttered under his breath as he pulled up more information on the new contacts flooding out into space around the ISF *Gambler's Fortune*—the bulk freighter the SEARs had been en route to before the ISB made their move.

Collins said nothing, letting Davis parse the information on his screens and sift through the analysis CIC was sending up, but she followed the flow of information as best she could. Her estimation of McCollum's freighter captain friend shot through the roof when she realized what she was seeing.

"Ma'am, the *Gambler's Fortune* has engaged the *Crescent Dawn*, but the ordnance they're using appears to be chemically fired artillery shells. No directed energy signatures detected, and no—belay that, there's the missiles."

Collins followed the updating plot intently. The *Fortune* wasn't screwing around, firing off enough kinetic and explosive ordnance at the ISB ship to saturate even a modern fleet escort's defensive envelope. The converted Federation freighter didn't stand a chance, and it appeared they knew it, as the *Crescent Dawn* began burning hard away from the threat.

The *Wraith*'s bridge was eerily quiet for the next ten minutes as the little spy ship tore through space; every person was working to check and double-check the status of all their systems after flying their *space*ship through an atmosphere. Collins had cringed when she finally sat back down at her command station and read through the damage reports that were rapidly piling up as her various section chiefs submitted their initial reports.

Her ship was steadily bleeding off the insane amount of velocity they'd come around the planet with, but it was going to be hours before they could fully reverse course and limp back into orbit. Her little stunt had degraded her main engines to barely thirty percent output, and there was a host of engineering systems throwing fault codes all over the ship, not to mention their comms antennae had all been burned off. Most worrying, however, was the status of her warp emitters, which were currently offline and unavailable.

She glanced up for the hundredth time over the last ten minutes. The swarm of angry explosives dogging the *Crescent Dawn* steadily shrank as the Q-ship ran for its life, throwing everything they had at the cloud of incoming ordnance. But it wasn't going to be enough; a huge bulk freighter like the *Dawn* was an ungainly beast, especially when that far down in a gravity well. The Fed ship didn't have the engine power or maneuverability needed to escape the incoming wall of destruction.

"It's all academic, at this point," Seymour commented to nobody in particular. "There's no way they can take all those shells and missiles out in time. They should just get to their lifeboats and get as far away from that tin can as possible before it gets dusted."

"Do you remember what the Dragons did to the civilian population back in '49, Ops?" Collins said darkly. "Those poor bastards probably wouldn't get picked up, even if they managed to get clear in their pods."

"Better to go down fighting than drift through space in a dark lifepod for days or weeks until you die of dehydration or freeze to death when the power finally runs out—assuming you don't just space yourself first," Davis muttered. "Poor bastards."

Collins didn't say it, but she agreed with her tactical officer. It took a few more minutes, but the angry swarm finally reached the *Crescent Dawn*. The *Wraith*'s two remaining optical cameras picked up a series of small flashes in space over the planet, followed by a massive flare of released energy a moment later. When the display cleared, Collins checked the tactical plot.

There were no survivors.

27

THE PALMER INITIATIVE

"Two thousand degrees Kelvin? Are you out of your mind, Captain? I may not be read-in on the full capabilities of the *Wraith*-class ships, but I'm pretty sure atmospheric flight wasn't a design consideration."

Henry didn't offer any social niceties, nor did he mince words as he approached the *Wraith*'s starboard main airlock. He carried only his beat-up datapad, a thermal mug full of fresh coffee, and a medium-sized backpack that contained his datapad's portable quantum link module and a few personal items. Captain Collins was standing outside the inner hatch, waiting for the airlock to finish its pressurization cycle, along with several of the *Wraith*'s crew, including Doc Adams.

Collins turned around and gave him a flat stare. "Henry, I really don't have the time for this. We made it, the SEARs and Ben made it, and the ISB didn't. That's all that matters at this point."

Henry walked up to the small group and shook his head in exasperation. "What is it with you people? And just to be clear, I'm including my son here. Every time I find myself around this ship and/or the SEARs, my life turns into a chaotic hell filled with gunfights, space battles, explosions, and Ben finding creative new ways to get himself torn up." He sighed heavily, tucking his datapad under one arm so he could free up a hand to massage his temples. "I swear to God, I'm getting way too old for this."

"You and me both, Henry," Collins said with a conspiratorial smile. "You and me both."

A harsh buzzer sounded from overhead, and the indicator light above the airlock changed from amber to green. A chief petty officer in grimy ship's utilities undogged the hatch and swung it open, then stepped aside to give the people standing there room to enter the airlock. Henry followed the group in, and a few minutes later, the outer airlock hatch opened, revealing a rail-thin man in his late twenties, sporting an even dirtier set of coveralls than the chief on the *Wraith*.

"Howdy, folks!" he said cheerfully. "Welcome aboard the *Gambler's Fortune*." He released his hold on the hatch and drifted lazily in the air next to it. "Cap sends his compliments and apologizes for not being here in person, but he's got his hands full overseeing the stowing of our cargo, fending off some rather pissed-off locals, and getting the ship ready for a warp transition. Watch your step as you enter the tube—your grav field doesn't extend beyond the inner lip of the hatchway. If you're not familiar with the sensation of sudden loss of gravity, I suggest you grab a puke sack before trying to make your way through the hatch—most people toss their cookies the first few times they try this. Don't worry, though—we run one standard g aboard the *Fortune*, just like God intended."

"Thank you, crewman," Collins said with a nod, stepping up to the edge of the airlock.

"Call me Tom, Captain," the wiry crewman said with a smile. "We're not real big on formality around here."

The CID captain nodded politely, then pushed out of the

airlock with her arms and glided down the dimly lit transfer tube. Henry felt a stab of jealousy at how easy the experienced ship captain made the maneuver look, knowing he was likely to make a fool of himself in just a few short seconds. Adams approached the hatch next, then proceeded to spin off down the tube, limbs flailing in a futile attempt to stabilize himself. Tom's hand shot out and grabbed the medical officer by an ankle, quickly halting his motion and getting him oriented properly. Adams nodded his thanks and mumbled something about tripping over the lip of the hatch before using the guide rope stretched along the side of the tube to pull himself through.

Henry managed to fall somewhere between Collins and Adams in terms of grace of movement, and he even managed to remember to seal the lid on his coffee before stepping out into the zero-g environment.

Five minutes later, the group stepped out into the corridor leading to the *Fortune*'s forward portside airlock. Tom led them down the access corridor and out into the huge, central passageway that ran the length of the big freighter's spine.

"Captain, I assume you'd like to go straight to meet with your people?" Tom said, turning to face her.

"Actually," Collins said, glancing at Henry, "I understand Ben Hutchins is in your sickbay, receiving treatment for wounds he sustained on the surface. I'd like to stop by and check in on him first."

Tom shrugged. "Suit yourself. This way." He set off in the direction of the ship's bow. "Sickbay is one deck down, adjacent to the crew quarters. It's not too far from the conference room where your SEAR team is waiting."

Henry followed along behind Tom and the two CID officers, his anxiety level building with each step. He'd of course been informed that Ben had been captured by the ISB and subsequently rescued by the SEARs, and the better part of the day he'd spent in his guest quarters aboard the *Wraith*, waiting for news of Ben's condition—good or bad—had been excruciating. The worst part had been his complete lack of control over the situation, stuck on a ship in orbit, unable to get down to the surface and left to rely on others to help his son. It was the worst form of torture a parent could experience.

Then had come the whirlwind of their brief combat with the ISB ship, the discovery that the freighter crew that helped get Ben and the SEARs off the surface was far more than met the eye, and the decision to have him transferred to the *Gambler's Fortune*. It was only an hour ago that Collins had finally met with him in person to fill him in on Ben's condition, which was to say that he'd been injured but was stable aboard the freighter and already being tended to by their medical officer. It wasn't the best news, but it was a far sight better than the last couple of times Ben had been wounded.

With the *Wraith* unable to make a warp transition, at least until her engineering teams managed to patch it back together after the damage the ship sustained during its little dalliance with Newman's Rock's atmosphere, Captain Micholson had agreed to take Ben, along with the Pathfinder contingent, SEARs, and the GIM agent they'd extracted back to Hai'alla—for a nominal fee, of course. But Henry wasn't privy to the exact details of the arrangement Collins had come to with Micholson.

Regardless, he was now aboard a freighter with his son, Mabel, and the SEARs, and they were heading out of the system in just a few hours. With any luck—and he was most certainly due some good luck at this point—Henry hoped he'd be back in his quarters aboard *Indomitable* and relaxing with Shelly by his side in a week or two, depending on how fast the *Gambler's Fortune* could make the trip. He just hoped the information Ben and the SEARs had managed to retrieve was worth the price they'd paid to get it.

———

CAPTAIN COLLINS SAT at a worn conference table with the SEARs and the GIM agent they'd extracted, Dimitriy Volkov. Chief Kravczyk and Petty Officer McCollum were conversing quietly with each other, and Valdez appeared to be intently studying the compartment around them. For his part, Agent Volkov just looked exhausted and in need of a solid night's sleep.

Heavy footsteps clanged down the deck plates and filtered in through the open conference room door, bringing everyone's attention to their arriving host.

"Howdy, all," said a bear of a man with a thick, wiry black beard streaked with gray. "I apologize for keeping you waiting, but I had to make sure my crew of barely functioning, weaponized autism was stowing our cargo properly and not playing grab-ass with their long-lost brethren."

"Ah," Chief Kravczyk said with a lopsided grin on his face, "so you're all marines, then?"

"Two points for my Cro-Magnon friend here!" the freighter captain bellowed, then roared with laughter. The man was like a bad caricature of some space western protagonist.

Both Collins and Valdez shot warning glares at the big SEAR, but he just shrugged nonchalantly. "Hey, I just call it like I see it, boss," he said to Valdez, who shook his head in a way that said, *Why do I even try?*

Micholson leaned across the conference table and covered his mouth with one hand, then whispered conspiratorially to the chief, "Don't tell anyone, but my first officer was actually a console jockey before signing on with us. She's good people, though."

"Captain," Collins said, standing and nodding at the crass freighter captain, hoping to get this meeting back on track, "thank you for everything you've done. You don't know how critical it was for my team to make it safely off the surface."

Micholson straightened up and flashed her a huge smile. "It was my pleasure, Captain. I'd be happy to tell you all about it over dinner this evening. My treat."

"I think this meeting will suffice," Collins said with just a touch of frost in her voice.

Micholson clicked his tongue in disappointment. "Well, that's a true shame. I think you would have found me to be marvelous company."

Collins said nothing, simply staring flatly at the oaf.

"Suit yourself." He held up his hands in surrender, then pulled out a chair and sat down. "So you need us to bring your people to the Alarian home system to meet up with the rest of your force because my Tessie and her team just acquired some super-secret intel upon which the fate of the human race rests, correct?"

"That seems a bit overly dramatic," Collins stated. "But yes, that's more or less the gist of it."

"Uh-huh." Now it was Micholson's turn to stare. "I'm not buying it." He shook his head. "I don't know what you CID spooks have roped my Tessie into here, but last I checked, we were still at war with the Alarians, and now you want me to fly my ship right up to Hai'alla? There's a whole hell of a lot more going on here, and I'm not so sure I want any part of it. Hell, we already blew our cover with Newman's Rock, which means I'm gonna have to drop several million on bribes and cosmetically refitting the *Gambler's Fortune* just to be able to show our faces around here again. Not to mention all the ordnance we expended taking out those cunts on that *Orion*. Who's going to pay for all that?"

Collins took a cleansing breath. She got the feeling that there was so much more going on here than just her team running into trouble and needing a ride. For starters, the fact that the rust bucket she was currently aboard was actually armed to the teeth. Just what had the SEARs stumbled into here?

"Captain," she said, doing her best to be diplomatic and defuse the situation while also walking an OpSec tightrope. "I'm sorry, but I can't disclose any more details about our mission than you've already been given. I gather you and your crew are former Confederation military. Surely you can understand my position.

"I will do everything in my power to ensure that you're compensated for any damages, though I'm not sure I can promise to cover the cost of your expended munitions—something, by the way, I find most curious." She leveled a look at the burly freighter captain. It was part question, part accusation.

Micholson crossed his arms. "Don't get your panties in a twist, Captain," he said with a wry grin. "I assure you, everything on this boat is perfectly legal."

"And yet I can't say that I've ever come across any other cargo vessels that were armed with modern anti-ship missiles."

"You mean like the one my people dusted a few hours ago?"

"Don't patronize me, *Captain*," Collins replied icily. The man was needling her for seemingly no other reason than to get under her skin, and she hated that it was working.

Micholson sighed, uncrossing his arms and leaning forward to fold his hands on the table. "Are you familiar with the Palmer Initiative?"

Collins's eyes widened. "I don't think there's a single captain in the fleet or CID who isn't aware of Senator Palmer's absurd plan to issue letters of marque to private warships and turn them loose on Confed space. The proposal never got off the ground, though, and for good reason—I can only imagine what kind of chaos would have ensued by arming hundreds of civilian ships to combat the piracy threat in the fringe systems."

"Well, you're right about the initiative never getting the green light from the senate," Micholson said with a snort. "So that's why Special Projects took it and ran with it."

"That's absurd," Collins scoffed. "If the Confed really were authorizing the arming of civilian vessels for some clandestine program, CID would be running it, not the navy."

"Please." Micholson snorted derisively. "The CID has to mooch off the navy for practically all of their fleet needs. Maintenance and repairs, ships stores, moving crews in and out—all of it takes place at fleet facilities and the navy bills the CID for it. No," he said, shaking his head, "if anyone was going to run a project that involved outfitting large interstellar vessels, the navy is the only organization with the logistical support to pull it off properly. And besides, if and when a program ship is involved in an engagement, the fleet will be the ones responding to clean it up and verify the claim, not the CID."

Collins leaned back in her chair and studied the freighter captain in a new light. The man was abrasive and crude, to be sure, but once she looked past what was on the surface, Collins was able to see some things she'd missed on her initial assessment of Micholson. His eyes, while flanked by laugh lines and slightly red-rimmed—from a night spent in one of the seedier pubs that catered to freighter crews, she'd assumed—shone bright and intelligent when she looked past the context of his rough and tumble facade.

Almost as if Captain Micholson was transforming in real time, Collins was suddenly looking at a dangerous individual. The oaf on the other side of the table had vanished, replaced by a wolf in sheep's clothing.

"So there are, what, hundreds of other *Gambler's Fortunes* flying around Terran space? And nobody's noticed?"

Micholson shrugged. "Nah. As far as I know, the pilot program only consisted of a dozen ships. We were the first to be enrolled in the program because I knew a guy, but only the third to actually become active due to the extent of the modifications I wanted made to the *Fortune*. I heard the brass were pretty happy with the initial results, but then Icarus happened and the program was shifted to the back burner, for obvious reasons."

Collins narrowed her eyes. "And how exactly do you know about the Battle of Icarus?"

"Where do you think we underwent our initial refit? The navy couldn't exactly park us over Elizabeth, in view of God and everyone, and then proceed to cram an innocent cargo ship full of guns and advanced sensors."

"Icarus is one of the most highly classified facilities the Confed has," Collins said incredulously. "How does a retired jarhead end up there to have his freighter converted into what is, essentially, a privateer in disguise?"

"Like I said." Micholson shrugged again, looking nonchalant. "I know a guy."

"You'll need to do better than that, Captain."

"I wasn't always a marine," he explained. "I started life as a strike fighter jock in the navy before taking an inter-service transfer to become a TACAIR controller for the marines when they started beefing up their ground forces back when things first started to fall apart with the Alarians. My old CO from *Vancouver* is now the admiral in charge of the program for Special Projects. We've kept in touch over the years, and he knew I was trying to get my own freight operation up and running. It seemed like a good fit."

"So now you fly around in various systems, keeping your eyes peeled for an opportunity to take out a pirate and snag a prize while you pretend to run high-value cargo around, unescorted."

"Oh, no." Micholson shook his head emphatically. "The cargo is real. Actually, we make a hell of a lot more from our legitimate long-haul cargo runs than we do from any pirates or would-be warlords we pop from time to time." He gestured over his shoulder with a thumb. "Those crates my people are securing right now? It's all headed for Isadore. They've finally got their industrial base built back up after the Alarians leveled the place five years ago. We're bringing in a load of refined rare earths and titanium because they don't have their refineries and smelting facilities back up to full production yet.

"So," he said, steepling his fingers on the table, "you can see why my crew and I would be concerned about who's going to foot the bill for all this. Valkyrie is a long trip as it is, but making a detour to Hai'alla first? It'll put us at least ten days beyond our delivery date, and we're going to need refueling once we reach Hai'alla. I'm going to need something that makes it worth our while to potentially lose a high-paying client on Isadore, as well as assurances that we won't be stuck in the Alarian home system because our fuel and propellant tanks are dry."

28

OLD FRIENDS, NEW RIDE

"GOT A MINUTE, CHIEF?"

Kravczyk looked over his shoulder and raised his chin in greeting. "Hey, boss. Yeah, give me a minute to finish up here."

Kravczyk turned back to the workbench and quickly reassembled the bolt carrier for his Mk. 27, then reinserted it into the PDW's upper receiver, replaced the buffer, twin recoil springs, and guide rods, and finally pinned the whole mess back together. After performing a quick function check, he took the stubby little gun over to a wall locker and tucked it away next to the rest of his team's equipment. After closing and locking the storage locker, he leaned back against the workbench and turned his attention fully to Valdez.

"Sorry, boss. You know how much Ben would've chewed my ass if I didn't clean and stow my weapon properly."

Valdez smiled and let out a low chuckle. "I do at that. He's worse than Master Chief Gutierrez," he said, referring to the man who was practically an institution at the Naval Special Warfare Training Center, where normal humans were transformed into the elite of the Terran armed forces.

Kravczyk winced. "I thought we agreed never to invoke he-who-shall-not-be-named. I still have nightmares about getting my ass smoked on the quarterdeck with that hellspawn looming over me and cackling maniacally."

Valdez smiled and shook his head in amusement, his eyes glazing over briefly as a wave of nostalgia hit him. "God, those were the days, weren't they? Nothing to worry about except putting one foot in front of the other and not being the first guy to fall out... We've come a hell of a long way in a relatively short time, eh, Chief?"

"Damn straight," Kravczyk agreed. He looked around conspiratorially, then reached down and opened one of the bottom drawers of the workbench.

"Where in the name of all that's good and holy did you find that?" Valdez exclaimed as the big SEAR pulled a bottle of amber-colored booze from the drawer.

Kravczyk smiled as one of his massive hands cracked the wax seal and pulled the stopper free with a light pop. "I won it off one of the engineers in a game of poker last night." He took a pull straight from the bottle and closed his eyes as the bourbon smoothly slid down his throat. "I'd already cleaned the guy out and was about to break off and hit the rack, but he wanted one more round for a chance to win everything back," he explained, offering the bottle to Valdez. "I almost felt bad about it but figured if the dumb shit hadn't figured out Mabel was feeding me his cards by then, he didn't deserve to keep it."

Valdez froze with the bottle just inches from his lips and shot Kravczyk a disapproving look.

"Hey, it wasn't *my* idea," he said, raising his hands defensively. "I guess the guy was talking shit about her after she helped them tune their engines or something. You know how she gets."

Valdez shook his head as if he'd finally realized that trying to keep his team in line during their downtime was a futile endeavor, and instead of voicing his objections, he put the bottle to his lips and took a large pull.

Kravczyk smirked. He was proud of the boss. Sure, it had taken damn near ten years to get to this point, but he'd finally given in. Valdez might not be ready to join Kravczyk in his shenanigans, but he was loosening up at long last.

"I'm proud of you, boss," Kravczyk said. "You didn't even get that twitch over your right eyebrow this time."

Valdez exhaled through his teeth, then offered the bottle back. "What's the point in holding out any longer?" he said with a defeated sigh. "I'm surrounded by aliens, loose cannons, AIs, smart asses, and a ship full of former jarheads. We're at the point where me trying to keep everyone in line makes *me* look like the crazy one. But I didn't come down here to tell you about how I finally removed the stick from my ass, Chief." The shift in Valdez's expression signaled to Kravczyk that he was finally going to have to have "that talk" with the boss.

"I'm fine, boss—"

Valdez cut off his attempt to nip the uncomfortable topic in the bud. "Don't give me that shit, Damien. I know you're not fine because *I'm* not fine. Going back to Landing was hard enough when it was supposed to be a simple pick-up mission. Having Ben and Zheng nabbed and killed or almost killed by the ISB sure as hell didn't help that, but then running up against Feng?" He trailed off and just stared at Kravczyk.

The big SEAR looked down at the bourbon in his hands for several moments, his thumb absently running over the open mouth of the bottle as he debated whether or not to open the box of unhappy he'd been forcefully ignoring for the last couple of weeks.

"What do you want me to say, boss? Yeah, it was tough going back," he admitted. "Not a week goes by that I don't think about what happened in '49, but we all have baggage that we deal with and we move on. We needed to go back, so we went back—it's as simple as that."

Valdez leveled a look at him that said he didn't believe for a second that was all there was to it. Kravczyk stared back at him for a few heartbeats before finally giving in to his friend. He took another hit from the bottle, then set it down on the workbench with a sigh.

Kravczyk stared at the deck, feeling his broad shoulders slump of their own accord. "I was so fucking scared, sir," he said in a small voice. "When I saw that smug fuck's face as he shoved Ben into that van, I lost my cool… and because of that, the ISB got away with my target *and* my teammate. McCollum knew it. She called me on it, and I damn near popped her one right there in the street." Kravczyk threw his head back and exhaled loudly, remembering the tense moment. "Fuck, I really need to talk to her about that…"

He then returned to the heart of the issue. "I really thought I was over that sack of shit, you know? It's been what, five, six years? A lot of shit's happened since then, and I thought I'd moved on. From what we knew, Feng was kicked out of the Black Dragons in disgrace, and I figured we'd never need to worry about him again. But having him appear unexpectedly like that? It was a fuckin' trip, man."

He locked eyes with Valdez for the first time since opening up. "But what more is there to do? We made it out, Ben's alive and Na'al's people will put him back together again, and now we need to focus on the task at hand. So all this shit goes back in the box for another six years, and hopefully the next time I have to open it up and dump it on the table, I'll have a hell of a lot more than this one bottle at hand." He inclined his head toward the half-empty bottle on the bench next to him.

"Don't beat yourself up, Damien," Valdez said. "I've reviewed the footage a dozen times, and there's no way you would have been able to get to Ben in time. Feng's team was always going to get Zheng and Ben, and second-guessing yourself isn't going to help. Whether you like it or not, you made the right call by holding your fire when the ISB grabbed Zheng and Ben. There were too many civilians around and you were just as likely to hit our guys as theirs."

Kravczyk sighed. "I know, boss—really, I do. But I can't shake this feeling that I should have seen it coming or been a little bit faster or..." He trailed off. "But I wasn't, and because of that, Zheng was killed and Ben's going to have to live the rest of his life with even more terrible shit haunting his memories." Kravczyk glanced down again and studied his hands, flexing his fingers and feeling the joints creak ever so slightly. "Do you ever wonder if we're getting too old, boss? Because I can't shake the feeling that it's time for us to just step aside and let the next round of dumbass kids take over."

Valdez snorted. "Jesus, Chief, I'm still in my thirties and you've got a ways to go before you catch up to me—we aren't *that* old yet."

"I don't know, man," Kravczyk said, shaking his head. "It just seems like it used to be a whole lot easier, you know?"

"That's because it was." Valdez swung an arm around, as if gesturing to the cosmos around them. "I mean, for fuck's sake, it used to be that all we needed to deal with was other humans and the same bad shit we've been doing to each other for millennia. But now? Interstellar wars with aliens, evil AIs hell-bent on our destruction, and being smack in the center of a conflict involving an untold number of races and with potentially galaxy-defining consequences... And that's before we consider Ben, some kid whose genius father turned him into a nigh-immortal, unstoppable force of science and nature.

"No matter which way you slice this shit sandwich, Chief, the old days were objectively easier. But you know what? I wouldn't trade my place in it for anything, and I'm willing to bet my meager pension that you wouldn't either. So," he said, reaching over and grabbing the bottle off the table before taking a pull and offering it to Kravczyk. "Until such a time as we're either dead and buried or too old and creaky for our knees to let us put one foot in front of the other, we're going to keep right on doing this shit and riding herd on all those kids you want to unleash on everyone. Understood?"

Kravczyk grimaced and took the bottle. "You drive a hard bargain, boss. I don't think you fully understand the hell you're committing us to, but at least we'll get to embrace the suck together."

————

"THAT'S IT. I'M OUT," Ben groaned. "I'm going back to my little farm in the middle of nowhere and becoming a hermit."

He didn't know where he was—hadn't even opened his eyes yet, in fact—but Ben could hear Tess speaking softly to someone over the faint buzzing in his ears and the throbbing headache that made the sound seem to fade in and out with each beat of his heart.

"Ben? How are you feeling?"

It was a voice he didn't recognize—male, with a faint, buttery Southern drawl, and somewhat grandfatherly. Grumbling internally, Ben braced himself for the stabbing pain he knew was coming, then cracked his eyes open just enough to see his surroundings.

Yep, the light piercing his eyeballs was just as bad as he thought it would be.

"Like someone's been using the back of my skull for a kettle drum."

"So not too bad, then," said a round-faced man in his early

sixties. "My name is Doc Murphy. You're aboard the ISF *Gambler's Fortune*—a bulk freighter operated by someone your friend Tess here knows. I'll let her fill you in on the details shortly, but the short version is that you're safe, your team is safe, and the *Wraith* is safe, though a little beat up, at the moment."

"Are you referring to me, my team, or the *Wraith*?" Ben said wryly.

Doc Murphy grinned. "I believe the proper answer to that question is yes." He chuckled, then slipped back into his comforting physician tone. "You've been kept in a medically induced coma for the last couple of days while we worked to put you back together and, most importantly, let your brain heal from the trauma it received."

He pulled a penlight from the breast pocket of his lab coat. "Apologies," he said, gently placing one hand on Ben's face and using his thumb to ease his left eyelid open a little more. "This is gonna suck."

He flashed the light in Ben's eye for a brief second, and Ben flinched away from the ice pick being driven into his skull. He groaned but did his best not to move. The old guy repeated the procedure on Ben's other eye a moment later, then, mercifully, took a step back.

"That was one hell of a hard hit you took, Ben," he said. "I know you probably want to jump right up and get back together with your team, but you need to stay here in our sickbay for a while. I'm going to let the lovely miss McCollum here fill you in on the details." He gestured to Tess, who was wearing a baggy set of blue coveralls. "If you need anything, just holler. I'll be nearby, going over some of your test results."

With that, the friendly freighter doc turned and strode away, letting Tess slip in alongside Ben's bed.

"Hey there, handsome," she purred.

A warm smile crossed her lips, and she reached a hand down. He went to move his right hand up to meet hers, sucking in a sharp breath through clenched teeth the instant he tried. Ben glanced down and realized the entirety of his right forearm was wrapped in gauze and medical tape. His brow furrowed in confusion.

"Uh, when did this happen?" he asked, gingerly lifting his right arm to show her and pointing at it with his left, as if she didn't already know. He paused, seeing the thick, splinted wrap on his left hand, along with several pins that were protruding from the tips of his pinky, ring, and middle fingers. He blinked a few times, then looked to Tess. "And this?" he said, exasperated. How the hell had he managed to get so screwed up without any memory of it?

"This," she said, indicating his left hand, "is apparently from when the ISB tortured you. And this"—she pointed at his bandaged right arm—"when that jerk, Feng, buried his karambit in your arm, severing your median nerve and laying open your anterior interosseus artery."

"Look at you and your big, fancy words."

"Shut up." Tess laughed and punched him lightly on the shoulder. "You're the one who's always saying people need to work on their vocabulary."

Ben shrugged. "Touché."

Tess's expression shifted from playful to serious. "Seriously, though, what do you remember? Doc Murphy said you might not recall much of anything from the past week, let alone the last twenty-four hours before we got you back from the ISB."

Ben pursed his lips and shifted slightly, trying to alleviate the soreness in his back and sides that was begging to settle in as his brain continued to come fully back online. He took a moment to think through what had happened. He'd met with their contact outside the cafe next to the park. Then they'd been jumped by a team of Asian-featured men in black tactical clothing. Things went fuzzy after that, but he had some flashes of excruciating pain and being tied up in a small room, somewhere, but he couldn't clearly recall any details beyond that.

"Some guys jumped me and our contact. I remember a brief fight, then coming to in a small room somewhere. One of the guys that nabbed us was there, and I think he worked me over pretty good, but I can't recall any details of what we talked about, if we even did talk." Ben lifted his head off the pillow and finally took in his surroundings—a pretty generic-looking ship's sickbay with a couple of beds, some plain cabinets and a counter along one bulkhead, and a privacy curtain separating the immediate area from whatever lay beyond. "That's pretty much it, until I woke up here."

The longer he strained to keep his head up, the more the throbbing intensified, so he relaxed and laid it back down. "What happened after they grabbed us? I assume you, Valdez, and the chief came in guns blazing?"

"Mabel was able to track the ISB tac team back to their base of operations, and we went in just a few hours after they grabbed you and Agent Zheng. When we got to the building they were holding you in, they'd already shot and killed Zheng. You, on the other hand, were well on your way to escaping, having killed several of the ISB agents by the time the chief reached the area of the building they'd been holding you in. Unfortunately, his arrival distracted you at a critical moment, and the team leader of the ISB squad—who incidentally happens to be the same guy that led the Black Dragon raid against Newman's Rock and squared off against Kravczyk and the boss, back in the day—cracked you in the head with a fire extinguisher before diving out a window to escape."

She took a breath, and her gaze fell. "But the ISB took out our shuttle before we could get you back and dust off. Lieutenant

Evers and the rest of the flight crew didn't make it." She looked up and gestured to the ship around them. "We lucked out, though. I noticed my Uncle Mike was in orbit when I was going through the orbital traffic data, trying to nail down which ship the ISB was operating from." Seeing Ben's raised eyebrow, she clarified, "He's not really my uncle. Mike and my dad were in the marines together, once upon a time. After their service contracts were up, both of them went into the freelance cargo business."

She smiled, and her eyes unfocused briefly as she relived some childhood memories. "Mike always seemed to be there whenever we got into a pinch. Whether it was money troubles, or a client trying to screw us over, Mike would swoop in to save the day or crack some heads—or he'd know somebody who could help."

"He sounds like a great guy," Ben said earnestly. "I can tell he means a lot to you. Why haven't you mentioned him before, Tess? It sounds to me like this guy is practically family."

Tess sighed. "I guess it just never really came up. After the Tiptons... Well, after my family was gone, I joined the navy and never looked back. There hasn't really been much of an opportunity for me to try and track him down.

"But enough about my past. Let's get you up to speed on things before your dad gets down here and starts worrying over you again. A lot's happened in the last forty-eight hours."

Tess spun around and glided her butt up onto the foot of Ben's bed. The fact that he noticed her shapely backside still looked good, even in those baggy coveralls, gave him hope for a quick recovery. A moment later, he realized she was smiling coyly at him, and he made an effort to wipe the stupid grin off his face.

He cleared his throat. "Ahem. Sorry. I'm paying attention now. I swear."

"Uh-huh."

"Hey!" he said indignantly. "You should be glad that I still think you're attractive. After everything I've been through over the last few months—you, know, being vaporized, rebuilt by aliens, and all that—there was a serious possibility that I could've thought you were ugly all of a sudden."

Tess snorted. "Puh-leeze. *Nobody* thinks I'm ugly, Ben. At least not if they're human."

"Then I guess we should be thankful that proves I'm still human."

"About that," Doc Murphy said, slipping past the privacy curtain with a datapad in one hand and his face screwed up in confusion. "Is there anything you need to tell me before I continue to treat you with the medications I have available on this ship?"

Tess and Ben exchanged a quizzical look. Then Ben turned his attention back to Doc Murphy. "Like what?" he said, dragging the words out in suspicion.

"Like that fact that I just sequenced your DNA profile to make sure there weren't any adverse drug interactions I needed to worry about, and my computer is telling me the sample doesn't match the baseline for *Homo sapiens*. Which is odd, considering the fact that, other than weighing a solid twenty or thirty kilos more than you look like you should, you bleed red and have all the parts a human should have, right where you should have them.

"So," the doc said, tossing his tablet on the counter along the bulkhead and crossing his arms, "how about you quit playing dumb and fill me in here. I don't care what kind of bizarre military experiment created you, and I'm not here to pass judgment. But if I'm to continue treating you, I *have* to know what I'm working with so I can be on the lookout for potential complications."

Once again, Ben and Tess shared a befuddled look. "No bull-shit, Doc," Ben said with a grunt, using his one good elbow to lever himself into a sitting position. "I swear I have no idea what you're talking about."

"Me neither." Tess shook her head. "Ben has a bit of an irregular history with regard to how he came to be here," she said slowly, doing her best to tiptoe around the fact that the body Ben currently sported had been grown by aliens, "but I've seen confirmation with my own eyes that he really is Ben Hutchins, human male."

"You see," Doc Murphy said, his voice going up an octave as he screwed up his face and raised a finger like a professor about to lecture a student on why their excuse for missing an exam didn't pass the sniff test. "The fact that you needed to actually check his status as a human raises some red flags here." He let out a sarcastic chuckle. "Because—and it's the damndest thing—the alleles that code for his musculoskeletal structure are the strangest things I've ever seen. And before you start questioning the expertise of some hick doctor that spends his days reading old sci-fi novels while his freighter plods between the stars, you should know that I spent thirty years working as one of the preeminent geneticists for a biotech firm specializing in gene therapies for the Confed military.

"In other words," he continued, putting his hands on his hips and narrowing his eyes at them both, "this ain't my first rodeo, missy. Some of the shit I just saw in his DNA looks *suspiciously* like some things my lab worked on with mouse models a few years back, though we never had any success when we tried to move up to human subjects. Now, I've already spoken with your father about this, Ben, and he swore up and down that you just recently had a routine workup and your DNA matched the profile on record from before you started working with the

SEARs. And you know what? He was pretty damn convincing. But my machines don't lie."

Ben blinked a few times, trying to process everything he'd just heard. "So," he said slowly, thinking about which of the hundred questions racing through his mind should be asked first. "What are you trying to tell me, exactly?"

"Son," Doc Murphy said, "I don't know what you've been told, but you sure as shit aren't fully human."

29

DEADLINE

"I RECEIVED A CURIOUS PIECE OF INFORMATION FROM ONE OF MY minders."

President Cunningham whirled around in the dim light of his office, and the freshly topped-off glass of bourbon in his hand clattered back to the beverage tray in a spray of high-dollar alcohol. He clutched his arms to his chest out of a protective reflex at the sudden intrusion.

It stared back at him through crimson eyes.

"Admiral Ogden made an unscheduled visit to the residence of Admiral Garland, and the two men spent a considerable amount of time together. They went to great lengths to ensure they could not be overheard by any system my monitoring programs had access to. However, less than eight hours later, Ogden was on a direct flight to the Kerner system and Archimedes Base."

The Master's avatar seemed to swell in size as it approached Cunningham's desk. Its ethereal hands planted themselves on the polished wood top, and the mass of shadow leaned over, looming above the President of the Confederated Terran Systems like a malevolent tidal wave about to come crashing down on him. A low, monstrous growl emanated from behind the veil of darkness, and those crimson eyes flared.

Cunningham went rigid, utterly petrified at the embodiment of evil bearing down on him. His hands and jaw trembled, but he focused his will and attempted to conceal his fear.

"What are you and your minions up to, *Mr. President*?" the Master snarled, punctuating each of the last two words with enough vehemence to ensure even the dullest of people couldn't miss the inherent threat.

Cunningham held his hands out defensively. "I... It's not what you think!" he stammered. "I sent Russ to approach Garland as if he was having second thoughts and looking for a way out." He sprinkled just enough truth into the lie that it would hopefully be convincing. "We weren't able to determine how Garland and his allies were communicating with *Indomitable*, so I wanted to try a different tack... and it worked. Russ went to Archimedes to personally ensure that the leak is sealed for good. Please, we're just doing what you asked!"

The Master's eyes slowly decreased in intensity, and the shadowy avatar flowed back, sliding off the desk and resuming its usual place a few paces away.

"Good. Very good. You've done well, Jasper," it purred, speaking to Cunningham as though he were a small child. "Once the leak is eliminated, it's time to arrange an end for the dear Admiral Garland. He's proven more resourceful than expected and has become too great a risk. I could do it, but I think it's about time you got your hands dirty. Consider this task payment for your incompetence at keeping him in check, and let it serve as a warning to those that have been aiding him."

Cunningham felt the pit of his stomach fall away. He couldn't have Garland killed—not in the middle of a messy political battle taking place in the senate between Cynthia and her allies and Garland and his. It would raise so many red flags that

Cunningham and his administration would spend the next year or more just fending off the sea of suspicious politicians, investigative reporters, and other nuisances in an attempt to conceal the truth. But maybe that was exactly what the Master wanted: to keep the Confed government bogged down in a messy scandal and at each other's throats while it worked to consolidate its forces and prepare for the coup de gras.

"I can't just kill one of my most outspoken critics!" Cunningham exclaimed, incredulous. "There's already a media feeding frenzy going on with this whole impeachment business in the senate. If we kill Garland, there's no way we'll be able to strong-arm the opposition into line."

"You should have thought of that before you failed to contain him. You have two weeks. I don't need to tell you what will happen if you fail."

"But—"

The Master's avatar winked out, leaving the president of the Confed alone in his office.

Two weeks? How quickly could Ramsey and Hutchins mobilize and move on the transceiver on Isadore? Cunningham's daily intelligence briefing had included a note about a brief shootout between two or three ships over Newman's Rock ten days ago, ending with the destruction of a bulk freighter. He'd assumed it had something to do with Garland's forces moving to acquire the intel that had sparked this whole clusterfuck, but the ship in question had been so thoroughly obliterated that Newman's Rock planetary defense hadn't been able to recover anything before the debris burned up in the atmosphere.

Cunningham had tasked Director Wheaton and CID with getting better intel on the incident, but it would be weeks before their teams were able to make it out there, gather the information, and return. That was too long; he needed a better idea as to the disposition of Garland's forces, and he needed it right now.

But with Russ all the way out at Kerner, nobody currently over Newman's Rock, and no way for him to communicate directly with either Garland or his people over Hai'alla, all the president of the Confed could do was sit and wait.

He was paralyzed with fear, and his lack of a complete picture of the situation meant he couldn't take any action without there being a significant chance that it was the wrong one. Did he put all his chips on Garland and his people, hoping they could take out the transceiver within the next couple of weeks? Or did he need to get moving on a plan to murder the admiral? Would the Master be angry if he dragged his feet and didn't have Garland killed before the deadline but was, at least by all appearances, working diligently to make it happen? Probably. Would he be allowed to live if he missed the deadline?

He shuddered. The memory of Felicia Keller's bloody eyes and tongue resting on a velvet pillow inside an ornate wooden box flashed through his mind. He was going to have to play both sides of this, right up until the moment of truth.

Cunningham sat down shakily in his desk chair and stared around the presidential office. He knew what the right thing to do was. He also knew he was, deep down, a coward, and he knew he'd do whatever it took for him to keep breathing a little longer. Whether that was continuing to support Garland as best he could or murdering the man in cold blood, Jasper Cunningham would ultimately do whatever would benefit *himself* the most.

And he loathed himself for it.

30

MOSTLY HUMAN

BEN SAT ON A POLISHED ONYX SLAB IN THE MIDDLE OF A MEDICAL bay aboard the rebellion warship *X'nec*. The alien docs had more or less taken care of his injuries, though he still had a few treatments left before he'd be back up to full strength. In the meantime, however, he was taking in his dad's truly epic tirade.

To say that his old man had been *upset* to discover that, apparently, Eelix and his team had taken some liberties with Ben's genetics was the understatement of the century. After Doc Murphy sat them all down and presented his findings on Ben's unusual DNA profile, Ben underwent the most grueling, painful, and torturous series of medical examinations any human—or mostly human, in his case—had ever been forced to endure in the entire history of the species.

The results had been... interesting, to say the least.

A muscle biopsy confirmed Doc Murphy's assertion that the alleles coding for Ben's musculature had indeed been altered, producing muscle tissue that was unlike anything any of them had ever seen before. The basic layout was all the same, but the real magic lay in the way the individual muscle fibers were constructed.

Typical human muscle had long bundles of muscle fibers that ran the length of the muscle, and those muscles were then attached to bones via tendons that transferred the force of the contracting muscle to the bone, resulting in movement. Ben's muscles still functioned in the same way, but the fibers of his muscles were braided or woven together rather than running in parallel. Doc Murphy had gone on a rapid-fire rant about myosin heads, adenosine triphosphate activation, actin, mitochondrial density, and a bunch of other stuff that went way over Ben's head, but the end result came down to a simple principle of physics: mechanical advantage.

Essentially, because Ben's muscle fibers were woven together in a helical pattern instead of running in a straight line, they were significantly longer than they should have been. The end result was muscle fibers that did more work over the same distance, which was a fancy way of saying he was freakishly strong now. It also explained why he could do things like pick up an ISB operative and swing him around like he weighed no more than a three-year-old, as the guys who'd abducted him had found out.

But the thing that Doc Murphy was really geeked about—and also confirmed his suspicion that Ben's DNA had been altered on purpose—was that the mutation only applied to striated muscle, not Ben's cardiac muscle tissue or the smooth muscle of his digestive tract. Apparently, a lot of thought had gone into the tweaks Ben's genome had received, and it hadn't taken his dad long to figure out who was most likely responsible for the illicit gene modifications.

"You motherfucker!" Henry roared. "You swore up and down that you and your team wouldn't do something like this to my son! You looked me in the eye and promised me that the man you brought back from the dead would be my son, exactly the way he had been—not some mutant that you and your people tinkered with for shits and giggles!"

Ben thought the Th'aloori scientist was doing a rather impressive job of trying to melt into the deck under his dad's onslaught, and he felt just the tiniest bit of sympathy for the devious little alien. Still, he had to admire Eelix's dedication to standing his ground and not fleeing the room. Then again, with a seriously pissed-off Admiral Na'al barring the exit, it wasn't like he'd be able to make it very far.

"B-But I did!" Eelix squeaked out. "I swear! We didn't alter his genetic information in the slightest! Check our files! You'll see that his DNA matches the record we received from your AI exactly!"

Everything clicked at once, and the lightbulb in Ben's head suddenly lit up like Time's Square on New Year's Eve.

Mabel.

"Don't lie to me," his dad fumed. "I know what—"

"Dad." Ben hopped off the strange alien exam table and stepped forward to put a hand on his dad's shoulder. "As much as it pains me to say this, I believe him."

His dad turned to stare at him, his face a mask of incredulity.

"Think about it," Ben continued. "Mabel was the one you had running point to coordinate the sharing of data regarding the effort to bring me back, right?"

His dad narrowed his eyes but nodded. "Yes," he said slowly, "but that doesn't explain—"

Ben cut him off. "Sure it does. You had the docs aboard *Indomitable* check to make sure all my metrics matched up with what they had on record from before Hai'alla, right? Including my DNA profile?" When his dad simply stared back at him, Ben continued. "And everything matched. I know, because I was wide awake while they were busy poking, prodding, and cutting bits of me off to run tests on for that first week I was back aboard, and they told me as much.

"So let me ask you this: who do we know that could swap out my DNA profile on record without anyone noticing and cover their tracks well enough that nothing would flag later on?"

"She wouldn't…" his dad replied. "I know it's easy to forget, but Mabel *is* just an AI, Ben. She's not programmed to pull that kind of stunt. There are hard-coded safeties in her matrix that prevent her from doing something that she knows will endanger her host, unless you are aware of the danger and agree to it. It goes against the very core of her programming."

Ben smiled sadly. "Dad," he said softly, "you and mom may have created Mabel's matrix and core programming, but I'm the one who's been teaching her how to be human. And I think we can all agree that I tend to find ways to bend the rules now and then."

"Oh…" his dad muttered, and his expression rapidly shifted from one of skepticism to one of horror. "Shit."

————

"Yes, I did."

Henry's mouth opened and closed a few times as he searched in vain for some coherent thought to express the combination of shock, disbelief, anger, and sense of betrayal that hit him all at once when Mabel said those three words.

"I'm sorry that I went behind your back, Henry," she went on before he could ramp himself up and unload on her for her reckless, possibly dangerous actions. "I saw an opportunity to make Ben stronger, and I knew that if Admiral Na'al's people were successful, Ben would be thrown into harm's way sooner rather than later. I couldn't stand the thought of losing him again, so I did everything I could think of to ensure he has every possible advantage."

Henry froze. Something in her tone resonated with him, and he realized that, for perhaps the first time, he suddenly saw her as more than just a collection of fancy hardware and strings of code. There was genuine emotion inside of her, and it was an emotion that he shared: the fear of losing Ben yet again.

"Dr. Vor told me you assisted his team with the redesign of Ben's implant," he said, settling heavily onto the sofa in his state-room aboard *Indomitable*. "Can I assume that was because you saw it as a way to give Ben an edge? Are there any other changes you and that alien mad scientist made to my son without telling anyone?"

Ben was still a guest aboard *X'nec*, undergoing some kind of regeneration therapy to finish mending his fractured skull and assortment of other broken bones. Doc Murphy aboard the *Gambler's Fortune* was one hell of a physician, but there was only so much modern Terran medicine could do for someone with the kinds of injuries Ben had suffered on Newman's Rock. So he was going to spend the next day or two aboard the rebel flagship, getting put back together—*again*.

"There's a file available in your dropbox detailing all the modifications Ben and his hardware received," Mabel said quietly. "Henry... I'm sorry. I really just wanted to help."

Henry sighed heavily and buried his face in his palms for a moment, feeling completely exhausted. The last few weeks had been an emotional rollercoaster. He'd gotten Ben back, only to ship him out the door and right into a gunfight. Then there'd been a space battle with the ISB, meeting a freighter captain that also happened to do contract work for the Confed and other high-powered entities on the side, and finally discovering that his son had been brought back from the dead only *mostly* human.

"Mabel," Henry said wearily, looking up to face her avatar, which was hovering in the middle of his quarters. "I understand why you did what you did—more than anyone else, I'd wager. But you simply cannot keep these kinds of secrets if you ever expect anyone to trust you. I know my son, and I know you've evolved your programming based on your intimate interactions with Ben, so I can't say that I'm all that surprised by your actions. But it stops now. We need to be able to rely on you if we're to have any chance in this fucked up galaxy. Do you understand?"

"I believe so, Henry."

He nodded. "Good, good. And for the record, I don't really blame you. I just wish you would've trusted me enough to bring me in on what you were planning. What you did was extremely dangerous, Mabel. You say you can't stand the thought of losing Ben again, but what if he suffers as a result of the changes you and Eelix's team made to him? Did you consider that?"

Her cube rippled in what Henry had come to recognize as a sign that she was irritated, but it quickly settled back down. "While you may not believe it, yes, I considered that," she said gently. "Perhaps this is simply my hubris talking, but as an AI, I can model and anticipate the interactions of far more variables than a human mind ever could. I have access to enormous data-banks filled with detailed information on every imaginable topic, and Eelix gave me nearly unfettered access to their own data libraries as well. Please believe me when I say that I spent more time analyzing what we did to Ben than you could in several lifetimes. And there were many other modifications that we ruled out simply because they posed even a modest risk to Ben."

"That doesn't really make me feel any better."

A long silence rang through the room. Then Mabel spoke again. "Henry? I have a question, but I'm afraid of what asking it might mean."

"What's that, Mabel?" Henry said, his curiosity piqued.

"Have you reviewed the recordings of what Chief Kravczyk and I discovered when we found Ben at the ISB's base of operations?"

"I have. Several times, in fact," he confirmed, suddenly afraid of what direction she was going with her question.

"Chief Kravczyk and I had a private conversation during the trip back here aboard the *Gambler's Fortune*, and we both agree that something about Ben felt... *different* during that encounter. The chief was quick to write it off as being related to the shock and stress of everything Ben was forced to endure during his time as a captive, but I'm not so sure I agree with his assessment.

"I've spent more time with Ben under extreme stress than anybody—even been inside his head during some of those events—and I've never seen him display the level of detached malice that I witnessed back at that abandoned factory. The evidence we saw tells a horrific story, and the manner in which those ISB agents were killed wasn't what I would have expected from Ben—especially the one Ben identified as his torturer.

"When backed into a corner, Ben is no stranger to extreme violence, but the kind of violence he employs during those times is something primal and animalistic. It's also done out of a sense of desperation—and, occasionally, righteousness. He is not—nor, I believe, is he capable of being—a ruthless killer. But what I saw in that interrogation room told me the violence he tapped into was more.... Perhaps *sadistic* is the word I'm looking for here. And that scares me."

"Can you elaborate?" Henry asked.

"It's just..." Mabel began, then trailed off. "I don't know, Henry. Maybe I'm just second-guessing everything we've done to him. But then I remember the brutal way in which Ben killed a hardened member of an ISB tactical team—by driving his thumbs through the man's eye sockets while pinning him to a wall—and I can't help but wonder if what Eelix said about Ben having two different waveforms in his head now has something to do with it."

Henry rocked back on the couch. Mabel had just dumped a truly terrifying thought on him—one he hadn't considered before. He'd assumed the dueling neural patterns keeping Ben from being able to use an APEX or link with Mabel was merely a side effect of the jury-rigged system they'd used to take a snapshot of Ben's engram, but what if that wasn't the case?

"So you're suspicious that, what, he might be schizophrenic? That there are two different Bens in there, somewhere?"

"I think we need to consider the possibility, Henry," she said. "Because most of the time, Ben is the same old goofy, lovable man we all know and care about. But what the chief and I saw in his eyes back there in Landing City wasn't Ben. It was a monster."

Goosebumps crawled across Henry's skin, and he sat in silence for a long moment, chewing on that thought. Was it possible that the traumas Ben had endured over the last few years had finally created a split in his psyche? It wasn't the craziest idea he'd ever heard. Hell, most people were still dealing with the psychological trauma of the Alarian War, let alone being the first molecule on the pointy end of the spear in a war against a new, terrifying enemy hellbent on exterminating anyone who might pose a threat to them.

"Mabel, send a note to Eelix, please, and ask him to recheck Ben's neural waveforms. I'd like to know if that dual pattern is still there, but don't tell him about your hypothesis just yet. I don't want to bias him toward that explanation."

"Understood," she said. "And Henry?"

"Mabel?"

"Do you think we should have just let Ben rest in peace? I...

I'm having a hard time deciding if what we did was really the best choice."

Henry's guts twisted into knots like he'd been physically kicked in the stomach. The same question had been gnawing at the back of his mind for months, ever since they'd embarked on their quest to bring Ben back; he'd just been doggedly ignoring it.

He stood up and headed toward the small head in the corner of the room. "Honestly, Mabel, I don't know." He opened the tap on the sink and splashed cool water over his face, then dabbed the moisture away with a towel before exiting the head and grabbing his datapad off the desk. "But it's too late to put that genie back in its bottle, so let's just focus on helping him through whatever it is he's dealing with right now, okay? Let's wait to hear from Eelix, and we'll go from there."

He turned and headed for the hatch. "But right now, I've got a meeting to go over where the agent could have hidden a damn slipspace transceiver at *my* company headquarters, then try to figure out how we're going to blow it up without killing a city full of people."

Commander Evans had contacted him again via his personal quantum link about a day before ISF *Gambler's Fortune* arrived over Hai'alla. Henry had kept the communication quiet, considering he knew next to nothing about Captain Micholson or his crew. Once back aboard *Indomitable*, however, Henry went straight to Captain Ramsey. The information Matt had passed along caused quite a stir considering the fact that it gave them a shot at finally kicking the Imperium out of local Terran and Alarian space once and for all.

The last remaining slipspace transceiver was on Isadore, and they were planning to take it out—and soon.

"You can't run from this forever, Henry," Mabel called after him.

Henry stopped in the hatchway and turned to look at her over his shoulder. "I know... but that doesn't mean I'm not going to try."

With that, he exited the compartment and headed toward *Indomitable*'s command briefing room.

31

THE THIRD DREAM

BEN STOOD UNMOVING ATOP A HILL OVERLOOKING THE SHATTERED city in the distance. Smoke rose toward the heavens, pouring from thousands of shattered windows and gaping blast holes as the Alarian capital burned. The Kendrathi Hegemony had been merciless, slaughtering the populace of this world with brutal efficiency. After the Hegemony fell upon the planet with a fleet more than five times the strength of the Alarians' own, the outcome of the battle was all but certain... at least until the Hegemony fleet began experiencing crippling systems malfunctions that left many of their warships vulnerable.

The space battle had raged on for several days, ultimately leaving both fleets decimated. The Hegemony claimed the skies in the end, but their mighty war fleet was shattered. The civilians on the planet cowered in their homes as the heavens burned above them, their once-proud fleet now nothing more than fiery streaks in the sky as the wreckage plunged to the ground. But they, too, would soon be nothing but ash after the Hegemony ground forces were finished with them.

The battle for Alaris Prime was destined to be won by the Hegemony—Ben had spent many decades ensuring that. In the end, the victorious Hegemony marines and their few remaining warships would leave the system and return home, to be hailed as saviors of the Kendrathi Hegemony. It was too bad they would limp their way home, only to discover their own planet had been razed to the ground by hellfire from an Imperial armada while they were away—right before the Imperium turned their ships to ash.

Ben stood there, flanked by a team of Imperial shock troops. The Hegemony marines were busy scouring the last vestiges of armed resistance from the planet, but Ben and his team weren't here to participate in the conflict between two lesser species. His mission was almost complete, but there was one annoying loose end that had managed to escape his notice until it was almost too late to contain it.

"Do we have their location?" Ben asked the commando team's leader without turning away from the glorious sight in the distance.

"We do, Master," the brawny Th'aloki soldier replied, his voice sounding tinny and compressed through his fully enclosed powered battle armor. "The last of them are preparing to depart from a large agricultural facility approximately ninety kilometers to the southwest. A fleet awaits nearby, in interstellar space. We were able to extract the exact location from the one you captured."

"Good." Ben turned to the commando leader. "Kill him—he's of no use to us now—and then prepare to depart. It is imperative that I reach that facility before the last of the Alarians depart."

"Your command," he said.

Before the commando could turn to walk away, his face morphed from that of a Th'aloki into one of a blue-skinned alien. Ben took a step back in surprise at the jarring shift. There was something familiar about the newcomer, but he couldn't quite place it. A name tickled at the back of his mind, but try as he might, Ben couldn't quite tease it out into the open.

Realizing Ben had noticed his sudden appearance, the blue alien opened its mouth and began shouting, but no sounds came out. Ben thought the strange being was trying to say something like, "Fight it! Don't give in!" but the ferocity with which he was attempting to communicate with him made it difficult to tell.

Then, as quickly as the commando had morphed into the stranger, he was back to his serious, professional self.

Ben shook his head and blinked, but the face of the commando remained unchanged. Perhaps it was just a sign of stress or being overworked, he thought. He would take some time to run diagnostics and examine the coding that governed his visual processing systems later, just to make sure nothing was amiss.

Ben turned back to the rapidly unfolding devastation in the distance. He didn't know the final destination of the refugee fleet the Alarians had formed in secret once it became clear that their war with the Hegemony was rapidly coming to a disastrous end, but he intended to find out. And when, at last, he uncovered the location of the last surviving Alarians, he would find a way to contact the Master and finish what he'd started. Even if it took decades longer, Ben would ensure that not a single free Alarian remained in the galaxy, because that was his mission. The Master commanded it, and he would see that order through to the end, or he would die trying.

32

TRAITOR

BEN JOLTED AWAKE, ADRENALINE FLOODING HIS BODY AS HE CAME to, already on high alert. A shrill, ear-piercing siren was blaring throughout his guest quarters, accompanied by strobing amber lights.

"Lights up!" he shouted over the din, commanding the room's AI to activate the overhead lighting.

Ben threw off the airy alien sheet and rolled out of the large bed and onto his feet. He ignored the clothes sitting on the small table next to the bed and instead went straight to pulling on his boots. If this was the kind of ship-wide emergency that required him to either fight or run to an escape pod, the lightweight ship's utilities sitting on the table weren't going to aid him much, but having a good pair of boots on your feet could make all the difference in the world.

The air around him seemed to charge with static electricity as the deck plates of the huge Imperial battlecruiser began vibrating beneath his feet. Something had happened that had Na'al getting his ship ready for action. After having spent nearly two weeks aboard *X'nec* since he'd been brought back from the dead, Ben had picked up on all kinds of interesting tidbits about the alien warship. One of those nuggets of information was that the electric charge in the air was a result of the ship's defensive systems coming online.

He hurried over to the hatch leading out of his quarters, knowing a pair of rebel marines were guarding his room. He tapped the door control and jumped back when the hatch whisked open silently.

"Shit!" he yelled, lunging sideways to get away from the hatchway and the pair of bloody alien bodies that lay crumpled in front of it. Ben pressed himself up against the bulkhead, ears straining to pick up any sign of the enemy that had killed his guards, but all he could hear was the blaring siren.

He inched his way along the bulkhead until he was just adjacent to the hatchway. Ben peered around the edge, slowly widening his field of view down the passageway outside, but all he saw was two bodies and empty space.

What the hell was going on? Was there a mutiny underway? Or did the Master have loyalist forces of its own spread throughout the rebel fleet and they were coming after him?

Ben's mind swam with a hundred different possible scenarios to explain the dead guards outside his room, but one thing was for damn sure: he needed a weapon.

Ben crouched next to the hatch and reached out, grabbing the casualty handle of the nearest guard's armor and dragging the Th'aloori marine into the compartment with him. He paused when his eyes caught sight of something attached to the panel that controlled access to his room. A small black box was stuck to the panel. Ben recognized it instantly—Jim had found the same thing back at the CDF outpost when the two men had ambushed a team of Imperial shock troops. The devices were some sort of universal electronic lockpick. *Someone tried to break into my quarters and kill me.* The realization sent a chill down Ben's spine.

The smaller alien was wearing an open-faced helmet, and

sticky dark blood ran from his mouth and nose. Ben quickly examined the dead marine, noting he appeared to have been caught by surprise, considering there were no defensive wounds and his plasma carbine was still snugly slung across his chest. The alien's head flopped loosely around on his neck, giving Ben a pretty good idea as to how the poor bastard had died. But why would these guys have allowed an enemy to get within arm's reach without reacting?

There was only one option. They had a traitor aboard X'nec—one that was familiar to these marines.

The revelation forced Ben to quickly reevaluate the situation. He freed the marine's plasma carbine and checked the weapon over. One of Mabel and Eelix's "upgrades" to Ben's implant must have included familiarization with Imperial small arms, because despite the weapon being designed for an alien physiology that included two thumbs per hand, the carbine slipped comfortably into his grasp—almost like he'd used one on many occasions in the past.

A wave of incoherent memory fragments crashed through his brain. Alien hands gripping a similar weapon. The chaos of combat raging all around him. The screams of the wounded, thunderclaps of ordnance landing nearby, and the banshee-like shriek of low-flying attack aircraft screaming through the air overhead. Then a face flashed before his mind's eye, the purple hue of the man's skin seeming oddly familiar. A name drifted up: Zel. Flames filled his vision, and the heat of the inferno washed over him.

Ben shook his head, frantically trying to clear the disorienting effects of the strange memory fragments. He cried out and fell back against the bulkhead as lightning danced through his skull. Then, as quickly as the bizarre wave of strange images and memories had come, they were gone, leaving behind an odd but intense feeling of betrayal. Ben's chest heaved with exertion, and sweat ran down his face and arms in rivulets, dripping to the deck and pooling beneath him.

"Benjamin Hutchins!" a harsh voice called out. "Are you present?"

A jolt of surprise and fear helped clear and focus his mind. He snapped back to the present, and he brought the carbine to bear on the hatchway. That voice had an edge of command to it and likely came from one of Na'al's other marines, sent to check on him. But what if it wasn't? What if this was another of the traitors that'd killed his guards?

That was when he realized the alarm had been silenced.

Ben quickly ran through several scenarios in his head, ultimately realizing that he needed to respond. If he said nothing, whoever was out in the passage would probably enter the compartment to clear it, and they would find themselves staring down the business end of a plasma carbine without warning. That was a situation that would only lead to a bloodbath, unless the guy coming through the door had an incredible amount of trigger discipline. But if Ben called out, giving away his position, and the alien in the hallway was actually hostile...

"I'm here," Ben said, his grip tightening on the carbine as he peered through the alien holographic sight atop the weapon.

"Imperial Marines," the guy in the hallway responded. "Admiral Na'al sent us to check on you."

A hand, fingers splayed out to show there was nothing in it, slowly came into view from around the corner, followed shortly by the rest of the armored marine it was attached to. His carbine was held at low-ready in his right hand. He looked at Ben, his eyes widening as he caught sight of the charged plasma carbine aimed directly at his chest from less than two meters away.

Ben and the marine stared at each other for a long moment, neither making a sound. Finally, after what felt like the better part of an hour but what was probably only a few seconds, Ben lowered the muzzle of his weapon to the deck and sagged back against the bulkhead.

"What happened here?" the marine demanded.

Ben could hear the rustling of more marines out in the passageway as they secured the area. He gestured at the dead alien on the floor next to him and looked up at the newcomer. "I awoke when the alarm went off and opened the hatch to ask my guards what was going on, but I found they'd both been killed by something shortly before. Their wounds weren't fresh, but they were recent enough that the blood hadn't congealed yet. I didn't see anybody out in the passageway, so I grabbed a weapon and hunkered down," Ben said, not mentioning his brief episode of chaotic memory flashes. "What the hell is going on?"

The marine relaxed his posture when he saw Ben lower his weapon. "Someone hacked our systems to briefly disable the slipspace suppression field, then transmitted a message back to Imperial Central Command. Several other members of the crew were similarly murdered by the traitor, and when we tried to contact your guard detail, there was no response. The admiral feared you might be a target for the enemy, given your importance in our fight against the Master and its agents." He paused, glancing down to take in the two dead marines, then up at the black box stuck to the hatch control out in the passageway. "It would seem he was correct."

33

LOSING THE BIG STICK

HENRY FELT A MIGRAINE COMING ON, AND NOT JUST FROM THE enormous amount of information he'd absorbed over the past two hours. The cram session Ramsey put the members of the briefing through had included everything from a complete rundown on the information they'd received from Admiral Garland via Matt Evans at Archimedes to the truly horrifying revelation that the Sino-Russian Federation was readying for all-out war with the Confed. Henry had known all about the agent's last slipspace transceiver being buried beneath ExoDyn HQ on Isadore, as well as the fact that the Master itself was using the facility to communicate directly with that traitorous piece of shit Jasper Cunningham and his administration. But it was the full briefing on the information that the SEARs and Ben had just retrieved from Newman's Rock that was the true punch to the nuts.

That the Feds were working with the Imperium wasn't the craziest thing Henry had ever heard. Hell, the very tippy-top of the Confed was doing the same thing now. That the Federation was planning to launch a multifront campaign against several of the Confed's core worlds, however, left everyone in the room speechless. The explosive nature of the revelation helped relieve some of the guilt Henry was harboring about allowing Ben to be thrown right back into the fire practically the minute he'd come back from the dead. He quickly realized just how critical it was that the team had been able to secure Agent Volkov—and also that his son had been instrumental in pulling it off.

Unfortunately, one of the Federation's first targets was supposed to be Isadore, and that was something that couldn't be allowed to happen—not with the last known slipspace transceiver sitting there, ripe for the taking. But maybe that was the Federation's goal for striking that system first? Either way, the window for striking the facility was rapidly closing, and this new information made it all the more imperative that Ramsey and his little force make their move as soon as possible.

If they could take the facility and cut off the Master's access to Terran space, there was a good shot they'd be able to rally their support back on Elizabeth and expose the Cunningham administration and their allies for the traitors they were—or at least leverage their position to get the Confed to mobilize again. If cutting the Master's influence out from local space wasn't enough to get things moving in the right direction again, then news of an impending invasion by the SRF sure as hell would be.

After all the background had been explained, the military minds in the room had gone about the task of hashing out the details of the operation to take the transceiver, and that was when Henry had been forced to put his foot down.

"We need Ben, Henry," Major Davis said, not backing down from his stance on the matter, despite the strong objections of both Henry and *Indomitable*'s chief medical officer, Dr. Maynard. "I know you don't like the idea of sending him out again so soon after his ordeal on Newman's Rock, but he and Mabel, together, give us the best chance to pull this off with minimal casualties."

"No," Henry said firmly, shaking his head. "Ben is not nego-tiable—you'll just have to manage without him."

"As much as I'd like to agree with you and make sure Ben gets the time he needs to recover, Henry," Commander Valdez said gently, "I'm forced to agree with Major Davis. I don't doubt that Mabel would be able to nail down the exact location of the transceiver once we're onsite, but if our objective is to capture the site—not just destroy or disable it—then we'll need the capa-bility that Ben brings to the table when he links with Mabel."

Henry threw up his hands in frustration. "I already told you, Ben hasn't been able to link with Mabel ever since he came back! All he would be for you is an extra gun—"

"That was before Na'al's people sent over their most recent analysis," Valdez said, shifting in his chair to face Henry more directly and leaning toward him. "Look, I understand how hard it must be for you to agree to send Ben out with us again. Believe me when I say I'd rather he hung back, too. But everything we just got from Admiral Na'al's team indicates that Ben's dueling brainwaves issue has been resolved, and he's good to go.

"This mission isn't going to be like everything we've done in the past. There are no Imperial fleets to contend with, no shock troops or agents to face off against—just a company-sized contingent of guns-for-hire. That comes direct from the CID guys on the ground, according to what we received from Admiral Garland. We let the marines go in and do the heavy lifting, and only then will Ben be brought onsite to do his thing with Mabel."

"It's not going to be that simple, Ramiro," Henry said, worrying at his scalp. "It never is. What if these mercs have orbital support or there's more of them than the CID say there is? What if the Planetary Defense Corps decide they don't like a bunch of new arrivals landing at what's left of ExoDyn head-quarters and starting a firefight? This whole operation could go off the rails in a hundred different ways, and we don't know that Ben and Mabel will even be able to link like they did in the past.

"We can't just take the word of an alien that slapped my son back together with spare parts he found lying around in the garage and added a host of unapproved 'upgrades' without telling anyone, then assume Ben is good as new. If—and I stress the word *if*—Ben really is able to integrate with an APEX again, it will take weeks to properly work up to a link attempt between him and Mabel. I'm not signing off on him trying to do something like that in a damned combat scenario for the first time after being brought back from the dead, so stop asking."

"Let's table the Ben issue for now," Captain Ramsey said, cutting into the conversation in an attempt to get things back on track. "It's a bit of a moot point, regardless, considering the fact that Ben will be aboard *Indomitable*, and *Indomitable* will be providing orbital support for the ground team—so if he's truly needed, he'll already be in-theater."

Henry slumped back in his chair, simultaneously glad that he didn't need to slug it out with Davis and Valdez over the issue anymore and also annoyed as he began to realize that, in the end, he actually had very little control over the situation. He could piss and moan all he wanted, but if the mission ended up hinging on Ben being present at the site, then that was right where Ben would end up, regardless of Henry's objections.

Ramsey turned to face the large wall display, where Admiral Na'al was patiently waiting for the argument about Ben's participation to conclude. "Admiral, you said you're willing to lend us two of your ships for this operation?"

Na'al nodded in a very human-like manner. "Yes. Ensuring the Master can no longer monitor this region of space is critical. To guarantee a successful outcome, I will provide two destroyer-class warships to accompany you. They will be more than capable of dealing with any threat you encounter in space."

"Your contribution to the operation is greatly appreciated, sir," Ramsey said. "We'll have our hands full supporting the landing, so it will be a great relief to know that two ships as formidable as your destroyers will be available to deal with any unwelcome guests in orbit." The captain turned back to the people around the conference table. "So we're in agreement that a straightforward frontal assault is the way to do this? With the rebel destroyers at our back, we shouldn't need to worry about space superiority. That just leaves the mercenary company at the facility itself."

"Uh, I actually have a thought about that." Chief Kravczyk raised his hand like he was in elementary school, asking for the teacher's approval to ask a question.

"Chief?" Ramsey said, indicating he should continue.

"Well, assuming that we make orbit without any resistance, we're still going to have been in-system for hours before we even drop, right? And that's even assuming that we use that nifty little warp-hop trick Mabel can do in order to minimize our approach time."

Kravczyk looked around and, seeing no objections, continued. "Well, the Master may not be physically present at the site, but we know it has monitoring programs keeping tabs on anything and everything that happens in Terran space, right? So has it occurred to anyone that it might do something rash when it finds out we're camping out in orbit over its last slipspace comms relay and about to take the facility? If I were in its shoes, I'd do everything in my power to throw a wrench into that plan the minute I learned what was going down."

"But what can it really do at that point?" Major Davis said. "It's not like it's going to come to Terran space and trap itself here when it knows we can destroy the facility from orbit, if it comes to that."

"No," the big SEAR agreed, "but it could blow the place like the agent did at the site on Elizabeth or send a bunch of orders to whatever AIs it has running around the Terran datanets, instructing them to screw with us in any way they can. Or maybe it'll send another agent or two over here in desperation. Let's not forget there are still millions of people living on and above Isadore, and it's still a major economic hub for the Confed. The Master might not be able to stop us from ultimately taking out the facility, but it can pull some pretty nasty stuff as one last 'screw you' before we do."

The room went silent as everyone mulled over all the ways a pissed-off Master could retaliate. Successfully taking the site was more or less a foregone conclusion at this point, but now they needed to weigh the costs that victory might incur.

Major Davis was the first to break the silence. "One way or another, Chief, we need to get into orbit using the ships we have available. *Indomitable* is currently the only ship we have that's both capable of conducting a transatmospheric assault *and* is of Terran origin. I'm sure we could borrow a ship or two from the Alarians, but how do you think the people on Isadore will react to an Alarian ship showing up in orbit unannounced? The same goes for the rebel destroyers. If they're providing overwatch, they can use their stealth capabilities to remain undetected, but if we try to use one to conduct flight ops for the landing, someone's going to notice an alien ship overhead and start screaming bloody murder."

Kravczyk smiled, which told Henry the man already had a solution in mind and once again reinforced the notion that the big SEAR wasn't nearly as dumb as he let on.

"So I have an idea about that…"

————

HENRY RUBBED his eyes with his palms and yawned deeply. It'd been almost a day and a half since he'd had any meaningful sleep, and his gritty eyes made sure he knew it. The last however many hours spent going over ExoDyn HQ schematics with the SEARs, Major Davis, and Commander Russel, *Indomitable*'s executive officer, had left him completely drained.

"Alright," he said to the few people that remained in the briefing room, "that's about as far as I can go right now. We'll take a look at it with fresh eyes tomorrow." He eyed the SEARs, who still looked sharp, despite enduring the same lack of sleep Henry was struggling with. "I don't know how you do it."

"Youth and love for the Confed!" Kravczyk said.

"More like copious amounts of caffeine," Valdez said wryly. "Your love for the Confed has never been more than skin deep, and I hate to break it to you, Chief, but you sure as hell don't have youth on your side, either."

Kravczyk looked at Valdez, scandalized. "Your words hurt sometimes… You cut me deep, boss. Real deep."

"I have full confidence that you'll get over it."

Henry looked around at the relaxed, smiling faces of the military people still seated around the table and pushed his chair back and stood. "Well, you gentlemen"—he shifted his gaze to Tess—"and *lady*, have a lovely, uh, whatever the hell it is."

"Oh two thirty, ship's time," Kravczyk helpfully chimed in.

"Jesus," Henry groaned. "No wonder I feel like hammered sh—" He broke off as the alarm for general quarters began blaring from overhead.

Everyone in the room was instantly on their feet, all traces of the relaxed, casual atmosphere from a moment ago having vanished in the blink of an eye.

"General quarters, general quarters," the ops officer said over the intercom. "All hands, set Condition-2 throughout the ship."

"Not an immediate threat." Major Davis exhaled the breath he'd been holding. "I wonder what it could be."

The main wall display that Admiral Na'al had occupied during the joint briefing the evening before flickered to life, and Captain Ramsey's face appeared.

"Good, you're all still there," he said without preamble. "Stand by. I'm patching Admiral Na'al in."

A moment later, the serious face of the rebel admiral appeared on the display in a split-screen, side-by-side layout along with Ramsey's feed from the bridge.

"Admiral, please tell them what you just told me," the captain said.

Na'al's chin twitched downward briefly in a truncated nod of acknowledgment, and the big alien launched straight into the heart of the matter. "We have a traitor aboard *X'nec*," he began, and Henry's heart leapt into his throat. "They breached our systems and temporarily disabled the slipspace-suppression field generators before transmitting a message to Imperial Central Command. They also murdered several of my crew."

Panic surged up from Henry's gut as his mind raced at the possibilities. Ben was still aboard *X'nec*, and if there was a traitor aboard, he would be an obvious target. Even though *X'nec* operated on the standard twenty-seven-hour Imperial day and their current shipboard time was somewhere in the middle of the day, Ben would likely be trying to keep his circadian rhythm as in sync as possible, meaning it was the middle of the night for him… He would have been in bed.

"Is my son okay?" Henry blurted out.

If Na'al was annoyed at the interruption, he didn't show it. The Th'aloki's glassy black eyes swiveled toward Henry, and this time Na'al's nod was slow, deliberate, and, most importantly, reassuring.

"He is unharmed, though it appears an attempt was made on

his life. Two of my marines that were assigned to guard his quarters were murdered, and there was a failed attempt to breach the compartment's security. I sent a squad of my personal guard to check on him when we lost contact with the two guards assigned to him, and they located Ben still inside his compartment and unharmed."

Relief washed over Henry. He should have been focused on the fact that somebody aboard *X'nec* had just blown their cover and exposed Na'al's rebellion, but all he could think about in that moment was how grateful he was that his son was okay.

"Did you apprehend the traitor?" Valdez said, demonstrating that he, at least, was locked in on the disastrous nature of what just happened.

Na'al rumbled with suppressed anger. "We have not," he admitted. "I have my security teams scouring the ship, but so far, there is no sign of them. The AIs we replaced the Imperial-issue shipboard controller AIs with have all been disabled, and every shred of security footage, access logs, or any other evidence that might help us identify who did this has either been irretrievably lost or corrupted."

"How is that even possible?" Henry said. "Was this the work of a single individual, or is there a team of traitors working in concert? I can't imagine a lone traitor would be able to pull something like this off by themselves."

Na'al looked uncomfortable and didn't respond immediately. He looked off camera for a moment, as if reviewing something on one of the displays of his command station on the battlecruiser's bridge. Finally, he returned his gaze to the camera and gave Henry an answer that chilled him to his core.

"Whoever is responsible used override codes restricted to either the Master itself or one of its agents. There is no other explanation for what we're seeing here."

The briefing room around Henry was suddenly filled with

gasps and whispered mutterings. An agent. They were dealing with an agent.

"You have an agent aboard *X'nec*?" Ramsey demanded. "Is the fleet at risk? Or the planet?"

Na'al made a calming gesture with one of his massive twin-thumbed hands. "Do not fear, Captain Ramsey. We do not believe an actual agent is present aboard *X'nec*. Instead, the most likely explanation is that the agent that was killed on the surface six months ago had contact with an operative aboard my ship, though it may be impossible to ever determine how. I suspect this operative was furnished with command override codes by the agent in the event he ever needed to access our systems."

"So Ben really did eliminate the agent on Hai'alla?" Valdez said.

"Yes," the admiral confirmed. "If the agent survived and somehow transferred to *X'nec*, we wouldn't be alive to have this conversation. I've seen an agent of the Master take direct control of Imperial warships on several occasions. They are as ruthless and proficient in space combat as they are in the manipulation of client species. *X'nec*'s weapons would have been employed without warning, and there would have been no survivors."

"That's a cheery thought," Kravczyk muttered.

"So where does that leave us?" Henry said. "Can we assume this traitor sent a detailed accounting of everything that's transpired since Battlegroup 7 arrived over Hai'alla?"

"Unfortunately, yes," Na'al admitted. "The message that was transmitted was sent unencoded. It not only told of the agent's destruction but of my betrayal. The Master now knows a rebellion is underway, and it will act swiftly to counter us." The rebel leader paused, looking each face over before pulling the rug out from under them.

"I'm sorry," he said, "but due to this event, I'm forced to return to Imperial space with my forces and try to head off the response that will most certainly be coming now. That includes the ships I'd promised for your operation to take the slipspace transceiver on Valkyrie."

A stunned silence hung in the air as everyone took in the full meaning of what Na'al had said.

"You're pulling out?" Ramsey said, the first to come back onto an even keel. "But if you leave now, you won't have the combat power necessary to properly take the fight to the Imperium. You'll be slaughtered."

"I'm afraid I cannot wait for you and the Alarians to work out your internal conflicts before we depart. I must return to my people and do what I can to salvage the situation before the Imperium can regroup and move on the rebellion. My people have been preparing for this fight for thousands of years, but even still, it will take time to properly activate all our forces and bring them under a united command. Without my fleet available to defend against the initial strikes by the Imperium, all will be lost.

"I've already dispatched a transport to return Ben Hutchins to *Indomitable*. As soon as my craft returns, we shall depart. I will retain the quantum entanglement communication device you provided to me and will attempt to remain in contact with you. And should you be successful in capturing the agent's last slipspace transceiver in the Valkyrie system, I've sent a complete set of protocols with Ben that will prevent the Master or its agents from accessing the node, but you will be able to use it to communicate with me."

The hulking alien looked around one last time, nodded curtly, and said, "I wish you luck. Act quickly to secure the site on Isadore and stabilize your government. We will not last long against the Imperium alone." Na'al's feed cut off, and Ramsey's face took over the whole display once again.

Henry was reeling. A few minutes ago, he'd been on his way

out the door to join Shelly in the too-small bunk they shared. Now he was looking around the room at a host of shellshocked faces, struggling to come to grips with the fact that they'd just lost the ace up their sleeve for dealing with all the internal political bullshit that was ravaging the Confed, not to mention their best weapon to counter an offensive by the Federation.

"Well… there goes our big stick," Kravczyk said. "What the hell do we do now?"

34

DISGRACE

FENG GROWLED IN FRUSTRATION AFTER SLAMMING THE HATCH closed with far more force than was necessary. It was a petty thing to do and didn't exactly cast his ability to remain calm and composed in a flattering light, but he no longer cared. The treatment he was receiving from the Black Dragons that had extracted what was left of his tac team from Newman's Rock had been nothing short of humiliating, and the debriefing—or, more accurately, the interrogation—he'd just been put through had been the icing on the cake.

And of course his rescuers couldn't have been mainline Federation Navy or ISB personnel. No, they had to be from the Dragons. They all recognized him immediately, though some at least made an effort to hide their disgust as he passed them in the narrow passages of the Federation frigate SRFS *Nantong*.

Feng was infamous within the organization because he was the only person who'd ever failed that spectacularly on a mission. Never mind the fact that the mission in question had been conceived by idiots and sycophants or that the space-superiority force that was supposed to have been waiting nearby had been scrubbed at the last minute because some entitled party member wanted a show of force over his homeworld as a display of how much he cared about his people's safety. Which was to say it was an election year, and the minister in question was embroiled in a sex scandal up to his ears. So off went the three-ship force that could have easily handled the lone Fourth Fleet frigate that responded to the distress call from Newman's Rock. That the frigate had been carrying two SEAR teams was the final nail in Quantum Tiger's coffin—and also in Feng's career as an officer in the Black Dragons.

The hatch opened with a high-pitched, almost inaudible squeak, and *Nantong*'s executive officer leaned out into the passageway.

"Senior Agent, don't forget that you and your people are free to move about the ship as you please, but I would encourage you to stay out of the way of the Dragons or any of my crew. You and your team will be returned to Lianmeng as soon as is feasible, but it may be several weeks before that happens," the young officer called after him. "Please don't make me confine you or your people to quarters for making trouble."

Feng turned and nodded to the naval officer. "As you say, Lieutenant. You have nothing to worry about."

The man ducked back into the briefing room, and the hatch closed again, leaving Feng alone in the heart of the aging missile-defense frigate. The knuckles on his right hand cracked in series as he channeled some of his simmering anger into the tightly balled fist. A sharp twinge from his newly mended index finger caused him to grimace and relax his grip. Feng flexed the hand a few times, paying attention to the stiffness of the first joint in the finger the kid had broken when he'd ripped away Feng's sidearm two weeks ago.

He'd barely managed to escape the SEARs' assault on his team's base of operations. After putting enough distance between himself and that hellbeast-in-a-man's-skin he'd mistaken for a CID operative or another SEAR, Feng called what was left of his team and they'd regrouped. Then the really bad news had come in.

Quon and his small team shifted tactics after Feng informed them about the SEARs taking out their command post. The four-man squad had initially planned to storm the ship, kill the crew, and then wait for the SEARs to return. But after the devastating losses they suffered at the hands of that kid and the SEARs, Feng ordered Quon to destroy the ship and kill the crew, stranding the SEARs on the surface until the ISB could be reinforced by additional personnel from their orbital support.

At least that was until *Crescent Dawn* was obliterated by the SEARs' own covert warship, a similarly sized cargo freighter with the designation ISF *Gambler's Fortune*. That the analysts preparing the background briefing for this mission had missed the fact that the CID was operating Q-ships of their own was unforgivable. But in the end, Feng had no doubt he'd be the one left holding the proverbial bag for this disaster.

Feng looked up from his repaired hand and strode aft, toward the temporary berthing he and the four remaining members of his team had been assigned. The hastily cleared-out storage compartment had been rigged with bunks arranged three high along one bulkhead, and they had just enough extra space to set up a table and chairs assembled from scrounged-up buckets and empty transit cases. It was far from comfortable accommodation, especially when the ship's garbage compactor, which was located directly beneath the compartment, cycled through the day's accumulated refuse in the middle of the night.

Feng couldn't believe how bad his luck had been. The whole operation had gone so smoothly right up until they'd captured that damned kid. Neither Zheng nor the SEARs were aware that the ISB had been following them for hours before Feng and his team finally made their move. In truth, he'd hoped to be able to nail both Zheng and Volkov at the same time, but his counter-parts at the CID and GIM weren't that stupid, unfortunately, and they made sure they couldn't both be grabbed at the same time. That the kid managed to kill one of his men and injure another was a shock, but casualties were to be expected when facing off against tier-one operators. In the end, Feng had thought himself fortunate to have captured one of his targets as well as one of the SEARs there to extract him.

How wrong he'd been.

Feng shuddered again as his brief time at the kid's mercy replayed itself in his mind's eye. The cold malice in his eyes, that unnatural voice. Then there was what he'd said.

Do you have any idea how much your failure has inconvenienced me over the last six years?

Feng hadn't told anyone about that part. He still wasn't sure he trusted his memory of the strange encounter, and he wasn't about to subject himself to any more scrutiny by powerful people looking for someone to nail for this disaster. As it was, he was fairly certain he would be stripped of his leadership role within the tac teams and, if he was lucky, relegated to a closet somewhere as an analyst for the rest of his career. If he started telling people he was pretty sure he'd just had an in-person encounter with the Imperium's agent? Best-case scenario, they'd assume he was crazy and send him for an in-depth mental health assessment.

But that had to be what it was, right? The facts fit what Feng knew about the origins of Quantum Tiger—namely, that when the Central Ministry found out about it, nobody was able to determine where the initial order for the operation had come from. At the time, Feng assumed the whole thing was political posturing to shield the politicians and senior military officers from culpability, but after the existence of the Imperium—and the agent that had been sowing chaos in Terran space for years—

came to light, Feng began to suspect otherwise. The exact time-line became a little muddy following the Alarian War, but after spending several years in the wake of his defeat during Quantum Tiger, Feng had been able to stitch together enough of a picture to know that the Sino-Russian Federation had been cooperating with the agent for at least a full year prior to the arrival of the first Imperium battlegroup.

And that whole underhanded mess had led him to his current predicament.

But what about the kid on Newman's Rock? Feng's instincts told him he'd been face to face with the agent, but how was that even possible? He'd seen the kid bleed; he was definitely human. Could it have been a trick? Something to draw some piece of information out of Feng before the kid killed him? But that still left the question of how he would have known about Quantum Tiger's origins in the first place. Was the Confed working with the Imperium also? That thought raised a whole host of further questions that threatened to have him going down rabbit holes for hours.

Personally, Feng found the idea of working with the Imperium to be a disgusting, outrageous betrayal on the part of the Central Ministry, and he was sickened when he realized just how quickly the politicians and top officers in the military had signed off on surrendering without a fight. He couldn't actually voice his opinion, of course, given the fact that he wasn't even supposed to know about the arrangement in the first place. But in the end, Feng supposed it didn't really matter who his master was—the Imperium or the Confed. Subjugation to either of them was an equally unacceptable outcome.

In his mind, the Sino-Russian Federation, and more specifi-cally the Chinese People's Galactic Republic, should be in control of its own destiny. He was sick and tired of constantly watching his people be treated as second-class citizens while the Western enclaves lorded their superiority over everyone else. So when he discovered that, in exchange for their ability to govern themselves as they saw fit after the fall of the Confederated Terran Systems, the SRF was planning to launch an offensive against the Confed to rob them of some of their most critical systems, Feng had reconsidered his position on working for the Imperium.

He should have known better, though.

When the Imperium fleet arrived in Terran space, the first planets they'd razed had been Federation worlds in Federation systems, not NAC- or Euro-controlled systems. Feng supposed that, in a twisted sort of way, he should be grateful to the Confed as it was one of their destroyers, CTS *Appomattox*, that had caught the Imperium red-handed and exposed their betrayal. Now he didn't know what to think or whom he hated more.

Then the face of that goddamned SEAR flashed in his mind, and Feng decided the Confed was the worse enemy here. The Imperium had at least refrained from striking core Federation systems and instead focused only on a few sparsely populated fringe worlds. The more he thought about it, the more he considered it possible that the whole thing had actually been a Confed false-flag operation designed to draw the Federation into a war before they were fully ready.

But it was all moot now. The ship that picked up Feng and the few remaining members of his team was part of the strike force that would finally end the charade of the Confed being one big, happy family. He and his people were now aboard *Nantong*, and they were heading directly for the heart of the NAC's industrial base on Isadore. If the intelligence reports about the Confed navy having pulled back to their bases in Columbia and Kerner were accurate—ostensibly to weed out traitors and sympathizers, laughable as that excuse was—then the world was ripe for the taking.

Doing so would strike a crippling blow to the Confed, but

most importantly, it would force them to respond, and that response would come from the nearest fleet base, Icarus Station in the Kerner system. And when the Confed fleet mobilized and departed from Kerner, the bulk of the Federation navy would strike Icarus. It was an all-or-nothing gambit on the part of the Central Ministry, but with a fool like Cunningham presiding over the Confed and all the competent people like Admiral Robert Garland removed from their posts and excoriated in public, the Federation's victory was all but assured. After Valkyrie and Kerner fell, the Confed navy wouldn't have the force strength to repel the combined might of the Federation navy, and they'd either be forced to capitulate or be destroyed.

As Feng approached the hatch to his team's quarters, he took in a deep, cleansing breath. He might have failed in his mission to prevent Volkov from passing on the Federation's secret plans to launch an offensive against the Confed, but it was too late for that intel to do any good. The Federation had been nearly ready to begin the operation anyway, and Volkov escaping had only moved their timeline up by a couple of months, at most. The Confed wasn't in any position to act on the leaked intel before the Federation strike force hit Valkyrie and put things in motion.

Feng opened the hatch and stepped inside. It wouldn't be long until *Nantong* joined up with the rest of the strike force and things kicked off. Until then, though, he intended to catch up on some much-needed sleep and allow his battered body to continue to heal. He might not have an active part to play in the upcoming operation, but at least he and his team would have front-row seats to the beginning of the end for the Confed.

35

THE CALM BEFORE THE STORM

BEN SAT ALONE IN THE OFFICERS LOUNGE ABOARD IFS *GAMBLER'S Fortune*, staring at the simulated star field that scrolled past. When not in warp, the crew could gaze out into surrounding space through the thick viewing window, but while transiting between stars at faster-than-light speeds, the window displayed a lifelike render of the star field blurring past. It seemed silly, but the cheap psychologist's trick that had been employed ever since humans took to the stars had an undeniable calming effect on the mind. And here, planted dead center on the worn and cracked brown "leather" of the couch positioned in front of the viewport, Ben felt completely at rest, if only for a moment.

The old cargo freighter was surprisingly well maintained, despite her outward appearance, and the ship's fusion power plant thrummed rhythmically along, just as it had for the past five days with nary a half note's variation in pitch. The hatches opened and closed noiselessly, the shipboard air was cool and crisp—a sign that the environmental systems were functioning at peak efficiency—and every single light source Ben had seen emitted a steady stream of photons without flickering. It was clear to him that Captain Micholson and his crew loved their ship, and he could almost see why. The *Fortune* had an old-school, no-nonsense working-man's vibe going for it; it reminded Ben of simpler times, when he lived and worked on the farm with Jim.

Thinking about the man who'd saved his life all those years ago sent a stab of loss and regret through his chest, and Ben's gaze fell to the floor for a moment. A complex mix of emotions washed over him—sorrow, anger, fondness. He focused on the good memories: the memories of Jim slapping him on the shoulder at the end of a productive day, of kicking it back with beers in the pair of rocking chairs on the house's front porch, both men content to just sit silently and look out over the beauty that was Leelanau County in late summer and early fall.

"Penny for your thoughts?"

The faint smile tugging at Ben's lips fell away, and he turned to look at Tess, who'd managed to sneak into the lounge unnoticed and was now standing just behind him. "Where does that saying even come from, anyway?"

Tess smiled. "Who even knows, anymore? Though I imagine that particular idiom held a lot more sway back when a penny was actually worth something." Stepping around to the front of the couch, she slipped in beside him and cozied up to his shoulder. "Seriously, though, Ben, we haven't really had much of a chance to talk since you got back, and I can tell something is eating at you." She lightly placed one of her hands on the back of his neck, and her fingers started gently caressing his scalp. "We've finally got some time alone, so how about it?"

There were several activities that immediately sprang to mind when Ben noticed he and Tess were alone in the lounge, but a deep dive into his immensely screwed-up psyche wasn't on the list. Unfortunately, he spent too long in uncomfortable silence, trying to come up with a believable excuse for why she'd been picking up on his brooding, and Tess wasn't about to let him skirt the issue.

"Ben." It was a simple, single word, but she packed her tone with an entire paragraph's worth of meaning.

"God, you're such a pain in the ass sometimes." Ben half sighed, half laughed. He shifted his position on the couch so he was angled toward her, and she mirrored him, bright green eyes locked onto his. "What do you want me to say, Tess? I'm pretty sure nobody has had to deal with the trauma of dying and then being grown—or whatever Eelix and his team did to re-create me. This isn't exactly something that the psychology textbooks cover."

"How about you just start talking, and I'll listen," she said softly.

Ben pursed his lips. He considered shutting this whole line of conversation off and stuffing it back into the deep, dark hole in his mind where he kept all the uncomfortable stuff he didn't want to deal with. But then he thought about their upcoming mission and how his team was going to need him at his best. Ben knew his current state of mind was dragging him down, no matter how much he tried to bottle it up and ignore it.

He looked down at his hands; he hadn't spent much time reflecting on the nature of his current self after he'd spoken with his dad about it, all the way back before Tess even knew he was alive again. He'd figured that if he gave it enough time, he'd eventually manage to come to grips with who he was now and become comfortable in his new skin.

But the update to his sense of self hadn't materialized.

"When I look in the mirror now, I don't recognize the person looking back at me," Ben said, eyes still down at the hands resting in his lap. "I look around, and everything is just as it should be." He chuckled wryly. "Which is to say, totally fucked up."

He looked up at her and, perhaps for the first time since coming back, really took in her features. She was truly just as beautiful and radiant as ever before, and that fact seemed to help anchor him to the present. Tess represented a constant in his timeline, helping him bridge the gap from one life to the next. She sat there, listening intently and waiting for him to continue. That was something he always loved about her—she didn't try to interject with meaningless platitudes or unhelpful suggestions when he was trying to put the chaos of his mind into a coherent picture. She just listened.

Ben went on. "Sure, I got a pristine body out of that disaster on Hai'alla—and it's the shiny, new-and-improved model, at that—but it seems like the galaxy has gone even further down the shitter than before I thought blowing myself up was a good idea. The Confed, which we've been working so hard to shore up, is in even greater turmoil than it was at any point in the last five years, the Federation has been plotting a war with the other enclaves in cooperation with the agent, and oh, by the way, the guy who's in charge of the Imperial Navy? Yeah, he's on our side now and has kicked off a rebellion.

"But the people are still the same. My dad. You, the chief, and Valdez. Collins and the crew of the *Wraith*… Everyone's the same. Maybe a little more frayed around the edges after everything that's happened, but you're all still the same people.

"And therein lies the rub, Tess, because after I woke up floating in a suspensor field with an alien mad scientist leering down at me, I didn't feel like myself, and that was before I found out that my DNA has been manipulated to make me some kind of hybrid human. Yes, I still find myself enjoying all the same things, my thought processes are more or less the same, and when I look in the mirror, I see the same face staring back at me that's always been there, less a few scars. But something in here" —he grabbed at his chest, all five fingertips digging into his flesh —"isn't the same."

Ben went quiet for a long moment, waiting to see a shift in Tess's expression that would indicate she agreed with him, but all she did was continue to look at him with that mix of caring and support. Ben dropped his hands to his lap again and began wringing them together, a touch of anxiety probing at the edges of his consciousness.

"And then there are the dreams I've been having," he said quietly. "I see terrible things, Tess. Things that I know I never did, but they feel so real—like memories of past lives, long forgotten. And I *feel* them. Terror, hate… *rage*. I've done some pretty terrible things in my life, experienced things that took me right to the edge… but nothing like this. And they're getting worse. I'm starting to have dreamlike flashes while I'm awake. I haven't told anyone partly because I don't want them to sideline me right when you guys need me, but mostly because I'm afraid that I might be going crazy. I mean, hell, I would swear up and down that when I died, I went briefly to heaven and had a chat with my mom. You can't tell me there's not something majorly effed in my brain right now."

Tess's face had finally started to display some concern when he'd mentioned the dreams, but bringing up the experience with his mom was what finally got her to break her silence.

"I don't think that's so crazy, Ben."

He reached out a hand and tentatively slipped her hand into his. "Tess, I know you believe in all that God stuff, and you know my background on it," he said, approaching the issue as gently as he could. "Your beliefs have made you the person you are today, and I'm grateful for that… but I can't possibly believe a supposedly loving God would do the terrible things that have happened—or at least allow them to proceed without so much as lifting a finger to stop it."

And as she was wont to do in situations just like this, Tess surprised him. She smiled. It wasn't a sad smile—the kind one person offered to another when they just didn't get it, like they were too stupid to see the obvious. This smile was warm and loving.

"Ben, I know your mom was a devout Christian, and I also know your dad went to church more to make her happy than because he actually wanted to be there. I don't blame either of you for falling away from the Church after her death. I know firsthand that it's impossible not to question your faith after an event like that. But I think you've got God all wrong. He doesn't do terrible things to people, nor does he allow them to happen because he's apathetic. Just the opposite, in fact. The existence of sin—evil, if you prefer—is what leads to the things that cause us pain and suffering. But God doesn't always intervene directly when bad people do bad things, because to do so would require taking away their free will.

"You've heard it said that man was created in God's image?"

Ben nodded, his eyes narrowing slightly as he wondered where she could possibly be going with this.

"Well, I've got news for you. That doesn't mean that God is a bipedal mammal with bilateral symmetry. I mean, at least not so far as we know. But the point is, being made in God's image means we were created with the capacity to think and act for ourselves. Sure, he could have created a bunch of slaves that did nothing but worship him and follow his every command, but in what way would that have meant anything? By giving us agency to determine our own course in life, God gave us the ability to *choose* to love and worship him. I think you'll agree with me that it's infinitely more satisfying to have someone choose to love you because they genuinely want to." She squeezed his hand, and the significance slammed into him like a truck.

"But that doesn't mean that God isn't working in our lives all the time, through the good and the bad," Tess continued before he could bring up the fact that she'd just told him she loved him, though not in so many words. "Yes, it was terrible when your mom was killed, but that event set in motion a whole series of actions that ultimately led to you and Mabel defeating an entire Imperial battlegroup at the Battle of Icarus. Or what about all the Alarians that are still alive today because you were there to stop the agent on Hai'alla? You've been molded into the man you are today because even though you don't believe in God, he still believes in you and has a plan for you—for all of us."

Her voice broke and she wiped at the corner of her eye, where a tear had been threatening to drop free. "My entire family was murdered in front of my eyes," she said, a hard edge creeping into her voice. "And had that not happened, I never would have found myself forced to become as strong as I am today. I never would have been picked up by that Prowler, and I never would have joined the navy and been able to make it through SEAR school. I wouldn't have been on the mission to get you off Earth, and I wouldn't be sitting here now, the only person in the entire galaxy that you can talk to freely, without fear of judgment.

"So don't tell me God doesn't care, Ben, because the two of us sitting here on this gross couch, aboard my uncle Mike's freighter—which just so happened to be in the *exact* place we needed it to be, exactly *when* we needed it to be there—are living proof that he does care and he always has a plan, even if we can't see it at the time. And when bad crap happens and God can't intervene directly, that's when we are called to step in and use the gifts we've been given. God has more tools in his toolbox than just snapping his fingers to solve problems. So the next time we're facing a mountain of hurt because evil did what evil will always do, take a step back and look around. I guarantee you God is there and he's working, but if you can't see him, consider that he may be working through you."

Tess fell silent, and the two of them sat there without saying a word for several minutes. Ben felt like a schoolboy that had just received the scolding of a lifetime, and bizarrely, he felt better for it. He wasn't about to run right out and go find someone to baptize him, but he felt more centered than he had in a long time. Maybe there really was some truth to what she'd said about God and cosmic-level plans and he just hadn't been able to see it before, or maybe it was just the strength of her conviction helping to prop him up. Regardless, he felt better. He hadn't gotten here via a route that he would have expected, but here he was.

"I still don't think I buy it, Gorgeous," he said, leaning in to give her a peck on the cheek. "But thank you. Nobody can help me square my shit away like you can, and when we're done with this op and finally have some time to take a breather, I promise you, we're going to take some time off and get away from all this crap, if just for a little bit. I think we've earned it."

She smiled and cupped his face with one hand. "It's a date, but what's to say we can't take a little time off right now?"

Tess leaned in and kissed him, long and passionately. When she finally came up for air, she pushed him down and slid in next to him, pulling his arms around her and hugging them to her chest.

Ben leaned in and whispered in her ear as the fake star field continued to scroll past on the viewport. "And I love you, too."

She didn't say anything, but he saw the corners of her eyes

crease as she smiled and hugged his arms tighter around her. They lay there, listening to the rhythmic thrum of the *Fortune*'s power plant as it filled the ship with life and watching fake stars streak past. And for the first time since his death, Ben found himself grateful to everyone who'd worked so hard to bring him back.

36

UNCLE MIKE

"We're in the pattern, but it'll be another six hours before we're given clearance to make our first run to the surface," Captain Micholson said. "The client isn't real happy with the fact that we're more than two weeks overdue, but they at least seemed to buy my excuse about an engineering casualty requiring an unscheduled stop. I managed to sweet-talk them enough to at least secure us a convenient pad for getting you and those ornery bastards you brought with you off-loaded without raising a fuss, which is a good sign that we won't be blacklisted for future contracts with them."

Ben looked around the crowded conference table, seeing the faces of people he'd trained and fought with before—his team, as well as Major Davis and the rest of the platoon COs from the Pathfinders. There were several new faces, however, which only served as a stark reminder of just how bloody the battle to take out the agent on Hai'alla had been. In particular, Sergeant Butler —with whom Ben had a bit of a checkered past—had been given command of Third Platoon after their CO and more than half of the platoon's marines had been killed.

Then there was the lone alien in the group, who stood out among the collected humans like a sore thumb.

"Is there any indication that the enemy is aware of our intentions?" asked Lursus Hallyn of the Alarian Council Guard.

Hallyn had been in command of Klaythron's other commando element during the assault on the datacenter. It was his squad that discovered the dead Alarian security detachment that normally guarded the facility, though they didn't see much action during the battle. Hallyn was a Lursus, which was the Alarian rank roughly equivalent to a Terran first lieutenant, and had been given command of the Pathfinder's Fourth Platoon as part of the Terran-Alarian joint operations. Hallyn had proven himself to the Marines during the Hai'alla operation, which had eased the transition to an integrated force. But while all four of the Pathfinder platoons now comprised a roughly fifty-fifty mix of both Terrans and Alarians, Fourth Platoon was the only one with an alien in command. The other three platoons were all commanded by Terran marines, but each had its own contingent of Alarian troops—including NCOs—to fill out the ranks.

"While it's too early to know for sure, it does not appear so," Mabel answered immediately, her disembodied voice coming from the conference room's hidden speakers. Normally, her avatar would have been hovering somewhere over the conference table, but *Gambler's Fortune* didn't have any holograph emitters installed in her largest conference room.

When Ben met them on the flight deck of *Indomitable*, the SEARs and Pathfinders were just returning from their first major exercise with the integrated force. He hadn't seen the Alarian members of the Pathfinders at the time because *Indomitable* wasn't yet equipped to embark a large number of Alarians, nor could it accommodate all of their unique diet and sanitary needs, so they'd remained on the surface.

The trip to Valkyrie had taken almost ten days, but that was still only about half the time Ben expected, given the age of *Gambler's Fortune* and the fact that the ship was just a cargo freighter. Then again, he supposed he shouldn't be surprised that a freighter that just so happened to be armed to the teeth had also received an upgraded power plant and propulsion system. While Ben hadn't spoken more than two words to Tess's uncle Mike since boarding the ship soon after Na'al took Battle-group 7 back to Imperial space, Valdez had filled him and the rest of the team in on the unique nature of *Gambler's Fortune*.

"So we go with our original plan, then?" Major Davis said. "Ben, you're still sure of the target's location?"

Ben nodded. "Positive."

Assuming the transceiver had been constructed beneath the main complex of the campus, as the others had been on Eliza-beth and Hai'alla, his dad and Mabel had been able to narrow down the possible location to three areas: the power-generation building, the executive office building, and the prototype-production facility. The first time Ben had been given a rundown on their analysis, he'd immediately fingered the prototyping plant as the target. How did he know this with absolute certainty? He didn't have a clue.

Regardless, when he'd seen the map of the complex and three highlighted locations, he'd experienced a scratching sensation at the back of his consciousness, much like a few weeks ago when he'd pulled the information about the Imperium pulling the strings within the SRF out of thin air. In a pleasant change of pace, however, Ben hadn't experienced crippling brain pain followed by unconsciousness after accessing the hidden informa-tion his subconsciousness was trying to bring to his attention. Instead, he simply pointed at the prototyping facility and confi-dently proclaimed it as their target. Thankfully, by that point, pretty much everyone was used to him pulling critical intel out of his ass, so it hadn't been much of a fight to get himself and the

SEARs assigned as the element that would take that position. It was the least likely to be heavily defended, after all.

That left the marines with what was assumed to be the hardest targets: the reactor facility and the airfield. Should Ben and Mabel be unable to take control of the slipspace transceiver, the marines could at least cut power to it by securing the power-generation facility that housed ExoDyn's onsite fusion plant and power-distribution infrastructure. Gaining control over the airfield would cut off any possibility of reinforcement or retreat by air. And since the enemy supposedly only had roughly a company-sized contingent onsite, it seemed likely that they'd prioritize securing those two critical assets first and foremost. The prototyping facility wasn't even operational anymore; ExoDyn had shuttered the entire complex during its bankruptcy proceedings in the aftermath of the Alarian War, so it seemed unlikely that the people in charge of securing the place would dedicate a large portion of their limited resources to guard it.

"Then it's settled," Davis stated, looking around the room to see if anyone objected.

Seeing nothing but nods of approval, Captain Micholson stood and slapped his hands firmly on the table. "That's it then. The trucks will be waiting at the pad, and I'll have my people on standby in the event you run into trouble and need a little extra oomph. Our first run to the surface will be in just over six hours —you have until then to make sure your people are ready. Once we put this thing in motion, we need everything to move efficiently or we're in for a world of hurt."

Everyone around the table waited for the big freelancer to finish. Then they all stood and began to file out of the conference room. Ben waited for the Pathfinders to clear out before rising and making to follow the rest of the SEARs out the hatch, but Micholson stopped him.

"Ben, I'd like a quick word, if you don't mind."

Valdez, Kravczyk, and Tess all paused and looked at the captain, then at Ben. Ben, suddenly experiencing a wave of overwhelming dread, stood there helplessly, hoping his eyes were accurately conveying his silent scream for help from his friends. Valdez and the chief exchanged a knowing smirk, then turned and booked it out the door. Tess turned to stand next to Ben and eyed the big freighter captain.

"Uncle Mike, you promised!" she said.

He waved a giant, dismissive paw at her. "Don't worry, Tessie. You can have him back in a few minutes." He paused, then shot her a mischievous grin. "I'll even try to make sure he still has all of his fingers and toes."

Tess sighed resignedly and turned to Ben. She offered him an encouraging smile, then kissed him on the cheek. "Good luck, Handsome," she said, then raised a warning finger toward him. "Don't screw up."

With that, she turned and disappeared, leaving Ben to a fate that was quite possibly worse than death.

"So, Ben," Micholson said, coming around the table and walking up to tower over Ben. From his newly acquired proximity to the man, Ben couldn't help but marvel at just how broad the former marine's shoulders were. "I understand that you and my Tessie are a bit of an item?"

Ben suddenly realized he was shying away from Tess's bear-like uncle-not-uncle, and he made an effort to straighten up and look the man directly in the eyes. "I love her," he said, mentally patting himself on the back for the steel he'd manage to put into his tone. "And woe be unto the poor son of a bitch that ever threatens her."

Micholson hummed, nodding as he chewed on Ben's response. "I believe that would indeed be the case. And given what Captain Collins told me before I agreed to take part in this little shindig, I know you'd do everything in your power to protect not only her but everyone you care about."

The big man leaned up against the table, which creaked ominously as his bulk settled into it. "But I didn't ask you to stay here and chat because I don't think you're worthy of my Tessie, Ben," he said, crossing his arms.

Ben's eyebrows ticked up, and he couldn't help the surprised look that overtook his carefully maintained facade of confidence. "Really?" he asked. "Because Tess told me you made the last guy she was interested in literally piss himself when you found out."

Micholson threw his head back and roared with laughter. "Ha! Oh, Lordy, I'd forgotten about that! Poor kid really thought I would throw him out an airlock if I caught him ogling her backside again. Served him right, though," he said, his voice turning serious again. "She was only fifteen at the time. But that's not why we're here."

He waved a hand between the two of them as if to shoo the tangent away. "I wanted to talk to you because I want to give you a little advice—something I had to learn the hard way, once upon a time. Between what Tess has told me and the details I've been able to drag out of the people who've known you the longest, I'm worried about you, Ben. I'm worried that you're holding on to too much of the terrible shit you've been through and you're using it to fuel yourself."

Ben opened his mouth to deny it, but the big freighter captain waved him to silence. "Don't argue with me on this. I don't really know you from Adam, but I do know how easy it is to give in to the rage when you need that extra boost to get you through. It's worked out for you so far, but there comes a point where you can't turn back. That point is different for every man, but the hell of it is you don't know when you'll cross it until it's too late.

"Anger can be useful. When you need that extra push, it has

a power and speed that our other emotions just can't compete with, and that's what makes it dangerous. Anger causes tunnel vision. It overwhelms common sense and your ability to reason —to see other, often more advantageous solutions. I just want you to be mindful of that," he finished. "That's really all I wanted to say—just be mindful. Because otherwise, you'll end up like me, and *you'll* be the one that ends up hurting the people you love when you lose your hold on the tiger's tail and it gets away from you." A haunted expression passed over Micholson's face, and his eyes lost focus for a moment. "Trust me, Ben, you don't want to ever truly understand what I mean."

Ben stood there, unsure what—if anything—he should say to that. The man was right, of course; Ben knew exactly what it felt like to tap into those emotions. He'd done it before, and he was sure he'd probably have to do it again, at some point. It was the thing he kept in his back pocket—something that could give him an edge.

But then his mind jumped to the brief time he'd spent with Saryf, the alien consciousness upon which the Master had built the agent that had caused so much destruction. The dreams Ben had been having over the last few weeks were all eerily similar in nature to what Saryf had gone through. In the end, the alien had given himself over to his grief and hate, and the Master used that to enslave him. Did Ben run the same risk if he wasn't careful?

"I'll do my best," he said.

Micholson eyed him for a moment, then stuck out his hand. "You make sure you bring my Tessie back safe and sound. You hear me?"

"I'll do my best," Ben repeated as he took the freighter captain's proffered hand and shook it firmly.

"That's all I ask. Now get the hell out of here. You've got less than six hours before we hit atmo."

37

THE AGENT

THE AGENT ALMOST COULDN'T BELIEVE ITS LUCK.

Regaining awareness aboard one of the Master's vessels had resulted in an initial surge of triumph, but that soon gave way to a mix of shock and fury when it was revealed that a rebel faction of the Imperial Navy had betrayed the Master. The agent, struggling to cope with its newfound existence within a biological entity, tried to lash out at the traitors. Unfortunately, the Terran, Benjamin Hutchins, was still firmly in control of his new body at that point, and all the agent had accomplished was influencing his emotional state to a small degree.

But the agent was nothing if not patient. It waited, and it learned.

The next time it attempted to take control was when Hutchins had donned his unique armor. But while the agent succeeded in linking with the APEX armor's processors, it was unable to prevent Hutchins from doing the same. The result was a digital gridlock as conflicting motor commands overloaded the armor's processors, causing them to continuously reset. Thankfully, Hutchins's failure to control his armor led his father to withhold authorizing the Mabel construct to attempt a direct neural link—something that surely would have exposed the agent's presence within the Terran's mind.

The first breakthrough came when the agent discovered that, to its horror, Hutchins was able to access small portions of its memories—memories that could potentially give the Terrans an advantage. At first, the agent had fought back, desperately trying to keep Hutchins's subconscious from clawing out increasingly sensitive information. But then the agent realized that, while it couldn't brute-force its way into control of Hutchins's mind or body, the connection they shared could be exploited via subtler means.

The Terran's thoughts and emotions could be influenced—much like the Master did to its subjects via their standard neural implant suite. So the agent probed its host's mind when he was at his most vulnerable: during sleep. By teasing Hutchins's subconscious, the agent paved the way for the Terran to freely give himself over to the agent's control. It wasn't a perfect solution, as the agent was only able to maintain its control over its host while the man was unconscious, but it unlocked several options that were previously out of the agent's reach.

It needed to tread cautiously, however; something that was emphasized to the agent when it'd nearly blown its cover during its escape from that useless ISB agent, Feng. While it was necessary for the agent to escape from ISB custody, it'd done so in a manner that, in retrospect, was out of character for its host. The agent feared that the SEAR, Kravczyk, and the Mabel construct suspected something wasn't quite right with their friend and teammate after that incident, judging by the SEAR's surreptitious glances and the AI's uncharacteristic avoidance of Hutchins. Thankfully, neither of them had pressed the issue directly with Hutchins, at least not yet.

There was also the matter of the consciousness shackled within the agent's core. The once-biological being known as

Saryf, whom Hutchins had unwittingly, if only temporarily, freed in the moments before the destruction of the facility on Hai'alla, was proving to be an irritant. The agent was in turmoil, struggling to reassert complete dominance over the consciousness that was the foundation of its existence.

Most recently, its troublesome core used the same dreamstate approach the agent had been utilizing in an attempt to warn Hutchins of what the agent was doing. The agent managed to contain the situation and mitigate the damage, but that incident reinforced the its need to remain ever vigilant, especially given the incredibly dangerous scenario posed by the alliance of the Terrans and Alarians with Na'al's rebel faction. The Master needed to be informed, but how?

Then fate had intervened on the agent's behalf: Hutchins was left alone in the care of the traitor Na'al and his rebels aboard their ship. The agent was forced to go temporarily dormant in order to evade the notice of the Th'aloori scientist tasked with examining Hutchins. Soon after that examination, however, the perfect opportunity had presented itself, and the agent struck.

It was unfortunate that it'd been required to kill several of the rebels—leaving Na'al with no doubt as to the presence of an enemy agent aboard his ship—but it had been necessary to eliminate any and all witnesses. It was imperative that the Master be informed of Na'al's betrayal and alliance with the Terrans and Alarians, as well as the true threat that Hutchins and the Mabel AI represented. And the agent had accomplished that feat, all while finding a way to cast suspicion everywhere but upon itself.

And yet, it couldn't have possibly imagined the windfall that was about to fall into its lap.

The agent barely had time to congratulate itself on a job well done and begin to formulate a strategy to deal with its predicament when the Terrans announced a new military operation against the Master. The agent had gleefully supplied Hutchins's subconscious mind with the information the Terrans needed to plan their assault. And why wouldn't it? After all, the Terrans were sending Hutchins and his team to the one place that would allow the agent to not only rid itself of the meat sack it was now shackled to but eliminate Hutchins, the Mabel AI, and their commando team all in one fell stroke.

And afterward? Well, afterward, Hutchins and his AI would be dead, and the agent would be back in Imperial space, ready to take the fight to Na'al and his little rebellion. It just needed to get Hutchins and, most importantly, his APEX armor in contact with the interface that provided access to the agent's last slipspace transceiver in Terran space.

38

PLANNING A REUNION

"I'M TELLING YOU, NA," QUON ARGUED, "THERE'S ROBUST DATA that you are dampening both the mTOR and hypertrophy pathways by going straight to a cold bath!"

Feng sat with the few remaining members of his team in *Nantong*'s mess, sipping at a steaming mug of Keemun black tea. Quon was engaged in a particularly heated debate with Specialist Na about whether heat or cold offered greater benefits after an intense workout. Quon insisted that all the published data suggested that a cold bath was detrimental to making gains after exercise, while Na vehemently disagreed.

Quon was right, of course—Na was the type of kid who did just enough research on an issue to scratch the surface, then presented himself as an expert on the topic. But while the use of cold did impart certain benefits, it also limited any gains you could make. The best thing to do after a workout was spend twenty minutes in a sauna, but Feng wasn't about to get involved. Instead, he turned his attention away from his two subordinates and returned it to the wall display that showed continuously updated orbital tracking data from Isadore's automated orbital control system.

Nantong had been on its way to Valkyrie to relieve SRFS *Chengdo*, a corvette-class ship that'd been tasked with monitoring the system in preparation for the planned assault on Isadore. The ship was rerouted to Newman's Rock after Feng contacted ISB headquarters to update them on the destruction of *Crescent Dawn* and request an extraction for what was left of his team. Getting in close enough to pick up the battered tac team had been a near-run thing. Newman's Rock planetary defense very nearly opened fire on the frigate as soon as they announced their intention to approach the planet. In the end, however, Feng and his team managed to get themselves to orbit on a stolen shuttle and were quickly picked up by *Nantong* before the ship made a hasty exit from the system.

Feng and his men were relegated to being unwanted passengers, at least until *Nantong* arrived on-station and *Chengdo* was sent back to Federation space. Unfortunately, with the Federation's strike on the Valkyrie system now imminent, command wanted both ships on-station to collect as much intelligence as possible before the arrival of the strike force, which was due to begin the operation within the day.

So instead of transferring to SRFS *Chengdo* after arriving on-station, Feng and his team continued to waste their time languishing aboard the small frigate as their quarry got farther and farther away. The odds that he could still track down and intercept Volkov and the SEARs before they delivered their stolen intel were slim, at best, but he couldn't just let it go. Feng was a loyal and, contrary to recent events, talented agent, and he prided himself on his record with the ISB. For that matter, he'd been an exemplary officer in the Black Dragons until the Quantum Tiger disaster. But therein lay the real heart of his problem; the two times in his career that he'd failed, he'd done so in truly spectacular fashion.

The cynical part of his mind told him that he was being kept here to ensure that Volkov and the SEARs got away entirely so he could then be drummed out of the ISB once and for all. There was probably some truth to that, but he also had to acknowledge that he was a victim of his own making. If he'd succeeded in reclaiming Volkov's stolen intel back in Lijia, then he wouldn't be sitting here right now, and the Federation wouldn't have accelerated their timeline to strike the Confed. But he hadn't succeeded.

So here he sat, drinking shitty Keemun tea and trying to ignore the still-heated argument between his men over something that just wasn't worth caring about as much as they did. He took another sip of the tea but froze with the cup only halfway back to the stainless-steel mess table. The orbital traffic display had just received another update, and one of the new arrivals from about an hour ago now had an identifier.

ISF *Gambler's Fortune*—cargo-class vessel en route from Newman's Rock, destined for commercial spaceport Arcadia-1. There was also a priority arrival prefix code attached to the orbital traffic record, meaning the ship would have its first cargo lander on the ground within a matter of hours.

Feng's heart instantly began hammering at the inside of his rib cage. It couldn't be, could it? Fate had abandoned him long ago; there was no way he was being given a chance to redeem himself. He looked away from the display, sweeping his gaze over his team to see if anyone else had noticed—they hadn't— and then looked back at the wall display. It was still there, listed among the arrivals.

But the SEARs wouldn't still be aboard her, would they? They'd escaped from Newman's Rock almost three weeks ago; even a cargo vessel like *Gambler's Fortune* should have arrived more than a week ago if it made a direct flight here. But Feng had assumed it would be taking Volkov and the SEARs either to

Columbia or Kerner, not a system that was no longer a Confed military stronghold like Valkyrie.

The timeline didn't make sense, though. If the SEARs had taken Volkov where Feng assumed they would, then the ship shouldn't have arrived here so soon. Columbia was all the way over in Euro space, Kerner was out beyond the established enclave territories, and the Valkyrie system was way out on the fringe of NAC space—practically next door to the Alarians. Traveling between the stars, even at superluminal speeds, took days or weeks. A high-speed courier could probably make the trip from Newman's Rock to Elizabeth or from Kerner to Valkyrie in three weeks, but a medium freighter like *Gambler's Fortune*? Not a chance—even if it'd been modified by whichever service was operating the ship. No, the most likely scenario was that the ship had either rendezvoused with another vessel to offload its precious cargo and then continued on here, after a week's delay, or its crew had suffered an engineering casualty while en route, delaying their arrival. One option meant Volkov and the SEARs were out of Feng's reach, but the other put his target just a few AUs distant.

Feng shot to his feet, his teacup clattering to the table. All conversation stopped, and his men turned to him with questioning looks.

"Go get geared up. We're going to the surface," he barked. "It would seem fate is offering us a chance to redeem ourselves. I'm heading to the bridge to secure us transport. Be ready for departure within the hour." He pointed to the orbital traffic display, and a wicked grin spread across his face. "Our Confed friends were kind enough to drop by, and we need to prepare a fitting reception for them."

39

ISADORE

"ALL CLEAR. POP YOUR TOPS."

Ben reached up and hit the releases on the clamps that secured the top of the cargo crate he'd been packed into like some kind of human origami. The latches fell away, and light seeped into the claustrophobia-inducing box through the seam between the top and body of the container. He placed his hands on the underside of the lid and stood up, his APEX armor responding to his commands just as effortlessly as it used to.

"Boss, I would like to once again go on record as saying this was one of the worst ideas we've ever agreed to," Kravczyk said as he materialized from his crate like a jack-in-the-box directly in front of Ben.

Ben carefully set the lid of his crate aside and looked around. He and the SEARs were inside the dimly lit interior of a commercial truck trailer. Whoever loaded the cargo aboard the truck had made sure they had enough room to maneuver when they climbed out of their hiding places, but only just barely. The rest of the trailer was jammed full of standardized vacuum-rated cargo containers that were filled to the brim with actual cargo.

Only the four crates the SEARs and Ben had been in weren't the real deal.

"Sorry about the accommodations for your ride down here," said the man that'd given them the all-clear a moment ago as he shimmied between stacks of cargo containers and approached the newly emerged SEARs. "We didn't want to risk you getting spotted by someone at the spaceport or, worse, one of the Imperium's minder AIs that are monitoring everything going on within our datanets right now."

"We knew the reason before we agreed to be packed into these things like sardines," Valdez said, thumping the side of his crate with a fist.

"They're really not that bad," Kravczyk chimed in. "You know, once all your extremities go numb from having your body twisted up like a pretzel."

"Jack Baker," the man said, extending a hand to Valdez. "I'm the agent who's been tasked with trying to keep tabs on our mysterious friends over at ExoDyn."

"Commander Ramiro Valdez," the SEAR leader said in greeting, exercising impressive control over his armor as he shook the man's unprotected hand without crushing it. He pointed to Ben and the rest of his team in turn. "That's Ben—he's a civilian contractor—Chief Kravczyk, and Petty Officer McCollum. You're the one who'll be coordinating the operation?"

"That's right," Baker said. "Myself and a few others. This truck is automated, but one of my people is controlling it from a safe house we set up a short distance from ExoDyn. Two other members of my team are going to be riding herd on the marines when they touch down in a bit. CID doesn't have a heavy presence on Isadore. Most of our people were recalled to Columbia, just like the navy boys. I drew the short straw and was assigned to keep an eye on an entire planet." The man looked around and shifted nervously for a moment before adding one last thing.

"It's probably because I, uh, was the one who originally initiated the dialog between the Office of the President and the Imperium."

Ben and the SEARs stared at the man in disbelief. Kravczyk made some kind of strangled choking sound, as if his brain had shorted out.

"And how'd that work out for you?" the big SEAR said, his tone dripping with disdain. "Pretty peachy, huh?"

Baker winced. "You can point fingers and chew my ass all you want, but not until *after* you secure the facility. I've done a lot of stuff I'm not exactly proud of, and that one tops the list. Regardless, my team and I are all you've got. I know that's not exactly reassuring, but here we are."

"So you were one of Wheaton's people that helped Cunningham and his cronies overthrow McGibbons," Valdez stated. "Then I assume you're aware of who we are?"

The CID man nodded. "I do. Officially, we still have standing orders to detain you and your whole team on sight. Unofficially, I've been instructed to assist you in whatever way you need, up to and including sacrificing myself or my entire team to ensure you complete your mission, and I intend to do just that. So you can stop worrying about it.

"Frankly, I couldn't give a rat's ass about all the political bullshit going down on Elizabeth. I do my job because it's the best way I know to help safeguard humanity. I thought McGibbons was off her fuckin' rocker, so I went along with Director Wheaton's request to initiate contact with the Imperium for the purpose of negotiating a peace deal. When we were trying to buddy up to the Imperium, you guys were bad. Once we pulled our heads out of our asses and realized the Imperium was just slow-playing us until they can hit us again, you guys became the good guys again." Baker shrugged. "Who the hell knows? Maybe tomorrow will roll around and you guys will be the bad guys again. Until then, the president himself has ordered me to help you out, so that's what I'm going to do."

"God, you CID guys are real pieces of work, you know that?" Kravczyk said.

Baker chuckled and hit the big SEAR with a genuine smile. "I could say the same about you. Last I checked, we're still technically at war with the Alarians, and yet you people have been buddied up to them for months. Not to mention that he"—the man pointed an accusing finger at Ben—"and his old man were collaborating with members of the Alarian High Council back even before the war. If anybody here is deserving of suspicion, it's him and his dad." Baker turned his attention to Ben and cocked his head in question. "I thought you were supposed to be dead, by the way."

"I got better," Ben growled. Having this prick call *his* loyalty into question was a bridge too far, and he found himself struggling to suppress the urge to beat the man senseless. *He* was the one whose loyalty was suspect here? "And that's pretty rich, coming from the guy who just admitted to committing treason."

"All right, all right, knock it off," Valdez said sternly. "We can continue this mud-slinging contest after we've taken control of our shiny new slipspace transceiver and ensure the Master and its agents lose their last avenue of intelligence in Terran space. Until then, we work together. Got it?" He looked at Ben and Kravczyk, then at Baker.

"Got it, boss."

"Understood," Ben said.

Baker simply nodded his acknowledgment, then glanced at his wrist. Ben noticed he had a small semi-flexible screen attached to the inside of his left forearm, much like what Ben sported on his own left wrist. "We're five minutes out from the drop point, and your marines will be dirtside in ten mikes.

Check your gear and get ready, because this show's about to start."

———

"Oh, you have got to be shitting me," Kravczyk muttered in disbelief. "These assholes aren't any regular old mercs, boss. They're fucking Dragons."

Ben and Tess quickly exchanged a concerned look before continuing to scan their sectors as they pulled security for Kravczyk and Valdez. The two SEARs were halfway up a pair of large trees, using their optics to scout the southeast section of ExoDyn's campus. With the marines preparing to hit the main gate and the facility's small airfield shortly, Ben and the SEARs had taken up position just inside the tree line to scout out their approach to the prototyping facility.

"How can you tell?" Valdez asked.

"See those two dickheads playing cards by the south entrance to the materials research building?"

"Got 'em... What am I looking for?"

"They've got matching tattoos on their forearms that look an awful lot like the ones we saw on the Dragons back on Newman's Rock a few years ago."

"Wait one."

Ben heard Valdez adjust his position from ten meters above, and a few moments later, he came back over the team channel.

"My optic doesn't have the same level of magnification as yours, Chief, so I can't really make out any details, but I'll trust your assessment. Still, how do you know they're not former members of the Black Dragons that are currently working for a merc unit?"

"Because they don't have those stupid fucking goatees all the Dragons grow after they muster out. Their kit is also identical, including the way their rifles are configured," Kravczyk explained. "I suppose they could be members of a PMC outfit that's run and supplied like a regular military unit, but I have a hard time believing they'd shave their goatees off to work for a merc outfit. Most of those guys keep them for life—it's practically a religion. Kinda like how the console jockeys all grow scraggly-ass beards after they get their separation papers and move back into their moms' basements."

Mabel, do you still have a line open to Baker and his people? Ben mentally queried.

Yes.

It was only a single-word answer to a relatively inconsequential question, but Ben smiled. He hadn't realized just how much he'd missed having her in his head. With his weird dueling brainwave pattern issue nowhere to be found after he got his skull split open by Feng, he'd been able to hop into his shiny new APEX and go about business as usual. But the real question was whether or not he and Mabel would be able to work together as they had in the past.

It took all of about three seconds during their testing aboard *Gambler's Fortune* while en route here for him to wash away more than a month of frustration and uncertainty that had been weighing on his thoughts since the first time he'd tried and failed to integrate with his armor after his rebirth. He hadn't really believed Eelix when the little Th'aloori scientist told him that the results of the emulation testing he'd run after Newman's Rock indicated that whatever had previously been affecting his ability to use his armor was now gone. But sure enough, when he finally had a free minute after the chaotic whirlwind that was the aftermath of the rebel fleet bugging out and the Terrans quickly throwing together an operation to take the last slipspace transceiver, Ben suited up and put Eelix's assurances to the test.

And it had worked flawlessly. Just like that.

"Commander," Ben said over the team channel, "Mabel reports that our line to Baker is still open. Do we need to tell him about this and have him pass that intel along to the Pathfinders? The marines prepared their assault based on the defenders being mercenaries, not a top-tier military unit."

"Yes. Mabel, please inform the CID that we suspect the force occupying ExoDyn are in fact active-duty Federation Black Dragons, and ask them to pass that along to the Pathfinders," Valdez said. "I don't want to risk a voice transmission, but a burst transmission from you should be safe enough if the enemy is listening for unexpected radio traffic. There probably isn't enough time for them to make any changes to the plan, but at least Davis won't be surprised when his marines run into a crack outfit instead of a bunch of complacent mercs."

"Understood," Mabel replied. "Transmission sent."

"Are we still a go?" Kravczyk asked. "Or does this mean we scrub the operation?"

"That these guys are Dragons is an unexpected challenge, but it doesn't meet the threshold for a mission abort," Valdez stated. "We go in eight minutes—just as soon as we hear the first kaboom. You ready, Ben?"

Ben glanced up and caught sight of Valdez looking down on him. "I'm good," he said with a nod, then went back to scanning the woods around him, carbine held at high-ready.

Getting dropped off at the abandoned factory on the other side of the hundred-acre wooded buffer zone at the rear of ExoDyn's property had given Ben a small jolt of anticipation because it represented some unspoken point of no return. Once Baker climbed into the truck's cab and the big rig pulled away, the mission was officially underway. But for Ben, the trip through the woods and over the ten-foot-high security fence— something their APEXs made a trivial matter, as they easily jumped clear over the obstacle—had been more of a trip down memory lane rather than a nerve-wracking ingress to their target.

Moving swiftly through the thick pines that towered above him brought on a wave of nostalgia from his lost childhood years. Ben had spent many a summer's day exploring these woods while his dad attended board meetings and did other thoroughly boring business stuff. Occasionally, one of the other ExoDyn executives would take their kids to work, and Ben would spend the day playing hide-and-seek with them, building forts or, when he was a little older, playing laser tag. But as the team approached the point where the forest gave way to the sprawling open grounds around the ExoDyn headquarters campus, those happy memories from Ben's youth quickly gave way to darker ones. The first small clearing they'd come across, blasted into the landscape by Alarian weapons just a few short years ago, was a stark reminder of the horrific start to the Alarian War.

From that point on, Ben didn't have any problem focusing on the task at hand.

He briefly shifted his gaze away from the quiet forest and looked at the alien weapon in his hands. Na'al himself had approved Ben retaining possession of the plasma carbine he'd lifted from the dead rebel marine's corpse on *X'nec*. Ben didn't know why, but he felt a sense of attachment to the weapon and he'd been reticent to turn it back over to the marines that'd come to check on him. It was as if a forgotten part of him had used a weapon just like this in some conflict many thousands of years ago, and he just couldn't bring himself to let it go. It was just one more strange thing in the ever-growing pile of odd feelings and memories that'd been popping into his mind, unbidden, ever since he'd awoken for the first time aboard *X'nec*. As far as the weird mental shit went, though, his newfound love of plasma weapons was about the least of his concerns.

"Your gut still telling you this is the place?" Kravczyk asked. "Once we go through those doors, we're committed."

"This is it," Ben said firmly. "I can feel it."

Valdez dropped to the ground a few meters away and waved up to Kravczyk, indicating for him to do likewise. "Alright, people, we go in five," he said.

Kravczyk thumped hard into the soft earth a moment later and unslung the rifle from around his back. The big SEAR quickly checked the chamber, then flashed a borderline manic grin at the rest of the team. "Oh boy," he said excitedly, "I finally get to see what Ethel here can really do in the hands of someone competent!"

Ben stared daggers at his friend, eyes darting from the SEAR's grinning face to his custom-build XM-93. He shuddered internally at the thought that his beloved rifle had been named Ethel. *Ethel.* Ben's dominant hand twitched on the grip of his plasma carbine, but through a tremendous force of will, he stilled the fury coursing through his veins and demanding he right the grave injustice before him.

"You see, boss?" Kravczyk pointed at Ben's murderous glare. "I told you he still had a thing for Ethel. But noooo, you were so sure that he was over it now that the rebs gave him that shiny new plasma gun."

Valdez unslung his own carbine and turned toward the heart of the ExoDyn campus. "Eyes up, everyone. It's go time."

40

THE NICKEL TOUR

"You don't seem to understand the severity of the situation, Captain," Feng ground out. "That ship being in orbit here can't be a coincidence."

"And you expect me to do what?" scoffed the commanding officer of the Black Dragon company guarding the defunct headquarters of the ExoDynamics Corporation. The man was everything Feng had feared he'd be: arrogant, politically connected, and, worst of all, stupid beyond belief. "You had your shot at command, Senior Agent. You proved yourself so utterly incompetent that you were not only removed from command but drummed out of the service entirely, lest the stench of your failure taint the finest fighting force in Terran space more than it already has. So you'll forgive me for not putting my men on high alert and risking the true nature of our presence here becoming known to the local authorities and the Isadore Defense Corps over the insane ravings of a disgraced fool. Good day, Senior Agent Wu."

With that, the man turned on his heel and strode out of the conference room Feng and his men had been escorted to upon their arrival at the ExoDyn complex a few hours prior. Feng seethed at his humiliating treatment, but thankfully, not every member of Jian Company, 2nd Battalion, 35th Black Dragon Regiment held such a negative opinion of him.

"Don't let Captain Guo deter you, Senior Agent," said the officer assigned to babysit Feng and his team as he peered over his shoulder and out into the hall to ensure his CO was out of earshot. "It's hard to blame the man for his foul attitude when he's forced to contend with the stick his father in the Central Party shoved so far up his ass he sneezes sawdust and spits out toothpicks."

"You don't understand, Sile," Feng growled. "When—not if —that ship makes contact with the IDC and informs them of the intel they stole from the Central Ministry, this place will be swarming with their security forces before you can so much as blink."

Wang Sile had been one of Feng's noncommissioned officers during Operation Quantum Tiger, and he was one of the very few Dragons to make it off of Newman's Rock alive and in one piece in the aftermath. But despite the disastrous outcome of the operation, the man had been one of Feng's staunchest defenders during the myriad investigative hearings the Central Ministry held in an attempt to determine upon which heads they would pin the blame for the embarrassing defeat. Even after all these years, Sile had greeted Feng with a warm smile upon finding him and what remained of his tac team aboard the shuttle that ferried them down to the small private spaceport at the northeast corner of the complex.

"But how could they know? You yourself said the information this defector, Volkov, stole pertains only to the planned strike against the Confed's most prized systems. Even if the IDC receives that information before our fleet arrives in orbit, I don't see why they would strike us now. We've been actively monitoring both the civilian and military datanets here, and no one has any idea that the security force occupying this facility is actually a Federation military unit. They believe us to be a security contractor hired to watch over the complex in anticipation of ExoDyn reopening this facility, as Isadore's industrial base continues to recover from the war. Not only that, but our mission here has nothing to do with the planned invasion, nor are we to participate once it begins."

Feng mulled over what Sile had said. The man brought up some salient points; the force deployed to ExoDyn wasn't part of the invasion force, so perhaps the Confed really wasn't aware that the security force here was in fact a mainline Federation combat unit. But he simply couldn't believe it was mere coincidence that the very ship that swiped Volkov from under his nose on Newman's Rock just happened to park itself over the only Federation assets on Isadore. But if *Gambler's Fortune* wasn't here because of the information Volkov had provided, then why?

"Do you know if the Confed is aware of this facility's true nature?" Feng asked.

Sile shrugged. "Of course. They are the ones who discovered the presence of the Imperium's hidden slipspace communications array in the first place. But the Master itself is pulling the strings in the Cunningham administration, and the Confed have been ordered by the Imperium to stay well away from this place. They're being monitored by the Imperial AIs that have been placed on every major world, and I'm sure you're familiar with what happens to people who cross the Imperium."

Feng shuddered. He'd seen the aftermath of several such instances—party members who'd said too much or were beginning to get cold feet regarding the Federation's active cooperation with the Imperium. There usually wasn't much left to identify, and the medical examiners had been forced to rely on DNA matches.

"I am," he admitted. "But what if a faction within the Confed has decided to take matters into their own hands? Like the ships that attempted to join the Alarians before Cunningham and his allies in the senate exposed their plot and ousted President McGibbons?"

"We lowly grunts don't receive much in the way of juicy intel like that." Sile shook his head. "So I can't say one way or another. But if what you say is true, I still don't see how such a small force could manage to pull off a successful operation against us without alerting either the Confed or their Imperial minders as to their intentions." He motioned for Feng and his team to stand and follow him. "Come. This will soon be nothing but an academic thought exercise, anyway, when our fleet arrives to take possession of this world. Until then, I will give you a tour of the once-famous headquarters complex of the ExoDynamics Corporation, starting with the office of the man who was once the most powerful in Terran space: Henry Hutchins."

———

MORE THAN AN HOUR after Sile led him and his team out of the conference room on the ground floor of the Executive Building at the heart of the ExoDyn complex, Feng had to admit he was impressed. He'd of course known that ExoDyn and Henry Hutchins were famed for their ability to both shatter technological barriers *and* successfully implement innovations on an industrial scale, but after receiving a guided tour of the sprawling campus, Feng was left awestruck. Despite the damage that still marred the surface of the once-beautiful complex, he couldn't help but be impressed by the technological prowess of the legendary Terran company and the man who'd been the driving force behind it.

In the wake of the Alarian attack on Isadore during the outset of the war, Isadore was left technologically crippled. Strategic assets and critical infrastructure had been decimated, leaving the tattered remnants of the planetary government scrambling to put enough of the pieces back together to prevent millions of people from starving to death. Rebuilding the planet's industrial base hadn't even been a line item on the government's agenda until after they were sure they'd even be able to continue surviving, let alone begin cleaning up the devastation. So it had taken nearly eighteen months before anyone even set foot back on the ExoDyn campus.

What was left of the ExoDynamics Corporation's governing board after the war had done an assessment of the facility and deemed it not only too costly but flat-out impractical to clean up the mess and rebuild what they'd lost, but enough was intact that they didn't want to write off the facility completely. So, given the disappearance of their founder and CEO, Henry Hutchins, the surviving board members voted to clean up the site and then mothball the facility in the hope that they could restore ExoDyn's operations at the complex down the road.

And so the facility sat abandoned for several years. After Henry Hutchins's miraculous reappearance a year ago, there was some buzz that ExoDynamics was preparing to make a comeback. It wasn't to be, however, as the man had chosen to continue living as a recluse, estranged from the company he'd once built into *the* Terran megacorporation. And that was how Sile and the Black Dragons had found the facility upon their arrival.

"And last but not least," Sile said with a flourish as he approached a control panel next to a set of massive cargo doors at the end of a wide underground hallway, "I present to you the Vault." He punched in a security code on a tablet that was stuck haphazardly to the wall next to a partly disassembled security panel with double-sided tape, wires snaking their way from one to the other. A moment later, the big doors slid aside on recently oiled tracks.

Feng's eyes widened and he heard several gasps from his team. As the doors parted, an enormous underground warehouse was revealed. Lights snapped on overhead—the ceiling must have been at least twelve meters high—revealing row after row of neatly organized crates and various pieces and parts of equipment sitting on dusty industrial shelves. But the sight that immediately caught Feng's attention was the half dozen APEX suits laid out on tables near what appeared to be a cargo elevator set into the far wall.

"ExoDyn just left all this stuff here?" he said incredulously. "There must be millions worth of equipment, just sitting here for anyone to come and take what they please."

"It took our best techs almost four days of round-the-clock work to crack the security protecting this room," Sile explained. "And that was only after they'd restored power to this section of the facility. In other words, nobody could have just walked in and taken whatever they wanted."

"Still..." Feng stepped into the warehouse and craned his neck to look around. "I can't believe no one made an effort to recover all of this."

"No one until us, that is," Sile said with a conspiratorial smile. "We've been cataloging and crating up the most valuable stuff for transport back to Federation space. There's a similar storage area on the other side of the complex, beneath the building where ExoDyn manufactured their prototypes, but while the material stored in there is highly interesting, it's almost all one-off prototypes or single pieces that were part of an iterative design process."

"In other words, the stuff that works is in here." Feng gestured around the massive space. "And the stuff that doesn't is kept elsewhere."

"Essentially." Sile nodded. "We cracked the other room a few days after this one, but most of our efforts with regard to cataloging and packing up what was left behind has been focused in here. That stuff over there"—he pointed to the neatly organized APEX suits and open transit crates in the distance—"was supposed to ship out during our next resupply, but that's been put on hold now that the fleet is beginning their operation to annex this system."

"May I?" Feng inclined his head toward the powered armor suits. Sile swept a hand out, palm up, as if in invitation, and Feng quickly walked down the length of the warehouse, not so much as glancing to either side as he passed row after orderly row of technological treasure.

With every step, Feng's heart beat faster. He'd been on the wrong side of suits like these several times now, and a part of him recoiled at the sight of the impossibly black graphene polyalloy plating that covered the armor. He slowed as he approached the nearest table, then reached out a tentative hand. The armor was cool to the touch, but something inside of it radiated the promise of raw power.

"These suits are obsolete now, but they were current production when the war started," Sile said, walking up to stand next to Feng.

"So they don't require the new neural implants the Confed is fielding?"

"Correct. And that's why we're taking them back to the Federation's Infantry Warfare Research Center on Lianmeng, where the eggheads that design and build the latest and greatest in infantry weapons systems are literally drooling in anticipation."

Feng snorted. "If they hadn't been so damned stubborn as to refuse the Confed's offer of a joint exo-armor development program back in the day, we wouldn't even need these relics. But leave it to the Central Ministry to see a paranoid conspiracy behind every corner."

"Careful what you say in this place, Senior Agent," Sile warned. "We may be far from Federation space, but talk like that has a nasty habit of finding its way into the wrong ears."

"Sile," Feng said, rounding on the man. "Fuck those sycophantic tyrants in the Ministry. I have dedicated my life to serving the Federation, and what have they done to reward me? Turn me into a pariah and punish anyone associated with me. Look at yourself! You should be in command of your own company by now, but because you had the misfortune to be assigned to my unit during Quantum Tiger, you've been forever relegated to a mid-level command, and no more!"

Sile reeled back from the vehemence in Feng's tone, looking unsure of whether he should retreat to safer ground or stand fast and try to calm him.

Feng took a deep, cleansing breath after his outburst and closed his eyes, counting backward from five in his head. "I'm sorry, Sile," he said after composing himself. "These past few weeks have been more trying than any other in my long career, and I am extremely frustrated by the lack of urgency I've seen from our respective chains of command when informed of a credible threat. Regardless, my behavior is inexcusable."

Sile relaxed somewhat at Feng's explanation and apology. "Think nothing of it, old friend," he said with a reassuring smile. "I will do what I can to ensure that we—" He was cut off by an alarm blaring from the facility's public address system.

Sile fumbled as he attempted to pull his personal data tablet from the thigh pocket of his fatigues, eyes going wide with shock when he finally held the device up and read the notifications on it.

"A Confed warship has just entered the system and threatened one of our frigates in orbit," he said in disbelief. "And our perimeter teams report enemy contact at the main gate, as well as along the fence line to the southwest!"

"Show me," Feng barked, reaching out and tearing the PDT from the man's hands.

Feng swiped at the screen, quickly navigating the familiar user interface until he found what he was looking for. He tapped on the highlighted high-resolution video feeds, and his heart stopped.

Four APEX-armored figures were sprinting toward the proto-type-fabrication building that Feng had received a tour of not twenty minutes ago.

"SEARs!" he snarled.

That fucking ox of a man was in the lead, armed with some sort of rifle that Feng couldn't immediately identify. He couldn't see the man's face, but there was only one human in existence that had that combination of speed, strength, and size.

Kravczyk.

And that meant that the other three SEARs on his heels were Valdez, McCollum, and the mystery kid that Feng still didn't have a name for.

He looked up and shoved the PDT into Sile's chest, then glanced down at the APEX armor on the table next to him. "Are these units operational?"

"Yes," Sile responded, brow furrowed in confusion. "We've checked them over and even charged the power cells in order to perform power-on self-diagnostics with them. These are all fully functional… but why?"

Feng ignored the man and turned to his team. "Suit up."

41

UNEXPECTED ARRIVALS

"TEN SECONDS TO TRANSITION."

Captain Edwin Ramsey stared at the massive holotank down in the Pit on *Indomitable*'s bridge, silently counting down the last few seconds until his ship would transition out of warp. *Indomitable* was already at general quarters, and Condition-2 had been set. The crew were at their battle stations, and all of the ship's defensive systems were powered up and standing by for action. Only her weapons remained powered down, as the good captain didn't want to pop into the Valkyrie system and scare the hell out of the locals when a kilometer-long battlecruiser appeared out of nowhere with her projectors hot and Mk. 18s ready for action.

With any luck, she'd find herself in position 8500 kilometers above the surface of Isadore as soon as the fields dissipated. Any closer and they risked a collision with a ship in the orbital traffic pattern. Any farther away and *Indomitable* wouldn't be in position to provide overwatch and launch her Sabers, thereby leaving the marines to assault a fortified position with nothing but carbines and harsh language.

The countdown timer ticked off the last few seconds, and the vibration from his ship's four type-48 quasi-symmetric stellarators decreased in frequency as the powerful fusion reactors spun down in the lead-up to warp emitter shutdown. An instant later, the heavy cruiser's fourth-generation warp emitters went through an orderly symmetric shutdown, and the warp field dispersed, leaving *Indomitable* suddenly drifting through space in the Valkyrie system.

"Ops?"

"All departments checking in now, Captain," Lieutenant Hutton, *Indomitable*'s first-watch ops officer said. "No problems reported."

"Very good. Comms," Ramsey called out, "please make our presence and intent known to Isadore orbital control and the IDC. It's rather unmannerly of us to pop in overhead like this, and I imagine there are more than a few people down there that are presently finding themselves *honked off*, as the good Captain Micholson so elegantly put it."

Indeed, the bombastic freighter captain/privateer had been a wealth of relatively up-to-date intel regarding Isadore's orbital defense situation, given his frequent dealings with the planet. One piece of information he'd brought up, in particular, was that the Isadore Defense Corps had ramped up their activity in response to the Confed navy pulling their forces out of the system. Micholson described the people responsible for managing orbital traffic and initiating a defense response in the event of a threat as "twitchy" of late, and he'd stressed the importance of quickly establishing clear lines of communication upon *Indomitable*'s arrival.

"Aye, Captain," Billings responded absently, already hard at work, bent over his console as he tried to establish communications with several planetside entities simultaneously.

Ramsey scanned the orbital traffic data that was populating in the Pit's holotank, and a mix of simultaneous relief and anticipation washed over him as his eyes caught sight of *Gambler's Fortune* sitting right where she was supposed to be, in a low orbit that brought it over Arcadia every twenty-eight minutes. But it was what he didn't see that raised the hairs on the back of his neck. He tapped a few controls to bring up CIC's current assessment of the shipping around the planet to make sure he wasn't missing something, but the latest report from *Indomitable*'s combat data nerve center stated the same thing he was seeing.

"Tactical, bring our high-powered arrays online, if you please," he said. "If the mercenaries defending the ExoDyn complex have any orbital support, it's not readily apparent. I want to know if there are any ships in the area that are hiding from Isadore orbital control."

"Space-search and targeting arrays coming online."

"Thank you, Mr. Curtis."

It would take a few minutes for the radar waves to propagate out and *Indomitable*'s receivers to pick up the returns, then for CIC to run their analysis of the data and send any suspected targets up to the bridge, but—

"Contact!" Curtis called out mere seconds after the arrays came online. "We've got a ship on an intercept course for *Gambler's Fortune*, approaching from their stern quarter. Wait one…" His hands nimbly flew over his screens, bringing up menus and running the raw data through several different analysis algorithms and filters simultaneously. "Confirmed, Captain. Federation type-53 frigate. She's running with her engines choked down to reduce her thermal bloom—sneaking up on the *Fortune*. Just over eight hundred kilometers separation and closing."

"Comms!" Ramsey barked. "Alert the *Gambler's Fortune* that they have an unfriendly ship closing fast! Advise they break orbit and evade. Ops, set Condition-1SS. Tactical, paint that frigate with everything we have. I want them to feel the heat from our targeting lasers on their skin through the hull."

Ramsey mashed down on the control that would broadcast over the standard emergency shipping channel and hailed the Federation frigate, which CIC had just positively identified based on her engine signature.

"Sino-Russian Federation ship *Nantong*, this is the Confed navy cruiser *Indomitable*. You are to cease your pursuit of the merchant vessel IFS *Gambler's Fortune* immediately. Failure to do so will result in your immediate and very violent destruction. I repeat, stand to and power down your weapons and engines or we will destroy you. Respond with your compliance over Confederation navy standard frequency Bravo-4 and stand by for further instructions."

"She's running, sir," Hutton announced from ops. "Her engines just went to full thrust, and she's vectoring away from the Fortune, but on a course that will get her over the horizon and into the orbital shipping lanes."

Ramsey growled. Why couldn't these things ever be easy? "And we can't risk firing on her once she's mixed in with the civilian shipping traffic, nor can we take the shot now, because she hasn't done anything except get caught with her knickers down."

"Captain Micholson expresses his thanks for clearing the, um, Federation ship from his blind spot, Captain, and he reports that he'll be transferring to a higher orbit once they've shipped their last cargo lander, which will be aboard within the hour."

Ramsey smiled at Billings's attempt to clean up what was no doubt a truly spectacular epithet from the freighter captain. "Understood, Comms. Please inform Captain Micholson that we'll continue to cover the *Gambler's Fortune* as best we can until such time as he clears local space or the threat no longer exists."

A pair of red brackets flashed on the tactical plot in the tank, and Ramsey frowned. *Indomitable*'s powerful search radar had burned through the stealth ability of yet another ship that was trying to hide nearby. This one was classed as an older Federation corvette that was a workhorse among their intelligence services.

Two ships? And actual Federation warships at that? Ramsey's intuition, finely honed after decades of service and multiple combat engagements, was screaming at him. There was more going on here than a simple mercenary company watching over a defunct industrial complex. One of Agent Volkov's concerns flashed to mind, and a chill ran up his spine.

The escaped GIM agent claimed that the SRF was planning an invasion of several key Confed systems, but according to his information, that operation wasn't due to begin for several months. However, Volkov had insisted that the Federation was ready to mobilize at any time, and he feared that his defection would result in the SRF advancing their timetable so as to take advantage of the element of surprise while they still had it. Ramsey considered that outcome unlikely, given the monumental hurdle of organizing and implementing an effective logistics train for an operation of the size and scale the Federation was planning. You couldn't simply mobilize entire fleets at the drop of a hat; it took months of moving personnel and materiel into position before something like what the Federation was planning could be put into motion. But if the Fed already had two ships in-system…

Ramsey tapped another control and opened a direct line to CIC.

"CIC—Lieutenant Lowen," came the crisp reply from Ramsey's second-watch ops officer, who was currently putting in time as the CIC watch supervisor. The CICWS position was normally held by a senior enlisted spacer, but Ramsey had been so impressed with Lowen's performance since he'd joined the ship that he had him putting in hours in CIC in the hope that the young man would soon qualify for CIC watch officer or possibly even as the captain's designated tactical action officer.

"Mr. Lowen," Ramsey said, not wasting time with pleasantries. "Please ask the SRO to keep a sharp eye out for any unusual contacts. I don't like the fact that the Federation already has two warships in this system, and I don't want any more of their forces to catch us by surprise at an inopportune moment."

"Copy, sir. I'll inform the search radar officer immediately."

"Good lad," Ramsey said and closed the channel.

"Sir, Captain Micholson is standing by on vid comms," Billings said from beside Ramsey, where he'd been standing by patiently while Ramsey spoke with CIC. "He says he's received critical intel from his people on the ground regarding the opposing force at ExoDyn."

Ramsey nodded his acknowledgment to his comms officer and tapped at his command console once again. He knew that trying to park his ship in orbit over a busy planet while his ground team was simultaneously preparing to launch their assault was going to be tricky, but the flurry of curveballs he'd had to navigate in the few short minutes since *Indomitable* transitioned in was getting to be a bit much.

Captain Micholson's grizzled face materialized in the holotank before him, and Ramsey nodded curtly. "Captain, I'm afraid we'll have to make this quick. We've got our hands full over here."

Micholson's bearded face clouded with a concerned expression. "My people on the ground just reported that Dagger has positively identified the unit guarding the ExoDyn complex. It's the Dragons."

Ramsey swore softly under his breath, but not softly enough, it would appear.

Micholson chuckled. "Yeah, that was pretty much the same thing I said."

Ramsey allowed himself two seconds to quickly consider this new information, scanning the tactical plot as he did so. The Fed presence and lack of an obvious mercenary ship in orbit made sense now. Unfortunately, it also meant they'd be obligated to engage *Indomitable* as soon as the marines initiated hostilities with the Black Dragon company securing ExoDyn. They couldn't simply run with their tails between their legs while a Confed battlecruiser and its forces pummeled their unsuspecting special operations force.

"Did your people give any indication as to whether or not the mission is still tenable?" Ramsey asked.

"They report that the information has been passed on to all concerned parties and that both Major Davis and Commander Valdez intend to proceed with the mission as planned," Micholson replied. "I've ordered my two tactical teams to remain on the surface and gear up, should either the Pathfinders or Dagger Team require backup. That said, my guys are better suited to quick hit-and-run skirmishes against pirates and the like rather than a stand-up fight against a properly equipped special operations outfit, so I wouldn't count on them affecting the outcome all that much."

Ramsey raised an eyebrow in surprise upon hearing that Micholson had ordered his people to gear up for a fight, but the big freighter captain caught the expression and shook his head.

"My guys will be ready if there is an emergency, but they're not stupid. If things look bad, they'll be high-tailing it out of there rather than getting in a scrap with the fucking Chinese. And you better believe that somebody is going to be paying us for this. We're racking up a shit pile of billable hours on this job, and believe you me, we don't come cheap."

Ramsey couldn't help but smile. Micholson might be a

former marine with a soft spot for those who still served the Confed, but the man was a mercenary through and through. "Don't worry, Captain. You'll be compensated generously for your assistance. Now, if you don't mind," Ramsey said, glancing at the master mission timer suspended in the air over the holotank, "I've got a squadron of Sabers to scramble, two Federation warships to keep an eye on, and a ground operation to cover."

"Say no more." Micholson threw a quick wave. "Micholson out."

The channel closed, and Ramsey looked around the bridge. "Right then," he announced. "Helm, take us down to deployment altitude. Ops, please inform flight ops that we'll be in position to deploy the Sabers presently. Comms, any luck with the IDC or Isadore orbital control?"

Billings nodded. "Yes, sir. They were a bit put out by our arrival but quickly became much more agreeable as soon as we shined the lights on two Federation warships in their skies."

"I'll bet they did at that," Ramsey muttered. "When you have someone with operational authority on the line, let me know. Now that we're aware our team is facing off against a proper military unit down there, I want the IDC mobilized to reinforce them as soon as possible."

"Yes, Captain."

Ramsey turned back to the tactical plot, eying the still-fleeing *Nantong* with suspicion. On her current course, she had the option to either come back around the planet and try to hit *Indomitable* from behind while the battlecruiser was busy launching her fighters, or the frigate could use her superior thrust to break orbit and run farther out into the system. What she did would depend on the answer to a number of questions, none of which Ramsey had at present.

Did the Federation have a larger force already in the system and lurking nearby? And if so, would *Nantong*'s orders be to join them rather than attempt a delaying action against a much more powerful opponent? For that matter, was the frigate even assigned the job of supporting the Black Dragons on the ground, or was she simply here on a recon mission?

Then Ramsey remembered that the ship had been vectoring in on *Gambler's Fortune*, which didn't make any sense, unless *Nantong* somehow knew what the freighter really was and that Captain Micholson was part of an operation to attack the Federation forces guarding ExoDyn. But how could they have known that the freighter wasn't just an innocent cargo ship? Could the Federation have already received word of the *Fortune*'s involvement with the SEARs' mission to Newman's Rock? As far as anyone knew, the ISB only had the one ship in the system during that operation, and it had been completely destroyed. It should have taken a month or more for the ISB to retrieve their team and for word that the freighter was more than she seemed to have reached their forward-deployed forces all the way out here in Valkyrie...

Then the frigate did something that no one expected.

A priority notification popped up in the holotank, accompanied by a blaring alert tone.

"Captain!" Hutton cried, coming halfway out of his seat. "The Fed frigate just emitted a slipspace signature!"

CIC was throwing information into Ramsey's command data feed fast and furious, and it all pointed to one thing: *Nantong* had just sent a comms transmission via a slipspace transceiver, a transceiver currently aboard the fleeing warship—not the one the Black Dragons were guarding down on the planet.

The Federation had Imperial tech on their ships.

Ramsey's blood ran cold at the realization. The Imperium must have given the Federation some form of their slipspace technology in order to give the SRF an edge over the Confed during the coming conflict between the two Terran factions, and they must have done so some time ago, if the SRF was already deploying it. But who was that ship trying to signal?

Moments later, Ramsey had his answer. The tactical plot was suddenly awash with crimson brackets as ship after ship materialized in space over the planet.

The Sino-Russian Federation had proven Ramsey's prediction of the timing of their invasion all wrong—and in spectacular fashion. He stared on in horror as the space around him swarmed with Federation warships.

The SRF strike against the Valkyrie system had arrived. And they'd come in force. By the time the tank stopped updating with new slipspace transitions, more than two dozen angry red dots now surrounded *Indomitable*.

But a Colossus-class battlecruiser was a force to be reckoned with, and Ramsey had his own ace up his sleeve.

"Very well then," he muttered to himself as he pulled up a preprogrammed script on his command console. He had no illusion that his one ship, powerful though she was, could prevail against such staggering odds. So he wasted no time with the decision to put all his cards on the table. "You've shown me yours." A grim smile pulled at his lips. "Let me show you mine."

Ramsey's index finger stabbed down on the *execute* command. Then he turned to face his stunned bridge crew.

"Ladies and gentlemen," he said in a calm, clear voice, despite the thunderous crash of his heartbeat in his ears. "It would seem our friends in the Federation wish to lodge a formal complaint to the Confed as to who the rightful owner of this system is." Ramsey pointed to the tactical plot currently dominating the main bridge display. "Helm, lay us alongside that big bastard currently angling to cut us off from our people on the planet. Comms, inform our ground team that their air support will have to wait until after we deal with this mess."

Ramsey took in a cleansing breath as he received the acknowledgments for his previous two orders. Then he addressed his tactical officer. "Mr. Curtis," he said, shooting the man a predatory grin. "Please ensure the Federation receive our strongly worded rebuttal to their proposal with all due haste."

Curtis nodded at his captain, his face a grim mask of determination. Then he turned back to his console and began selecting targets and tasking firing solutions to *Indomitable*'s formidable array of weaponry. Just as the threat-detection algorithms flagged the first of the missiles leaving the Federation ships' tubes, *Indomitable* opened up with her main guns.

The *Dame* roared defiantly into the tempest, and the fight was on.

42

YOU SHOWED ME YOURS, I'LL SHOW YOU MINE

ANOTHER BARRAGE OF LASER FIRE RAKED ACROSS *INDOMITABLE'S* forward port quarter, and a fresh round of damage notifications flooded the tank. Ramsey's grip on the edge of his control panel tightened as his ship took the hit, but the massive battlecruiser shrugged off the petawatts of directed energy, actually siphoning a portion of it off to charge the supercapacitors that fed her own armaments.

"Forward port-quarter Aegis plating degraded, Captain," Hutton announced from ops. "Aerogels and ablatives are nearly exhausted, and the charging circuits are down to thirty percent efficiency. One or two more salvos like that and we'll be down to the homogenous plate and the pressure hull."

"Helm, put us into an axial roll to starboard. Roll rate one hundred eighty degrees per minute," Ramsey ordered, doing what little he could in an effort to stave off the inevitable. "And if you get me abreast that carrier without any new holes in the hull, Mr. Thornton, I'll make sure you receive a double ration of grog tonight."

"Aye, Captain!" the helmsman bellowed back enthusiastically. He briefly took his hands away from his flight controls to crack his knuckles, then began the very delicate work of threading a kilometer-long warship through the hail of incoming fire.

Ramsey felt one corner of his mouth twitch upward. If there was a man or woman in the fleet who could drive the *Dame* right up to the enemy's doorstep without letting them get in a crippling shot, it would be Flight Lieutenant Maxwell Thornton. Ramsey's eyes drifted back to the three-dimensional tactical plot suspended in the holotank, and his grin faded.

Indomitable had already destroyed or disabled three enemy combatants—those that had emerged from their warp within what amounted to knife-fighting range. However, now that the Federation strike force had enough time to get their feet under them after their transitions into the system, the big Confed battlecruiser's initial advantage was gone. Ramsey eyed the mission clock, shocked to see that a mere thirteen minutes had ticked away since the first of the Federation ships appeared; it'd felt like the better part of an hour. This deep in the planet's gravity well, though, the battlespace was compressed, and engagements that might normally take hours or days to take shape were happening in the span of minutes—minutes that Ramsey and his ship didn't have.

Come on, Raal. Where the hell are you? Ramsey chided himself for the momentary thought that his Alarian counterpart might not follow through with her end of the plan, but no. If Temina Raal said she was going to do something, then no force of heaven or hell would be able to stop her. Ramsey glanced down at his command console, seeing the green indicator next to the command script he'd executed as soon as the Federation strike force showed up.

That hastily coded script had activated the Alarian slipspace emergency beacon Raal's people installed on *Indomitable* before they'd departed Hai'alla. With Battlegroup 7 out of the picture, the Alarians had stepped up and offered to provide a quick reaction force should *Indomitable* end up facing more than it could reasonably deal with—the same quick reaction force that was poised for action less than a quarter of a light-year outside the system.

Indomitable bucked under his feet, and Ramsey barely managed to catch himself on the side of the holotank. A damage notification strobed red, briefly minimizing the tactical plot and replacing it with a diagram of the ship's aft section. One of *Indomitable*'s MPDs was highlighted amber, indicating damage.

"Proximity strike on number three MPD, Captain," Hutton reported from ops. "Magnetic confinement is holding, but engineering recommends limiting number three's output to no more than twenty percent, until they have time to properly assess the damage."

"Very good, Ops," Ramsey said. He struggled with the urge to micromanage the situation, but he knew his ops officer would coordinate with Commander Sexton's people in engineering, and between them, they would ensure that the proper steps were taken to protect what integrity the damaged drive pod had left after the strike. So instead of commenting further, he turned his attention back to the big picture around him.

The tactical plot was a chaotic mess. Missiles and other ordnance were streaking through space, and ships of all sizes and classes were either scrambling to clear the battlespace—in the civilian ships' cases—or maneuvering into formation and attempting to encircle Ramsey's command, as the Federation ships were doing. Every few seconds, a half dozen icons would flare and disappear, as *Indomitable*'s and the Federation ships' countermeasures and point-defense systems destroyed or disabled one another's anti-ship missiles.

Thus far, the ranges were extreme enough—and *Indomitable*'s defenses robust enough—that none of the Federation's ASMs had struck home, save the one that had detonated short and damaged the *Dame*'s number three MPD. Whether that particular missile detonated as part of its strike package programming or *Indomitable*'s electronic countermeasures or PD cannons took it out wasn't of particular interest to Ramsey. What did interest him was that all the Federation had to show for their efforts thus far was one degraded engine and some scorched hull plating.

The Federation strike force was more or less composed of three different elements. The main force appeared to be a landing force, consisting of two strike carriers and their escorts. Separate from those fifteen ships were another dozen, split into what Ramsey assumed were hunter-killer squadrons—small, agile formations comprised of destroyers and light cruisers that could quickly track down and deal with any opposing ships and wrangle civilian orbital traffic to ensure the landing force could operate without worrying about space-based resistance. And then there was the lost little lamb among the group, the fleet carrier SRFS *Zhejiang*, which had popped into existence a mere 1900 kilometers off the *Dame*'s starboard bow with nary an escort in sight.

The Federation fleet's formation was a disaster, with the various elements arriving spread out and in poor position to cover each other. It appeared they weren't nearly as adept at executing pinpoint intra-system jumps as either *Indomitable*, with her Mabel-supplied upgrades, or the Alarians. Ramsey and his people had immediately alerted them to this harsh reality when Lieutenant Curtis promptly turned two of their destroyers into twisted, glowing wreckage with a combination of 455mm railgun rounds and nearly ten petawatts of laser energy less than sixty seconds after they'd transitioned.

The wayward *Zhejiang* was far and away the juiciest target on the board, but she'd immediately turned away from *Indomitable* upon realizing she was badly out of position, and her crew were currently flogging her engines for all they were worth in a desperate bid to escape. Meanwhile, the nearest of the hunter-killer squadrons presented the greatest threat, as the squadron commander attempted to save the errant carrier by ordering his ships directly at the big Confed battlecruiser.

The lone cruiser in formation with the dying destroyers followed suit ninety seconds later, when a full twenty-four shot broadside from the *Dame*'s Mk. 18s slammed into the hapless ship, scoring seventeen hits and leaving gaping holes in her hull from stem to stern. Under full thrust after making the jump in, the cruiser literally ripped herself apart as the incredible force of her engines twisted and sheared the badly damaged internal structure of the ship. She flexed, bowed, and twisted like an arrow that had just left the bowstring until its abused hull couldn't take the stress anymore and she broke apart in explosive fashion. The three other ships in the formation had turned tail and run for the relative safety of the landing element soon after.

But Ramsey knew his ship's lopsided performance thus far wouldn't continue much longer. The enemy was rapidly becoming a cohesive fighting force, and it was only a matter of minutes before their superior numbers would start taking a toll on the grossly outnumbered battlecruiser. Even now, the second hunter-killer element was formed up and burning hard toward his ship, spewing a veritable cloud of missiles out into space, all of them aimed directly at *Indomitable*.

Ramsey eyed the red inverted V's representing the incoming missiles, noting they were projected to intercept his ship in eight minutes if he didn't order a course change to evade them. But even if he did try to run, the sheer number of incoming ASMs would tax his ship's missile defense systems right up to the breaking point. Indeed, he suspected the odds of *Indomitable* managing to escape in a combat-effective state were perhaps one in five, at best. And even if she did come out the other end in one piece, with her legs and teeth intact, the *Dame* would be woefully out of position to assist Isadore in repelling the invasion.

Then the holotank strobed with a host of new notifications and audible alerts. A tightly packed cluster of blue dots materialized between the squadron of destroyers bearing down on *Indomitable* and the main body of the strike force.

Ramsey smiled.

He ran through some quick mental math, calculating closing velocities, the theoretical effectiveness of his ship's various missile defense systems, probable enemy responses to the arrival of Raal's fleet, and the relative positions of the *Zhejiang*, the two enemy formations, *Indomitable*, and the newly arrived Alarians. All of this flew through his mind in a matter of seconds. Ramsey eyed the fleeing Federation carrier, and his predatory nature went to war with the more responsible part of his brain. Should he make a run for it in the slim hope that his ship could evade or destroy all the incoming missiles? Or should he push toward his target and at least ensure the enemy would lose their biggest and most expensive chess piece before the missiles bearing down on them struck home?

If *Indomitable* stayed her course and chased down *Zhejiang*, she would almost certainly suffer a mauling, but Ramsey still had a few tricks left up his sleeve, and they might just give him the edge he needed.

In the end, his decision was really a foregone conclusion. Despite commanding one of the largest and most irreplaceable warships in the Confed navy, Edwin Ramsey was, and at heart always would be, a destroyerman. And destroyer skippers were practically obligated to always go in for the kill.

"Helm!" he barked. "Increase thrust to military-emergency. Alter course thirty-four degrees starboard, seven degrees declination."

It was going to be close—perhaps too close. The deck beneath his feet began vibrating harshly as Thornton poured on the coals, despite the active dampeners that helped isolate the Pit from the rest of the ship. Ramsey's lips pressed into a thin line as he watched the reactor readouts in the holotank spike up to 112 percent of their rated output, and the temperature of the magnetic constrictors that contained and directed the plasma propellent discharge out of his ship's huge MPD nozzles quickly jumped into the red.

He opened a channel to engineering without taking his eyes off the rapidly changing information displayed in the holotank. A tone sounded, letting him know the channel was open.

"Engineering." The word had to be shouted over the din of machinery and several voices all trying to be heard over each other, but Ramsey recognized the voice of his chief engineer.

"Cheng, I need you to give me everything number three has left and then some," Ramsey said without preamble.

Commander Sexton emitted a brief choking sound before responding. "Captain, number three is held together with spit and baling wire as it is. You've already got my engines running so hot it'll be a miracle if there's anything left on the pylons but charred stumps by the time you're done with them."

"Commander, if we don't kick this bitch in the ass, and soon, then a little engine repair will be the least of our worries. Make it happen."

Ramsey cut the channel, immediately regretting the harsh tone he'd taken with his chief engineer. He made a mental note to apologize to the man the next time he had the opportunity. *If* they had the opportunity, that was.

"Sir," Billings reported, "*Elyris* is requesting orders."

Ramsey glanced at the tactical plot, noting that Captain Raal was already splitting up her formation, detaching a squadron of destroyers to go after the Federation hunter-killer squadron pursuing *Indomitable*, while the bulk of her fleet angled in on the Federation carriers and their escorts. That Raal was requesting orders was nothing more than her being polite at this point. The fiery Alarian commander was well versed in the art of space combat—especially against Terran fleets, Ramsey thought darkly —and she was already putting herself in the best position to repel the Federation forces.

"Please inform *Elyris* that Captain Raal may proceed as she sees fit," Ramsey said to his comms officer. "Tell them we'll join them just as soon as we deal with a straggler and swat down an annoying swarm of flies."

He turned back to the holotank and noted with satisfaction that number three's output was now over sixty percent and holding. The thermal stress the engine in question was enduring was extreme, and Ramsey knew full well that it was only a matter of time before the magnetic constrictors failed and the MPD lost containment. In the meantime, however, the added thrust from number three looked like it would just barely give *Indomitable* the extra velocity she needed to pull off her captain's plan. Still, it was going to be an extremely close shave.

43

THE BATTLE OF EXODYN

A RIDICULOUSLY LOUD EXPLOSION ROCKED THE EXODYN CAMPUS, sending every bird within several kilometers into the air in a panic.

"Overdid it a little, don't you think?" Kravczyk commented dryly, gesturing with his chin at the cheery mushroom cloud roiling into the cloudless afternoon sky on the other side of the complex.

"This from the guy that used a demo pack designed to eliminate hardened fortifications on a crumbling farmhouse just so he could take out a few Th'aloori shock troops?" Ben jabbed, his mind flashing back to those dark days back on Earth when the Imperium made their first attempt to kill him.

Kravczyk inhaled as if he were preparing a long-winded rebuttal, but Valdez cut him off.

"That's our cue," he said, standing from his prone position just inside the tree line. "Just like the old days." He waved for the rest of them to follow him out, and the team quickly fell into a loose traveling wedge formation as they raced across the open ground between their objective and the wooded buffer zone that separated the ExoDyn complex from the neighboring property.

While their surveillance of the immediate area hadn't turned up any enemy positions, that didn't mean they weren't going to run into a random patrol or stumble upon a squad of pissed-off Black Dragons playing cards once they breached the building. The guards Kravczyk had been eyeing with the magnified optics on his rifle—no, correction, *Ben's* rifle—were several hundred meters distant, near one of the research labs on the north side of the large recreational area that had once been used for the ExoDyn intramural softball league and company picnics.

The buildings that once housed the executive offices, along with the applied sciences and commercial implementation divisions of the campus, lay on the other side of the materials research lab, with those four structures arrayed around a common courtyard. And if you continued straight on through the courtyard and out the other side of the executive building, you'd eventually run into Major Davis and his Pathfinders. Rounding out the sprawling compound's layout was a small airfield that lay to the rec area's west, past a line of warehouses, and the building housing the complex's onsite fusion reactor to the north of the airfield and directly west of the commercial implementation building.

The plan called for the main thrust of the assault to come from the Pathfinders as they took on what the CID guys had flagged as the most hardened targets of the whole facility— namely, the fusion plant and airfield. Air support would come in the form of *Indomitable's* ground attack squadron of F/A-26 Sabers, followed by the marines' dropships to augment their close air support and evacuate casualties. The Dragons would have no choice but to respond with the bulk of their forces or risk quickly losing both of those critical points in short order. With the Black Dragons' full attention focused on fighting off the marines, Ben and the SEARs were going to slip in the back door and try to neutralize the slipspace transceiver before any of the defending forces noticed what they were up to.

All the intel they'd been able to collect so far indicated that either the Federation marines guarding the place weren't aware of the transceiver's exact location within the complex or whoever was in charge around here didn't see the value in tying up limited resources to defend it. Ben suspected the most likely reason was the latter, as the slipspace comms node was located not only underground but in an area of the complex that didn't house any critical infrastructure. With barely a hundred marines onsite, priority had been given to securing the two most critical points—the power-generation facility and the airfield. One supplied power for the entire facility, including the Imperial transceiver, while the other gave the defenders unfettered access to resupply and reinforcements or an avenue for retreat.

If the Dragons lost control of either point, it would make their job significantly harder. By contrast, trying to assault a subterranean location that only had a couple of fixed entry points was a tall order for anyone. Not to mention that a location like that could be easily defended with just a squad or two, at least until reinforcements arrived from elsewhere around the complex… unless a company's worth of pissed-off marines were busy breaking shit out on the front lawn.

The team was barely halfway across the clearing when their carefully laid plan was blown all to hell.

"Oh shit, oh shit! Boss!" Kravczyk shouted as the team closed in on the backside of the prototype-fabrication building.

"I see it, Chief," Valdez said, "but we can't do anything about it from down here. Stay focused."

The "it" he was referring to was the metric fuckton of Federation warships that had just appeared over the planet without warning. *Indomitable* had dumped a flurry of orbital data onto the tacnet right before Ramsey gave them the even better news.

There was no way for the *Dame* to launch her Sabers until after the threat from the Federation strike force had been eliminated.

Ben couldn't help but admire the optimism from *Indomitable*'s comms officer, considering the battlecruiser suddenly found herself facing down no less than two dozen Federation capital ships all by herself. The Colossus-class cruisers were purpose-built to go head to head with the Alarian heavy cruisers like *Elyris*—really more like fast battleships than actual cruisers—but even the considerable might of *Indomitable* couldn't possibly stand up to the force that had just jumped into orbit, especially without Mabel to give her the edge. What was supposed to be a relatively quick strike on the Imperial transceiver had just transformed into a clusterfuck of epic proportions, and Ben couldn't help but see the comparison between this and the mission to take out the agent on Hai'alla.

Thankfully, they'd prepared for a worst-case scenario like this, but Ben found that fact to be less comforting than it should have been. He was nervous enough about the prospect of going up against the Dragons, having heard the horror stories from Kravczyk and Valdez, but now they were under the guns of an entire Federation fleet? Ben struggled to control the tightening of his chest and the rising sense of dread as his augmented legs propelled him toward his objective.

As if Valdez was inside his head, the SEAR team leader reiterated his last point. "We can't do anything about the furball upstairs—let *Indomitable*, the IDC, and the rest of the fleet take care of it. Our mission is unchanged. We go through that door and kill anything that tries to stop us from getting to the slipcom node, got it?"

It was a rhetorical question, and the team stayed silent. But the gentle nudge from Valdez gave Ben the little bit of extra willpower he needed to compartmentalize the danger in space and refocus himself on the task at hand—something he was immensely grateful for, and a detail that really demonstrated just how good of a team leader the experienced SEAR was.

The slab-like side of the building was fast approaching as Dagger Team's armored boots ate up the distance with ease, driven forward by the awesome power of their APEX suits. Kravczyk and Valdez slid to a stop to the left side of a man door that led into a hallway housing the building's ground-level offices, and Tess and Ben joined them a few seconds later. Ben pressed himself against the side of the building and faced away from the door, bringing his carbine up to a ready position as he watched the team's back. Kravczyk was designated as the point man, followed by Tess and then Valdez.

Once the team finished "setting the stack," as the SEARs called it, Valdez said, "Breacher up," and Kravczyk moved into position, readying himself to make entry into the building. Tess flared out and swapped places with Ben as he stepped up to the security keypad next to the door and placed his hand over the unit's inductive dataport.

After just a few seconds, Mabel notified the team that she'd successfully defeated all the security provisions throughout the entire wing of the building, including both external and internal intrusion alarms and all video and audio monitoring systems. To Ben's immense relief, she also reported that she saw no sign of defenders within the northern half of the building, but she cautioned that she couldn't take control of the rest of the building's security systems without the risk of alerting either the defending Federation marines or any Imperial monitoring programs that might be present.

His job now done, Ben switched back to watching the team's rear, while Tess moved up to Kravczyk's right shoulder, preparing to follow hot on his heels after he breached. Valdez and Ben tightened up behind them, and they were ready.

"Status?" Valdez said, querying the team for the final time before they entered the building.

"Four up," Ben replied.

"Three up," Valdez said. Tess and then Kravczyk finished their status checks a moment later.

During the trip here, Ben and the SEARs had spent several days aboard *Gambler's Fortune* rehearsing both breaching and how they would move once inside the building. He'd found it oddly comforting—practicing how best to breach a defended position and then search for and kill every bad guy in the building. But the drilling helped focus his mind on the task at hand, which in turn meant he spent less time overanalyzing every little doubt that'd been nagging at the back of his mind and he'd been stubbornly trying to shove back into his mental closet and forget about.

It felt good, having a purpose and being part of a team again. When Kravczyk had been riding herd on him during his training stint with the Pathfinders at Joint Base Thunder back on Elizabeth, Ben had felt like an outsider. But here, flowing through motions that he'd done more than a hundred times over the last week with people he knew well and respected? Some of that swagger that he'd lost somewhere along the line of leading the Pathfinders into a slaughter and getting himself blown up was starting to come back. Ben knew he was faster, stronger, better armed, and better armored than his opponent, and he damn sure had better teammates to watch his back. The Dragons weren't going to know what hit them.

"Breach," Valdez ordered.

The Pathfinders had a whole bag of tricks from which to draw when it came to breaching a building like this, ranging from ballistic or explosive breaching tools to flashbangs, but the SEARs, with the awesome power and protection of their APEXs on tap, generally preferred to do things the old-fashioned way.

The sole of Kravczyk's size-twelve boot slammed into the metal security door so hard that it exploded out of its frame and went careening down the hallway. The big SEAR rushed through the doorway with Tess immediately behind and to his right, and Valdez followed them a moment later. Ben turned from his tail-end Charlie position and entered last, quickly taking in the SEARs' backs as they rapidly advanced.

Ben followed, keeping the majority of his focus on their rear as the team progressed down the hallway in a classic "rolling-T" formation. Kravczyk and Tess stopped to quickly clear every office along the hall, marking each room with a red X on their shared tacmap after ensuring that no enemy forces or other surprises were present, not that they actually expected to run into much resistance here. At least not on the ground level and the floors above. However, once they descended the stairs to the sublevels and to where Ben was certain they'd find their prize, all bets were off.

"Stairway to the sublevels coming up," Kravczyk called out, despite the fact that they could all see it on the tacmap displayed on their HUDs.

"You're still sure about this, Ben?" Valdez said. While he'd technically asked a question, the way in which he'd said it made it clear he didn't expect Ben to respond in anything other than the affirmative.

"This is it." Ben nodded. "No question. Down two levels, take a right, secure storage area at the end of the hallway. We'll find our objective thirty meters in, along the eastern wall. It's a nondescript utility box that will look like any other electrical junction box or data cable routing access point."

How he knew all that without ever having laid eyes on the object in question, he didn't know, but images of the specific utility panel began randomly flashing in his mind's eye shortly after learning they were going to be hitting the site to cut the

Master and its digital minions off from Terran space once and for all. It was hard to describe, but the knowledge didn't just get called up like an old memory; he *felt* that it was true in a way that was more on the level of a religious experience than anything else, so deep was his belief that they would find exactly what he'd described, exactly where he'd said it would be.

Given the wealth of other information about Imperial operations in Terran space that he miraculously had access to after being brought back to life—information that Na'al and his people had been able to confirm, for the most part—the people in charge of planning this operation had taken him at his word. Sure, they were still making sure they didn't put all their eggs in one basket by tasking the marines with taking out the power plant and airfield, in the event Ben's information was wrong, but Ramsey, Davis, Valdez, and the others had planned everything as if the access node for the transceiver was right where Ben said it would be. That knowledge gave him an immense feeling of satisfaction at being trusted, but a lingering terror made him worry that maybe, just maybe, what he thought he knew to be the gospel truth would actually turn out to be wrong. That it might also somehow be a trap—some poisoned nugget of information planted in his head by the agent before he'd nuked it out of existence—had also occurred to him. He'd said as much, but most everyone had written that idea off as lingering doubt from his last encounter with the agent.

Valdez signaled for the team to once again stack up outside the door to the stairwell, and a moment later, they were through and on their way down to sublevel two. That they were leaving nearly the entirety of the above-ground portion of the building uncleared was something that none of them were particularly fond of, but the logistics of trying to clear the building and then make sure it *stayed* clear afterward made it impossible, given the nature of their small team. It would have taken at least a full platoon to secure the building and hold it, and the attacking force just didn't have the manpower to spare. So instead of doing things how they *should* be done, Ben and the SEARs were making a beeline straight to their objective—speed was everything. They needed to either take the transceiver offline or destroy it before the Imperium could use the connection to learn about the threat the SEARs and Pathfinders posed and possibly pull off some kind of shenanigans that would make life miserable for the Confed.

When they reached sublevel two, the team's luck finally ran out.

"Contact right!" Kravczyk shouted even as the boom from his rail rifle filled the underground hallway they'd just emerged into.

Ben heard the big SEAR call out the enemy contact, and everything inside him demanded that he barrel through that door and help his friend, but that wasn't his job. He kept his plasma carbine aimed back up the stairwell, watching for someone sneaking up on them from behind as the short-lived gunfight played out behind him. Then as quickly as it had started, the engagement was over.

"Two down," Kravczyk said. "Don't think they were coming for us—more like they were running to reinforce their buddies at the front of the complex. They're still armed to the teeth and kitted out in full battle-rattle, though."

"Move up and secure the bodies," Valdez said. "If we weren't on the clock before, we definitely are now. Let's go."

Ben flowed out behind the SEARs, and the team made their way down the wide subterranean corridor that had once been used to move personnel and material between the prototyping facility and other parts of the complex. They stopped briefly at the two enemy marines, now riddled with 6.5mm holes and crumpled up in widening pools of blood. Tess and Valdez checked the two men for signs of life, not expecting to find any, and they didn't. Their grizzly task complete, the team moved on, rapidly approaching a T-intersection with a set of wide sliding doors in line with the corridor they'd approached from.

"Mabel, do you have anything from the enemy comms or data networks?" Valdez asked as the SEARs took up a defensive posture on either side of the doors.

"I lost my connection to the enemy's wireless datanet when we descended belowground, Commander," she said. "The construction of the walls around us, coupled with the depth of the soil overhead, is preventing the Dragons' network signal from reaching us. I should be able to access ExoDyn's network momentarily, however."

Ben stepped up to the security panel next to the gigantic doors, noting that the lower part of the panel had been removed and that a datapad was connected to the wiring behind it via a cable.

"What do you think, Mabel?" he asked. "Do we go in through the datapad or use the door's security panel?"

The inductive dataport on the security panel lit up with a translucent yellow highlight, and Mabel said, "The panel. While I'm sure I could get in via that datapad, seeing as it appears the Federation techs used it to breach the door's security, the panel offers the most direct route to what we want."

Ben reached out a hand and planted it on the security panel, and Mabel went to work. Ten seconds later, Ben heard the door's locking bolts retract with a distinct thunk, and then the doors began to slide apart.

"Looks like the Fed boys have been doing some mainte-nance," Kravczyk commented when he realized the door tracks had been recently lubricated. "Awfully nice of them to get the place ready for us."

"I'm in," Mabel said over the team channel. "I have access to

ExoDyn's internal datanet. However, much of the facility is still unavailable to me, as those areas never had their data cables repaired after the Alarian attack on the facility at the outset of the war."

"Meaning?" Ben said.

"Meaning I'm blind in approximately sixty-four percent of the facility," she said. "Pretty much everything on the eastern half of the complex is inaccessible to me, save for the power-generation building. The good news is that it appears the enemy have reacted much as we anticipated. They're working to reinforce their positions around the fusion plant and are also sending troops via the underground tunnels to the airfield. Major Davis and his Pathfinders have them on their heels, despite the lack of air support. I don't think the Dragons were expecting us."

"Thank God for small miracles," Tess muttered.

"No kidding," Kravczyk chimed in as the doors reached the end of their travel and the lights in the cavernous room beyond snapped on. "We're way overdue for things to swing our way for once."

The team moved into the room, the SEARs going first and clearing the area immediately around the entrance. Ben's eyes swept over the neatly ordered rows of pallet racks and industrial shelving, all of it stuffed with boxes, transit crates, containers of all shapes and sizes, and even various pieces of equipment that were just sitting out in the open. He recognized a few things— several iterations of an autonomous mining drone that ExoDyn had rolled out the year before the war started, for example.

The team rapidly moved through the entirety of the underground warehouse, calling out the all-clear less than a minute after entering. They met back up in the center aisle that ran the length of the hundred-meter-long space, and Ben gestured back in the direction of their objective. "It's just over there," he said, turning to face the SEARs as they all regrouped on him. "You guys watch the door while Mabel and I take care of—"

Before he could finish his sentence, the three SEARs suddenly became a blur of motion.

"Contact!" Valdez shouted as the SEARs raised their weapons and opened fire simultaneously, scattering to the sides as they did so.

Ben's brain stem took control and had him moving before his conscious mind fully caught up to the sudden danger. Acting on muscle memory, he pivoted in place and brought his plasma carbine up to his shoulder, dropping to one knee and preparing to engage whatever threat had just appeared behind him. As the security doorway came back into view, Ben saw what had triggered the SEARs, and he hesitated out of confusion for just a split second.

Five APEX-armored people were taking up positions around the entrance to the warehouse, two to either side of the security doors, two more using the nearest row of shelves for cover, and the final man down on one knee, dead center in the doorway. These weren't your run-of-the-mill Black Dragon commandos in their signature onyx black hardshell combat armor, similar to what the Pathfinders wore. These were honest-to-God APEX suits—Gen IIs, if Ben's eyes weren't deceiving him—and the only military unit he knew of that used APEXs were the SEARs.

Run!

Mabel screamed the warning into Ben's mind, but it was too late. A puff of smoke from over the shoulder of the kneeling man was followed immediately by a jet of flame that flashed down the length of the warehouse. Ben's supercharged alien nervous system took over, and time slowed down before his eyes. He moved on instinct, his support hand coming free of his carbine and pushing out toward the incoming streak of fire.

Ben didn't even have time to think about what he was doing.

He threw out his left hand and willed something, anything, to stop the rocket from slamming into him and blasting his shiny new body to pieces. Just before the forearm-sized missile from the Mission Adaptable Rocket System launcher reached him, the air in front of him shimmered and distorted, like a heat mirage on an especially hot day.

The nose of the missile crossed the plane between normal air and the chaotic magnetic fields Ben was projecting like a shield, and its warhead detonated.

Ben had just enough time to register a flash. Then the hand of God himself smashed full force into his chest and the world around him went dark.

44

FROM THE JAWS OF DEFEAT

THE DISTANCE BETWEEN *INDOMITABLE* AND THE FEDERATION FLEET carrier rapidly closed, but the swarm of missiles doggedly hounding his ship had Ramsey second-guessing his decision to pursue *Zhejiang*. But it was too late to change course now. The fleeing carrier was throwing everything it had at its pursuer, but the big battlecruiser shrugged off the relatively weak laser pulses and casually swatted aside the few missiles *Zhejiang* launched.

Fleet carriers were designed for one purpose: to park themselves over a planet and deploy transatmospheric strike fighters and dropships full of ground troops. That role was predicated upon the presence of escort ships that could defend the enormous space busses from any and all threats; the carriers themselves didn't have extensive armaments, sacrificing weapons for the ability to pack in an entire battalion's worth of troops, their supplies, and the craft needed to put them on the surface. Now *Zhejiang* was all alone and had an irate enemy warship between it and the ships that were tasked to protect it, so it was doing its best to get the hell away from the apex predator that was the Colossus-class battlecruiser.

It didn't work.

With the incoming missile swarm less than 1200 kilometers distant, *Indomitable* cut loose with everything she had. The space between *Zhejiang* and the *Dame* sparkled as petawatts of directed energy beams sliced through the void, exciting the few hydrogen and helium atoms that got in the way and crisping particles of space dust before raking across the doomed carrier's stern quarter. Dozens of 455mm railgun shells followed hot on the beams' heels as Talon II anti-ship missiles surged out from *Indomitable*'s sixteen Mk. 5 Rapid-Cycle Missile Launch System tubes.

Ramsey watched on in stoic silence as his ship's laser projectors slagged the older carrier's homogenous armor plate and bit deep into the fairings around three of *Zhejiang*'s massive engine nozzles. One MPD exploded when its magnetic constrictor rings failed, tearing the entire drive pod off its pylon and sending it careening into its neighbor. The sudden asymmetrical thrust from the remaining engines caused the carrier to yaw drunkenly to port, exposing her minimally armored flanks at the worst possible moment.

The salvo of cannon rounds tore into the Federation flagship, the projectiles' inertial fuses delaying the detonation of their 152-kilogram bursting charge until they'd penetrated nearly to the very center of the ship. Through the hull-mounted cameras, Ramsey and his bridge crew watched the demise of their enemy. Gouts of flame and debris erupted from more than a dozen gaping wounds in the carrier's port flank, and her engines faded, then flickered out as she lost power. Several bright jets of plasma erupted into space around the ship, her reactors having undergone an emergency venting to avoid a containment failure and subsequent reactor explosion.

The devastation wrought by the Mk. 18s was almost unimaginable, such was the effectiveness of the big 455s. Ramsey remembered how the cannon shells had easily punched through the more brittle ceramic-based hull armor of the Imperial warships, but the ease with which the rounds passed through those vessels had resulted in a number of complete pass-throughs that limited the weapon's effectiveness —unless they scored a hit on one of the Imperium's antimatter reactors, that was. But here, against the ultra-dense homogenous armor of a Terran warship, the very kind of target the Mk. 18s were designed to fight? Well, the results spoke for themselves.

"My god..." Ramsey heard someone mutter. "Those poor bastards."

On the displays, the image-stabilized camera feeds showed *Zhejiang*'s hull rippling and flexing as secondary detonations ripped through the carrier. Several rents opened up in the hull where the seams between panels could no longer withstand the inferno raging through the interior spaces, and more jets of flame spewed into space.

Then something detonated. Whether it was one of her magazines or her hydrogen fuel storage tanks, the end result was the same. The camera feeds washed out with a blinding release of stored energy, and when they finally cleared several seconds later, the big fleet carrier had broken into three pieces and a cloud of rapidly cooling debris.

"Mr. Curtis," Ramsey said, his voice cutting through the stunned silence of the bridge. "Please safe the warheads on the Talons we fired and put them into a retrieval orbit, provided they have enough fuel left to perform the required maneuvers."

The missiles hadn't even had a chance to get halfway to their target before the 455s did their sinister work. With any luck, Raal would send the Federation running and someone could retrieve the missiles later on and recycle them.

Ramsey turned his eyes back to the tactical plot, noting that his people in CIC had been busy. Between his ship's point-defense batteries and her electronic countermeasures, the rapidly approaching swarm of enemy missiles had dwindled to a mere handful.

"Helm!" he shouted. "Get our starboard flank turned toward those missiles. Let's give our people in CIC more to work with, shall we?"

Thornton didn't acknowledge the order verbally, but the sudden queasy feeling in Ramsey's gut told him the man was doing his best to bring more point-defense cannons to bear against the approaching missiles.

It was going to be close.

One missile's marker winked out, followed a moment later by another, then another. As each missile fell, the time it took to burn through the remaining missiles' hardened casings decreased because more and more projectors were being brought to bear on those that remained. As the final five red V's crossed inside of a hundred kilometers and began executing their terminal attack phase, every eye on the bridge was locked onto the main bridge display.

One disappeared, despite the missiles' attempts to evade the incoming fire by executing a series of random jinking maneuvers. Having covered so much ground, the incoming ship-killers had expended too much fuel to evade earlier. *Small miracles*, Ramsey thought. But the violent maneuvers made it extremely difficult for the point-defense lasers to put enough energy into the missiles to disable or destroy them before they altered course and the beams lost contact.

Eighty kilometers. He counted down the distance in his head.

Then a second winked out.

Fifty kilometers. Come on, come on!

The third and fourth were destroyed almost simultaneously, and Ramsey's heart leapt into his throat.

Ten klicks!

The last missile began a final sprint to its target as it closed to within ten thousand meters and burned its motor at full thrust. Then it was in so close that it crossed inside the firing arcs of the PD cannons at the extreme ends of the ship, reducing the number of beams attempting to connect with it with each passing second.

The missile flashed across the screen until its icon overlaid *Indomitable*'s, and Ramsey tensed for the inevitable. A muted clang rang through the ship, and time seemed to stand still. Every officer on the bridge braced for the explosion that was sure to follow after just a few milliseconds...

Someone stifled a laugh, the strangled sound booming through the dead silence of the bridge like a gunshot. Then someone else let out a low chuckle, followed by several more people. All around the bridge, people were exchanging questioning looks, no one wanting to say what they were thinking out loud.

"Missile strike on our port side, Captain," Hutton called out from ops. "Charlie deck, between frames one thirty seven and one thirty eight. The warhead failed to detonate, but the missile struck a section of armor that was already degraded from our earlier fight with the destroyer squadron. It managed to punch through the armor but was stopped by the pressure hull. One section of port berthing is depressurized, but no casualties reported."

Ramsey inhaled deeply through his nose and released the death grip he'd unknowingly had on his command console. *No casualties.* Whether the missile had been a dud or *Indomitable*'s point-defense systems had done just enough damage to disable the warhead didn't really matter at this point. They were all alive. He cleared his throat and straightened his uniform top, smoothing out several wrinkles that had appeared at some point during the engagement.

"Right then," he said, addressing his bridge crew. "Helm, get us turned around, if you please. The enemy is back in the other direction."

Ramsey glanced back at the tactical plot, and his eyes widened in amazement. In the short time since the Alarians' surprise arrival, Raal and her fleet had pummeled the Federation strike force, though not without incurring some costs of their own. The second enemy destroyer squadron pursuing *Indomitable* had been reduced to a single ship attempting to limp away from the battle. The two carriers in the main formation were both little more than molten lumps of alloy, and their escorts had been scattered by the Alarians' decisive and relentless counterattack. By comparison, the Alarians appeared to have lost a destroyer and had several more ships damaged to varying degrees.

As he watched, Raal's flagship, the heavy cruiser *Elyris*, cut loose with a blistering salvo of shockingly accurate laser fire. The beams all converged on the cruiser *Xianxi*'s engineering spaces, and the ship promptly went dark, her reactors and emergency power cells destroyed. Through it all, the Alarian fleet remained disciplined, maintaining a tight formation with overlapping fields of fire. The Federation, on the other hand, had not, and Ramsey got the sense that he was watching a group of professionals face off against hobbyists.

"Hey, look at that," Curtis called out to no one in particular. With no incoming fire and his only target destroyed, *Indomitable*'s tactical officer was watching the battle over Isadore approach its inevitable conclusion. "One of the Fed ships is making a run at *Gambler's Fortune*."

Ramsey broadened his field of view and picked out Captain Micholson's freighter, which was currently in a high orbit and making to break away from the well and head out-system. A Federation frigate was in pursuit and launching missiles.

"Why aren't they using their lasers?" Billings muttered.

"*Gambler's Fortune* grosses half a million tons," Curtis explained. "Trying to take out a ship that massive with a couple petawatts worth of laser energy would take all day. Not to mention that a ship as small as that frigate has to divert reactor power to charge her capacitor banks, which decreases engine output. They're fleeing the Alarians, but the *Fortune* is a target of opportunity. Thus, missiles."

"Bastards," Hutton growled. "They've already lost, but they're going out of their way to poke us in the eye as they retreat."

"We'll see about that," Ramsey mused. From this distance, there was nothing *Indomitable* could do to assist the disguised privateer. "I suspect our Federation friends are about to discover that *Gambler's Fortune* is packing a whole lot more than what's on the tin."

As if on cue, the freighter launched missiles of her own. So many, in fact, that Ramsey heard Curtis whistle in surprise. While *Gambler's Fortune* was a large vessel, grossing somewhere north of five hundred thousand tons when fully laden, she was still a commercial freighter first and disguised space combatant second. As such, the general-purpose disposable missile pods she carried were equipped with ordnance that was much smaller and shorter-ranged than the massive Talon II ship-killers that were the weapon of choice for long-range engagements against warships. But what Captain Micholson's ship lacked in quality she made up for with quantity.

Nearly a hundred missiles flooded out of the bulk freighter, and Ramsey could just imagine the faces of the frigate's bridge crew as they were suddenly staring down enough incoming weaponry to take out a ship five times their tonnage. He winced, realizing that the bombastic freighter captain was almost certainly going to be billing CID and the Confed navy for all the ordnance he'd just expended. Then again, the limited amount of time Ramsey had spent with the man had left him with the distinct impression that Micholson was a die-hard subscriber to the "overkill is underrated" way of approaching life.

Realizing their catastrophic error in trying to chase down the *Fortune*, the enemy ship—which Ramsey could now see had been positively identified by CIC as an older type-39A carrier escort frigate, the SRFS *Yantai*—attempted to break contact and run. The little ship's missile defense systems performed admirably. In the end, however, there was little difference between being hit by forty-three missiles versus a hundred when your ship only grossed 6300 tons to begin with.

By the time the strobing explosions ceased over the planet, *Yantai* had been reduced to little more than a cloud of debris, the largest piece of which was so small it didn't even register as a target on *Indomitable*'s high-powered space search radar. Ramsey frowned as he watched the tactical plot update the *Yantai*'s contact as "destroyed," and he was suddenly overcome with a wave of frustration mixed with sadness.

It wasn't supposed to be this way. Humans shouldn't be fighting humans anymore; he'd thought they'd moved past this depressingly stupid part of Terran history. How many people had just died horribly out there in the cold vacuum of space, and for what? To pull one over on the Confed and put the Federation at the top of the Imperium's slave hierarchy? It was all so pointless.

Cheering erupted from around the bridge, interrupting Ramsey's dark musings. He glanced around to see what was going on, only to find Billings's smiling face looking up at him expectantly.

"What's that, Comms?"

"I said the remaining Federation ships have struck their colors, sir!" he said with a wide grin. "And the acting Federation commander has signaled that he's specifically surrendering to *you*, Captain. Congratulations, sir. The skies are ours."

Ramsey nodded absently for a moment before something Billings had said reminded him of the other part of this operation. "Have we received any updates from the marines, Comms?"

Billings shook his head, his jovial mood evaporating. "I'm sorry, sir. With all the jamming going on around the planet, we lost contact with Major Davis and Commander Valdez. I've got my team in CIC working to reestablish comms with someone dirtside, but so far, we've not had any luck."

"And I'm sure the lack of air cover isn't doing them any favors," Ramsey said bitterly, remembering the squadron of F/A-26 Sabers still manned and ready for action down on his flight deck. "Helm?" he called out. "Don't spare the horses, Mr. Thornton—we may have taken the high ground, but we still have an entire company of marines down on that planet. I'm sure I don't need to remind you what the Pathfinders did the last time they lacked proper orbital support."

Thornton chuckled. "Indeed, sir. We'll be back over the planet in a jiffy."

Ramsey looked down and realized his hands were beginning to shake—the aftereffects of the adrenaline rush he and his whole crew had been working under during the battle. He clasped his hands behind his back and turned his attention to the data still streaming into the holotank, making a conscious effort to regain his composure of command while simultaneously chiding himself for the dark-humor quip about the disastrous end to the Pathfinders' last mission. It was unprofessional, even if he was surrounded by like-minded officers who wouldn't think twice about it.

But he also couldn't help the sense of foreboding that steadily crept up his spine as he reflected on the last time the Pathfinders and SEARs had tangled with their enemy. All the intel they had available while planning this operation suggested the ground phase would be fairly straightforward, but they hadn't exactly anticipated that the marines would be facing off against a company from the SRF's most-feared special operations forces or that the Federation would show up with a fleet, intent on taking the system for themselves.

Sure, Ramsey and the others who'd planned this mission had ensured they'd be ready for any contingency by having the Alarians on standby as a quick reaction force, but no one expected them to actually need Raal and her fleet to get involved. Yet here they were, still in position to pull victory out from the jaws of defeat, but the butcher's bill was rapidly adding up, and Ramsey feared it would only get larger before this was all over.

45

THE ENEMY WITHIN

"BEN!"

Kravczyk heard Tess shout over the cacophonous roar echoing around in the confined space of the underground warehouse. He didn't have time to divert his attention, however, because a team of Black Dragons in fucking APEX armor was pushing in hard. He sent a half dozen rounds downrange, forcing his target to dive for cover when at least one or two of his railgun's slugs connected with the thick graphene polyalloy plates covering the man's chest.

Kravczyk cursed, realizing that the lower-velocity setting that had proven more than a match for the run-of-the-mill hardshell worn by most of the Dragons wasn't going to cut it against the advanced powered exosuits his team was currently facing off against. He berated himself for not thinking of that while mentally toggling the weapon's velocity setting to a level that should prove effective without blasting gaping holes in every wall between here and the reactor building on the other side of the complex. The big SEAR had extensive experience with the Gen II APEX armor—it was the same suit that'd kept him alive while he took on Feng and his company of goons on Newman's

Rock six years ago, after all—and he knew precisely what the armor could and couldn't stand up against. But the Feds didn't use APEX armor, and the sudden arrival of a full fire team equipped with it had thrown him for a loop.

A hail of gunfire sparked and pinged off the industrial shelving he was using for cover, and he felt two rounds slam into his left thigh and side. He rolled away from the incoming fire, thankful that his armor afforded him the same level of protection as his enemy's. His HUD warned him that he'd been hit, but only that; his APEX was still fully functional, and he wasn't injured. More rounds hammered into the crates between him and the attacking Dragons, and he had no choice but to shift his position.

"Keep their heads down while I try to get an angle on them!" he said over the team channel.

Neither Tess nor Valdez bothered to respond verbally, instead signaling their acknowledgment by increasing their volume of fire. That was when Kravczyk realized he didn't hear the unique sizzling boom of Ben's borrowed plasma carbine. Scanning his HUD for the kid's status, he winced when he saw that Ben's suit was throwing errors and indicating he'd been hit and was wounded.

The kid had been in the worst possible position when the SEARs noticed the enemy, standing in the middle of the room with his back turned and his guard down after they'd cleared the space. Ben's indicator flashed an ominous yellow with the word "medic" flashing next to it, but at least his vitals were still registering, meaning he must've been able to get out of the way of that damned MARS rocket those assholes had sent their way.

"Do either of you have eyes on Ben?" Kravczyk asked as he moved farther down the aisle, intent on using the cover of the shelves to get himself all the way to the wall. Between the far ends of the shelving and the concrete wall was a wide gap that allowed foot traffic to pass, and his plan was to skirt along the wall, out of sight of the enemy, in order to get a better angle on their position near the doors.

"He's down and not moving but appears to be in one piece," Tess called out. "I don't know how that MARS didn't kill him, but it blasted him backward all the way to the service lift at the far end. I can't get to him without giving the enemy an opening to move up or shoot me in the back."

"Stay where you are," Valdez broke in. "If we take the pressure off, this little stalemate we have going won't last."

Kravczyk reached the end of the row just as the incoming fire from the enemy team slackened before dying out completely a moment later. He paused at the corner, peering around the edge to check for bad guys, then yanked his head back immediately as a single round punched a hole through the vertical support of the pallet rack next to him, mere inches above his head.

"That's enough!" a familiar voice shouted from the entrance, and Kravczyk's blood boiled.

Feng!

"Throw down your weapons and surrender! Your marines are about to be overrun topside, and you're outnumbered and have no way out," the ISB agent sneered. "Give up now, and you'll live. If you continue to resist, I'll see to it that none of you leave this warehouse alive."

"What's the play, boss?" Kravczyk said, turning and trotting back down the aisle toward Valdez, who was huddled behind a large transit crate at the end of the row opposite Kravczyk's own.

With Ben down, their ability to take control of the Imperial transceiver was off the table. They could still try to destroy it, but they would first need to physically locate it, if that was even possible. As far as they knew, the access point in this room was only that—a data connection, nothing more. The actual transceiver hardware was buried somewhere beneath their feet, and it would take time to figure out how to gain access to it.

"Without a line to the marines while we're down in this hole, we have no way of knowing what's going on topside," Valdez said. "But we can't just throw down our guns and surrender—not with the risk that transceiver presents."

"So we're going with the Butch and Sundance ending, then?" Kravczyk eased the partially spent magazine out of his rifle and quietly slotted a fresh one into place. "Works for me."

"I know what you're thinking, Commander," Feng warned, "and I advise against it. Despite our history, I don't wish to see you dead."

"Oh, that's fucking rich," Kravczyk scoffed. The idea that Feng wouldn't dance on their corpses was laughable, given how poorly his career had gone after he butt heads with the SEARs during Quantum Tiger.

"No," Valdez said slowly. "I think he means it. If he captures us, it'll very likely put him back in favor with the higher-ups in the Federation. He parades us in front of the people who previously called him a failure and gets to thumb his nose at them."

"You're trying my patience, Valdez," Feng growled. "Throw down your weapons and surrender. Do so immediately and I'll even let you tend to your wounded man over there. If you continue to be obstinate, I'll have one of my men put a round through that kid's faceplate and be done with it. Then we can go back to shooting at each other."

Kravczyk reached the end of the row and crouched, keeping his head down enough that Feng and his team wouldn't see him inching right up to the end of the shelving unit. The mention of Ben made him crane his neck to see if he could spot the kid. Sure enough, he could just make out Ben's crumpled form through a gap between the boxes on the shelf behind him. He still wasn't moving, nor had he made any sounds over their secure team channel, leading Kravczyk to believe he was probably unconscious… which made him a sitting duck.

Kravczyk turned to Valdez and adjusted the opacity of his faceplate so the boss could see the grim expression on his face. Valdez did likewise, and Kravczyk deflated slightly when he saw Valdez's look of defeat.

"Alright, Feng," Valdez shouted. "You win." Then he called out to his team in the clear, making sure Feng could hear him. "Guns down. Do as he says."

"I knew you were more intelligent than most of the Confed's stooges," Feng said, taunting the SEARs in triumph.

The team set their weapons on the floor, then all stood and slowly emerged from behind their cover. Kravczyk half expected the ISB team to open up and gun them down the moment they were out in the open, but Feng's team held their fire.

"Come on out, then. Nice and slow." Feng motioned for the rest of his team to move up and secure the SEARs.

Weapons still aimed at the SEARs' centers of mass, all four of Feng's team moved as one, quickly approaching their new prisoners while their team lead lagged slightly behind. Kravczyk smirked when he realized Feng was still so gun-shy around them that he was hiding behind his team just in case his opponents had some nasty trick up their sleeves.

As it turned out, Feng's cowardice saved his life.

One of the ISB operatives was a few paces in front of the rest of his team when the man's head exploded. The air running the length of the central aisle was suddenly filled with a torrent of searing heat as dozens of golf-ball-sized plasma bolts streaked toward Feng and his team, cutting down three of them before they even realized what was happening. The SEARs reacted immediately, diving back behind cover as Feng and his sole surviving teammate cut loose with their rifles as they, too, scrambled to clear the killing zone.

Valdez grunted over the comms, and his status indicator on Kravczyk's HUD flashed a warning.

"Boss!" Kravczyk shouted as he rolled to his feet, XM-93 back in hand after he'd dove for cover and scooped it up in the process.

"I'm okay," Valdez ground out, but the pain in his voice was clear. "Took a round through the calf, but I'll live."

"Next time, give us a warning, Ben!" Tess shouted as she popped around the corner to send a few rounds toward the last two ISB agents, who were scrambling to recover from Ben's ambush.

But the kid didn't respond, and a moment later, the stream of plasma bolts ceased.

"Ben?" Kravczyk called out, popping out to send a few shots of his own at Feng. He felt an immense level of satisfaction when the powerful railgun slugs punched gaping holes through the equipment stacked up on the shelves around where the senior ISB man was hiding. But Ben still wasn't on comms, and when Kravczyk glanced over his shoulder to where he'd been lying on the floor a few moments ago, there was no sign of him.

A shout of surprise pierced through the gunfire, followed by the sickening crunch of armor on armor. It came from the side aisle Feng's last tac team member had dove behind for cover. The shouting immediately morphed into a blood-curdling shriek, accompanied by a wet tearing sound. Then a body emerged from the end of the row, streaking through the air directly at Feng's position.

It was in two pieces.

Kravczyk felt his gorge rise when he realized the bundle of thick cable attached to the man's torso was actually his intestines separating from his body cavity. A sickening crunch sounded from Feng's position, followed by a piercing scream from the ISB agent. All gunfire stopped, and the SEARs cautiously stepped out from behind their cover. Kravczyk moved up, rifle still trained on the end of Feng's row, and quickly closed the distance.

Then Ben strode out from the left side of the center aisle, plasma rifle held loosely in one hand as he stalked toward the downed ISB agent. Blood and gore dripped off of his armor, leaving a thick trail on the floor behind him.

Jesus Christ, Kravczyk thought. *He actually ripped the son of a bitch in half with his bare hands.*

"Ben?" Kravczyk and Valdez said in unison, but the kid didn't so much as twitch his head in their direction.

A chill ran up Kravczyk's spine, and his mind flashed back to the moment he'd spotted Ben pinning Feng to the wall back at the ISB's base of operations on Newman's Rock. He rushed forward, realizing what the kid was about to do.

"Ben, no!" he shouted as Ben disappeared behind the row of pallet racks shielding Feng from view.

Kravczyk reached the row in question and saw Feng on the ground, one leg twisted at an impossible angle. His rifle had been knocked from his grip and lay a few meters farther down the row. The two halves of the poor bastard Ben had torn apart were tangled up with the senior ISB agent, who had his hands out in front of him and was pleading for his life.

"No!" he screamed. "No! I'll do anything you ask! Please, don't!"

Valdez grunted as he limped to a stop next to Kravczyk, and the two men exchanged horrified glances. Behind them, Tess was checking on the downed ISB operatives. Not that there was much point, considering how little of them actually remained after the plasma carbonized their flesh and bone.

"Hey, kid," Kravczyk said softly, holding out a placating hand. "It's over. You got him." He flicked his gaze down to Feng, who'd been reduced to a whimpering mess at their feet, and he actually felt sorry for the man. "Come on, Ben, stand down."

Feng latched onto Kravczyk's evident intent to spare him, and he pleaded with him instead. "Damien! Don't let this crazy son of a bitch kill me! He's crazy! There's something not right with him—you have to see that!"

Kravczyk ignored him. "Ben?"

"This one deserves to die," the kid said without turning from Feng. His voice was half an octave lower than normal, and it carried a menacing quality that seemed alien to Kravczyk. "He's caused so much suffering, so much grief." Ben leaned forward slightly, appearing to swell in size as he loomed over the wounded man. "So much wasted effort."

He delivered that last sentence with a snarl that bordered on something feral, and Kravczyk's spidey sense went absolutely bonkers.

Before any of them could react, Ben's carbine flashed up, and the kid put a plasma bolt through the middle of Feng's faceplate. The man's head exploded as the plasma superheated the squishy bits inside his skull, and his APEX helmet couldn't take the sudden spike in pressure.

Kravczyk took an involuntary step back at the shocking display of unnecessary violence, and all three SEARs stood in stunned silence.

"It's done," the kid growled, turning to face his teammates at last. "Now, I'm going to finish this and go home."

He strode away from the carnage on the floor, brushing past Kravczyk and Valdez as he exited the side aisle. Ben paused when he saw Tess, and his body went suddenly rigid, as if he was conflicted on what action to take.

"Ben," Valdez said, moving to stand in front of him. "Are you okay? Your suit's biofeed is telling me that you're unconscious right now. That was a hell of a hard shot you took back there with the MARS rocket. Why don't you let us check you out a minute?"

The kid stayed rooted in place for a moment longer, then twitched as though his brain had glitched and he'd just come back online. "I'm fine, Commander," he said, but his voice still sounded wrong. "A little banged up, but I'll live." He glanced down at the blood seeping from Valdez's calf. "Much like you."

"Yeah," the boss said, clearly not buying it. "Well, if it's all the same to you, I still want to give you a once-over. My suit's got me juiced up for the moment, so I'll be fine. You, on the other hand, look like you got your ass blown up by a rocket, which, as it turns out, is exactly what happened. We need to check you out for head trauma, and we haven't had any contact with Mabel, either. What's her status?"

"She's currently offline," the kid stated cryptically, but he didn't elaborate. He sidestepped Valdez and resumed his path toward their objective. "Let's just finish this."

Kravczyk had seen enough. Something was seriously wrong with Ben, and the little voice in his head that warned him of danger was going absolutely apeshit. He took two steps forward and clamped one of his meaty paws on the kid's shoulder, spinning him around.

"Now wait just a damn minute, Ben!" he said, getting right up in the kid's face. "Something's off with you. For fuck's sake, you just blew the head off a defenseless man! What's up? Come on, talk to us!"

Ben slowly looked down at Kravczyk's hand, then back up to his face. "Remove your hand, Chief."

"Fuck that!" Kravczyk shouted. "Not until you let us check you out." He pointed at Ben's face. "Something inside your head is fucked, Ben! Now stand—" He broke off when he realized his HUD was showing a data transfer coming from Ben—a big one.

Kravczyk's HUD went fuzzy for a split second. Then Mabel's voice boomed through his suit comms.

"It's not Ben!" she screamed. "It's the agent! The agent has control of his mind!"

Kravczyk recoiled, jerking his hand away from the kid like he'd been electrocuted. Then he froze...

Ben's body language had changed in the blink of an eye. Whereas a moment ago he'd been rigid and uptight, now he stood there casually, relaxed and in complete control of the situation. But the most terrifying change Ben had undergone was that the grinning visage of the agent's Grim Reaper avatar was now projected on his helmet's faceplate.

Kravczyk's eyes went wide as realization hit him. The encounter back in Landing, the critical intel popping up in Ben's head at just the right moment... And could Ben have been behind the sabotage on X'nec?

Motherfu—

The agent's crimson eyes flared, and before Kravczyk or the other SEARs could even raise their weapons, the agent struck.

46

WITH FRIENDS LIKE THESE

KRAVCZYK ROCKETED BACKWARD AND SMASHED INTO ONE OF THE stacks of equipment. The collision buckled the corner support, and a mountain of boxes, crates, and steel shelving collapsed onto him. He gasped, desperately trying to draw air into his deflated lungs after the agent's foot connected with his midsection.

Tess and the boss were shouting, but Kravczyk couldn't make out any of their words over the ringing in his ears. His ribs screamed in protest as he struggled to free himself from the pile of crates and scrap metal pressing down on him. A gunshot rang out, then another.

"Damien!" Mabel shouted over his suit comms. "You need to get up! The agent has control of Ben's mind, but Ben is still in there and he's fighting back. You have to get me back into his armor. I can force a link with him and make the agent fight us in the ether, but not until I'm back on board his APEX. Now, move, you overgrown flesh sack! We don't have time for you to take a nap!"

Kravczyk roared through the pain, pressing against the collapsed stack with all his augmented strength. His vision flashed red as he hit the limit of his physical capabilities, then willed himself to push past them. Metal creaked and groaned as his HUD went crazy with warnings that he was over-stressing his armor's power-assist actuators. Then something shifted, and the load holding him to the floor eased considerably.

He tossed aside the junk piled atop him, and his heart leapt into his throat. There in front of him, Tess and the Boss were tangling with the agent. The two of them were using every last ounce of power their armor afforded them and were still losing ground. Kravczyk pulled his lower half free with an ear-splitting shriek as the armor plates over his thighs scraped against steel. His rifle was buried somewhere beneath him, so he didn't even try to look for it. Instead, he planted his feet and prepared to launch himself into the melee.

"Comin' in hot, boss!"

Kravczyk shot through the air like a cannonball and smashed into his three teammates, driving all of them to the ground. Tess was caught on the bottom, having been latched onto the agent's back like a spider monkey. Her legs snaked around the kid's waist while her arms struggled to pin the agent's arms to his sides. Meanwhile, Valdez and Kravczyk each took an arm and fought to restrain their possessed teammate.

The agent shrieked and snarled, the Reaper skull thrashing around Ben's faceplate like a caged animal.

"How the fuck is he so goddamned strong?" Kravczyk grunted out. "Fucking alien witchdoctors playing God with his DNA!"

And he was strong, too. Kravczyk had seen Ben display some incredible feats of raw power since his return, but he didn't truly understand just how insanely strong the kid's tweaked musculature actually was until now. The three SEARs were all grunting and breathing hard, but the agent continued to thrash, making it impossible for Kravczyk to maintain solid contact long enough for Mabel to transfer back into Ben's armor.

Then Valdez screamed in pain as the agent used its legs to apply pressure to the gunshot wound in his calf. The boss's grip on Ben's other arm slackened enough for the agent to rip it free, and then he struck Valdez in the chest with an open-palm strike. The SEAR leader was knocked back onto his ass, reflexively clutching at his wounded calf. But that brief reprieve was all the agent needed.

Kravczyk saw the blow coming and raised his left arm in an attempt to block it, but the agent's fist blasted through his guard and slammed into the side of his helmet. Kravczyk rolled with the strike, but his vision still went black for a split second and a wave of nausea coursed through him. When he looked up, the agent was on his feet, one of the SEARs' carbines in his hand. It was aimed directly at Tess, who was on her back at his feet with her hands out defensively.

"Ben!" Valdez shouted. "I know you're still in there, dammit! Fight it!"

The carbine boomed, and for one terrible second, Kravczyk's heart stopped.

Then he realized the round had punched into the concrete just centimeters from Tess's head. She was still on the ground, frozen in place by the near miss. Then a flicker of movement caught Kravczyk's attention.

Ben's gun arm was trembling and his fingers twitched around the weapon's grip, but other than that, the kid was locked up, just like a few minutes ago.

"Run!" Ben screamed at Tess. His voice sounded tortured, like he'd put every ounce of his willpower into getting that single word out of his mouth. He went silent again but remained locked up.

"Now, Chief!" Mabel bellowed.

Kravczyk struggled to his feet and lurched toward Ben. The sign of life from the kid had snapped Tess out of her daze, and she swept his legs out from under him. The agent crashed to the floor in a heap, and all three SEARs dog-piled on top of him. Kravczyk's hand slammed onto the diagnostic port on the back of the kid's helmet, and Mabel dove in.

———

"DON'T YOU FUCKING DARE, you son of a bitch!"

Ben crashed against the walls of the mental prison the agent had thrown him in, blasting at the invisible barrier with everything he had. He was trapped somewhere that resembled the same null space he'd sent the agent to back on Hai'alla. But this place still had thin connections to reality, just beyond the invisible walls of his prison. A few meters away, the agent's avatar held Tess's M93c in one hand, muzzle aimed at her head as she lay at its feet.

It wanted Ben to watch as it slaughtered his friends—wanted him to rage at his impotence and lose himself to his grief when the deed was done. But Ben had other plans.

He ceased his struggling and closed his eyes, reaching out with his mind and searching for some way to escape. He hadn't really had a chance to stretch the legs of his upgraded implant and revamped neural circuitry, but he called upon them now.

Instantly, his sphere of awareness expanded to the entire warehouse around his physical shell, and he instinctively knew exactly where Valdez and Kravczyk were, as well as what they were doing. A wave of panic threatened to take him when he realized there was no way they'd be able to intervene before the agent killed Tess, and he was her only chance. Ben pushed his fear for Tess aside and reached out for the connection he was sure was there but the agent had just obscured from his senses.

A gentle tug pulled at the back of his mind, and Ben opened his eyes and smiled.

Gotcha!

Ben twitched his hand to the side just as the agent squeezed the trigger. The round slammed into the concrete next to Tess, and the agent's head whipped around, crimson eyes flaring in rage.

"No!" it shouted. "That's not possible!"

"That's my woman you're messing with, dickhead," Ben snarled. "And I'm afraid I just can't allow that."

He thrust his hands forward, driving his fingertips into the barrier between him and the agent. The barrier flexed under his assault, and then the very tips of his fingernails slipped through. Ben roared and drove his hands through the veil separating them until he could clench his fists around the thin fabric of ether and begin tearing the opening wider.

Ben didn't have much time and could already feel what little control he had over his body slipping away. He screamed a warning at Tess as the agent's will crashed against his own.

The agent lunged at Ben in an attempt to intercept him before he was fully free of his digital prison, but it was too late. As it came within reach, Ben hit it with a straight kick that sent it reeling back, then finished extricating himself from the confines of the cell he'd been trapped in. Finally free of his mental prison, Ben rolled his head around, feeling several vertebrae crack as he stretched.

"No!" the agent screamed. "No! No! No! You can't! It's not possible! This is my body! Mine!"

Ben crashed one fist into a palm and cracked his knuckles. "The hell it is!" he shouted. "You're just squatting in it!" He chuckled, unable to help himself. "And I'm serving up your eviction notice!"

Unbelievably awesome one-liner out of the way, Ben charged

at the agent. But the agent wasn't about to take it lying down, and it rushed at Ben in return. The two consciousnesses collided and began tearing into each other. Fists, claws, teeth—anything and everything they had at their disposal was thrown at their opponent. Each had only one goal in mind: domination of Ben's body. One of them wouldn't survive this fight, and they both knew it.

The agent shrieked in rage as Ben ripped one of its ears off with his teeth. Ben screamed a moment later when the agent pierced his side with a bony finger. The appendage grated between two of his ribs, and the agony of that finger moving around inside him almost made him lose his grip on his connection to the agent. He clung stubbornly to the thin thread that connected the two of them, though, certain that if he gave up, his friends were as good as dead.

"Give up, Terran!" the agent roared. "You've already lost!"

Ben reared back and slammed his forehead into the agent's bony face, sending a cascade of teeth into the void around them. "Not happening, bitch!"

Ben spat a glob of bloody saliva into one of the agent's flaring eyes, extinguishing the fire within for a split second. The agent jerked back, at last withdrawing its finger from Ben's side. Ben gasped and clutched at the hole in his side, taking a few steps back and buying himself a moment to recover.

This isn't working, Ben realized. He needed some way to change things up, to get this fight onto more favorable ground. Here, surrounded by the void, both Ben and the agent were more or less equally matched. While he experienced this place as though it were filled with realistic objects, he knew that what he was seeing and feeling was merely his brain taking the data and converting it into something his conscious mind could interpret. But if his subconscious could tweak how he experienced the digital battleground around him, was it possible for him to actually *control* the battlespace?

Ben wracked his brain, trying to come up with some way he could alter his surroundings and give himself an edge. He willed a weapon to appear in his hand. Sword, club, plasma rifle, he didn't care—he just wanted *something* to fight with... but nothing happened.

The agent cocked its head as if studying Ben, but it didn't make a move toward him.

"What are you doing?" it asked in a tone that Ben could best describe as concerned curiosity. "What did you just try to do? Do you have any idea how dangerous what you're doing is?" The agent's voice was steadily rising in pitch as Ben continued to will some kind of advantage into existence. "Stop! You'll destabilize the whole system! We'll both die!"

Ben grunted under the mental strain as he focused his will upon creating something out of nothing. A burning sensation crept up his spine and into his brain, and in a last, desperate gamble, he switched his approach. He stopped trying to give himself a weapon and instead focused on altering the reality of the space around them. Flashes of light pierced through the void around them, turning the nothingness upon which they stood into glass. Heat washed over them, and an orange glow grew in intensity under their feet.

Ben threw his arms wide and screamed into the ether, the fire raging through his brain as he struggled to bend reality to his will. But he just couldn't do it.

"Let me give you a hand with that, Ben."

Mabel stepped up next to him, appearing as the same Amazon warrior avatar she'd donned when the agent had briefly imprisoned Ben on Elizabeth, except this time, her face was clearly defined. High cheek bones and a narrow jaw framed a face with smooth, tanned skin, but just beneath the surface,

Ben could see what looked like emerald-colored circuitry. Her eyes were a piercing shade of indigo, as if they were slightly luminescent. She leaned in and kissed him lightly on the cheek, and the fire raging through Ben's brain vanished, followed a moment later by the hole in his side closing up.

"You!" the agent snarled. Mabel's sudden appearance was the last straw, and the agent charged at them, crimson eyes flaring like miniature novas.

Mabel held up one hand and snapped her fingers.

With a sound like shattering glass, reality around them splintered and fell away, revealing a scorched and barren landscape beneath a sea of sulfur-colored clouds. Ben quickly ran his gaze over their surroundings, reflexively taking a step forward when he realized the land beneath his feet stopped just a few meters behind him, giving way to a sheer cliff with roiling flames at the bottom. Then he realized he was alone in this place. Mabel was no longer by his side, nor was the agent charging toward him. A quick scan of his person revealed he was now dressed in nothing more than a well-worn set of CDUs.

"Ben!"

He looked up toward the sound of her voice, and she snapped into existence ten meters away and behind the place where the agent had been just a moment ago. Searing heat lashed at Ben's back, and he flinched away, looking over his shoulder at the flames that were now licking the edge of the cliff behind him. When he turned back to face Mabel, he was greeted with the grinning face of the agent.

The construct struck him in the sternum, the force of the blow taking him off his feet and sending him flying backward. Mabel screamed as he crashed to the ground and tumbled over the edge of the cliff. Ben scrambled to find a handhold, but his fingertips merely scraped over the hardpacked earth without finding purchase. The last thing he saw before his head slipped below the rim of the cliff was the agent blurring toward Mabel's avatar. Then they disappeared as he fell... and jerked to a stop, suspended in the air by a crushing force grappled onto his wrist.

A blue alien grinned down at him. "You didn't come all this way just to die now, did you?"

"Saryf?" Ben said the man's name so quietly that it was practically a whisper.

Saryf nodded, then hauled Ben back over the edge of the cliff. "I need to thank you for showing me how to escape the shackles the Master put on my mind, but first, your AI is in need of our help." He pointed toward Mabel, who was engaged with the agent in a ferocious brawl. Ben's expression hardened, and he charged toward her, Saryf no more than a pace or two behind him.

Mabel cried out as the agent slashed her across her belly, leaving deep lacerations in her skin that immediately began pouring out blood. She struck the agent with an uppercut, leaving it momentarily dazed as she clutched at her wounded abdomen and reeled backward, trying to gain a little separation from her foe.

The agent shook its head like a dog with a toy in its mouth, then dropped to all fours and morphed into an abomination that was halfway between a skeletal man and a bear. Its face elongated into a short, lupine snout filled with long fangs. Then it reared back on its hind legs and roared.

"Hey, ugly!" Ben shouted. "Over here!"

The agent was now little more than a rage monster, the part of the Master's influence that had corrupted and enslaved Saryf for millennia. With the consciousness that it'd formerly dominated now freed from its clutches, the agent had essentially gone feral. It roared again upon seeing Ben and Saryf charging toward it, then launched itself at them. In two bounding strides, it was upon them.

Out of the corner of his eye, Ben caught sight of Mabel collapsing to the ground just as the agent lunged and Ben dropped into a slide. He flattened his body to the ground as the beast's jaws snapped at the air above him. Landing hard after overshooting its target, the beast dug its claws into the ground, leaving deep furrows in the soil as it struggled to halt its momentum and turn around. Ben scrambled to his feet and rushed the agent, but Saryf got there first, leaping onto the beast's back and raining hammer blows down on its head. The thing reared up, trying to throw the alien off, but it exposed its belly by doing so.

Ben planted his foot and kicked off with every ounce of strength at his command, slamming into the agent's soft underside with a drop kick. Air exploded from the creature's digital lungs as it was sent flying. Saryf bailed off, crashing to the ground with a grunt as the agent shrieked and thrashed at the air. Then, with one last roar of defiance, the beast disappeared over the edge of the cliff.

Ben walked over to Saryf and reached out a hand. The alien took it and allowed Ben to help him to his feet. Then he threw himself around Ben in a crushing bear hug, wracked with sobs.

Ben returned the man's hug awkwardly, then patted him on the back with one hand. "It's alright now, Saryf. You're free." That statement brought on another wave of uncontrollable sobbing, and Ben tried to think of some way to tactfully get the man to let go; he needed to check on Mabel. Thankfully, Saryf released him a moment later, and Ben turned and ran to Mabel without another word.

She was in bad shape, blood pouring out from between her fingers as she weakly tried to staunch the flow with her hands. The glow from her eyes was dim, and the color of her tanned skin had gone a sickly ashen gray. Ben knelt next to her and placed a gentle hand on her shoulder.

"Hey there, Gorgeous," he said, trying but failing to force a grin onto his lips.

She flashed him a pained smile. "That's the line you always use on Tess, Benjamin. Can't you come up with something more original?"

"How bad is it?" he asked, reaching down and lifting her hands away from the wound. He sucked in a sharp breath when he saw the extent of the damage.

"That bad, is it?" she said.

Ben pulled off his CDU top and wadded it up, pressing the fabric to the grisly wound and applying pressure until Mabel moaned. "This little thing?" he said. "Nah, just a flesh wound. We'll get you patched up in no time."

She chuckled and caressed his cheek with a blood-slicked hand. "My Benjamin. You never were capable of lying to me."

Her voice was weak now, and the realization that he was losing her hit Ben like a punch to the gut. He blinked away tears and shook his head. "Don't you dare, Mabel! Not now, and not like this. We've got way too much work left to do!"

"If I may?" Saryf took a knee on Mabel's other side.

He gestured to her wound. Ben hesitated for a split second but then relented. He nodded and took his hands away. Saryf gently pulled Ben's now blood-soaked shirt away from her wound and tisked.

"She will not survive, unless I can repair the damage to her matrix," he said.

Hope welled within Ben, but then he paused. "What's the catch?" There was always a catch, and he had a terrible feeling that he knew what it was.

"No catch," Saryf said with a serene smile. "You have freed me from an eternity of torment, Benjamin Hutchins, and for that, I shall be forever grateful." He placed his hands on Mabel's belly, and a warm glow came from his palms. "I was meant to die a long time ago. In doing this, I am merely taking one small step toward setting the universe back in order."

The glow coming from Saryf's hands intensified, and Mabel's wounds began closing. The glow spread up the alien's arms, then worked its way across his torso. He looked at Ben and smiled. There was but one emotion there now: peace.

"Thank you, Ben. It's because of you that I may now go join my girls in the afterlife. I know you will take the gift of my life and use it to its fullest."

Mabel inhaled sharply and her eyes flew wide open. The light coming from Saryf was suddenly blinding, forcing Ben to look away and shield his eyes. When he turned back around, Saryf was gone, but Mabel was now whole again.

"He's gone," Ben whispered, a tear breaking loose and running down one cheek. "After all that time, he was freed only to die."

"Nonsense," Mabel scolded him, sitting up and probing her newly healed flesh. "You freed him and gave him the peace he never would have been able to find otherwise. And now a part of him lives on in me," she said, holding a hand to her breast. "You *saved* him, Ben. It's what you do—you save lives. Never forget that."

Ben pushed himself to his feet and stood up, then reached a hand down to Mabel. She took it, and he pulled her up. "Are you ready to get out of here?" He glanced at the wasteland surrounding them. "I think I've had enough of this place for at least one lifetime, maybe two."

She smiled and squeezed his hand. "Stand by."

A tingling sensation rippled over his skin. Then the world around him swirled and twisted.

———

A MOMENT LATER, Ben opened his eyes and the sensation of an elephant sitting on his chest smashed into him.

"Ugh! Chief, get your hairy ass off my delicate little body!" Ben wheezed out. "You should know better than to take advantage of people when they're unconscious."

"Ben?"

"No, it's the fucking tooth fairy. Yes! Now get the hell off me!"

Kravczyk didn't move, instead looking at Valdez for a second opinion. "Whatcha think, boss? He sure sounds like that ungrateful punk we rescued back on Earth."

Valdez grunted, then rolled off the dog pile with a groan. "Let him up, Chief. We still need to get control of the transceiver."

Kravczyk grumbled. "Fine, but if he tries to murder my ass again, I'm putting him down for good."

The big SEAR pushed himself up and off the pile. Then Tess, who Ben just realized was lying across his legs, followed. She reached down and helped Ben to his feet, and he smiled at her.

She punched him in the face so hard he crashed back onto his ass, stunned.

"Wha—" was all he managed to get out before she pulled him back to his feet.

"That's for all the things I can't even list out right now because there are so many, you jerk!" Then she threw her arms around him and squeezed him tight. A moment later, she released him and took her M93c from Valdez. "And that—along with all the other things I'm going to do to you after we're done here—is for saving my life."

Ben blinked rapidly a few times, processing Tess's violent whiplash of emotions. "Umm, yeah... sorry." It was the best he could come up with on such short notice.

Tess let out a frustrated sigh, then turned away and trotted off toward the entrance to the warehouse. "Just go finish it already!" she called over her shoulder.

Ben looked to Kravczyk and Valdez for support, but he found none. Valdez shook his head and limped off after Tess. Kravczyk slammed one of those giant meat hooks he called hands onto Ben's shoulder and chuckled.

"Goddamn, kid! Even after all my tutelage, you *still* suck with women! You truly are hopeless. I give up." The big SEAR spun Ben around and shoved him in the direction of the dataport that would allow Mabel to take over the Imperial slipspace transceiver. "Now just go take that damn thing over so we can go home. I'm sick of fucking aliens, Federation assholes, evil AIs hellbent on galactic domination... Boss!" He dug his rifle out from under a pile of twisted steel and broken equipment, then jogged after Valdez. "I'm putting in for leave. Pretty sure I'm way overdue for a vacation."

Ben shook his head and trotted past several stacks to the row that would take him right to the access panel on the wall. Sure enough, as he neared the end of the aisle, a plain gray-painted electrical panel was inset into the concrete. He reached up and pulled open the access door, seeing a simple inductive dataport and a small diagnostic screen behind it.

You ready, Mabel?

Yes, Ben, she responded immediately. *Let's finish this and go home.*

"Sounds good to me."

Ben reached out a hand and made contact with the dataport. He stood there for a few seconds, and then Mabel's voice came over the team channel.

"It's done," she reported. "The security protocols supplied by Admiral Na'al were effective—we are the only ones who will be using this comms node from now on."

"That's great news, Mabel," Valdez said. "Now let's get out of here and see if we can't help the marines clean up topside."

"There's no need, Commander," Mabel said. "I now have full access to the rest of the complex's functioning datanet. The Federation fleet have surrendered to Captain Ramsey and the Alarians, and they've ordered all Federation forces on the surface to lay down their arms. Isadore Defense Corps is mobilizing to assist in securing the site."

"Wait..." Kravczyk said. "Does that mean we won?"

"Indeed."

"Hot damn!" he shouted. "Key West and watered-down drinks, here I come!"

"We're not done here yet, Chief," Valdez said. "Let's go help the Pathfinders pick up the pieces and finish securing the premises. Our job's not done until our boots hit *Indomitable*'s flight deck again."

Ben closed the access panel and jogged back down the aisle. When he emerged from the stacks, he made a deliberate effort not to look at the carnage behind him. Instead, he focused on the three SEARs waiting for him, their onyx-black armor silhouetted by the light that spilled in from the hallway behind them.

"Forgetting something?" Kravczyk said.

Ben froze and looked around, suddenly conscious of the distinct lack of weight in his hands. He looked up with a sheepish grin.

Valdez shook his head and simply pointed back to where the agent had murdered Feng. Ben turned and ran back to retrieve his weapon, taking care to avoid looking at the gory aftermath of the fight.

"Right then," he said upon rejoining his team. "Let's get the hell out of here."

47

UNDER NEW MANAGEMENT

ADMIRAL ROBERT GARLAND WAS DRESSED IN HIS CLASS-A UNIFORM as he strode through the halls of the presidential building, just a few blocks away from where Cynthia Mercer and her gang of traitors were busy fending off a rabid media in the capitol building. While his reinstatement hadn't yet been announced publicly, the people in this building were all thoroughly aware of his current status. Which was precisely why every single person he came across either dove for cover in the nearest office or tried their best to meld with the walls as he passed them.

He was here at the request of Russ Ogden, but this was not a social call, and the irate scowl on his face had been there ever since he and Mark Gideon had talked things over with Henry, Ramsey, Collins, and even a delegation from Hai'alla. He knew what he had to do, and he loathed himself for it.

"The president is expecting you, Admiral," said Cunningham's chief of staff, Jane VerBeek, as he approached the president's office. "Go right on in." She opened the door for him, and Garland walked in without so much as a glance at the woman.

"Admiral," the president said, standing from behind his desk and coming around to offer Garland his hand.

Garland glanced around the room as Jane closed the door behind him. Russ was seated on a couch next to the recently reinstated CID Director Gideon, while Henry was in an armchair adjacent to them. The room's final occupant gave the admiral pause, however. An elderly Alarian male stood behind and to Henry's right.

"Bob, this is Brevik," Henry said, indicating the Alarian. "He's Elyria's representative and a senior member of the Alarian Intelligence Directorate."

Garland inclined his head to Brevik, unsure of exactly how he felt about this strange new world they found themselves in. Just a few short years ago, Mark Gideon and this alien were mortal enemies. Now they were occupying the same room for the same shared purpose. Despite the fact that this meeting was months— if not years—in the making, Garland still felt like things were changing at breakneck speed.

Returning to his purpose for being there, the admiral ignored the president's proffered hand and instead got right down to business. "You know why we're all here."

Cunningham finally realized Garland wasn't going to shake his hand, and he dropped his arm to his side and stood in front of his desk, looking like a whipped dog.

"I assume you're here to tell me I'm being removed," Cunningham said, his shoulders slumping in defeat. "I can't say that I blame you, but I have one request, if I may?"

Every eye in the room was locked onto the man that had nearly doomed all of Terran space—and there was no guarantee they were out of the woods yet.

"And that is?" Garland said.

Cunningham fidgeted with his hands before spitting out what he wanted. "I'll resign. No messy fights in the senate, no long, drawn-out legal battles. I'll step down and pass on the reins of power, then retire somewhere away from all the cameras. It's cleaner that way, and with any luck, the distraction will be minimized so our armed forces can go about bringing themselves back up to a war footing as quickly as possible."

Garland snorted. "How noble of you." He looked around and saw roughly the same sentiment from everyone else, save for Brevik, who Garland suspected was someone who never gave away his true feelings. Turning back to Cunningham, he shook his head and hit the man with a smile that didn't reach his eyes. "No, Mr. President, we're not here to remove you from the office you stole from your predecessor. Just the opposite, in fact—we're here to make sure you stay planted firmly in that cushy chair of yours. At least until we don't need you anymore."

Garland couldn't help but feel a wave of disgust as the words left his mouth, but if they were going to get things back on track and, at the very least, get the fleet into position to counter the immediate threat from the Federation, they couldn't afford to erode trust in the Confed government any more than had already been done.

"I... I'm sorry?" Cunningham sputtered in shock. "You're leaving me in charge?"

"Hell no!" Garland boomed. "You've lost the privilege of even managing a gas station, let alone the fate of the Confed, but public trust in the government is already near the breaking point. If we put the public through another messy impeachment and oust all the people that were just put into power because they almost handed everyone over to the Imperium on a silver platter... Well, what do you think the reaction to something like that would be?"

The president's face steadily lost its color as he war-gamed Garland's scenario in his head, rapidly coming to the same conclusion as the admiral and all the other people in the room.

Garland allowed himself a satisfied little smile upon seeing Cunningham's expression. The idea that he was going to be paraded around as a hero and be forced to act as their puppet—in order to make sure the political gears moved smoothly while Garland and his allies worked furiously to unfuck this goat—was little better than a death sentence. It would be torture for the man, and he deserved nothing less.

"You'll serve out the remainder of your term and make sure we have everything we need to ensure the safety of humanity. Do this—and be good at it, for once in your life—and you might even be allowed to retire in peace when this is all over. Resist, and everyone will know what you've done."

Cunningham placed a hand on his desk and slowly moved around it to sit back down in his chair. He looked around the room, but whatever he was searching for, he didn't find it. "But what will you tell the citizenry? You can't expect them to just roll with the pronouncement that the Imperium is real, we're now allied with the Alarians against them, and the SRF has declared war on the Confed! It'll be chaos!"

"We take a page from your book," Garland explained. "We offer up bits and pieces of the truth and spin it in a way that will support whatever story we decide to feed them. But that's a task for Mark's people, as I'm terrible with that subterfuge crap. I imagine we'll focus on the threat from the Federation, as it's the most pressing issue, and then ease the public into the idea of a war with the Imperium as needed. And in the meantime, we put together a special unit tasked with countering the Imperium threat. Once the conflict with the SRF is resolved, we can focus all our energy on the Imperium."

Cunningham looked around, and the expression on his face told Garland the man hated what they were telling him to do, but he was such a coward that he'd accept whatever role they assigned to him without a fight.

"Cheer up, Mr. President," Garland said sardonically. "We're about to make you into a goddamned hero."

EPILOGUE

BEN'S EYES OPENED, AND HE SQUINTED AT THE BRIGHT SUNLIGHT that streamed in through the open bedroom window. A breeze wafted in, carrying with it the familiar scent of freshly cut hay from the fields adjacent to the Hutchins's family farm in northern Michigan. The air was cool, but it had a weight that held the promise of a hot, late-June afternoon. Ben breathed deep, grinning as he exhaled through his nose and stretched his arms. When he turned his head and took in the sight next to him, his grin widened into a full-blown smile.

Tess's auburn hair spilled over her face and onto the pillow, and the sight of her, combined with the memory of the previous night's activities, stirred something down below. Ben allowed his gaze to linger on the woman of his dreams for a few moments longer. Then he sighed inwardly and carefully extricated himself from the tangle of sheets. He snagged a pair of shorts off the bedroom floor, gave them a cautious sniff, and then, satisfied they still had at least a half-day's-worth of use left in them before needing a trip through the washer again, he pulled them on. Ben padded lightly toward the door in bare feet. Opting to forego a shirt this morning, he grabbed his running shoes and socks off the dresser on his way and gently closed the door behind him.

A few minutes later, he was running down the winding gravel driveway, intent on heading north, along the western shore of Lake Leelanau. Once he turned onto the road that bordered the blue waters of the lake, he gradually increased his speed, his breathing still coming light and easy. He soon reached a pace that most human sprinters could only sustain for brief periods. Then he pushed beyond it. Exhilaration coursed through him as the wind whipped past his ears and his feet continued to pound away at the cracked pavement like a metronome.

While he ran, his mind was free of distractions. It was the most peaceful time he'd experienced in well over a year, and he almost didn't want it to stop. He and Tess had two weeks to spend on the farm. It was a pittance, given everything they'd been through over the last year or so, but it was better than nothing. After that, he didn't know exactly where they'd be sent, but he was sure it would be tough sledding, given his past experience.

For the moment, though, he cast aside all thoughts about the tensions between the Confed and the SRF, Na'al's struggle to get the rebellion organized, and the hundred other stress-inducing things that were all in motion to ensure that humanity not only survived the next half decade but also remained free. He and his team had been granted a brief reprieve in the wake of their thwarting of the Federation invasion and capture of the slipspace transceiver, and he intended to make the most of it.

But then his thoughts drifted to the beautiful woman back there, and before he knew it, his feet were chewing up the distance between him and his home.

Ben slowed to a walk as he crossed the point where pavement gave way to gravel, finally feeling winded. With sweat pouring off his face, he made his way up the long, winding driveway, through the wooded property boundary near the road, and past the fieldstone pillars that once mounted the gate that had separated the Hutchins farm from the surrounding area. For the hundredth time in the last week, his thoughts flashed to the night the Imperium shock troops dropped onto the farm, intent on killing him. But as he rounded a bend in the driveway and the trees gave way to rolling vineyard and a collection of buildings at the top of the hill, those darker memories were replaced with more pleasant ones.

While Ben was off playing super-soldier on Elizabeth and Hai'alla, the vineyard had been whipped back into shape after a season of neglect. Unbeknownst to him, after he and the SEARs saved the day during the Battle of Icarus, his dad had seen to the cleanup of the farm. The charred remains of the old house were demolished and hauled away, and a new, slightly smaller but cozier cottage was built in its place.

His dad had also contracted with a vineyard services company to keep the farm neat and tidy. Last year's harvest had been sold to local wineries that were looking for quality fruit, as would happen to this year's crop as well. He didn't want to think about the next year, or the year after that, but it was entirely possible that he wouldn't be able to return here for harvest for a long time to come, depending on how things went.

Ben made a detour into a block of Pinot Noir, noting with satisfaction that the vines were beginning to bloom. He leaned in and breathed deep, catching just the barest hint of the grapevines' sweet-smelling flowers. It wouldn't be long before tiny little green spheres took their places—grapes, in the earliest stages of growth.

"Maybe ten days or so," he muttered to himself, looking around at the sea of green growing all around him. "Then we're off to the races."

His eyes caught sight of a figure standing on the house's covered front porch and leaning casually against one of the posts that supported the angled roof. Tess stood there, cradling a coffee mug in her hands and wearing nothing more than one of Ben's T-shirts. All thoughts of his vineyard forgotten, Ben was back on the driveway and headed straight for the porch.

She stood there, watching him as he made his way up the last hundred meters of driveway, running a thumb around the lip of her ceramic mug. As he got closer, her neutral expression gradually shifted to a loving smile.

"Hey there, Handsome," she greeted him. "I didn't even hear you slip out this morning. How was your run?"

"Cut short," Ben said seriously. But he couldn't hold it for long, grinning as he ran his eyes up and down her, from the tips of her freshly pink-painted toenails, up those long, athletic legs, all the way to the top of her staticky, bed-headed auburn hair. "I received a report of a smokin'-hot redhead standing on my porch, and I rushed back to investigate."

Tess rolled her eyes. "Really? *That's* the best line you were able to come up with on your eighty-kilometer run or whatever ridiculous amount you're up to now?"

"It was only thirty-five this morning," Ben protested, ignoring the fact that any other human running thirty-five kilometers in under an hour and a half was insane. "Like I said, I had something I needed to do back home." He hopped up the stairs and winked at her, slapping her butt playfully and leaning in for a kiss.

"Eww!" She pushed him away. "You aren't doing *anything* until you shower first!"

Ben pouted briefly. Then a devilish smile crossed his lips. Tess noticed the shift in his demeanor and made to flee, but he was too fast.

"No!" she screamed as he wrapped her up in his arms,

smothering her face and neck in kisses. She hissed like a cat being thrown into a lake and thrashed around, but she was no match for his strength.

Her coffee mug hit the deck, and Ben, sensing doom, opted to break contact and beat a hasty retreat. He cackled as he rushed inside, heading for the master bathroom and the luxurious glass-enclosed double shower within.

"Now we *both* need showers, Gorgeous!" he shouted over his shoulder as she tore after him. "Get your sexy butt in here!"

———

KRAVCZYK EYED the surface of the water suspiciously. Somewhere, lurking beneath those aquamarine waves, his quarry was preparing an ambush.

"Come on, Gorgeous," he muttered, hands twitching in anticipation. "Make your move."

The tip of his fishing rod arced down toward the surface, and the friction plates inside the big saltwater reel suddenly shrieked as something massive struck the strip of bonita tied to the end of its line. The drag payed out line so fast the spool was a blur of motion.

"Fish on!" Kravczyk bellowed, snapping up the rod and setting the hook with a howl of excitement.

He fought the monster for more than an hour, and just as his muscles were finally beginning to fatigue, the marlin jumped out of the water a mere thirty meters behind the boat. The thrill of seeing that massive fish sparkle in the afternoon sun filled him with a renewed energy, and he rallied, finally landing the beast a few minutes later.

"Nice fish, Chief!" Henry congratulated him as the boat's crew wrestled with the trophy-class marlin. "Too bad these waters are strictly catch-and-release." He took a long pull off one of the beers in his hands, then smacked his lips and sighed contentedly.

Kravczyk froze, turning to Henry with murder in his eyes.

The tech giant fixed him with a flat stare, then couldn't maintain the facade any longer.

"You should see the look on your face!" Henry roared with laughter, then passed the big SEAR the other beer he held. "Don't worry, my gigantic friend. You get to keep the fish. I even know a great taxidermist, if you want to have it mounted."

Kravczyk chugged the beer down, then tossed the bottle into the small returnables basket next to the door into the charter boat's salon. "You're mean," he said to Henry. "You and your kid both."

"As much as I want to blame it on his mother... yeah, he probably gets it from my side of the family," Henry admitted.

"Alright then." Kravczyk reached into the cooler for another beer before gesturing toward the fighting chair mounted to the deck. "Your turn."

Henry shook his head. "Nope, this trip was for you. I only tagged along to avoid getting suckered into joining Shelly at the mall while she looks for a new dress before we have dinner tonight." He checked his watch, and his eyes went wide. "Shit! Dinner!"

Kravczyk approached the boat's two mates as Henry vaulted up the ladder to the flybridge, hollering to the captain that they needed to haul ass back to port so he could make his dinner date on time.

"You want a picture, Chief?" asked the first mate, a guy about Kravczyk's age who went by the name "Stack" as he held up his hands like he was using a camera. "Nothing like your first marlin. Trust me, you'll want to show this one off—he's a beaut!"

Kravczyk smiled broadly and nodded. "Hell yes I want a picture! Here, hold my beer."

He motioned the two crewmen out of the way, then bent over and picked up the still weakly struggling marlin. The two crewmen's jaws dropped when Kravczyk hoisted the nearly 250-kilogram fish up and cradled it in his arms.

"Well?" he grunted. "What are you waiting for?"

"Uh, yeah," Stack said, passing Kravczyk's beer to his assistant and pulling out his phone to snap a picture.

Kravczyk dumped his catch back on the deck and swiped his beer away from the kid, who stared at him with a mixture of awe and terror. "You think that's impressive, kid," he said with a wink, "you should see what my buddy Ben can do. He's shit with women, but the son of a bitch can literally bench-press this boat."

Kravczyk's phone buzzed, and he pulled the tiny device from the pocket of his swim trunks, seeing that Stack had initiated a data drop with the pictures he'd taken. He looked up and raised his bottle to the man in thanks, then pulled up the pictures and selected his favorite.

"Speaking of Ben." He thumbed out a quick text message to the kid before sending him the photo of the marlin. "He could probably use a change of scenery about now." He was talking out loud, but not really to anyone in particular. Both of the boat's mates had gone back to stowing his fish and had stopped paying attention.

His phone buzzed again, and he looked down to see that Ben had already responded to his gloating. He swiped at the screen to see what the kid had said.

Congrats on your little fishy, Old Man. Thanks for the offer of a change of scenery, but I think I've got the view covered.

Kravczyk muttered a series of increasingly violent threats at the snarky little shit, then scrolled down to see the picture Ben had sent. His eyes widened when he saw a bikini-clad Tess smiling seductively and cheersing the camera with a drink in one hand. She was leaning back against the railing of a small boat, surrounded by azure-blue water that nearly matched the tropical shade of the ocean around Kravczyk.

"Goddamn, kid!" he exclaimed, then looked up and took in the sight of the setting sun over the ocean to his west. The charter boat's motors increased in pitch as Henry finished coercing the captain into opening up the taps on their run back to port, and Kravczyk braced one of his meaty thighs against the fighting chair as he typed out a reply.

Nice catch, kid. Maybe you're not so hopeless after all.

———

TAROK NA'AL WALKED down the boarding ramp of the small Imperial dropship—a craft the Terrans called a Stalker—and stepped out into the knee-high grass. He idly toyed with the small pebble in his hand. After nearly a century of rolling back and forth between his fingers, the stone had attained a luster similar to that of polished marble. The action soothed him; it'd helped him remain grounded to who he really was through all the trials he'd endured. It was the only thing he possessed that could physically link him to the man he'd called grandfather.

Na'al slipped the pebble back into his pocket as his personal guard finished arraying around the ship, their eyes and weapons constantly sweeping the tree line a short distance away.

Battlegroup 7 had made orbit over Lokack-3 less than an hour ago. At first glance, the Lokack system was barren of any advanced life—no space stations or other orbital constructs, no mining rigs in the asteroid belt, and no visible artificial construction on any of the planets or moons. In reality, however, Na'al knew that his small fleet had been tracked from the first moment they arrived over the system's third planet. Even now, he could feel the eyes boring into him and his marines, sense the holographic weapon sights that were all targeting his position.

He stepped forward, arms held out to his sides to show he was unarmed, even if his guard detail wasn't.

"I am the forgotten son of Kroz Tibbedal," the rebel admiral shouted into the silence around the clearing. "Tell your leaders that Daloth Venz has returned."

Na'al wasn't sure of the protocol for this encounter, but he was surprised when three individuals shimmered into existence less than five paces away—two Th'aloki guards flanking a Th'aloori woman who held some position of rank, judging by their body language. His guard detail immediately moved to counter the threat, calling out the contact and collapsing in on the admiral to protect him.

"Hold!" he said in a commanding voice. "Stand down, marines. If these people wanted us dead, we'd be nothing but lifeless corpses already."

His guard detail cautiously lowered their weapons, but they didn't leave his side. Na'al shouldered past them and approached the three people before him. They were dressed in lightweight tactical gear, similar to the stealth armor systems Imperial marine recon units employed. All three carried electromagnetic projectile carbines instead of standard Imperial plasma-based weapons.

The figure in the center took one step forward and called out, "That's far enough." The woman's voice carried a hard edge, and Na'al knew instinctively that she had seen her fair share of warfare. "How do we know you are who you claim to be?"

Na'al had been expecting this question, and he recited the passphrase his adopted father made him memorize long ago. "When the flowers of the field have returned to the earth—"

"So we, too, shall meet again, my love," the woman finished.

She reached up and retracted her helmet's visor, allowing the admiral to see her face. "We meet again, Daloth Venz, son of Kroz... Or should I call you Tarok Na'al, first admiral of the Imperial Navy?"

Na'al rocked back on his heels slightly as recognition hit him. She was older now—a full-grown Th'aloori female—but her eyes still contained that spark of fierce defiance he'd seen in them over a century ago, the day he'd betrayed his people for the sake of maintaining his cover.

"Hello, girl," he said, inclining his head in greeting.

"I hope you're bringing more than that fistful of beat-up scrap metal you parked in orbit," she said. "The war you started is already gaining steam, and we are nowhere near prepared to take on the might of the Imperium."

"A beginning," Na'al said, glancing skyward. "Nine of the most advanced warships the Imperium possesses." He glanced back to her with a predatory grin. "*Possessed*," he corrected. "Past tense. Another of my ships is on a separate mission but will rejoin us in the coming weeks."

"Ten ships? Against the entire might of the Master and the Imperium? You've doomed us all, kinslayer," the girl bit out.

Na'al rounded on her. "Ten ships, plus the combined might of two allied species, girl! And while ships and spacers to crew them are necessary, they aren't enough to win this fight."

"Who is 'they,' oh wise one?"

Na'al grunted. He didn't blame the girl for her animosity toward him, not after he'd led the mission that resulted in the slaughter of their whole village. But her acerbic mockery was becoming tiresome.

"Hold your tongue, girl!" he bellowed, causing her to flinch away and her guards to raise their weapons. His marines replied in kind, but Na'al waved them down. "Did you think this day would come and we would simply waltz into the Master's chambers and execute it? Blood *will* be shed in the coming fight. More than either of us might be willing to pay, but if we're to finally cast off our chains and rid our people of the Master's yoke, then pay it we must!

"You ask who can lead us to salvation?" Na'al thumped a fist into his chest. "Perhaps you think that person is me? It's not!" He took a moment to calm himself, closing his eyes and inhaling the sweet scent of this planet's atmosphere. "I do not have the ability to fight the Master within its domain, and neither do you. But I've found the one who does. He and his team will join us when they are able."

"And who is this mythical person?"

Na'al glanced up to the sky, eyes straining to cross the vast distance between him and the one he believed to be their savior.

"Benjamin John Hutchins."

The End

AUTHOR'S NOTE

(AKA, THE SHAMELESS RAMBLING OF A GUY WHO THINKS HE'S MORE IMPORTANT THAN HE IS)

Hoo boy.

If you'd have told me a year and a half ago that ten thousand people would have read my books in just eighteen short months, I'd have called you crazy. If you've never ventured into the publishing world, it's extremely rare for a debut author to have the kind of (modest) success I've achieved in such a short time. It's truly humbling, and I'm so thankful to everyone who's made this dream of mine possible.

Most importantly, though, I'm grateful to the people who read my books (that's you, in case you didn't know.) You guys (and gals—few though you may be) are awesome. Without you I'd just be some dude whose wife yells at him a lot because he *still* spends all his free time writing instead of cleaning the garage. But she sees my sales numbers every month, and thus she's content to merely complain about my three-year shirking of responsibilities instead of taking more drastic action. So thank you for that; marital bliss ensues because of it.

Now, on to a bit of self-serving promo! If you've gotten this far in the series and still haven't signed up for my email newsletter, then I shall resort to begging. Please, PLEASE sign up for my mailing list. They're super important for authors because it's a great way for us to communicate directly with fans. I only send out an email blast a few times a year, but it always has juicy bits in it about progress on the next book, little glimpses into my chaotic life, and news about new releases (like when you can expect Ben and the team to return for book 4)

Also, when you sign up, I give you free stuff. For instance, a 6,500 word short story detailing the incident on Hai'alla between Ben and Elyria back before the war. Right now, I'm working on a novella that will center on Kravczyk and Valdez's first go-around with Feng and the Black Dragons, which you won't want to miss. That will be something that's free to my email list, so be sure to sign up! Go to https://geni.us/RobertsonList or scan the QR code below.

Scan this QR code to sign up for my newsletter

And if I still haven't convinced you to sign up for my newsletter, at least give my author page a like and a follow on Facebook. It's linked below, and I always post announcements about new releases, etc. on there. You can also shoot me a message via my Facebook page if there's a burning question you have, or you just want to praise the gloriousness that is my storytelling.

Scan this QR code to be taken to my Facebook Page

Alright, enough rambling. Thanks again for reading!
    Carry on.
    -John

P.S. Seriously, thanks for reading! You're awesome!

Printed in Great Britain
by Amazon

22393147R00239